The Forgotten Marines

"The Capture of John Brown"

by

Dale Lee Sumner

The Forgotten Marines, "The Capture of John Brown"

Copyright © 2004 by *Dale Lee Sumner*

All rights reserved. No part of this book may be reproduced or transmitted in any form by any means, electronic or mechanical, including photocopying and recording, or by any information storage and retrieval system, without permission in writing from the author, except in the case of brief quotations embodied in critical reviews or articles. Requests for permission should be made in writing to:

> Dale Lee Sumner
> 104 Rainbow Dr., PMB #440
> Livingston, TX, 77399

ISBN: 978-1461144861

Third Edition: May 2011

Front Cover: *"Capture of John Brown at Harper's Ferry"*
Painting by Colonel Charles H. Waterhouse, USMCR, 1991
www.waterhousemuseum.com

Back Cover: *"Harper's Ferry Marines"*
Photo by Jim Wassel, October 2009, Wassel Photo and Design

CONTENTS

Dedication		iv
Acknowledgements		v
Preface		vi
Chapter One	"WARNING"	1
Chapter Two	"ALARM"	5
Chapter Three	"PREPARATION"	13
Chapter Four	"TRAVEL"	49
Chapter Five	"ARRIVAL"	115
Chapter Six	"RECONNAISSANCE"	131
Chapter Seven	"ENTRY"	171
Chapter Eight	"WAITING"	185
Chapter Nine	"ACTION"	215
Chapter Ten	"AFTERMATH"	239
Chapter Eleven	"CLEAN-UP"	257
Chapter Twelve	"REWARDS"	291
Appendix		299

Dedicated to
all of the Marines I have known
and proudly call 'Friend' and 'Shipmate'.

Especially two former Marines,
both of whom, at different times,
had a significant impact on my life.
They shall always remain my lifelong friends.

Robert Gary Posey
Staff Sergeant, USMC
(A two-tour Viet Nam veteran)

and

Robert Owen Wagner, Jr.
Corporal, USMC
(Injured during the Mayaguez Incident)

Semper Fi

ACKNOWLEDGEMENTS

I am deeply indebted to Mr. David M. Sullivan, historical author of a non-fiction series, *The United States Marine Corps in the Civil War* – each of his four volumes encompasses one year of the war. (Shippensburg, PA: White Mane Publishing Company, 1997-2000) Because of his invaluable resource help and encouragement, this novel stepped out of the starting block. I strongly recommend his volumes to anyone who wishes to learn more about the United States Marines during this history rich time period of our country.

I am especially indebted to many good friends who read my drafts as this novel was taking shape. Their eager anticipation of the "next installment" was a constant inspiration. I greatly appreciate those who kept referring to this work as historical "FACTion" rather than historical fiction. Thank you one and all.

I am most especially appreciative of my wife, Cindy. Although she dearly disliked being a 'writing widow', she was always my foremost fan, consummate critic, and exacting editor. Without her daily assistance and patience, this story would never have been put to paper. Thank you, "P" -- 1-4-3!

For additional perspectives of the Harpers Ferry story, I suggest *The Raid* by Laurence Greene (1953) and *Thunder at Harper's Ferry* by Allan Keller (1958). Both novels provide excellent insights into the "other" sides of the story. Greene focuses on the town and its residents, while Keller spotlights Brown and his insurgents.

A historically concise account can be found in <u>John Brown's Raid</u>, a 70 page pamphlet published by the National Park Service (1973). It is still available from the U.S. Government Printing Office, Washington, D.C., 20402, or at the Harpers Ferry National Historical Park.

PREFACE

Oddly enough, the role of the United States Marines during the capture of John Brown at Harper's Ferry has been completely overlooked and essentially forgotten - even by the Marines themselves. Most modern history books, within a quick line or two, exultantly refer only to Colonel Robert E. Lee, "commanding Marines", and assisted by First Lieutenant J.E.B. Stuart, as capturing John Brown.

Is this an accurate depiction of the bona fide story? Not quite! Colonel Lee did not directly command the Marines as implied. The inter-service rivalry of the day, as well as the Military Act of 1834, Section 2, would not have allowed an Army officer to command any personnel from the Marine branch of service, except at the specific direction of the President. Lee was sent as the overall commander of Army forces, comprised of Militia units from Virginia and Maryland. The Marines sent to Harper's Ferry were 'Regulars' and commanded by their own Officer-in-Charge, First Lieutenant Israel Greene, USM. (His name is often found in most historical writings without the final 'e'.)

Why were the Marines sent? Who were they? How were they organized? How did they prepare for the journey to Harper's Ferry? (**Harpers Ferry** is our modern spelling of the town's name. No one seems to know what happened to the apostrophe in "Harper's" after the Civil War.) What actually took place after they arrived there? What kind of a wooden ladder could do what three heavy sledgehammers could not? How and why did the sword that struck down John Brown bend? As one looks into the Marines' involvement in this bygone confrontation, more and more questions present themselves and demand explanation.

Now, one hundred and fifty years after the event, this novel offers an in-depth look at the actions of those heroic, but forgotten Marines. Although fictional dialogue has been incorporated to give 'life' to the story, historical accuracy has been preserved as correctly as possible.

In 1996, Bob Wagner and I co-founded the Civil War reenacting unit, "U.S. Marine Detachment, Washington Navy Yard, 1859-1865". When we first 'hit' the field in our period correct Marine uniforms, we were constantly asked, "What are you guys?" Our proud answer of "Marines" usually drew the disparaging comment, "The Marines didn't exist during the Civil War." The sting of those words still smarts. (Ask any modern Marine and s/he will proudly inform you about the Marines' "...honorable and continuous service since first established on November 10, 1775.") To help dispel the unfortunate, but common, misconception about Marine participation prior to and during the Civil War, I have injected information throughout this novel to give the reader an appreciable knowledge of the Marines of that period.

While researching this story, I discovered that all written accounts of the action within the engine house were sketchy at best. Most left significant question as to how 1stLt Greene's sword became bent. Supposedly, in a wild thrust, the point of the blade struck a relatively small breast buckle on Brown's cartridge belt, and the force of the blow caused the blade to bend. To me, the physical reality of that happening just seemed to be extremely improbable. Greene, himself, admitted that he "wasn't sure how it happened. The struggle had taken place too fast." I offer in this novel a more plausible explanation. It is the result of many hours spent with modern Marine combat veterans and Civil War re-enactors; thoroughly discussing, carefully analyzing, and role-playing what "could have logically happened".

In early 1999, as the 140th anniversary of his death neared, I became especially interested in Luke Quinn, the Marine who died at Harper's Ferry. Information about Quinn is scarce. Just locating his gravesite proved to be a difficult task. It turns out that many current residents who have lived and worked in Harpers Ferry most of their lives can't identify its location. Not knowing at the time that Quinn was Roman Catholic, Bob Wagner and I doggedly began our search by looking at each and every tombstone in each and every cemetery at Harpers Ferry.

After many long hours of scrutinizing epitaphs, we finally found it. It was honestly the second to last tombstone that was left for us to look at.

In October 1999, our re-enacting unit performed a commemorative memorial ceremony for Private Quinn - the first U.S. Marine killed relative to our Civil War. This novel was also written to further acknowledge him, the only non-resident involved in the events of the 1859 raid who still remains at Harpers Ferry. (In 1899, the raiders killed at Harper's Ferry were exhumed and reburied at John Brown's farm at North Elba, near Lake Placid, NY.) Except for the location of his grave, nothing else is known about Quinn's burial. I detail in this novel what I believe to be a proper funeral for our silent, fallen hero. If his funeral didn't occur as described herein, perhaps it should have.

"Rest-In-Peace, Luke."

Dale Lee Sumner
1 May 2011

About the Editions

The First Edition (October 2004) -- the original printing of the story.

The Second Edition (July 2008) -- the result of a change in printing format and layout, with some minor grammatical corrections.

This Third Edition (May 2011) -- the result of a change in publisher. In addition, this Edition contains all of the pertinent historical information that has been discovered and validated since the book's first printing in 2004. Various style and language edits have also been incorporated.

Why an Appendix to a novel?

Over the years, I have 'devoured' many books of all types. While the majority of the novels I read were, indeed, entertaining, the ones I enjoyed the most often included photographs or prints of some sort (even if only on the flyleaf). For me, the visual stimulus always seemed to enhance the story even more because my mind's eye would take the provided reverence point(s) and significantly assist my imagination in encompassing the whole imagery of the written narrative. (Sometimes, a book cover just doesn't do it.)

I have included an Appendix in this novel to provide just such visual aid reverence points, as well as to provide educational material that will enhance my readers' enjoyment beyond the storyline and, hopefully, entice each of them to seek out more information about the historical facts presented herein.

I wholeheartedly recommend previewing the Appendix <u>before</u> starting to read this account of John Brown's capture by the Forgotten Marines. I am sure you will refer back to it quite often.

Enjoy!

CHAPTER ONE

"WARNING"

August 25, 1859, 2:10 p.m.

Tick, tick...tick. The lanky, timid man tapped ever so lightly on the opaque pane of the open office door and stood nervously at the threshold with an envelope and a folded piece of paper in his hand. The gilt lettering centered on the door's glass proclaimed 'John B. Floyd'.

"Ex-x-cuse me, Mister Secretary, b-but I have a very interesting communication here that was forwarded from the Cincinnati P-Postmaster. I thought you might want to see it r-right away."

"Come in, Johnson. What is so important that you're stammering again?" The Secretary had always taken great pains to ensure that he did not rattle his administrative clerk. The man tended to be a nervous Nellie, but he was by far the most efficient member of his support staff.

Quickly and silently, Johnson shuffled up to the front of the Secretary's desk, leaned forward, and placed the articles of concern on top of the other papers the Secretary had been working on. His right arm retreated to his side as soon as his fingers released their unwanted captives.

The Secretary picked up the envelope first and looked at it intently. "Hmmm, addressed to me in care of the Postmaster of Cincinnati, but with no return address," he said. "And no markings at all by the Postal System. I really should discuss that sort of thing with the Postmaster General." After glancing at the envelope's blank backside, he added, "Nothing interesting here, either," and placed it aside.

He then picked up the folded piece of paper. It was a common bond with no unusual watermark. The handwriting inside was clear and strong. Obviously, he decided, written by a man. With a firm voice he read aloud,

"August 20, 1859.
 Sir: I have lately received information of a movement of so great importance that I feel it is my duty to impart it to you without delay.
 I have discovered the existence of a secret organization, having for its object the liberation of the slaves of the South

by a general insurrection. The leader of the movement is *old John Brown*, late of Kansas. He has been in Canada during the winter, drilling the Negroes there, and they are only awaiting his word to start for the South to assist the slaves. They have one of their leading men (a white man) in an Armory in Maryland - where it is situated I have not been able to learn. As soon as everything is ready, those of their number who are in the Northern States and Canada are to come in small companies to their rendezvous, which is in the mountains of Virginia. They will pass down through Pennsylvania and Maryland, and enter Virginia at Harper's Ferry. Brown left the North about three or four weeks ago, and will arm the Negroes and strike the blow in a few weeks; so that whatever is done must be done at once. They have a large quantity of arms at their rendezvous, and are probably distributing them already.

As I am not fully in their confidence, this is all the information I can give you. I dare not sign my name to this, but trust you will not disregard this warning on that account."

He reread it again to himself. After pondering for several moments, he then stated, "Well, Johnson, I see nothing of importance here. It is just like so many other letters we receive from crackpots. Why," he twisted the letter around into Johnson's view, "it's not even signed. And, besides," he huffed rather matter of factly, "there is no U.S. Armory in Maryland." He shook his head faintly. "Just another alarmist trying to make something happen over nothing." After making this last comment, he returned the letter to his own perspective and paused. "Oh," his eyes closed momentarily and he inhaled a short breath, "just put it in the usual receptacle and carry on with your duties. I am satisfied in my own mind that a scheme of such wickedness and outrage could not be entertained by any citizen of the United States." He flicked the paper aside and it landed on top of the envelope.

For just an instant, Johnson cocked his head slightly to his left side, simultaneously raised his eyebrows, and crookedly pursed his lips. Suppressing a deep shrug of his shoulders, he stepped around to the side of the large oak desk and retrieved both articles. "Yes, Mister Secretary." He wheeled around and left the room as swiftly and quietly as he had entered.

John B. Floyd, a staunch Democrat, former Virginia Governor, and current Secretary of War, returned to the work of managing the standing Army for James Buchanan of Pennsylvania, the fifteenth President of the United States.

CHAPTER TWO

"ALARM"

Monday, October 17, 1859, 10:30 a.m.

BANG! BANG! The door glass rattled violently and a very intent Johnson thumped right up to the front of the large oak desk. "MISTER SECRETARY! An urgent wire from Mister John Garrett, president of the B and O Railroad!" His arm extended straight out. He was grasping a telegram firmly. The edge of the paper was just inches away from Secretary Floyd's nose. Johnson's hand was steady. The paper did not move at all.

Startled by Johnson's bold demeanor and the suddenness of his entry, Floyd jumped to his feet. His chair fleetly squeaked against the floorboards, tipped, and crashed backwards. Neither man heard the sound.

"Wha...What's happening?" stammered Floyd as he reached for the telegram.

"INSURRECTION, SIR!" stated Johnson in a clear and firm voice.

"Where?"

"Harper's Ferry, Virginia, sir. It's the Armory!"

"What?" Floyd did not comprehend what he had just heard. He drew the telegram closer to his chest and began to read aloud. As he spoke, some of the words came out as mere movements of his lips while others were vaguely distinct.

> "A formidable Negro insurrection at Harper's Ferry..."
> "United States Armory...and bridges are in full possession of large bands of armed men said to be abolitionists..."
> "Two hundred and fifty Whites and a gang of Negroes..."
> "Guns planted on the railroad bridge..."
> "Telegraph wires cut..."
> "Militia men assembling..."

At this point, he added, "Aaahah!" and then continued with clarity,

> "The presence of United States troops is indispensable. Can you authorize the government officers and military from Washington to go on our train at 3:20 this afternoon to the scene?"

As he was reading, Johnson circled unnoticed behind the desk, uprighted the large, padded leather chair, and positioned it behind the Secretary of War.

Stunned, Secretary Floyd plopped down into his chair and jabbered, "Negro insurrection...Abolitionists..." As a native-born Virginian, his mind was swimming with a variety of dreadful thoughts. "Johnson," he said, looking up, "do you remember the Nat Turner bloody revolt back in Thirty-One?"

"Honestly, no sir. I was just a young lad back then."

"Ah, well, it was a horrific slave uprising. It happened in Virginia's tidewater region during my father's term as Governor. A slave named Nat Turner and perhaps forty or so of his followers had stabbed, shot, and clubbed at least fifty-five white folks to death in a single night. Regardless of their age," he continued shakily, "men, women, and children were killed as they slept." He repeated, "Women and children...as they slept, mind you!" His head began moving slowly from side to side. "It was terrible, just terrible!" Jumping up to his feet he continued, "Another slave uprising...on this large of a scale must not happen." He banged his fist on the desktop and shouted, "It CANNOT happen!" For the first time in his nearly incompetent tenure as Secretary of War, John B. Floyd was galvanizing into action. "Whoever is responsible for this outbreak WILL be put down and put down QUICKLY!"

He then turned to his right and moved toward a large map on the side wall of his office. "Johnson, who and where are the closest Regulars that we can send to Harper's Ferry?"

"Uhhh..." Johnson's thoughts flashed through lists in his head and seized on the necessary information. "That would be the Third Artillery Regiment commanded by Colonel Gates at Fort Monroe in Virginia, sir."

Floyd placed his finger on the tip of the James Peninsula near Norfolk, Virginia. Checking the relative distance to Washington, he asked over his shoulder, "Is there no other substantial body of soldiers any closer?"

"Not U.S. Army Regulars, sir." Johnson was well aware that, with an army of just sixteen thousand soldiers, most were scattered along the Pacific coast, as well as in Utah and the Southwest. This dispersion was necessary to guard the United States' newest, most distant borders and fight its Indian wars.

Only a mere one thousand members of the standing Army were posted anywhere East of the Mississippi River – most posts were scattered along the Southern Atlantic and Gulf coasts, as well as a few on the northern border.

"All right, then. Take down a telegram." Floyd spun around and paced as he dictated.

> "Colonel Gates. You are hereby ordered to put three full Companies of troops aboard this evening's boat to Baltimore for immediate service at Harper's Ferry. Signed, etcetera, etcetera."

He started looking for something on his desktop as he waved his hand dismissively. "Get that off to the War Department telegrapher, immediately." As Johnson was heading toward the door, Floyd looked up and added, "And ask Colonel Drinkard to please attend me as soon as possible."

Shuffling through papers and files on the top of his desk, Floyd mused, "Now where is that blasted report..."

Shortly, Colonel Drinkard, Chief Clerk of the War Department, appeared in the doorway. "Yes, sir. You sent for me?" He entered the room without further ceremony and immediately approached the side of the Secretary's desk.

"Yes, Colonel. I am looking for a report that you sent me last Friday or the day before. It had to do with U.S. Army officers who have reported their presence in the Washington City area for whatever reason. Do you recall it?"

"Yes, sir, I do. Was there any particular officer that you had in mind?"

"I am looking for a senior field officer with sound judgment and preferably with battle experience. Was there anyone on that list that you could recommend for some serious business at Harper's Ferry? Here," he picked up Garrett's telegram and held it toward Drinkard, "read this and you will better understand what I am looking for."

Colonel Drinkard scanned through the message quickly. With full comprehension of the Secretary's needs, he stated, "We have just the man right across the river." He pointed in the general direction of the Potomac. "Brevet Colonel Lee has recently returned from court-martial duty up in New York City (the location of Army Head Quarters). He is a distinguished

Mexican War veteran. He lives here and is spending a few days at his home, *Arlington*, before returning to his post with the Second Cavalry in Texas." He returned the telegram to Secretary Floyd.

Floyd sat down at his desk and leaned forward on his forearms. "Yes, yes...a Virginian...and an excellent officer." He was retrospective and starting to feel a little calmer. "As I recall, he was stationed at Fort Monroe during the nearby bloody revolt and subsequent manhunt for Nat Turner." Convinced that Lee was, indeed, the man he was looking for, he turned to his Chief Clerk. "Please send a special messenger to request that Colonel Lee report here immediately."

"Yes, sir!" As Drinkard started to turn, he suddenly remembered a young cavalry officer who had been waiting outside his office for several hours. "And, if I can catch him, I think I have just the right 'special messenger' to send, too. Excuse me, sir, I shall be right back." Drinkard left the room at a half trot.

Secretary Floyd sat back in his chair and twisted his body toward the wall map. His mood was thoughtful. His eyes were looking, but not seeing. He reflectively figured that it would be more than two full days for the Fort Monroe troops to get to Harper's Ferry and that transit was further delayed because they would not be able to start until later that evening. "I cannot believe," he said to the map, "we're losing nearly three days for the lack of expedient transportation."

"I beg your pardon, sir?" It was Drinkard. Floyd did not realize how long he had been gone or that he had even returned.

"Ah, yes, Drinkard." The Secretary returned to his feet and started pacing again. "I have just realized that the troops from Fort Monroe will not be effectively in position until at least mid-morning Thursday. The Governors will undoubtedly call out the State Militias, but I am not entirely comfortable with emotionally charged Militiamen performing this task. Colonel Lee is certainly up to the leadership assignment, but a Federal military presence is required at the Harper's Ferry Armory at the earliest possible moment."

"Yes, sir. It is Federal property and we need to regain it as a matter of honor!" exclaimed Drinkard.

"Right you are, Colonel." He thought carefully for a few

seconds more. "I absolutely hate the idea of it, but I am going to have to ask the Secretary of the Navy for his help. He has a Marine Barracks near the Washington Navy Yard. They're Regulars and could probably be enroute in a matter of hours." Looking at the floor, he shook his head, "Mmmm, Mmmm, Mmmm. Asking the Secretary of the Navy for help. Now that's a problem for honor." He suddenly faced Colonel Drinkard. A look of horror was on his face. "Oh, my!" he exclaimed. "Marines doing the Army's job!" He swallowed hard. "I fervently pray that this doesn't set a precedent for the future."

"Absolutely not, sir!" replied Drinkard. He probably felt the same rush of fear in his loins as Secretary Floyd had.

"Yes, well...uh, I shall first brief President Buchanan of this whole situation and get his blessing relative to approaching Secretary Toucey about the use of his Marines." With that statement of intent, Secretary of War Floyd removed his hat, overcoat, and umbrella from the hall tree. "If Colonel Lee arrives before I return, please update him about these events." And he exited his office.

Monday, October 17, 1859, 11:15 a.m.

"Oh!...excuse me...ahh, good morning, Mister Secretary." It was Charles Welsh, the Chief Clerk of the Navy Department. He had barely averted a collision with Secretary Floyd in the hallway just outside of the Secretary of the Navy's office. The entryway was very close to a busy corridor intersection and the cause of many such mishaps. "Are you here to see Secretary Toucey?"

Floyd was jolted out of deep thought. During his walk from the White House to the Navy Department across the street, he had been internally rehearsing his comments for Toucey and had been walking along in a trance. "Oh, good morning, Welsh. Yes, I am here on the gravest of matters. Thank you." This last comment was in response to Welsh's courteous act of opening the door and standing aside to allow him in. Floyd walked toward the inner office door, stopped before a desk next to it, and was about to indicate to the attending administrative clerk why he was there to see Secretary Toucey. Before any words were exchanged, Welsh swooshed the second door open and announced his arrival.

"Mister Secretary, Secretary Floyd is here to see you, sir." The Secretary of the Navy rose to meet his guest.

"Good morning, John, an unexpected surprise to see you on such a gray and rainy day." Toucey walked from behind his desk. His left hand extended toward a side chair. "Please, be seated. It's a rare day when either of us visits the other's office." A rare day, indeed, in spite of the fact their offices were only a city block apart. "What can the Navy do for the Army, today?"

"Thank you, Isaac. I've just left the President and am here to provide you with information concerning a very urgent matter." He sat down on the edge of the proffered chair and, leaning forward, began expressing to the Secretary of the Navy the thoughts that he had so carefully rehearsed enroute. Isaac Toucey and Charles Welsh had both taken seats and listened intently. Several tense minutes passed. "...So, as you can see, the time factor involved with the Fort Monroe contingent is a clear case for sending Marines to Harper's Ferry as quickly as possible." John Floyd sat up slightly in the chair. "What say you, Isaac?" He was emotionally exhausted and his eyes clearly begged for a positive response to his request.

Secretary Toucey smiled, stood up, and walked toward Floyd. "Indubitably, John. I shall write the orders immediately and Charles, here, shall hand carry them to Colonel Harris posthaste." As Secretary Floyd stood up Toucey grasped the man's right hand with his own and placed his left hand on Floyd's right shoulder. The two started walking toward the door as they shook hands firmly. John Floyd was visibly relieved.

As the Secretary of War was departing the outer office, Toucey requested that the administrative clerk prepare to take down a message for Colonel John Harris, Commandant of the Marine Corps. He dictated,

> "Sir: Send all the available Marines at Head Quarters, under charge of suitable officers, by this evening's train of cars to Harper's Ferry, to protect the public property at that place, which is endangered by

riotous outbreak. The men will be furnished with a proper number of ball cartridges, ammunition and rations, and will take two howitzers and shrapnel. The Commanding Officer, on his arrival at Harper's Ferry, will report to the Senior Army Officer who may be there in command. Otherwise he will take such measures as in his judgment may be necessary to protect the Arsenal and other property of the United States. I am respectfully, etcetera, etcetera."

To the clerk he added, "Please prepare that for my signature as quickly as possible."

As they waited in the Secretary's office, Toucey and Welsh discussed the matter at hand and, briefly, the nature of a future recompense for this unaccustomed debt owed by the Army. While the events of the day were sufficient cause for temporary cooperation between the two Presidential Cabinet Members, the interservice rivalry was deep and long standing and, indeed, as many military men are fond of saying, "paybacks can be hell".

CHAPTER THREE

"PREPARATION"

Monday, October 17, 1859, 11:50 a.m.

Chief Clerk Welsh paid the driver and stepped down from the hackney. He started running across the street toward the sentry station at the main entrance arch of the Marine Barracks. Three Marines were present. Two Privates with long arm weapons and a Corporal. They were in the process of relieving the watch. The Corporal's back was to the approaching visitor. His primary interest was focused on the uniform appearance of the on-coming watch stander. He was just about to say something about a not so white waist belt when the watch stander leaned slightly forward and whispered, "Foul wind, Corp, top hat astern." The Marine Private then snapped to ramrod stiff Attention and, looking straight ahead, called out in a clear voice, "Attention On Deck." The Corporal gave the Private an evil eye. Knowing that his 'look' conveyed the possibility of retribution if this was a false alarm, the veteran calmly came to Attention and executed a smart Right About Turn.

Recognizing the visitor, he flashed a flawless salute and said, "Good day, Mister Welsh. Corporal Gilbert, sir. Corporal of the Guard. How may I assist you, sir?"

"I must first meet with your Officer of the Day and then I have urgent business with Colonel Harris," replied Welsh.

"Aye, sir. Right this way." The Corporal made a right facing movement and, when it was completed, continued to turn his head even further to the right to address the two Privates. "Private Roy, assume the watch. Private Allen, you are relieved. Carry On." He stepped off. Both Marines voiced, "Aye-Aye, Corporal!" as he led the visitor toward the Duty Office.

Following the Corporal, Welsh thought to himself, "*I do like how these boys are disciplined. I must discuss with Secretary Toucey about maintaining the minimum Marine recruitment age at twenty-one. It makes perfect sense to do so.*"

Corporal Gilbert rapped twice on the open door as he stepped inside and to the right. He snapped to Attention and announced, "Lieutenant Greene, Mister Welsh from the Navy Department, sir."

First Lieutenant Israel Greene stood up behind the Duty

Desk. He was meticulously dressed in the latest regulation 'undress' (working) attire for company grade officers. His uniform consisted of a single breasted dark blue frock coat with evenly spaced buttons. He also wore dark blue trousers with a red stripe down the outer seam. Passing across his right shoulder, between his stand-up collar and the four inch, fore and aft, by one inch shoulder mounted rank-insignia, crossing to his left waist and under his white sword belt was his crimson silk sash tied behind his left hip. The sash worn in this manner was a clear indication of his position as Officer of the Day. He started to speak but was cut off by Welsh.

"Quickly, how many Marines do you have available for immediate duty?" queried Welsh.

Greene instantly picked up his duty roster and started checking. He was a little flustered by the sudden presence of the Chief Clerk of the Navy Department and by his brusque demeanor. He flipped through the pages twice, calculating numbers in his head. "Sir, I cannot give you an exact number, but we have about twelve Non-Commissioned Officers (Non-Coms/NCOs) and ninety Privates, more or less, at the Barracks and on duty in the immediate vicinity."

"Is that all? I thought there were more assigned here," retorted Welsh.

"There were, sir. But a Detachment of thirty-nine Marines left this morning for Brooklyn," responded Greene.

"Oh...yes, I had forgotten about those orders. Thank you, Greene." He spun about and exited the room. "Come Corporal, to the Commandant's office if you please."

Greene watched from the doorway as the crafty little Corporal caught up with and slipped around in front of Welsh. He heard the Corporal's gentle "This way, sir" redirect Welsh to the right. John Harris had only been Commandant for slightly over ten months, but at sixty-six years of age and with forty-five years as a Marine, he was a man of quintessential military habit. He was undoubtedly preparing to adjourn to his quarters at the stroke of Eight Bells (Noon) to partake dinner. Corporal Gilbert knew this and was taking Welsh toward a side entrance to the Head Quarters building. This act of forethought would allow them to intercept the Commandant if he had already departed his office.

Greene wanted desperately to know what sort of trouble was afoot. However, as Officer of the Day and with the imminence of Twelve Noon, his movement was restricted to the immediate proximity of his post. As he returned to the desk, he spoke out loud to himself, "Sit tight, Marine, you'll find out soon enough." He picked up his fatigue (undress) cap and sword and prepared himself for the Noon Parade. Not even the light rain that had been falling all morning was going to spoil the established tradition of the United States Marine Corps' parading to the Noon meal.

Monday, October 17, 1859, 12:00 Noon

Moments before, Colonel John B. Harris, the sixth Commandant of the Marine Corps, had been viewing the parade ground from his second story office window. He had been reflecting about the rain apparently stopping for the time being when he spotted Welsh exiting the Duty Office. He had therefore delayed his departure for dinner. There was no doubt in his mind that something critical had occurred. This was the first time that the Chief Clerk of the Navy Department had arrived without prior notice. The visit was also peculiar since Welsh seemed to be in a hurry and was without umbrella or overcoat on this cool, and now, overcast day. Harris met his visitor in the anteroom to his office.

Welsh was the first to speak. "I have a most important dispatch for you from Secretary Toucey." He fumbled in his coat pocket, retrieved the dispatch, and handed it to Harris.

Harris accepted the dispatch. "Thank you, Mister Welsh. Please come inside and warm yourself by the fire." He followed Welsh into his office, sat down at his desk, and began reading. The contents of the dispatch confirmed his suspicions.

Addressing Welsh, Harris said, "Secretary Toucey says he wants "suitable officers" sent with the Detachment. That might present a bit of a problem. Brevet Major Terrett, the Commander of the Marine Barracks, is still on leave of absence. First Lieutenant Greene is next in seniority and will therefore command the expedition. There are two other officers available...Second Lieutenants Henderson and Jones. One should accompany Greene, leaving the other behind in charge of the Barracks." He paused and grimaced, "However, Henderson has been reporting himself sick lately and is simply not up to performing either assignment. Jones will have to remain in charge of the Barracks and Greene will take the Detachment by himself."

"Have you any other leader to send?" asked Welsh. His coat was visibly steaming as it was drying from the heat of the fire.

The sight of a 'fuming' Chief Clerk mentally startled Harris. He gestured a mild 'halt' sign with his right arm. His elbow was bent. His hand oscillated quickly from left to right and back again. "No," he continued, "As you are aware, both the Sergeant Major and I are restricted by law from leaving the Washington area." He paused. With a slight bend of his head, his bearded chin rested lightly on the curved forefinger and thumb of his raised right hand. His thought finished, he continued, "Under the circumstances, the best that I can do is send Orderly Sergeant McDonough to assist Greene. He is my own right hand man here at Head Quarters. He was at Chapultepec with the Marine Brigade during the Mexican War and has commanded quite a few ship's Guard in his time."

Welsh acquiesced. "Very well. Lieutenant Greene will take the Marine Detachment to Harper's Ferry with Orderly Sergeant McDonough as Second-in-Command." He went on to explain Secretaries Floyd and Toucey's plans regarding time of departure, rendezvous with the Army officer who would command the Militia at the scene, as well as other details of the expedition. When he had finished, he took his leave and returned to the Navy Department office.

Harris started drafting orders to Lieutenant Greene.

> "Sir; You will take command of a Detachment of Marines and proceed by the 3:20 PM train to Weverton, Maryland. On your arrival there, you will communicate with the senior officer of the Army, who will either be there or in its vicinity with such instructions as he may have to give you in carrying out his orders from the President of the United States. You will take with you two 12-pound howitzers with such ammunition as may be necessary to serve them efficiently in case of them being required for use. Very Respectfully Yours..."

"Orderly Sergeant," said Harris. His voice was no louder than his usual conversational tone.

"Yes, sir," responded a booming voice from the outer office. Orderly Sergeant McDonough was famous for his seemingly cat-like hearing. He, of course, had overheard most of the conversation between Welch and Harris and was currently standing just outside Harris' door. He waited several heartbeats before framing himself in the doorway.

Dressed per the prevailing Uniform Regulations of the day, he was immaculately attired in an enlisted 'fatigue' (working) uniform consisting of a sky-blue, single breasted, short length coat (also referred to as a shell jacket). It reached about an inch or two below his waist and had a standing hooked-up collar, three inches high. The coat had no color trim, but it did have a shallow, horizontal pocket low on each of the front panels. It was made of kersey wool, as were the matching sky-blue trousers, also without color trim. The coat had nine buttons in the front and one button per cuff, as well as one button per shoulder strap. The buttons were uniquely 'Marine' with an arc of thirteen stars above an eagle with outstretched wings holding a loop of anchor cable in its beak and grasping the ring and stock of a slanting fouled anchor. The buttons also had a lined background within a raised circumference border.

As a Marine Sergeant, his rank insignia was denoted by the wearing of two plain stripes of yellow worsted lace on each arm starting just above the sleeve cuff, placed diagonally on the outer arm from one seam to the other, the outer points inclining towards the elbow. As a means of signifying his elevated status for having commanded ship's Marine Guard Detachments at sea, he was designated as Orderly Sergeant and, unlike a regular line sergeant, wore a red worsted sash under his white waist belt.

"Please convey my compliments to Lieutenant Greene and ask him to report to this office as soon as the Noon Parade is done." Harris could still hear the Musicians on the parade field.

"Aye-Aye, sir!"

Monday, October 17, 1859, 12:30 p.m.

Greene knocked three times on the doorjamb, entered the

room, and stood at Attention before the Commandant's desk. "Good afternoon, sir. I have the pleasure to report that the replacement Detachment departed for Brooklyn on time and without event at Ten-Thirty, the Noon Parade has been completed in a satisfactory manner, the mid-day meal is being served to all hands, and the Noon Watch work assignments have been properly detailed for completion."

As Greene was making this official report, Harris was mentally noting his physical characteristics. Greene was short. Maybe five foot four compared to Harris' own height of a quarter foot beyond six feet. He was athletically built. He also possessed a masculine face, dark hair, and a robust moustache. "Thank you, Greene. Please be seated." While Greene positioned himself in the closest chair, Harris speculated that the junior officer was about thirty-five years old.

Harris sat back in his chair. "Tell me, Greene, when were you first commissioned?"

"Back in Forty-Seven, sir. About the middle of the War with Mexico," replied Greene. "Unfortunately, not early enough to have participated in any of the ground action."

"And your current date of rank?"

"July, Fifty-Five, sir."

"Sea assignments?"

"Three, sir. One as second officer and two in command."

"Am I correct in remembering that you have recently acquired artillery training?"

"Yes, sir. At the Military Academy (West Point) in Fifty-Seven, sir."

"Excellent," said Harris, "excellent." Greene had been reassigned to the Marine Barracks when his last ship returned from an African tour a little over six months ago. From his personal observations, Harris had rated this officer with all high marks. He saw Greene as dedicated, enthusiastic, competent, and correct in his military bearing and attitude. And now, Harris figured that Greene's twelve years of Line experience would certainly serve him well for this upcoming assignment.

Satisfied that Greene was the right Marine for the job, Harris said, "Well, Greene, we have a bit of an adventure in the making. There is an extraordinary sort of insurrection occurring at Harper's Ferry, Virginia. Here are your official orders." He leaned forward slightly and held out the document for Greene to retrieve.

Greene quickly read the orders. A smile grew wide across his face. "Yes, sir!" His excitement could hardly be contained. It was a strain on his self-control to regain his seat. When he did, he was merely poised on the front edge of the chair.

Harris picked up a pen and proceeded on. "Now then, to start with, Lieutenant Jones will stay to command the Barracks in your absence. As Lieutenant Henderson is still on the Binnacle List (sick list), my Orderly Sergeant McDonough will be your Second-in-Command. From the Barracks, Orderly Sergeant Mundell will also be assigned." He was checking off the names from a list in front of him. He paused to let Greene make mental notes of the names. "So, without stripping the Barracks absolutely bare, what can we spare for this Detachment?"

Sans notes, Greene quickly responded, "Well, sir, our list of able bodied and available men tallies out to four Sergeants, three Corporals, two Drummers, one Fifer and seventy-four Privates. A few Non-Commissioned Officers and Musicians too sick to travel, and Privates just enlisted will stay behind." Greene had obviously done his homework since Welsh had left the Duty Office.

"Hmmm..." Harris was running a sum. "Looks like a Detachment total of eighty-seven, including yourself." He chuckled. "Secretary Floyd has called out three Companies of Artillerymen from Fort Monroe." He shook his head slightly. "And heaven knows how many State Militiamen are responding." Leaning back in his chair, he continued, "But I tell you, Greene, eighty-seven Marines sounds like just the right number to me."

Greene chuckled at the joke, too. "Yes, sir, just right, sir."

Harris spent the next several minutes telling Greene all the information he had received from Welsh. Finally, he stood up, signaling the end of the meeting. "Form your Detachment, Lieutenant. And make sure that you take along a proper mix of rounds for the twelve pounders. Enough to knock down the whole confounded place if you have to." He nodded resolutely. "Carry on, Lieutenant. Fortitudine!"

"Aye-Aye, sir! Fortitudine!" As Greene left the office,

Orderly Sergeant McDonough, now accoutered with his sword, fell into step behind him.

* * * * *

"I'm telling you boys, something big is in the making." Private Allen was standing in the middle of the Barracks' berthing area and had an audience of about twelve other Privates around him. As the off-going watch stander, he was excused from the Noon Parade and authorized to eat his midday meal before the normal serving time. He had done so, quickly, and had been eagerly waiting for his Barracks mates. He had a juicy bit of scuttlebutt (gossip) to pass on to them.

"Yeah, sure. What's a Fresh Fish (newcomer to the Corps) like you going to know?" quipped Private Quinn.

"I know enough to know that a top hat named Welsh showed up at Sentry Post Number One, all excited, had to see the Officer of the Day immediately and then had urgent business with the Commandant," replied Allen. Raising his hands high on his chest, he placed his thumbs behind his linen braces (suspenders) and held on to the fronts with his fingers. He looked around the small crowd with an air of smug importance.

"AND..." chimed in several of his comrades.

"And, do you know who this top hat Welsh is?" He posed an index finger and, circling, pointed at the faces around him. He was truly enjoying the suspense of the moment. Satisfied that no one knew the answer, he continued, "Well, I asked the cook in the galley who this Welsh fellow was. And do you know what he told me?"

"Come on, man, spit it out!" The closet man to him had grabbed his braces and had given him a little friendly shake.

"MIS-TER Welsh is the Chief Clerk of the Navy Department." The answer was loud and clear, but it had not passed Allen's lips. Everyone turned around to identify the speaker. It was Corporal Gilbert. The crowd of men moved toward him. Everyone started talking at once.

"What's going on, Corporal?"

"Has a war started somewhere?"

"Did something happen to the replacement Detachment that

left this morning?"

"How did you know who this fellow was?"

"Come on, Corp, talk to us."

"Yeah, what do you know?"

"PIPE DOWN ALL OF YOU!" Corporal Gilbert commanded.

"Please, Corporal, you escorted the man around the Barracks. Surely you know something about what's going on." It was Allen. For all of his bravado, he, too, was only capable of guessing and wanted to know something. They all did.

Gilbert walked up to Allen. "Allen," he said, "you're still a Fresh Fish in this sea going outfit. Sure, you are a little smarter than most and, in fifteen or twenty years, you might even make Corporal. But the best thing that you could do right now is to learn how to 'sit tight'. You'll find out soon enough." He spun around and addressed the whole group. "Now, carry on with your duties. There are Noon Watch work assignments waiting to be done." He started toward the exit. "Let's move it you Jack Tar rejects, or there will be no liberty call next Sunday!"

As men were shifting away toward their appointed places of duty, Allen gently grasped the arm of Private Quinn. "Quinn, you've been with the Marines for quite a while. In the three months that I've been in so far, I've heard 'sit tight' more often than I can count. Is there something more to this phrase than meets the eye?"

"Yes, my fishy young friend, there is," replied Quinn. "Sit down for a minute and I'll tell you the story." They both sat down on the edge of one of the wooden bunks. "During the War with Mexico, there was a sea battle between one of our ships and one of theirs. A Marine Private was assigned to the magazine to help fill powder bags for the gun crews. The battle was hot and furious. Several fires had started. One of those fires was very close to the magazine. The air was filling with ashes and sparks." Quinn looked at Allen seriously. "Now, you know that ashes, sparks, and black powder don't mix well in a ship's magazine, right?" Allen nodded. "Okay, well then, this Private couldn't find the lid to the barrel of black powder that he had been dipping into to fill the powder bags." He clapped his flat right hand over the rounded thumb and forefinger of his half-closed left fist. "So he covered the barrel with the biggest thing he had available." Quinn dropped his hands. "A little later, when the fires were out, a Naval officer stuck his head into the magazine to check on things. Of course, this officer was a wee bit upset to see a Marine calmly sitting on a powder barrel, softly singing a merry tune. When the officer asked what the Marine thought he was doing, the Marine calmly replied, 'Just sittin' tight, sir'." As he gently rocked his head from side to side, the crooked smile on his lips parted just enough to allow a soft chuckle to escape. "Of course, it took a moment or two before the officer realized what had happened and what the Marine's comment actually meant." Suddenly, Quinn stood up. "So, to make a long story short, our ship won the battle and the Private soon found out that his quick thinking had probably saved the ship from exploding. He also found out that he was to be immediately promoted to Corporal." Quinn gave Allen a little slug in the arm. "Now hurry up to where you're supposed to be before Corporal 'Powder Pants' Gilbert catches you." And he dashed toward the exit.

Allen was puzzled for a few seconds. "Powder Pants?" he mused. Suddenly realization dawned, his eyes widened, and he yelled after Quinn, "You mean that the biggest thing he had available was his backside?" Quinn had stopped at the doorway and was grinning broadly back at Allen. After a quick wink and a firm nod, he ducked through the portal. Allen laughed. "Well I'll be switched. Old Powder Pants, huh?" His head swayed with amusement. "Corporal Gilbert, you are one sly sea dog."

Moving off the bunk, he pursed his lips and tried, "Fort-a-two-day-nine..." He shook his head. *"Maybe,"* he thought, *"I'll get that word right one of these days."*

A genuinely 'new' enlistee passing by asked, "Say, what is that funny sounding word?"

Allen stood up tall, straightened his shoulders, smiled, and replied, "Well, Fish, that funny sounding word is Latin and it's the Marine Corps' Motto. I can't say it just right, yet, but it means 'With Courage'." As he spoke these last two words, he clenched his right fist, tensed his upright forearm, and gently shook both with conviction. He then relaxed and continued, "It's a big part of who we are. So, you'd better start learning to get your tongue around it as soon as you can." Allen strutted off toward the exit chuckling and saying to himself, "Fort-a-two-day-nine."

Monday, October 17, 1859, 12:40 p.m.

Lieutenant Greene and Orderly Sergeant McDonough walked quickly down the passageway. Lieutenant Greene was deep in thought. As they encountered the top of the stairs, he said over his shoulder, "Please ask Lieutenant Jones and Orderly Sergeant Mundell to report with yourself to the Duty Office at the double quick."

"Yes, sir."

Turning on the landing, Greene could actually see the Orderly Sergeant and paused momentarily, "Oh, yes...and be so kind as to advise Lieutenant Jones that he will be assuming the watch as Officer of the Day."

"Yes, sir."

As they approached the main entrance foyer, Greene checked his pocket watch. "Yes..," he reflected. Passing through the door and onto the porch he added, "And please have the Non-Coms round up all hands for a muster on the parade ground at One O'clock. No specific uniform. They should come as they are." At the bottom of the steps, he stopped, turned about, and faced his Second-in-Command. "Carry on, XO." He used the familiar form for Executive Officer.

McDonough grinned widely and replied, "Aye-Aye, Skipper." He saluted and started trotting off. His responsive use of the familiar form for Commanding Officer clearly indicated his mutual respect for the Lieutenant and his leadership.

Greene returned the salute and angled off toward the Duty Office. Since first reading his orders in the Commandant's office, thoughts at the back of his mind had been playing with various logistic needs. A great deal of organization and preparation had to be accomplished within the next hour and a half. He possessed a very strong analytical ability and truly enjoyed this sort of problem solving. Organization was his specialty and he sometimes marveled at how easily things seemed to fall into place when he thought about them.

The excitement of an unexpected command opportunity,

the thrill of pending action, and the challenge of organizing the Detachment all combined to exhilarate him to an unaccustomed height. His feet felt as though they were barely touching the earth. Time seemed to be standing still. Everything he was thinking was absolutely clear and concise. A euphoric "Yes!" escaped his lips as he bounded from the walkway and cut directly across a wide grassy area toward his objective.

Upon arriving at the Duty Office, he quickly sat down and withdrew paper and pencil from the desk drawer. He paused and reflected. "...Seventy-four Privates...four Sergeants...three Corporals..." Staring into space, he absently tapped the pencil point on the paper. His thoughts raced. Although anticipating action, "...Two twelve pounders...seven man crews..." he plainly did not know what they were heading into. "...Have to be ready for anything..." He began jotting down numbers. Within a few moments, half-finished calculations dotted the paper in front of him. "Yes..." he nodded, "Three sections of twenty and one of fourteen..." He started listing supply information in several different columns. "...Rations ...ammunition...equipment..." A smile of satisfaction began cracking across his face as his pencil flashed across the paper.

A huffing and puffing Lieutenant Jones appeared in the doorway. "You sent for me, sir?"

"Yes, Jones. Please sit down and catch your wind." The junior officer did so. Greene laid his pencil down. "You will assume temporary command of the Barracks immediately." Jones knew that something was up because he would be assuming the OOD duties, but this news stunned him. He just sat there with his mouth open. "Here, lad, this will give you more information." Greene handed his orders over to Jones.

Knock, knock, knock. Orderly Sergeants McDonough and Mundell had arrived and entered the room. Greene signaled them to be seated. "Excellent," he said. "Lieutenant, when you are finished reading the orders, please pass them to the Orderly Sergeants." Jones passed the paper to McDonough who immediately passed it to Mundell who merely leaned forward and placed in on the edge of the desk.

Greene suppressed a smile and stood up. "Yes... uh...well then, it appears that everyone is somewhat aware of what the rising wind is all about. So, let's get right to it. We have a great amount of work to accomplish in a very short period of time." He picked up and handed the duty rosters to Jones.

"Lieutenant, I annotated these rosters earlier. The names that are checked are men that will be staying here at the Barracks under your command. The remainder will be marching with the Detachment." Greene's gaze redirected to the Orderly Sergeants. Both men had already taken out small notebooks and pencils from their pockets. They were confident and they were ready.

Greene picked up his jotted notes. He began, "Excluding Musicians, our main body will be made up of eighty-one men. Four Sergeants, three Corporals, and seventy-four Privates. We will also be taking two howitzers, two limbers and eight or twelve horses. The Detachment will be organized into four Sections. Three infantry...Sections A, B, and C, and one artillery...Section D."

"Orderly Sergeant Mundell, pick your best gunnery Sergeant from the four available Sergeants. He will command the artillery section. Assign to him ten of your best gun handlers and four teamsters. Advise him to prepare his ammunition for any eventuality – solid shot, shrapnel, canister, and grape. We're not sure of what size force we'll be up against."

"Yes, sir," responded Mundell. "And, sir, we can get by with just eight horses. That'll mean less fodder and grain to worry about."

"Umm...hmm," Greene nodded acknowledgement and said, "Very well, thank you." He continued, "So, with those fifteen assigned, that will leave us with one Sergeant, one Corporal and twenty Privates for each of the remaining Sections." He leaned forward. "I want all three of you to work on this. We need to assign the men carefully. Each Section should be a balance between Shellbacks (old hands) and New Fish. Make sure that each Section is as strong as the others are. If there's any hot work to be done over there, I can't be worrying about Section capabilities." All three in his audience nodded agreement and understanding.

Greene leaned back and referred to his notes. "Now then, concerning preparations. We'll send Section A to the galley to help prepare ninety sets of rations for three days. Section B will collect everyone's cartridge box and sling and take them to the Armory. They will fill each cartridge box with forty rounds. Caps will be distributed to the men while enroute to Harper's Ferry. Section C will be split up. Half will draw haversacks and canteens from the Quartermaster Sergeant and report to the galley to assist Section A. The second half will draw knapsacks and distribute them one to a bunk. They will then assist Section B. When the ammunition is ready, distribute the cartridge boxes one to a bunk. The same will pertain to the haversacks and canteens when they are full." He looked around at the three men. "Any questions?"

"No, sir," chimed his audience.

"Very well. Orderly Sergeant McDonough, you will please oversee the galley preparations and Orderly Sergeant Mundell, please oversee the Armory preparations. After all else is ready, have the men prepare their knapsacks and greatcoats."

"Aye-Aye, sir," chorused back.

"I shall be leaving the Barracks shortly to facilitate travel arrangements with the B and O railroad. Lieutenant Jones, as Officer of the Day, you will be overall responsible for the coordination of preparations until I return."

"Yes, sir."

Greene moved toward the doorway and checked his watch. "I shall address the men in about five minutes. That should obligate an additional five minutes." He closed his watch and looked up. "Gentlemen, that affords you ten minutes to prepare your Section lists. Please join me on the parade field when you are finished." As he stepped out of the office, he could hear the screeching of chair legs on the floor and the shuffling of feet. Greene was confident that his able Non-Commissioned veterans would know what to do and would get it done quickly. He smiled as he slowly headed toward the assemblage of men on the parade field.

Monday, October 17, 1859, 1:00 p.m.

"Marine Barracks, ATENNN..SHUN!" Sergeant Davis looked first right, then left down the front rank of Marines. Satisfied that the assembly was squared away, he executed a smooth right about turn. When Lieutenant Greene was within six paces of him, he snapped a salute and reported, "All present or accounted for, sir."

Greene returned the salute. "Thank you, Sergeant." As the Sergeant was positioning himself one pace beside and slightly behind the Lieutenant's right arm, Greene surveyed his Detachment. The Sergeants had obviously cleared the Barracks of Marines and had sent for the daily duty men at the kitchen, stables, latrine, and elsewhere. They were dressed in a variety of uniforms and work clothes as well as various stages of dress and undress. At this moment, the one thing they all had in common was the look of intense interest on their faces.

Greene barked, "In Place, Rest." As one, their right feet slid back slightly behind their left heels, their body weight shifted back to their right legs and their left hands crossed over and held onto their right hands in front of them.

"Men, today is not going to be a normal Monday. Today, we are about to embark on a great adventure."

"I knew something big was in the making," whispered Allen under his breath.

"An insurrection of an undetermined size has been reported at Harper's Ferry, Virginia. The Armory there has apparently been seized." A general murmur started between some of the men.

"Silence in the ranks!" hissed Corporal Gilbert from behind the formation.

"The Marine Corps has been called upon to provide an armed force capable of putting down this insurrection and to protect the property of the United States. It will be our honor and privilege to answer this call."

"HUZZAH!" Nearly a third of the assembly cheered at once. Greene waited patiently as the Non-Commissioned Officers restored order.

"In order to prepare ourselves for this challenge, a great many things must be accomplished in a very short period of time. I shall require that each and every Marine put forth his best effort until such time that we return triumphant to this Barracks."

"HUZZAH!" This time over half of the assembly cheered.

Greene held up his arms to signal 'silence'. It occurred quickly. "In a few moments, Orderly Sergeants McDonough and Mundell will be announcing your Section and duty assignments. Listen carefully and follow their orders." Greene paused as he withdrew his sword from its scabbard. "As our preceding Comrades-in-Arms exhibited during the battles in Tripoli," his tempo and volume were slowly escalating, "and also during the assault on Chapultepec Castle and Mexico City...the very Halls of the Montezumas...we shall venture forth to meet this new challenge with the same valor and determination." He held the sword out, away from his body, the point upward. As if he were admonishing them, he smoothly shook the fist holding the grip toward the assembly. His speaking volume again increased. "Prepare well, Marines, for we will soon march onward to glory." He thrust his sword upward toward the sky and the intensity in his voice increased even more, "For God, Corps, and Country." And, then, circling his sword above his head, he shouted, "For-da-tu-da-nee!"

"FOR-DA-TU-DA-NEE! HUZZAH! HUZZAH! HUZZAH!" Now the whole assembly cheered, including the Non-Coms. The men were jostling each other, their mood was playful, and some were even throwing their caps into the air.

Lieutenant Greene was exhilarated by the surging excitement of the assembly. His pulse was racing and he felt lightheaded. He returned his sword to its scabbard. He then glanced toward the Commandant's office. The Commandant was standing in the center window. Greene smiled wildly and tossed a half salute in that direction. The Commandant actually waved back. He thought to himself, *"Dear God, I love this life!"* Sobering quickly, he turned around to look for his Second-in-Command. Lieutenant Jones and Orderly Sergeants McDonough and Mundell were approaching from the Duty Office. He turned and headed in their direction.

As Greene approached the trio, Orderly Sergeant Mundell peeled off toward the cheering assembly. As only an experienced Barracks Sergeant can, he ordered, "AAAA-TENN-SHUNN DEEE-TACHHH-MENT!" The assemblage was immediately as frozen and quiet as a startled church mouse.

Lieutenant Greene returned the salutes from Lieutenant Jones and Orderly Sergeant McDonough. McDonough gave Greene a knowing nod and discretely held out several pages of paper. Understanding that the Section lists were ready, Greene said, "Well done, gentlemen." To McDonough he said, "XO, please carry on with your duties. Form the Detachment for departure at Two-Fifteen."

"Aye-Aye, sir." In a lower tone, he added, "That was a first-rate speech if I may say, sir. The boys are rightly fired up. They'll never realize how hard they've worked until long after we depart." He saluted.

Greene grinned and returned the salute. To Lieutenant Jones he said, "Lieutenant, please escort me to the main gate." The junior officer turned about and fell into step with Greene. Behind them, they could hear the XO.

"Attention To Orders. When dismissed, the following men will report to Sergeant Woodfield for duty in Section D..."

"Jones, I shall be off immediately to the B and O agent's office. It is absolutely imperative that this Detachment be fully prepared and ready to march no later than Two-Twenty. I am relying on you to ensure that this objective is fully realized. Our Orderly Sergeants are extremely competent, but, if an unusually perplexing situation should arise, or if a command decision must be made before I return, you must weigh out all of the options and make the correct decision for me. Is that understood?"

"Yes, sir."

"Good," said Greene. "Now then, a personal request. Please ask the Wardroom servant to make up my valise with the following items -- Two fresh shirts, two pair of drawers, four pair of socks, a blanket, my shaving items, and a pair of my black leather gloves. Do you have all that?"

"Yes, sir."

"Thank you," continued Greene. "If the valise and my boat cloak are brought down to the Duty Office, it will save me immeasurable time." He had reached a spot just inside the main gate and stopped. He unbuckled his sword belt and handed it to Jones. He then unknotted his sash and removed it from his shoulder. With a couple of deft movements, he rearranged the sash around his waist. He retrieved his sword belt and repositioned it quickly. Greene then detached his brass scabbard encased sword and handed it to Jones. "Please retain this in the Duty Office as well." He pulled down on the lower edge of his frock coat to straighten it. After brushing off unseen lint from his sleeves, he straightened to his full height and said, "You have the watch, Lieutenant. Any questions? No? Good. I shall return as soon as possible." He exited through the main entrance arch and turned up Eighth Street toward Pennsylvania Avenue.

"Yes...sir..." Lieutenant Jones suddenly felt exhilarated and deflated at the same time. He had just received his first Command assignment, and he felt extremely proud of the trust that Lieutenant Greene was placing in him. However, he was commanding the home guard and all the action would be happening elsewhere. "I sure wish young Henderson wasn't feeling so sick." He shook his head. "Sit tight, Marine. A bigger chance will be coming along, soon."

As he headed toward the Duty Office, he hefted Greene's sheathed sword in his hand and appreciatively noticed how light it was. "Hmm," he pondered. "Not exactly regulation weight. Feels more like something one would wear to a fancy dress ball." He shrugged his shoulders. "I guess that makes sense. Why carry around a heavy sword when just performing post duties. It's only a badge of office around here anyway." He drew the lightweight Mameluke sword out and tested it for balance. "Verrry nice. I'll have to see about getting me one of these." Smiling, he resheathed the weapon and entered the Duty Office.

Monday, October 17, 1859, 1:15 p.m.

Greene covered the three blocks to Pennsylvania Avenue at a quick pace. On the North side of the street an elderly man was sitting on a bench under the broad shade tree that protected the omnibus pickup stop. After crossing the street, Greene addressed the man. "Excuse me, sir, but have you seen an omnibus go by here recently?"

"Yes, Lieutenant, the last one went by here about five minutes ago, as I was approaching this bench." He was a weathered man, about seventy years or so in age, white hair, a small white beard, and the cane he carried was more likely for function rather than style.

"Thank you," replied Greene to the man. To himself he cursed. He knew the transportation company's schedule was erratic, but their interval, somehow, was not. Another omnibus would not be coming along for at least fifteen more minutes. He began surveying both directions of the avenue for other transportation. As he did so, he realized that the man had addressed him by his rank. He queried, "You are familiar with the rank and uniform, sir?"

"Well, the uniform style is new, but I supposed the single gold bar at each end," his index finger oscillated back and forth in an arc, "of the bright blue field of your rank-strap still meant the same." Greene stopped and faced the man. His eyes narrowed slightly as he reassessed him. The man smiled. "Why, long before you were born, Lieutenant, I was one of the lucky Marines with Andy Jackson down in New Orleans, back in January of Fifteen." The elderly man reached out with his cane and tapped it across the shin of his right leg. The sound was wooden. "Lost this one just below the knee during that little fracas."

"I am truly sorry to hear that," replied Greene. He was delighted to know that this man had been a Marine, but saddened about the injury.

"Don't be," remarked the man. "God, Corps, and Country, you know." His face beamed. "It was my pleasure to be there." As he spoke, Greene could hear the sounds of a carriage off to his right. It was a hackney heading toward Capitol Hill and it was empty.

Greene bowed slightly. "Excuse me," he said and turned to flag down the carriage. The driver acknowledged the hail and directed the horse to the bench. Greene addressed the elderly man, "Please, sir, won't you join me in this carriage?"

"Why, thank you kindly, Lieutenant." Greene helped the man into the carriage.

"Driver, to the train depot if you please. And kindly be as direct as you can." As the carriage began to move out, Greene settled in next to the elderly man. He was curious to learn a little about the 'Old Corps' from his unexpected guest.

Monday, October 17, 1859, 1:30 p.m.

The man laughed gently. "And that, Lieutenant, was how we managed to fight one more battle after the peace treaty had already been signed." The hackney came to a gentle stop in front of the train depot.

"Fascinating," said Greene. He had been enthralled during the whole ride. Hearing stories from any veteran whose adventures took place long before his own had always intrigued him. "Pray tell sir, if you please. What advice do you have to give to a modern Marine officer?"

The elderly man leaned back slightly and took a hard appraising look at Greene. He began speaking in a tone of a wise, old father, "Only two things." He held out a hand with one finger extended. "Look out for your men. You must consistently treat them with a fair and even manner in all things. Make sure their needs are taken care of." He extended another finger. "And always lead by example. Don't ask another man to do something that you're not willing to do yourself." He relaxed his hand. "If you are steadfastly that kind of an officer, your men will follow you into the fires of Hell." He paused, letting his words sink in. After Greene blinked, he continued, "As the great John Paul Jones once said to his young Marine officer, "To be well obeyed, a commander must be perfectly esteemed." He paused again. "Fortitudine, Lieutenant." He leaned forward and patted Greene lightly on the knee. "Now, off with you. I believe you have important business to attend to."

"Yes, sir. And thank you, sir." Greene smiled broadly and offered his right hand. They shook hands warmly, like old friends.

"Thank yooou, Lieutenant. I have enjoyed the ride immensely."

Greene stepped out of the hackney and paid the fare. He gave the driver an extra twenty-five cents. "Please take this gentleman to any location he desires." He backed away from the carriage wheels and saluted the occupant. As the carriage rolled past him, Greene was totally surprised to hear the man ask the driver to return him to 'his bench'. Greene just stood there shaking his head and grinning. "And number three," holding out three fingers, he said to himself, "NEVER assume anything, either." As he watched the hackney turn the corner, he suddenly realized that he had not even learned the man's name or his rank. He shrugged his shoulders slightly, turned, and proceeded toward the depot door. As he ascended the steps, he thought appreciatively of the man and what he had said. He mused, "Without a doubt, once a Marine, always a Marine." Opening the door wide, he entered the depot.

"Good afternoon, sir, may I help you?" inquired the ticket clerk as Greene stepped up to the window.

"I'd like to see the station manager, please," replied Greene. He was directed to an open door with 'Thomas H. Parsons, Agent' labeled above it. Greene walked in and stood before the desk. A man in his mid-forties was seated behind it. He was reading one of many telegrams that seemed to cover the top of the desk. "Excuse me. Mister Parsons?" The man looked up and nodded. "I am First Lieutenant Greene of the United States Marines. I believe that you will be expecting us for your Three-Twenty train departure."

The man stood up, pushed his chair back on its wheels, and walked around the desk. "Yes, yes I am." He looked past Greene into the station area. "Are your troops here with you, now?"

"No sir, not just yet. They are in the middle of preparations, but will march in less than an hour. I have come to address transportation planning with you."

"Good, good," replied the man. He moved a chair close behind Greene and signaled him to sit. He then seated himself behind the desk again. Even before his chair stopped rolling forward, he asked, "How many troops will be coming? I have a crew waiting to assemble the necessary cars."

"Our Detachment will have a total of eighty-seven men with knapsacks and long arms. We will also have two howitzers and limbers, and a total of eight horses," replied Greene as he watched the agent take down hurried notes.

Parsons made some quick mental calculations and stated to the paper he was writing on, "Looks like we'll need a total of three, no...make that four cars. Two standard fifty-six passenger cars, one boxcar for the horses and a flat car for the cannon." He tapped his pencil point triumphantly on the page and look up to Greene. "Will a couple of your men be able to travel with the horses?"

"Yes," replied Greene, "we will have four teamsters."

"Good. I'll have my crew start assembling the cars right

away. How soon can you get your people here and start loading?" Parsons stood up again.

Greene also stood up and looked at his watch. "I shall be walking back to the Barracks to verify the travel time. However, I am estimating no more than thirty minutes to do so. We shall march out at approximately Two-Twenty. That should put us here around Two-Fifty or Two-Fifty-Five. Will this allow sufficient time for loading?"

"It'll be cutting it close," replied Parsons as he moved toward the office door. Greene followed. "I'll have the cars ready and a cargo crew standing by. Ramps will be in position for the horses and cannon. If your men can muscle them up into place, my men will anchor everything down for travel. Your best approach will be down the right side of the depot and then up the ramps." He pointed toward the appropriate side of the building for reference. "Your cars will be the last in the line right after the caboose. We'll be detaching you at Relay Station and hooking you onto a special military train coming out of Baltimore and going West from there. Any questions?" They were near a door that led to the 'working' side of the train depot. Parsons' hand rested on the doorknob.

"Actually, yes. Do you happen to have any printed information about the Harper's Ferry area?" Greene knew that, once, during its construction, Harper's Ferry had been the western terminus for the B&O railroad. He was hoping to find some intelligence about his destination.

"As a matter of fact, we do. There should be some brochures on the rack over there in the far corner." He pointed. "If there aren't any out, just ask the ticket clerk to find one for you. We have plenty left over from two years ago." He shrugged. "Big marketing scheme dreamed up by the boss at the main office. Didn't ask anyone in the field...if you know what I mean." Parsons winked. "Anything else?"

"No, thank you. That will be just fine." Greene offered his right hand.

Parsons grasped it and shook it firmly. "Right, then." He looked at the large clock on the waiting room wall. "See you again in about an hour and fifteen minutes." He opened the door and exited.

Greene walked over to the rack indicated to him. He

readily located the brochures in question. As he reached for one he could not help but think, *"E Pluribus Unum,"* as indeed there were many. He unbuttoned two middle coat buttons, placed the brochure into an inside breast pocket, and refastened the buttons. After pulling down the lower edge of his frock coat, he turned and headed toward the telegrapher's window. Once there he picked up a blank telegram form and a pencil. After pausing for a moment to compose his thoughts, he wrote,

"Mrs. Israel Greene, c/o Edward C. Marshall, Jr., Berryville, Virginia. Dearest Edmonia, Significant and potentially dangerous events occurring at Harper's Ferry. Strongly request that you, the children, and your mother leave immediately to visit your cousin in Richmond. Imperative you travel South via Front Royal vice North to avoid possible growing hazard. I am ordered to Harper's Ferry. Will contact you in Richmond upon my return. Your Husband, Israel."

Satisfied, he slid the form across the counter top to the telegrapher and waited to pay the applicable fee for the number of words he was sending. He even paid an additional twenty-five cents to have the message delivered immediately.

His wife, six-year-old daughter, and two-year-old son were visiting her mother at his wife's brother-in-law's farm. He felt optimistic knowing that Berryville was more than twenty miles Southwest of Harper's Ferry, but he did not want to take any chances. He also knew his wife was very familiar with the Manassas Gap Railroad depot at Front Royal, as well as the appropriate train connections for Richmond. She would not have any problems making this trip. If this was a false alarm, she could at least enjoy her cousin's hospitality for a brief visit. He even hoped that the trip would mollify his mother-in-law for a little while. As the matriarch of the Taylor family, 'Ma Maw' was still a little miffed about her eldest daughter marrying a Northerner eight years earlier.

Outside again, he checked his watch. It indicated 1:45. He reviewed the return route in his head, nodded, pocketed his watch, and started down the steps. *"Thirty minutes,"* he thought. *"Don't rush, must maintain a pace that can be duplicated by a marching unit."* He was oblivious to the looks that his uniform and military bearing attracted. He was a man on a mission and his demeanor indicated every bit of it.

Monday, October 17, 1859, 2:05 p.m.

When he finally made a right turn off of Pennsylvania Avenue onto Eighth Avenue, Greene again checked his watch. He had meticulously maintained the standard twenty-eight inch stride all the way. "Excellent time," he said to himself. "Four more short blocks and this whole junket will be completed in less than twenty-five minutes. We'll probably be able to march back even quicker. A marching unit won't have to dodge townspeople along the roadside or carriages in the middle." He soon reached the main entrance. Satisfied with his overall planning and preparation, he bound into the Duty Office.

"Hello, Lieutenant, I have returned." The officer sitting in the duty officer's chair turned around slowly to face him. Greene stopped dead in his tracks. It wasn't Jones! It was Major Russell, a member of the organizational staff at the Navy Department. He was the Paymaster of the Marine Corps.

As he stood up, the Major said, "Hello, Greene." Heavy smoke from his cigar wafted around him.

"Hello, Major," responded Greene. "Have you seen Lieutenant Jones, sir?"

"I believe he is checking on a few things with one of the Orderly Sergeants. Something concerning ammunition or some such thing." As he was responding, Russell was retrieving a piece of paper from his inside breast pocket. He handed it to Greene. "Chief Clerk Welsh made Secretary Toucey aware that Colonel Harris was shorthanded for officers. I have been ordered to...umm...accompany you on this expedition." He smiled broadly. It was one of those smiles that just doesn't come across as sincere.

Greene accepted the paper and slowly read the orders from Toucey to Russell. He could not believe what he was reading. *"What the devil is he doing here?"* he thought. *"Russell is a Marine and he outranks me...yes. He also has five years seniority...yes. But, he IS A STAFF officer."* Greene's mind was screaming, *"This is a Line operation. He has no business here!"* His gut wrenched with anxiety. Nonetheless, he concentrated hard to maintain a calm composure. He slowly looked up at Russell.

Russell spoke first. His left hand waved the cigar around as he did so. "Of course, as a staff officer, I shall only be accompanying you in an advisory capacity."

He had heard of the pending expedition and had talked Secretary Toucey into sending him along. He was fully aware that, by law, he was prohibited from exercising command, but this was an opportunity that he could not pass up. The potential for personal reward was too great. Russell's argument to Toucey had been, "My presence will undoubtedly steady the young officer." It had worked and he was here under orders. He took a triumphant draw on his cigar and exhaled slowly.

"Yes...of...course." Greene replied deliberately and sarcastically. He was livid. He felt a flash of anger within himself. He was definitely taking the Paymaster's presence as an affront to his own professionalism.

"Calm...down," he thought. *"You are the more experienced officer. You have twelve years of field and sea service while Russell only served eight years before being appointed Paymaster on the Staff of the Corps."* His mind searched for more information about Russell. *"And don't forget, he has some very influential political connections on the 'Hill'."* A vague thought crept to the front. *"There has even been a rumor or two that Russell is backroom maneuvering to be named Commandant."* Another flash of anger welled up. *"That's it! He's counting on enhancing his reputation and political standing by way of this expedition!"* Greene's moral makeup was not favorable toward this type of political maneuvering within the Corps. He wanted to spit!

Instead, he managed to swallow and civilly say, "Very well, Major. The Detachment shall be marching out in approximately ten minutes. Please be ready. I shall be making a few last minute checks before formation is called." He placed Russell's orders on the desk corner. As he silently retrieved his sword, boat cloak, and valise from a side table near the doorway, he mentally thanked Lieutenant Jones for his thoroughness. The thought of Jones caused him to suppose that he had probably left Russell's presence on the same pretext as his own. He paused for a moment, faced the Major, and said, "By your leave, sir." Without waiting for a response, he spun around and exited the duty office. Russell's smile only seemed to enlarge around the cigar clenched in his teeth.

Once outside of the Duty Office, Greene took ten quick paces toward the parade field and stopped. He shook off the panicky feeling of claustrophobia and took several deep breaths. He relaxed as the fresh, cool air filled his lungs. He looked up to survey the low gray clouds. "Well," he said, "if Lady Luck comes back to us, we'll be aboard the train before it starts raining again."

He looked down and saw Corporal Gilbert heading toward him. Greene was very happy to see the little Corporal. "Our old reliable war horse," he mused. He waited for Gilbert to halt in front of him.

Gilbert saluted. "Good afternoon, Lieutenant. Welcome back. May I take those for you, sir?" He held out his arms to accept the items Greene was carrying.

Greene said, "Thank you, Corporal," as he handed over everything but his sword. Once his hands were empty of the bigger items, he reinserted the brass scabbard into the sliding frog (leather holder) and positioned it to hang in its normal position. While gently patting the Mameluke's unique cross guard to fine-tune the scabbard's alignment, he asked, "How has everything been progressing?"

"Absolutely as smooth as the ocean near the Doldrum Islands, sir. Everything is ship-shape, squared away, and ready to roll." He leaned slightly forward and with a low voice said, "The boys are just hiding out until Assembly is played. They want to make a bit of a show of falling in." Gilbert's habitual grin was as broad as ever. He straightened back up. "With your permission, sir, I shall take these," he indicated his armful, "and see about getting them stowed for travel." A quick nod from Greene was enough to send him on his way.

Monday, October 17, 1859, 2:15 p.m.

Orderly Sergeant Mundell stood at the far North end of the parade field near the Commandant's house. He tugged first on his left cuff to straighten the sleeve, then his right. He next pulled down the front of his fatigue coat, squared his shoulders, and flexed his neck and chin to distend his collar. Once ready, he stepped off toward the Adjutant's 'position' on the parade field. As he passed by the second of five Officer's Quarters that formed the Eighth Street (front) 'wall' of the Barracks, two Drummers and a Fifer quietly appeared and fell in behind him. At the appropriate location and in proper sequence, they all made a smart left turn and marched uniformly to a spot just short of the exact middle of the parade field, where they halted. The Drummers each sidestepped two paces outward from the center. The Fifer was one pace to the right of the right most Drummer. After a hesitation of several heartbeats, Mundell commanded, "Drummers...Beat...Assembly."

The single structure that contained the enlisted quarters and associated office spaces made up the back wall of the Barracks. It was a two story, rectangular brick building with a portico extending the whole length of the lower level. The spaces between the columns were filled three quarters of the way up with mortared bricks. This facade shielded the first floor windows from the view of the parade field, but allowed essential ventilation. The percussion roll on the drums rattled rhythmically off the brick walls of the whole structure. The sound was voluminous.

From behind the portico walls, evenly toned and forceful commands could be heard. From the left side of the entryway, "Section A, Forrrwarrrd...March." Simultaneously, from the right side, "Section D, Forrrwarrrd...March." The initial crunching sound of boots striking the bricks echoed stereophonically from behind the portico. A brief pause. Again from the left, "Section B, Forrrwarrrd...March." Echoing from the right, "Section C, Forrrwarrrd...March." With smooth precision, hidden Marine columns marched toward each other from opposite sides of the Barracks entryway. They were marching two by two. Together their footsteps sounded like a single, heavy giant marching on a brick pathway.

Seemingly on a collision course, the Sergeants of Sections A and D suddenly came into view. Three paces behind them and slightly to their left or right followed the stolid Sections. When they were eight feet apart, the sergeants stopped. As one, they echoed, "By Files, Right", "By Files, Left," respectively. When each Section's lead file was just one pace away from the two Sergeants, the Sergeant of Section A barked, "March." On the next requisite footfall, the men in the lead files of each column made ninety-degree turning movements around their

Sergeants. As the men accomplished their turns, the Sergeants executed their own facing movements and stepped out with them. Sharply uniformed Marines followed in close order behind the lead files. The two separate columns continued on a parallel course, straddling the flagpole, toward the parade field.

Precisely twelve feet onto the parade field, the Sergeants again gave turn commands. This time the column heads were ordered away from each other toward opposite ends of the parade field. The drum roll continued.

First Lieutenant Greene was approaching his Commander's 'position' from the end of the parade field opposite the Commandant's house. Orderly Sergeant McDonough was two paces behind him. As Greene was advancing, he was watching this extraordinary marching formation with true admiration.

This spectacle was, indeed, something new and unusual. Normally, the 'Fall In' or 'Assembly' commands were carried out with a flurry of men moving toward accustomed positions from all directions and at varying speeds. It usually looked something like organized mass confusion. It was never smooth and precise like this formation's proficient movements.

Additionally, only an educated observer would have noticed that Sections C and D were marching in reverse height order. They were formed up with the shorter men at the front, graduating to taller at the end. With Section A as the lead marching Section of the Detachment, this lineup would ultimately place Sections C and D men in their correct height order without additional maneuvering after the final facing order.

Greene said over his shoulder to McDonough, "Now, this is impressive."

To which McDonough responded, "Aye, sir, that it is. That it is." At the appropriate point, they both executed smart right turns and stopped at their corresponding 'positions' several paces behind the 'Adjutant'.

The drum roll changed in timbre as the last files of Sections B and C made their final turns onto the parade field. After two heavy signal beats, the drums stopped and the marching stopped without voice command. An eerie quiet settled over the whole parade field.

As Orderly Sergeant Mundell slowly withdrew his 1827

regulation sergeant's sword from its scabbard, a long, faint, nerve-grating scrape of metal on metal could be heard. With his arm down by his side, he briefly held the sword grip firmly in his hand. The blade's tip pointed toward the ground almost forty-five degrees from the line of his upright body. With a smooth, practiced flick of the wrist, he brought the sword to the carry position. At this unusual angle, his fingers could just lightly grasp the sides of the sword's grip. The blade rested gently against his upper arm, angling past his right shoulder with the tip pointed skyward beyond his right ear. To a parade formation, a drawn sword is a clear indication to all present that the possessor is the sole individual from whom all orders would next originate.

Orderly Sergeant Mundell quietly inhaled and commanded with forceful intonation, "Detachment, Face, Front." As one man, the four Sections faced toward him. Sections A and B made facing movements to the left, while Sections C and D faced right. Each of the Sergeants made additional sharp maneuvers to position themselves two paces in front of their Section's center.

Mundell surveyed the formation standing at Attention before him. All of the Marines were distinctively unvaried in appearance. Each man was clothed in a sky-blue greatcoat over his fatigue uniform. Their coat shoulder capes were folded back and buttoned behind them at the second lowest of five buttons. While this rakish 'fashion statement' seemed to bestow the appearance of folded wings, it functionally prevented interference with movement while performing a manual of arms with the muskets they carried.

Their dark blue fatigue caps (also referred to as wheel hats) were all squarely positioned on their heads. This cap was similar to the Army version, but it had its own unique 'Marine' differences. In the front center of the cloth headband, above the black chin strap and nearly vertical, leather visor, were three block letters - U S M. Each letter was two inches high and made of brass. The ten inch diameter crown of the cap was stiffened with a whalebone hoop. This gave the top a ship-shape, flat appearance, rather the floppy, careless look of the Army's cap.

Their white cartridge belts crossed from their left shoulders to the attached black leather cartridge boxes just behind their right hips. Crossing from the opposite shoulders were their white baldrics, which ended with an attached black leather scabbard and inserted bayonet, just behind the left hips. Oval, solid brass buckle-plates on the baldrics were neatly positioned above the intersection of the two crossed belts. Both of the belts were held in position by white waist belts with rectangular, solid brass, buckle-plates. A black leather cap box was suspended from the waist belt just to each man's right of center.

Canvas haversacks painted black and 'Japanned' (covered with heavy black lacquer) metal canteens were both slung from the right shoulders across to the left hips. Their leather knapsacks were mounted across both shoulders atop all of the other belts and straps and under the capes for protection from the weather.

Every Marine present carried a caliber .69, Model 1842, smooth bore musket. Ironically, most were probably manufactured in the Armory at Harper's Ferry. Their weapons were without slings -- a Marine tradition established well before 1800.

They carried their weapons at a shoulder arms position different from the Army's. In accordance to the instruction of the Marine Corps' Manual of Arms, the weapon was placed on the left shoulder. When shifting from a starting position of Order Arms to Shoulder Arms, each man maintained his left upper arm against his body. As he shifted his weapon upward with his right hand from alongside his right leg and across his body, he elevated his left forearm to a position parallel to the ground and grasped the butt of the weapon's stock with the left hand. This gave the weapon an angle of tilt that both assured symmetry down the line as well as precluded striking the man behind the carrier when turning or maneuvering in formation.

Satisfied that all hands were squared away in proper Marine fashion, Mundell next commanded, "Report," and turned his head toward the Sergeant of Section A.

Sergeant Buckley saluted horizontally across his body to a point where the fingers of his down-turned right hand just touched the barrel of his weapon. He turned his head slightly toward the adjutant and responded, "Section A all present, sir."

Orderly Sergeant Mundell replied, "Very well," and

returned the salute with his sword. He then turned his attention the next Section in line.

Sergeant Callahan saluted and reported, "Section B all present, sir."

In his rotation, Sergeant Davis saluted and reported, "Section C all present, sir."

Sergeant Woodfield stood before a Section that was merely half the size of the others. He saluted and reported, "Section D all present or accounted for, sir." As he finished his report, the sounds of shoed horse hoofs, trace chains, and metal-banded carriage wheels grinding gravel under a heavy load could be heard just outside the Barracks gate.

With the same realization as everyone else, Mundell mentally registered that the howitzers were being positioned for departure by Section D's 'accounted for' men. "Very well," he said and cut away another smart sword salute.

Mundell paused for a short time, took another deep breath, and commanded, "Preeesennnt, Arms." The command was executed with a flourish of snap and pop. When finished, each man was holding his weapon vertically in front of him. Mundell performed a right about turn and saluted Lieutenant Greene. Holding his sword in the final position of the salute's downward sweep, he reported, "Sir, the Detachment is formed."

Lieutenant Greene returned a hand salute. "Very well, Orderly Sergeant. Assume your post."

Orderly Sergeant Mundell raised his sword to the carry position and proceeded to a location one pace to the right of Orderly Sergeant McDonough. Upon settling in at the appropriate spot, he sheathed his sword. When the guard slammed against the head of the scabbard, Lieutenant Greene smoothly withdrew his own sword and brought it to the carry position.

Greene inhaled and commanded, "Shoulder, Arms." As one, the Detachment members suddenly twisted their weapons up and away from the center of their bodies. While they gently returned the weapons to their left shoulders with their right hands, they positioned their left hands to catch and grasp the butt of the stocks. Their final motion was a smooth swing of their right arms to their sides.

Greene continued, "Without Doubling, Right, Face." Each

man now turned ninety degrees to his right. Instead of automatically forming into the normal files of four abreast during such a facing, they maintained their double ranks.

He was about to give his next command when, to his left, the unexpected motion of men moving into a line ahead of the column caught his attention. His head snapped in that direction. He was starting to mouth "Wha..." when he spotted Corporal Gilbert among them. He closed his mouth, faced forward, and anxiously watched out of the corner of his eye for several seconds.

When the movement stopped, he commanded with lower volume, "Staff, Forward, Left Turn, March." He then stepped off and made his left turn. Greene was marching his staff to a position at the head of the column. The Orderly Sergeants and Musicians followed behind him. Their formation resembled the shape of an arrowhead -- Lieutenant Greene, followed by the two Orderly Sergeants, and the three Musicians behind them.

Looking toward the head of the Detachment line, Greene could clearly see that the additional men had formed into a file of three abreast. The two on the outside were holding flags. "Amazing!" he exclaimed. He had quickly deduced that Corporal Gilbert had put together a previously unthought of and unplanned for Color Guard! As he marched nearer to them, Greene could make out the other two faces, but not their identities. From all appearances, Gilbert had rousted out a couple of the newest recruits and whipped them into satisfactory enough shape to be a temporary Color Guard. A smile cracked wide across the Lieutenant's face. "Our old war horse, again," he said half aloud. "So now you are a Color Guard Corporal, too." He made eye contact with Gilbert and winked. Gilbert's facial expression was as resolute as his assumed position required, but the twinkle in his eyes spoke volumes about the gratification he felt for having pleased his commander.

As the staff marched past the Color Guard and neared the North end of the parade field, Greene's attention was suddenly attracted to a new movement just ahead of him and to the left. The Commandant and the Sergeant Major were approaching the edge of the parade field from the Commandant's house. The sight of them started his mind racing. *"Wait a minute!"* he thought.

Greene croaked, "Staff, halt." As he glanced over his right shoulder toward the Color Guard he prayed, *"Please, don't let it be so."* He needed to confirm something that his brain had just registered. Sure enough, there they were, as plain as day. The Colors being held aloft were the very Colors from the Commandant's office. One was a National Ensign with a special canton and emblazoned with gold lettering that proclaimed 'U.S. Marine Corps'. The other was a very distinctive presentation flag given to the Marines by 'the grateful citizens of Washington City'.

Corporal Gilbert was standing ramrod stiff and staring straight ahead. His face was an unreadable mask. Greene closed his eyes, and, as he was rotating back around, groaned in a sinking whisper, "Oh, my..."

Thoughts began buzzing like bees in Lieutenant Greene's head. *"Greene, you're a dead man!"* . . . *"This could wash both of our careers right out the scuppers."* . . . *"Wait, Gilbert wouldn't do something that stupid."* . . . *"Okay, he has a reputation as a sly old sea dog, but he's always been straightforward."* . . . *"Hold on, the Commandant has stopped outside of the marching area. Is that a good sign?"* . . . *"Well, dooo something!"*. . . *"Get this parade moving. We have a train to catch."* . . . *"Oh, lord, what a way to start an expedition."*

He closed his eyes and silently prayed, again. *"Let us hope that it is easier to ask for forgiveness than it would have been to ask for permission."* He swallowed hard, opened his eyes, raised his sword in the air, and commanded, "Detachment, Forwarrrd." He paused, and then, bringing his arm down, "Marrrch." The column moved forward. As it neared the corner of the parade field he added, "By Files, Left, March." When the column reached an appropriate point, he commanded, "Staff, Forward, Left Turn, March." His timing was perfect and the Detachment was now in its full and proper marching formation. The Drummers were tapping out the cadence and all were in step.

As they neared the Commandant's position, Greene commanded, "Detachment, Eyes, Right," and he saluted with his sword. The Commandant and the Sergeant Major both returned hand salutes. Greene searched the faces of both men for signs of anger or displeasure. He found none. In fact, both men were smiling. *"Well,"* he thought, *"maybe Gilbert did everything right after all. The Sergeant Major is responsible for those Colors and he looks as pleased as punch. Oh happy day, it's on to Glory!"* A smile returned to his face.

When several measured paces beyond the Commandant, Greene returned his sword to the carry position and called out, "By Files, Left, March." They were now heading toward the main gate of the Barracks.

When they were about half way down the parade field, Greene could see Major Russell standing in the open doorway of the Duty Office. *"Just stay there, Major, and let us proceed on this mission without you,"* he thought. He tried desperately to avoid any eye contact with the Major. When he spotted Lieutenant Jones standing near the sentry at the main gate the task became much easier. He blocked the Major completely out of his mind.

As they neared the South end of the parade field, Greene commanded, "By Files, Right, March." The Detachment was now heading directly toward the main gate. Meanwhile, Major Russell was edging his way toward the moving formation. Just as soon as the staff passed him, he stepped in between the Musicians and the Color Guard. After falling into step, the Major flashed a sneer of victory toward Greene's back, but unbeknownst to Russell, Gilbert was giving him the evil eye behind his own.

Greene returned Lieutenant Jones' salute as he passed through the gate. He glanced left to verify that the howitzers were indeed ready to move out. Satisfied with what he saw, he commanded, "By Files, Right, March." The Detachment was now heading North on Eighth Street toward Pennsylvania Avenue.

When Greene heard the starting calls of the teamsters and the familiar sounds of rolling gun carriages, he knew that, finally, his whole Detachment was fully formed and on the move. He spoke over his right shoulder, "Musicians, 'The Girl I Left Behind Me' if you please." The Musicians immediately struck up the familiar tune.

After the Musicians completed the first pass through the melody, the veteran Marines started singing,

> "I'm lonesome since I crossed the hill,
> And o'er the moor and valley,
> Such heavy thoughts my heart do fill,
> Since parting with my Sally.
> I'll seek no more the fine and gay,
> For each but does remind me,
> How swift the hours did pass away,
> With the girl I left behind me."

It was the old English folk tune that American military men regularly sang when departing from their home base into the unknown. This select tradition had been inherited from the British military during the French and Indian War. The Marines continued with gusto,

> "Oh, ne'er shall I forget the night,
> The stars were bright above me,
> And gently lent their silv'ry light
> When first she vowed she loved me.
> But now I'm bound for Brighton camp,
> Kind Heav'n may favour find me,
> And send me safely back again,
> To the girl I left behind me."

As they reached Pennsylvania Avenue, Lieutenant Greene commanded, "By Files, Left, March." He also scanned the area around the bench for his 'old' Marine. A pang of sadness touched him when his search was unsuccessful. The column turned and the singing did not skip a beat.

> "The bee shall honey taste no more,
> The dove become a ranger,
> The dashing waves shall cease to roar,
> Ere she's to me a stranger.
> The vows we've registered above,
> Shall ever cheer and bind me,
> In constancy to her I love,
> The girl I left behind me."

The Marines were in a jubilant mood. This adventure was a welcome relief from their daily Barracks routine. The veterans marched and sang with pride. The Fresh Fish attempted to emulate the vets with their own bravado. Deep down many felt the excitement and apprehension of going into harm's way.

CHAPTER FOUR

"TRAVEL"

Monday, October 17, 1859, 2:50 p.m.

"What is all of this? Why are all of these people here?" Lieutenant Greene could not keep the words in his mouth.

The three blocks from the unfinished Capitol building to the train station had been lined with people. They were cheering, beseeching, and wishing them well, all at the same time.

"Hurray for the Marines!"

"Go, gettum, boys!"

"Put them back in their place, fellas!"

"Do your duty, lads!"

"Stop the rebellion before it spreads!"

"Good luck, men!"

"Huzzah, huzzah!"

Some men were waving their hats. Many ladies were either crying into their handkerchiefs or waving them. Little boys were running up and down the line of Marines, whooping and hollering for all they were worth. Little girls were hanging onto their mother's coats and, for the most part, hiding their faces. Older girls were pointing at the Marines, whispering to each other and giggling. Younger men, as well as older boys who were standing away from their parents, were all wishing they were going along, and looking for an opportunity to do so.

The mood was festive, yet somber at the same time. Washington was a very Southern community in its attitudes. The current administration was made up of mostly Southern Democrats. Word of the insurrection was spreading quickly around the city. Trepidation concerning a massive Negro insurrection was not being openly discussed, but it was deeply imbedded in the psyche of the citizenry. A great many of the men and women lining the streets had very intent, searching looks on their faces. They were seeking reassurances that the Marines were capable of handling the task ahead of them. The impressive martial appearance, demeanor, and weapons of the Marines satisfied many.

As they approached the train depot, Greene recognized Agent Parsons when he stepped out from the crowd and approached him. Walking beside Greene, he leaned close to be heard and said, "Right on time, Lieutenant. Take your men down the next alleyway on the right." He pointed. "My boys are keeping the path open. We're all ready for you. As I mentioned earlier, the flatcar is at the end of the train. Ahead of it is the boxcar for the horses. The next two cars will be for your troops. We have ramps positioned so you can load everything from the right side of the train. Our regular passengers will be loading into the other cars from the platform on the left."

"Thank you, Mister Parsons," responded Greene. They were almost at the opening to the alleyway. Greene mentally measured the distance and commanded over his right shoulder, "By Files, Right, ...March." Parsons jumped out of the line as the Detachment executed the turn.

The alleyway passed between two buildings and continued on. Just past the collision barrier (the bumper) at the railroad terminus, the pathway curved ninety degrees to the left and then paralleled the tracks for about two hundred yards beyond the depot.

Greene marched his Detachment to a point alongside the train where he was almost at the forward end of the foremost car designated for the Marines. Here, he commanded, "Detachment, Halt." He turned around and addressed Mundell, "Orderly Sergeant Mundell, have the men fix bayonets and stack arms."

Mundell responded, "Aye-Aye, sir," saluted and departed to carry out his order.

Greene next addressed McDonough, "XO, please have the Musicians board this first car." Upon looking past the Musicians, he added, "Oh, and please invite Major Russell to do the same. Thank you." Major Russell had casually stepped out of the formation, away from the train, and was milling about smartly on the far side of the pathway.

"Aye-Aye, sir," responded McDonough, who also saluted and departed to carry out his order.

Greene next turned his attention to the Color guard. He approached them slowly and deliberately. He stopped in front of Gilbert and starred at him for a few seconds. With a tone of mock irritation, he asked, "Color Corporal Gilbert, am I to assume that you have made arrangements to ensure that these colors are indeed returned to the Commandant's office in a safe and expeditious manner?"

Gilbert responded without fear, "Aye, sir, just as safe and as quick as possible."

Greene leaned closer and again mocked, "And just how sure are you that these untrained and unknown New Fish are reliable. Are you sure enough that they won't misplace them or maybe even sell them to some souvenir seeker?"

"Well, sir," replied Gilbert, "sure enough to promise these men that the Sergeant Major is waiting for them with monetary chits for drinks at the widow Abel's tavern. And the sooner they get back to him with these flags, the sooner they will get their chits and time off enough to use them, sir." Gilbert finished with a grin that spanned from ear to ear.

Greene snickered, but quickly put on a stern face. "Very well, Color Corporal, you may dismiss your Color guard." As he turned away, he could hardly keep from laughing out loud. The widow Abel's tavern was a fictitious establishment, rumored to be somewhere near the Washington Navy Yard's main gate. Its embellished wonders were often revealed in sea stories told to uninitiated recruits while they were undergoing their first months of training. The promise that only the best were allowed to enter the tavern is surreptitiously used to induce superlative performance from the occasional sluggard recruit.

Greene walked toward Orderly Sergeants McDonough and Mundell who were standing in front of the formation, just between Sections B and C. The Detachment was facing toward the train. With bayonets attached at the end of each barrel, their weapons were neatly stacked upright in front of them. Each stack was made up of three weapons forming a tripod with a fourth weapon leaning against it. The tripods had been 'locked' together with a distinctive manipulation involving the affixed bayonets.

Greene surveyed the Detachment and said calmly, "Orderly Sergeant McDonough, please have the men unship their knapsacks and place them near the weapon stacks. Sections A and B will help load the howitzers onto the flatcar. Section C will assist with loading the horses into the boxcar. Railroad men will anchor the howitzers to the flatcar. Orderly Sergeant Mundell, you will please double check their work."

"Aye, sir. With discretion, of course, sir," replied Mundell.

"Yes, thank you," nodded Greene. He continued, "After the howitzers and horses are loaded, reform the men to board the passenger cars. Direct Section A to the front car with the staff, Musicians, and half of Section D. Sections B and C with the rest of D in the other." He was pointing as he assigned the cars. He pointed last to the boxcar and said, "The four teamsters will ride with the horses." He paused as he retrieved his watch and checked the time. "We must be fully loaded and boarded in twenty minutes or less. Any questions?"

"No, sir," the Orderly Sergeants chimed.

"Very well." Greene replaced his watch. "I shall meet briefly with the railroad agent and then repair to the first car. Please carry out the assignments." All three men saluted at the same time.

The two Orderly Sergeants turned to carry out their orders and Lieutenant Greene climbed up the steps onto the closest passenger car. He passed across the car's rear platform and onto the depot's platform on the opposite side. Once inside the depot, he found Agent Parsons sitting at his desk pondering over more telegrams.

"Have you received any additional information from Harper's Ferry?" he asked.

"Not, yet," responded Parsons. "The telegraph lines are still down in Harper's Ferry and no trains have passed through in either direction." Holding onto one particular telegram, he stood up and added, "I have, however, just received a message from the War Department requesting that I detain the Three-Twenty train. Apparently their designated senior officer is still meeting with the President and will be delayed." He looked again at the telegram and shook his head. "I won't be able to give them much time, maybe ten more minutes. The cars ahead of yours are going to be filled with some very powerful businessmen, Senators, and Congressmen, as well as their family members and servants. These high-level people are very influential. Mister Garrett has personally assured them an expeditious exodus. I can't delay the train's departure too long, or there will be nothing but the devil to pay from the main office." He crumpled the telegram and shook his fist with disgust. "Don't you just hate politicians?"

"Can't really answer that. I work for the number one politician," answered Greene. When Parsons gave him a puzzled look, he continued, "The President is my Commander-in-Chief."

"Oh, yes," replied Parsons sheepishly.

"Was there any mention as to the identity of the Army's senior officer?" asked Greene as he indicated the crumpled telegram in Parsons' hand.

"Wha..? Oh..." He smoothed open and reviewed the telegram. "No. Just that he would be delayed." He started moving toward the door. "I'd better respond right away and let them know the circumstances."

Greene stepped aside and spoke as the distracted agent passed by. "Thank you, Mister Parsons."

Moving into the main waiting room, Greene spotted a newspaper boy who had just entered the area to sell his papers to the outgoing passengers. *"Might be a good idea to see what the printed page is saying about all of this,"* he thought. He called the boy over and paid him three cents instead of the usual two for the paper.

Rather than reading the paper, he folded it under his arm and strolled about, observing and nodding to many of the Baltimore bound passengers. He concluded that they were an unusually well-dressed and smartly groomed collection of people with equally unusual deportment about them. They were not the regular sort of passengers to be riding in nominal coach cars. *"Mister Parsons will, indeed, be hard pressed to delay the train for any amount of time,"* he mused as he exited the door on the train side of the depot.

Standing by the train, he could see that his men had finished their loading tasks and were boarding the passenger cars. He could also see Orderly Sergeant Mundell weaving in and out of the gun carriages and limbers, looking very intently at the wheel chocks and anchoring chains. *"Good,"* he reflected, *"everything seems to be in order."* He checked his watch, was satisfied with the time, and headed for the first 'Marine' car.

Onboard, the seats were arranged in such a way that two pairs of passengers sat opposite of each other with a common space for their legs and feet. Greene deliberately bypassed

Major Russell who was sitting by a depot side window in the first section of seats in the car. Instead, he sat on the window side of Orderly Sergeant McDonough in the opposite section on the right. They were facing aft, but, like most sea veterans, riding backwards did not cause them any motion sickness.

Everyone's attention was instantly attracted to the clamor of feet and voices. The 'regular' passengers were boarding the train. Greene instinctively said, "Looks like it won't be long, now."

McDonough tapped the Lieutenant on the arm and quietly directed his attention toward Major Russell. Greene watched Russell as he exited the car, waved to someone, and crossed the platform. Russell approached and shook hands with an impressively dressed, rotund, and bearded man. The two of them were smiling and conversing amicably. Surrounded by an entourage of nodding and smiling minions, they began walking toward a car farther up the train. "Interesting," said Greene as he turned back around. To himself, he added, "*Maybe Lady Luck and his big whig friend will keep him away from us for the whole trip.*"

In the true fashion of all military men, Greene decided to rest while he could. He stretched out his legs, settled down in his seat, and shoved his cap forward over his eyes. Within seconds, he was asleep.

Monday, October 17, 1859, 3:30 p.m.

With two long blasts on the whistle, a flurry of steam near the drive wheels, and a sudden lurch, the locomotive began pulling away from the depot. The cars behind echoed clanging and clunking reverberations as each was jolted in sequence from a dead stop and obediently dragged along. Many passengers instinctively reached for a steadying object or person nearby. A few were so surprised that they cried out and began looking around warily for assurances that everything was all right. Quickly realizing what had happened, most smiled sheepishly at having been caught unprepared, while a few cursed the railroad company for scaring them. Almost to a man, the Marine Privates cheered the train's start.

Lieutenant Greene simultaneously opened his eyes and removed his cap to his lap. As he was straightening up in his seat, a train conductor entered the car and seemed to be searching for someone. Orderly Sergeant Mundell raised a hand and signaled him over. As the conductor neared their section of seats, he asked, "Are you Lieutenant Greene?" Mundell politely pointed out the Lieutenant.

Greene leaned forward and said, "Yes, sir, at your service."

"Lieutenant, Agent Parsons asked me to tell you that the Army's man did NOT make it." The conductor seemed a little unsure as to how this information was going to be taken. He nervously held out an envelope and added, "And I'm to give this to you."

"I understand, thank you," responded Greene. Smiling, he accepted the envelope and continued, "Can you tell me, sir, when the next train will be departing Washington?"

The conductor was delighted to get back to something that he knew. Flashing a grin of relief, he responded, "Yes, sir, that would be Five O'clock."

"Five O'clock?" Greene was surprised by the answer. "Why so late?" he queried.

"Well, Lieutenant," the conductor swayed gently as he settled into the rhythm of the rocking train, "this stretch of track we're running on is a point to point branch rather than a main stem. There is only one set of tracks from Washington City to Relay House and no sidings. That means that we can only move one train at a time on this branch." He removed a large silver watch from his vest pocket and made a quick mental calculation. "We should be arriving at Relay House in about forty-five minutes or so. Once we are on the main stem, the next scheduled Southbound will be able to get by. She's an express and will only need about thirty-five minutes to reach Washington. Add on another fifteen minutes to discharge and embark passengers as well as turn the locomotive, and that should put you at Five O'clock." He checked his watch again and clucked, "We'll need to make up some time if she's going to make her scheduled departure." Finished with his explanation, he pocketed his watch. "Anything else I can do for you?" he asked.

"No, sir. Again, I thank you. You have been most

informative." Greene stood up and offered his hand. They shook quickly and the conductor returned to his paying passengers.

Greene sat down and examined the envelope. It was from the Navy Department. He opened it and read,

"Sir; As there may not be sufficient time before the departure of the cars for Colonel Harris to give you full instructions for your guidance as the Commanding Officer of the Marines to be sent to Harper's Ferry to protect the public property there, I transmit herewith a copy of the Department's letter to him of this date upon the subject by which you will be guided. I am respectfully, etc., Isaac Toucey."

Greene then read the orders. When he was finished, he pocketed the papers.

"Anything new?" asked McDonough.

"Actually, no," replied Greene, outwardly. "Just the Navy Department making sure that we are aware of our instructions." Internally he was thinking, *"It seems odd that Secretary Toucey would have sent such a letter. Is he second-guessing Colonel Harris' instructions? What else might he have intended?"* He pondered this for a few moments. His mind was testing several possible answers. Finally, he reasoned, *"The only logical explanation is that he may have had second thoughts about sending Russell along and is using the letter to reiterate that I am indeed in Command of the Detachment. Nothing else makes sense. That's got to be it!"* More than half satisfied, he opened his newspaper and tried reading to take his mind off of the subject.

* * * * *

"Huzzah!" The Marine Privates of Section A were thrilled by the start of the train. Even Sergeant Buckley's admonition to them concerning 'silence on deck' while the Commanding Officer and Staff were present was temporarily forgotten. This had been a day of multiple excitements and they were like little children anxious for the next sight or sound to delight them.

The exuberant members of Section A occupied most of the fifty-six-passenger car. They had removed their knapsacks and stowed them in the overhead storage cribs. Each man was seated with the butt of his weapon resting on the floor and the barrel rising upward between his knees toward the ceiling. Most maintained the upright balance of the familiar piece with just one hand. Some of the Fresh Fish were fearful of Corporal Gilbert's "Heaven help the man if any part of his weapon other than the butt should touch the deck or even bumps into anyone or anything else" and held on tight with both hands.

The car had fourteen rows of seats on each side. The first four rows of seats on the left, as well as the third and fourth rows on the right, were empty. This effectively isolated the Staff's first two rows on the right into a traditionally unapproachable area known as 'Officer's Country'.

Corporal Gilbert and Sergeant Buckley had arranged themselves into seats on opposite sides of the aisle in rows five and ten, respectively. From their strategic polar positions, each NCO could clearly see the other. In addition, each was within hearing, and order giving, distance of different halves of the Section.

With the exception of the Privates sitting next to the NCOs, the remainder of the Privates sat in pairs. Privates Quinn and Allen were sitting opposite of Corporal Gilbert and another Private, facing forward. Quinn, as the 'senior' of the two in their row, was next to the window.

The Musicians sat facing forward in the back rows on either side of the aisle. The Drummers were together on the left, their drums between their feet. Behind them was the forward wall of the lavatory. The Fifer sat alone on the other side. Behind him, in the open corner opposite the lavatory was a potbelly stove and a box of split wood. Because the Fifer's 'weapon of sound' was the least cumbersome of anyone's onboard, Sergeant Buckley had designated him as the fire tender. A crackling fire was already burning and the radiant warmth was slowly drifting toward the rows of seats.

Quinn leaned toward Allen and said, "Now, isn't this much more enjoyable than standing two more inspections today?"

"Well, I do have to admit that four full uniform inspections a day is a bit on the bothersome side," responded Allen.

"Ha!" laughed Gilbert. "Just you wait until you're aboard ship, lad. The inspection routine you've been conducting at the

Barracks will seem like a picnic compared to the rigors of shipboard duty. Right, Quinn?"

"Right you are, Corp." Quinn grinned and added, "And there's a bully chance that I'll never see shipboard duty again, too."

"And just exactly what is that supposed to mean?" asked Gilbert.

With an air of mock indifference, Quinn responded, "Well, Corp, my enlistment is just about up and I haven't exactly made up my mind about shipping over for another hitch."

"Oh, to be sure," mocked Gilbert right back as he shifted his weight and twisted his body away toward the aisle.

Quinn glanced at Allen, winked, and looked back to the Corporal. "So, Corp, what wonderful words of enticement do you have for me?"

Gilbert slowly returned his posture toward the window. His gaze rested on Quinn. Raising his right hand into the air in a 'halt' sign, the Corporal grimaced his face, rocked his head in the negative and replied, "Sorry, lad. No great enticements or promises." He lowered his hand and continued, "You know full well, that, as an Irish immigrant, you have found a good home here in the Marines." He waved his left hand in a circling movement around the car. "You've made some good friends here, too." He pointed his right index finger toward Quinn's face. "You like being out in the fresh air and not breaking your back for a living like you used to." He lowered his finger toward Quinn's chest. "That uniform you wear is better than any clothing you've ever owned before." He opened his hand, palm up, fingers spread. "The six dollars a month pay isn't all that bad," he paused, then closed and shook his hand slightly, "and regular, too." Gilbert reached back and scratched his temple for a second. "I can't actually remember hearing anything about you refusing or being disgusted with the daily grog issue. And," he pointed his finger again, "you certainly aren't complaining about getting hot meals and a cot every day, either." Gilbert dropped his hand and shook his head again. "No, lad. Why would I want to bore you with some kind of long shipping over lecture? YOU are in for life like the rest of us, and you know it." The little Corporal flashed his customary toothy grin, rocked his head up and down, and chuckled.

Gilbert knew he was right so he diverted his attention to checking out the behavior of his other charges. He immediately noticed that the Private sitting diagonally across the aisle from him was staring in his direction. The Corporal flashed an evil eye and snapped, "What are you looking at?" The Private immediately jerked his eyes and head toward the front and froze. Satisfied, Gilbert momentarily grinned in amusement and then assumed a look of unconcern as he continued to survey 'his half' of the car.

Quinn chuckled and said to Allen, "Well, that all may be true, but I'm still keeping my options open. Time will tell, Fish, time will tell."

"How much time do you have left on your enlistment?" queried Allen.

"I'm not really counting, mind you, but something like a month and seven days." Quinn reflected then added, "These past four years have gone by rather quickly, though. I might stick around for another hitch or two, but not for life like the Corp says."

"Why is that?" wondered Allen.

Quinn looked at Allen intently for a second. "Yes, I guess you don't know that much about the Marines, yet, do you?" Allen's blank stare prompted him to continue. "It's simple. In order to be promoted to Sergeant in this outfit, you have to know how to read and write. Something that I can't do." He paused in reflection again. "Not much call for that sort of thing as a stone mason apprentice."

"I could teach you if you'd like," volunteered Allen.

"And just how did you learn reading and writing working in the coal mines?" Quinn looked quizzically at Allen. "Isn't that what I heard, you're from the coal mines out West near Pittville or someplace like that?"

"Actually, it was Pittsburgh...Pennsylvania," corrected Allen. "My mother was a Methodist. She taught both my sister and me. She was a strong believer in being able to know God's word as it was written. Would you like to learn?"

Quinn flinched a little, "Well," he said slowly, "maybe reading, but not any Methodist preaching, okay? I'm a Roman Catholic."

"Okay, I promise," snickered Allen.

"Were you a coal miner?" asked Quinn. "You certainly have the look of strength about you. I would say that swinging a pick for a couple of years has built you up pretty good."

"Yes," was the reply. Now it was Allen's turn to be reflective. "My Dad was one. Mom wanted me to be a preacher. I became a miner when I was fourteen. Dad was killed in a cave-in. To keep the family together, Mom started taking in a couple of boarders. She also did some laundry and such for others, but to help make ends meet, I had to become a miner." He gulped. "I hated it. Just couldn't stand not seeing the sun and not being able to breathe fresh air."

"I know what you mean. I couldn't stand the smell and taste of stone dust," commiserated Quinn. "The only days that it wasn't so bad was when it rained, but then working in the rain or snow wasn't great, either."

"Yeah, mines are always cold and damp, too." Allen gave an involuntary shudder.

"So how'd you get out of the mine and into the Marines?" asked Quinn with genuine interest.

Allen shifted his position to find a little comfort in the hard wooden seat and continued, "About a year ago, my mother passed away. My sister, Eugenia Grace, and I continued on as best we could. Then, about five months ago, she married one of the boarders. He's a nice fellow who works in the company store, not an actual miner.

"I came East with the hopes of seeing the ocean. Figured that it was the largest wide-open space that I could find. The stories that I had read made life at sea seem like a great adventure.

"When I was in Philadelphia I met a fellow at church who directed me to a Navy Recruiting Rendezvous. Seems as though the Navy people were looking for 'new hands', as they called them, and I figured that sounded like a good idea to follow up on. Turns out that they were looking for men to be coal haulers on these new steam ships of theirs. Well, sir, when I found out about that, you can imagine what my response was.

"It just happened that a most agreeable Marine Sergeant overheard my little 'discussion' with the Navy fellows and asked if he could have a word with me. We went to a tavern next door and, over a couple of beers, he explained how I could have all of the benefits of an ocean voyage without all of the evils of being a sailor...mainly handling coal and the like. As you can figure, I bought off on the representation and here I am."

Private Ruppert, sitting across from Quinn, laughed heartily. "Sounds like I met up with the same sort of recruiting Sergeant. Mine was a little on the sly side, too."

He leaned forward and continued, "I'm just nineteen, but big for my age." He peeked at Corporal Gilbert furtively. "My recruiting Sergeant says to me, "Not to worry me Bucko," and hands me two small pieces of paper with numbers written on them. He then tells me to take off my shoes, put one piece in each, and put them back on. When I asked him what for, he says, "Well, Bucko, the number twenty-one is written on those pieces of paper. With your shoes back on and you standing on the pieces of paper, when the enlisting officer asks you if you are over twenty-one, you be sure and tell him, 'Yes, sir, without a doubt.' As for truth, you will be 'squarely over' the number twenty-one."

Allen laughed out loud. "Ho, ho, that's funny." Even Corporal Gilbert snickered and had trouble keeping a straight face.

Quinn added, "You'd be surprised to find out how many fellows in the Marines could tell you a similar sort of story. The idea of 'a few good men' doesn't seem to hold too strong for the ones doing the looking." Corporal Gilbert signaled his displeasure by coughing and clearing his throat with exaggerated loudness.

Not wanting to incur the Corporal's wrath, Quinn quickly changed the subject. "We usually don't use first names in this outfit, but mine is Luke. What's yours?"

Allen looked a little sheepish. "My given name is Balford, but my family called me 'Bal'. When I was working in the mine, the men there just called me 'Al'. With all of the noise down in the hole, I guess they didn't hear the 'B' when I said it. They must have figured 'Al' had to do with my last name."

"Bal..ford." Quinn rolled the name off his tongue and listened to the sound of it. "Must be an old family name."

"I think it was my father's grandmother's maiden name," offered Allen.

"I know how it is being a namesake. Mine was originally Lucas. I've been told that my father didn't follow the normal Celtic naming plan when he named me after his little brother. Seems as though my 'uncle' drowned when he was a young lad, long before I was born. My father must have loved him dearly and wanted to keep the name alive." Quinn was nodding his head slightly. "I changed it slightly when I came here from Ireland. I was nine and eager to be more American."

"Where is your family, now?" asked Allen.

"All gone," he said quietly. "It's just me to carry on the family name." With a slight jerk of his head, Quinn pointed toward Gilbert. "The Corp's right about a couple of things, though. I HAVE found a home in the Marines, and these shipmates ARE my family." He scooted down in his seat.

After a contemplative moment, he continued in a subdued tone, "Yes, this is much better then starving in a potato famine, or breaking a heavy sweat trying to make a living straining my back ten to twelve hours a day."

The four men sitting together all nodded affirmation in some small way. The rhythm of the train rocked them gently to-and-fro. The colorfully mixed yellow, orange, red, and brown autumn leaves on the trees passing by the windows painted a continuous panorama of beauty and tranquility. Wordlessly, each man surrendered to his innermost thoughts, dreams, and fears.

Monday, October 17, 1859, 4:15 p.m.

Sensing that the train was slowing down, Lieutenant Greene looked out of the window to verify his suspicion. A short blast emanated from the train's whistle. "*Yes,*" he thought, "*that's a clear indicator.*" He applied his seaman's eye to gauge the speed of objects passing by the window. With assurance, he said to no one in particular, "We certainly are slowing." He looked to Orderly Sergeant Mundell and said, "We should be approaching Relay House. This is where they'll transfer these cars to another train going West."

While starting to stand, Mundell replied, "Yes, sir. I'll see if I can locate the conductor to find out exactly what will be happening next."

"Thank you, Orderly Sergeant." Greene then looked about the car to see how his Marines were doing. Satisfied that they were traveling well, he said to Orderly Sergeant McDonough, "XO, after the cars are successfully transferred to the other train and we are underway again, you may pass the word for the men to prepare and eat a supper if they so desire. Once we arrive at Harper's Ferry, it will be difficult to say when they will eat a proper meal again."

"Aye, sir," responded McDonough. He understood full well the Lieutenant's meaning. At the '8th' and 'I' Barracks, a light breakfast of coffee, bacon, and bread was usually served around 5:30 a.m. The large, sustaining meal of the day was dinner, which was served at Noon. Supper, a civilian tradition, was a light fare, meant to tide one over until breakfast the next day. Supper was an unofficial meal for Marines on Barracks Duty.

A few moments later, Major Russell entered the car ahead of the conductor. Mundell was immediately behind them. Russell returned to the seat he had previously occupied. McDonough stood in the aisle as the conductor addressed Greene.

"Well, Lieutenant, as I was just saying to the Major, here," he twisted half around and pointed with his thumb, "we are arriving at Relay House. This is the transfer station onto the main stem." The conductor glanced out of the window to mark his bearings. "We're pulling onto a side track to allow the Southbound by. While we're waiting for her to clear, we will unhook your cars and this train will continue on to Baltimore." To emphasize the cars next movements, he started gesturing with his right hand as he continued, "A small yard locomotive will pull you back down the branch." Holding his arm out in a curve to the right, he pulled it back until his hand was by his chest. "Then it will push you onto the main stem behind a special Westbound that is waiting." He pushed his arm out in a curve to the left. "You will feel a little jolt or two when you are hooked up. The whole transfer will probably take about fifteen minutes or so."

Another short blast sounded from the whistle. The conductor again looked out the window and said, "Well, got to go, we're about to stop on the siding. It's been a pleasure, Lieutenant." He nodded and turned toward the Marines. Waving as though he was signaling an engineer, he shouted, "Good luck, boys! Give'um what for!"

The veteran Marines shouted back a rolling unsynchronized "Fortitudine!" The newer men joined in as they realized what was happening. Rattling from different parts of the car, the cheers ended with a 'knee' of varying volume, intonations, and lengths.

The conductor was stunned by the response. His eyes widened. He hastily searched around for understanding. "Err, uhh...yes." He looked back toward Lieutenant Greene and stammered, "G-Good luck, Lieutenant." He made a small waving motion with his right hand.

Greene replied, "Thank you," but he was not sure that the rapidly departing conductor heard him.

Monday, October 17, 1859, 4:30 p.m.

With a louder and harder jolt than expected, the Marine cars were coupled with the Westbound. Within a minute, a Militia General and a civilian entered the car. The General quickly spotted Russell sitting alone. Recognizing the Major's gold oak leaf on his shoulder rank strap, he assumed that he had located the commander of the Marines. Pointing a finger toward his quarry, he said, "Ahh, Major, I am Brigadier General Egerton of the Second Light Brigade, Maryland Volunteer Militia, out of Baltimore."

Russell stood up to greet the General. "Good evening, General, I am Major Russell, United States Marines. A pleasure to meet you, sir." He grasped the General's hand and pumped his arm.

"Yes, yes, a pleasure," said the General absently. He extricated his hand politely from Russell's grasp and indicated the gentleman next to him. "This is Mister Smith, Transportation Master for the B and O railroad. He is Mister Garrett's right hand man and personally responsible for assuring our safe passage to Harper's Ferry."

The railroad man acknowledged both statements with a nod

and said, "We have received a telegraphic communication and understand that the Army's senior officer is not aboard your cars." As he was speaking, Egerton was gazing about the car. It was difficult to tell if the General was searching for the missing Army officer or simply assessing the Marines.

"Yes, I suspect that his meeting with the President took longer than expected," replied Russell. He had accentuated the 'his', implying that he, too, had possibly had a meeting with the President.

Egerton's attention suddenly returned to the conversation, "Oooh...Well, then," he continued to Smith, "I recommend that we push on West as soon as possible." To no one in particular he said, "Insurgents wait for no one, you know, and it will be more than two hours before the Army's commander can arrive at this station." He withdrew his watch and said to it, "Yes, time is of the essence." As he pocketed the watch, he looked to Russell, "Don't you concur, Major?"

General Egerton was indeed desirous to get moving. His two hundred and fifteen officers and men had been cooped up in their stationary passenger cars for over three hours. Although the orders from his Governor were to stay on and protect Maryland soil, he was apprehensive that the insurrectionists would move out of Virginia. He was especially anxious to ensure that the whole dangerous affair was confined to his neighboring State's side of the Potomac River.

Momentarily distracted by movement on the opposite side of the aisle, Russell glanced over the General's shoulder in that direction. Greene was on his feet and had an expectant expression on his face. Ignoring the Lieutenant's presence, he said, "Yes, General, time is of the essence."

"Good, good," beamed Egerton, "We'll find the conductor and get things rolling." He started to turn for the door and paused, "Oh, Major, won't you please join me in my car. I would like very much to discuss the possibilities of 'hot' action upon our arrival."

"Thank you, sir," replied Russell as he followed the General through the door, "I am honored." Honored, indeed. Russell was fully aware that a posting as a Militia General was a traditional and time-honored reward for significant political support or contributions rendered to the incumbent State

Governor.

Greene was inflamed by Russell's snub and moved to interject his opinion into the decision process. He stepped into the aisle and followed the three men out of the door. Once on the car's platform, he stopped and stood still. As he watched the proceeding trio enter the next car, the evening air quickly engulfed him. Its moist, cooling effect helped smother his burning anger.

"Okay," he thought. *"The 'good' Major overstepped his authority."* He shook his head 'no' slightly. *"I have to let that go. Can't let the Militia see any wrong face of the Corps."* He inhaled deeply and exhaled slowly. *"After all, my orders allow me to take such measures that may be necessary to protect United States' property at Harper's Ferry. Getting there without further delay doesn't violate those orders."* He closed his eyes, inhaled deeply again, and held it for a long moment. *"And besides, Major Russell is, once again, away from us for a while."* As he exhaled, his body released all of its anger and frustration.

Two long blasts on the train's whistle roused him from his contemplations. He braced and waited for the lurching start of the train. After the car was in motion, he turned about and reentered the door.

Monday, October 17, 1859, 4:45 p.m.

Orderly Sergeant McDonough looked toward Lieutenant Greene and said, "By your leave, sir, I shall start instructing the men about field rations."

"Very well, XO, carry on," replied Greene.

McDonough stood up and started walking aft. When he arrived near Gilbert's seat, he stopped and spoke to Allen. "Private Allen, I heard you say that you can read. Is that true?"

"Uhh...yes, Orderly Sergeant!" Allen was stunned. He had never spoken to anyone higher in rank than a Corporal. It was unheard of for a Private to even think about talking to a Sergeant, let alone the famous Orderly Sergeant McDonough. He worked directly for the Commandant and was allocated god-like status even by Corporal Gilbert.

"Good." McDonough handed Gilbert a folded newspaper. "If you ask Corporal Gilbert real nice, he just may allow you to read the news after he is finished with the paper."

"Yes, Orderly Sergeant!" responded Allen as McDonough continued aft. He looked to Gilbert and stammered, "How...how did he know?"

Gilbert grinned widely. "Orderly Sergeant McDonough is well known for his remarkable hearing." He nodded 'yes' slightly and continued, "That's the way it is in the Corps, the higher the rank, the better the hearing." He leaned closer to Allen and suggested softly, "Watch what you say, lad, watch what you say. Even when you can't see us, NCOs hear everything." He leaned back, tucked the newspaper between his hip and the armrest, and folded his arms.

Allen spun around to Quinn for confirmation. In all seriousness, Quinn was nodding his head in the affirmative, as was Ruppert. "Wow!" exclaimed Allen in a long, low whisper.

McDonough stopped near the middle of the rows containing Marines. "Listen up, men." He paused to allow the men sitting with their backs to him to turn around. "A great many of you have not been required to live on field rations before." Oscillating his body slowly from forward to aft as he was speaking, he projected his voice clearly and commandingly. His volume was such that he was loud enough to be heard by all and yet not so loud as to be screaming or straining. "In your haversacks is enough food to last each of you for three days." He held his aloft.

It was roughly a twelve-inch-by-twelve-inch canvas bag that had been painted black on the outside as a waterproofing. The back and front pieces of the bag were attached to a three-inch wide strip that ran across the bottom and up the sides. This gave the haversack its depth. A semi-circle shaped flap attached to the top of the back piece was flipped over to the front to cover the opening. Attached at opposite sides of the top of the back piece was a forty-inch long and two-inch wide black painted, canvas carrying strap.

"As you have probably noticed, your filled haversack weighs around twelve pounds. About ten of that is food." As he lowered his arm, McDonough circled around slowly and made eye contact with as many as he could.

"The idea is to ration yourself and make the food last for three days. Longer if possible." He paused to let that fact sink in. "For those of you with hearty appetites, this food could be gone in one day." He escalated his volume, "DON'T LET THAT HAPPEN!" Several Privates in the direction that McDonough was suddenly pointing jumped with surprise. "It will be easier to stretch your food out than it will be to go hungry. IS THAT CLEAR?" He pointed toward another group of Privates.

"YES, ORDERLY SERGEANT!" chorused back from all the Marines.

"Very well, then. Open your haversacks and let's take a look at what's in there." McDonough waited.

The Privates struggled with their muskets. Some were indecisive about what to do with them or where to put them. Most figured out some method or another to securely stabilize the weapon while they shifted their haversacks around from their left hips to their laps. A few actually managed to unloop their haversacks from around their necks and place them on the floor in front of them. Each man ultimately started to unbuckle the single leather strap that held the flap down.

"All right, now," continued McDonough. He was holding the haversack open by the cover flap and up above his waist so he could see into it easily. "The first thing you will probably notice is your mess furniture. On top is the tin cup." He took his out and held it high with his right hand. "This is more than just a drinking cup." He circled around. The majority of the Privates had removed their cups and were also holding them high. "This is your stew pot, your soup pot, your coffee pot, your creek dipper, your rain catcher, your wash basin, your shaving cup, and, if necessary, your shovel." As he was listing off the many uses, most of the Privates started lowering their arms and looking at the cups more closely with renewed interest.

This field cup was very different. It was large. It had a diameter of four inches with a flat bottom, and a straight sidewall four inches high. The 'C' shaped handle on the side was big enough that an average man could hold onto it with three fingers inside the loop. Its full measure capacity was twenty-eight liquid ounces – three and a half cups

McDonough hooked the cup handle over his little finger on his left hand and reached into the haversack again with his right. This time he withdrew his knife, fork, and spoon, and held them aloft. "I will assume," he chuckled, "that, by now, everyone here knows what these are for." A few friendly jabs and snickers speckled the group. The fork was not a commonly used utensil for many prior to their joining the Marines.

The utensils were of the everyday variety. The knife was nine and a half inches long. It had a five and half inch flat, spatula shaped blade that was rounded at the end and a four-inch wooden handle. The blade was initially one inch wide to accommodate many sharpenings. The fork seemed tiny in comparison. It was merely seven inches long, the wooden handle being half of it. Its three simple tines extended from a base that was a little over a half an inch wide. The spoon, on the other hand, seemed like a small spade. It was all metal and eight inches long. The working end was three inches long and almost two inches wide.

McDonough slipped them back into the haversack. He next withdrew a tinned iron plate and held it up. It was a nine-inch basin-like affair that had a two-inch side that angled slightly upward from the bottom of the plate. "Just one word of caution," he said. "This plate is great for holding stews and soups, but DON'T try to use it to cook with. It DOESN'T work." He lowered the plate and scowled around the car. "And the devil WILL take the man who tries to prove otherwise on this expedition." He crammed the plate back into the haversack.

McDonough knew that the plates really could be used as frying pans but he did not want these Privates trying it. There were two inherent problems. Most of these plates were new and therefore 'unseasoned'. Cooking meat on them now would badly scorch the unprotected upper surface and potentially damage them beyond effective use. Additionally, if the Privates used them to cook over a fire that was too hot, they would unwittingly be attempting to reforge the plates, thus destroying them entirely for future cooking or eating use. McDonough wanted to protect Marine Corps property. He did not think these men were ready for fry cooking and its inherent dangers to the equipment. Boiling their food would have to do for now.

"Now then," he continued, "let's take a look into the inner bag." A smaller cotton bag was attached three quarters of the way up the inside of the haversack by three buttons. Two buttonholes near the top of the bag were toward the back 'corners' and one in the middle of the front piece. This suspended bag was the actual part of the haversack that held the food.

"In here you will find about three pounds of hard bread, also known as ship's biscuit or pilot bread." He paused while the men stared at their pieces of hard bread. They looked like large crackers. Each one was about two and a half inches square and a little over one quarter inch thick. "Just so you'll know, there are about ten pieces of hard bread in a pound. That gives you a daily ration of four pieces for each of your two meals and two pieces to nibble on later." He tapped a piece on the top of one of the seatbacks and chortled as it made a hard clunking sound, "If your teeth are that good."

"You will also find in here a three pound piece of salt pork." McDonough reached in and pulled out a piece of the meat. It was not wrapped in paper or in a bag of any sort. It was just there in his hand. He continued, "A smart man will cut this into six equal pieces. That will give him about a half a pound of meat for each meal over the three day period." A few of the Privates eyed their pieces of salt pork to figure out the best way to cut them.

"Of next importance, you will find about a quarter pound of coffee beans in there." He looked into his haversack for a split second. "You'll have to move the hard bread around to see them. They usually settle to the bottom of the bag."

As the sound of shuffled crackers could be heard throughout the car, he carried on, "While you are digging around in there, you will also notice two small, cotton, tie bags." McDonough held up one such bag. It was closed with a drawstring. "One of these has about a half a pound of salt in it, and the other holds the same amount of sugar." He dropped the small bag into the haversack and smiled slightly. "For those of you who may have forgotten, sugar grains are brown in color, salt is white."

McDonough now pointed into the haversack. "In order to add a little flavor to your meals, the Barracks cook was able to provide each of you with a potato, an onion, two carrots, two apples, and some ginger cookies as a treat." He dropped his cup inside and started to buckle the top flap down. "I will now turn you over to Sergeant Buckley for your cooking lessons."

At this point, Sergeant Buckley stood up and commanded, "Attention, Section." All of the Privates squared away in their seats and froze. McDonough nodded to Buckley and headed toward the next 'Marine' car to indoctrinate its occupants.

Sergeant Buckley stepped to the position where McDonough had been standing, looked around, and said, "Rest." The seated Marines relaxed. Those who needed to, turned around to face the Sergeant. Many took the opportunity to finish buckling down their haversack flaps.

"All right, listen up," started Buckley. "The most important and easiest meal to prepare is breakfast." He paused while several Marines concluded their adjustments and quickly gave him their undivided attention. "As for the coffee...that will be easy on this expedition. The beans you were issued have already been roasted. Normally they're 'raw' and green in color." Buckley lowered his voice slightly. "You drew a lucky card this time. But the cooks, who had recently roasted a large quantity of beans at the Barracks, drew a joker." He grinned, implying that something devious had been accomplished and that he was pleasantly pleased with himself about whatever it was. Raising his voice again, he proceeded on with the instruction, "All you will have to do is crush them up, add water, and sit tight while it boils.

"For those of you who like regular strength coffee, you should just cover the bottom of your cup with one layer of whole beans." He held up his index finger to reinforce the concept of one. "The rest of you can add or take away as necessary for your tastes." He turned to the closest Marine and said, "Fisher, hand me your bayonet and get your cup out." Taking the bayonet and holding it with the tip toward the overhead, he continued, "The easiest way to crush the beans in the field is to leave them in your cup and use the socket end (the cylinder shaped part that attaches around the muzzle end of the barrel) of your bayonet." He took hold of Fisher's cup with his left hand and, holding onto the bayonet above the socket with his right hand, he repeatedly lowered and raised the socket end inside the cup, twisting his right hand to simulate a grinding motion.

Buckley handed the bayonet back to Fisher. "Once all of the beans are ground up, fill your cup with water up to about here." He indicated about three-quarters full with his finger. "Next, you will place your cup in some coals near the edge of the fire." He simulated placing the cup in a fire by placing it next to Fisher's shoulder.

He admonished, "If you put it in the flames," he held the cup above Fisher's head, "your fingers will pay dearly when you try to remove it. Not to mention dropping the cup and spilling everything in the fire." With exaggerated fright, he opened his hand wide and the cup dropped into Fisher's lap. The Sergeant fanned his hand as though his fingers had been singed as he looked around to ensure that everyone understood the warning. Many of the Marines were nodding their heads up and down. "Okay, so you put the cup near the edge of the fire and you let the water boil until," his speech slowed significantly, "it's a nice," he paused between each word, "deep, rich, dark brown color." Buckley was obviously a coffee lover of long standing. His eyes had closed and his face turned slightly upward as he inhaled the aroma of a perfect cup of coffee that was brewing in his memory.

He shook himself from his reverie. "Anyhow, with several open fires, all of you will be able to boil some coffee and cook your ration of meat at the same time." He pulled the ramrod partway up on Fisher's weapon. "The quickest way to cook the meat will be to use your ramrods as a skewer. This will allow you to use the open flame of the fire to cook in while your coffee is cooking in the coals." He again looked around to make sure that everyone got the idea. With the experience of a long service veteran, he gently pushed the ramrod back to its locked position.

"Any questions?" Buckley looked around the car. No one indicated a need to have anything explained. "Very well," he barked. "Each set of facing seats will make up a mess unit." He pointed at two facing seats near him for emphasis. "For those of you who would like to make coffee or attempt some cooking," he paused, "one," he held up his index finger, "I repeat, one member of each mess will be designated as the mess cook. Only the mess cook will be allowed to use the heating stove at the end of the car." Buckley then admonished, "Keep that area shipshape. Do you understand?"

"AYE-AYE, SERGEANT!"

The Sergeant circled slowly around the car with an inspective eye. Satisfied, he then bellowed, "THE SMOKING LAMP IS LIT!" And followed with, "CARRY ON!"

Monday, October 17, 1859, 5:15 p.m.

Lieutenant Greene stood up and retrieved his boat cloak from the overhead storage crib. As he moved toward the aisle, he commented to Mundell, "I shall be on the car platform to take some fresh air, Orderly Sergeant. Please advise Orderly Sergeant McDonough of my whereabouts upon his return."

"Aye-Aye, Sir."

Once outside, Greene stopped in the middle of the platform and swung the cloak around his head and down upon his shoulders. He breathed deeply, and exhaled slowly several times. The crisp chill of the Fall air refreshed him. As his eyes adjusted to the night's darkness, he made his way to the edge of the platform and leaned against the body of the car.

Looking out from under the platform's roof, he checked the blackened heaven for stars, but was unable to find any. The earth was still overcast with rain-laden clouds. The dim lantern light from within the cars was just enough to enable him to make out some trees and bushes as the train passed by them. Greene ruminated aloud, "T'was a dark and gloomy night as the king's men slowly rode to the morrow's battle. Each man pondering if the gods would be favorable."

"A very interesting presentment, sir." From the next car's platform, the voice had suddenly reached out through the darkness. "Is it the beginning of a soldier's prayer or perhaps a quote of some sort?" The voice was non-threatening, balanced in masculine pitch and inflection, yet gentle, perhaps even friendly. Greene spun around toward the sound. His eyes searched to find the source. Deep in the shadows, he could just make out a small, glowing amber. It moved up in an arc, stopped, and for a moment intensified in brightness. Greene froze. Staring intently, he could almost make out a man's face before the amber suddenly fell in a downward arc.

Slowly from the shadows, a figure emerged. It was a man of medium height. He appeared to be wearing a uniform. At least the hat and the metal shoulder devices seemed to indicate so. As the stranger approached, Greene could also see that the man was holding a small cigar in his right hand. He estimated the other man to be in his early to mid-Twenties.

"I do apologize for startling you, sir." The voice sounded sincere. "I undoubtedly enjoy an unfair advantage as I have been out here for some time and my eyes have fully adjusted to the dark." He stopped a half pace away from Greene.

"Allow me to introduce myself." He shifted the cigar to his left hand and extended his right. "Captain Richard Gary Byrd, of the Flying Rifles. More formally Company D, Second Light Brigade, Maryland Volunteer Militia."

"A pleasure to meet you, sir." Greene grasped the man's hand and shook it politely. "First Lieutenant Israel Greene, United States Marines."

"Ah," said the man with a sense of recognition. "Then you must be the Second-in-Command of the Regulars."

Greene bristled slightly, but continued courteously, "Actually, Captain, I am the Commander of the Marine Detachment."

"Oh, yes. Marines. Sorry." Byrd first exhibited regret for his blunder and then a look of confusion. "And the 'Marine' Major that I met earlier?"

"Yes, that would be Major Russell, the Marine Corps' Paymaster. He is a staff officer and accompanying us in an advisory capacity at the application of the Secretary of the Navy." Greene was, as before, fully aware of service discretion and said no more.

"Oh, I see." Byrd nodded with an air of understanding. "Another one of those infamous political entanglements." He smiled ruefully. "Very similar, I suppose, to me being posted as a Captain over the other officers who have been a part of the Militia much longer than myself." He shrugged. "Not really sure what's going on or what to do if anything happens, but I am here none the less."

Greene did not respond and Byrd continued, "This whole Militia thing was my father's idea. He's a State Senator, you see, and quite anxious for me to follow in his footsteps." He looked out over the shadowy, passing landscape. "Afraid, though, that I don't have the insatiable ego needed for politics." He flipped the cigar away from the car. The glowing amber tumbled erratically into the darkness. "No, my desires lie in the field of medicine. I would much rather help mankind than try to control it." He continued to look out into the darkness and remained quiet for several seconds.

Byrd returned to the present moment with a quick turn toward Greene. "So, Lieutenant, pray tell what was that little soliloquy of yours about?" His mood was upbeat and his interest heartfelt.

Greene grinned sheepishly. "Oh, something I seem to remember reading or hearing somewhere. It might have been from one of Shakespeare's plays." He shook his head and shrugged his shoulders slightly. "It just seemed to fit the current situation."

"How true," agreed Byrd. "How, true."

"Is this your first sojourn into harm's way?" asked Greene. He attributed the man's talkativeness to nerves. He was not sure why, but he had taken an immediate liking to the young Captain and was partial to the idea of helping him calm down.

"Why, actually, yes." replied Byrd, hesitantly. He had not been aware that it showed so readily. He quickly considered changing the topic of conversation, but there was something resolute and personable about this new 'Marine' friend. He instantly felt that he could trust him. "I must say that I have very mixed feelings about all of this. On one hand, I am as excited as a schoolboy about the adventure. Yet, on the other, I have strong feelings of trepidation." Byrd was holding out both of his hands and moving them up and down like a scale seeking a balance point. "Are you feeling this sort of turmoil?" His facial expression indicated that he was seeking an honest answer.

Greene responded in a very careful tone. "At the present time, no. But, I do know about the feelings of which you speak." He gazed steadily into Byrd's eyes. He could see the young man visibly relax. "With your permission, I would like to tell you a little story about when I did feel that sort of turmoil."

Byrd chuckled and asked, "Will this be one of those 'sea stories' you nautical folk are so well known for?"

Greene also chuckled and shifted about slightly on his feet to establish an authoritative posture. "Well, now, Captain, that depends. Do you know the difference between a fairy tale and a sea story?"

The Captain pondered for a few seconds, decided that he did not and said, "Apparently not. Please, continue."

"Very well," said Greene. "As you may well remember from your childhood, a fairy tale always begins with," he elevated his voice as though making an announcement to a large group, "Once upon a time..." Greene even raised his right hand and swung it outward. As the young Captain nodded, 'yes', Greene retracted his hand and continued, "But, a great sea story always starts with a sly look around to see who might be listening," Greene moved his head slowly left then right with a slight ducking motion to imitate the action, "and then it begins with," he paused, leaned closer, and hoarsely whispered, "I jest you not, but THIS," he pointed his forefinger toward the young Captain's chest for emphasis, "really happened...."

Greene was having a hard time keeping a straight face. The look on Byrd's face was priceless. First came confusion. Then, with an expression of sudden realization, Byrd exclaimed, "There is no difference! It's just the delivery!" Both men snickered and quickly progressed into roaring laughter.

Greene slowly regained his composure. It felt good to relax and enjoy himself. He had not realized how much of a strain he had been under since receiving his orders earlier today. "Well now, Captain, my story goes back to July Eighteen Fifty-Three, when I was in the steam frigate *Mississippi*."

"Excuse me," queried Byrd, "did you say 'IN' the ship?" His look also questioned the use of the word in Greene's statement.

"Yes," responded Greene. "In nautical terms, members of the ship's company are IN the ship since they are an integral part of the vessel the same as the planks, masts, or sails. On the other hand, passengers or guests are said to be ON a ship as they are temporary visitors and not permanent." Greene shook his head slightly and said, "Trust me...it's one of those subtle Naval traditions of perplexing vocabulary."

"Ahh," mused Byrd. However, a look of minor mystification remained on his face.

Greene continued, "We were the flagship for a squadron of ten ships, all well armed and presenting a formidable firepower of one hundred and forty-four guns. Commodore Matthew Perry commanded the squadron. The Commodore was carrying a letter from President Fillmore to the Emperor of Japan seeking to negotiate a commercial treaty. His task was especially difficult because Japan had barred entry of any outsiders to their country since Sixteen-Forty. They were generally known to kill any foreigner who set foot on their shores even if by accident of ship wreck."

Byrd grimaced. "I say, a rather tough bunch, these Japaners."

"Yes, undeniably," agreed Greene. "However, within two weeks of our arrival, the Commodore had shrewdly negotiated an opportunity to meet with a high level Japanese official to formally deliver the President's letter." Greene unconsciously gripped the hilt of his sword with his left hand. "This was to be our first time ashore and we had to be prepared for anything."

"Exactly," agreed Byrd.

"I can remember the day as though it was just yesterday," said Greene thoughtfully. "At daybreak, the *Mississippi* and the *Susquehanna* steamed close to land and anchored in such a way as to present a full broadside of guns toward the shore. The enlisted men had drawn lots the night before to determine who would go ashore. All of the Marine Officers and as many Naval Officers as could be spared were to go ashore." Greene pondered for a moment. "As I recall, the Commodore's honor guard consisted of one hundred Marines, one hundred Sailors and forty Musicians. Why, even the Commodore's personal bodyguards were two splendidly tall and powerfully built Negroes, both heavily armed." Greene lightly brushed off the front of his frock coat. "The Marines outdid themselves preparing their uniforms and weapons for the occasion. They wore blue coats, white cross belts, white trousers and pomponed shakos (a tall, cylinder shaped hat with a visor). I don't think I've ever seen a finer looking troop of Marines since."

"Wouldn't you say you had a superior looking outfit with you, now," commented Byrd.

"A superior looking outfit, yes. But not as beautiful as they were in Japan on that day." With a proud little smile and a wink of the eye he continued, "I am referring to magnificence here, Captain."

"Ahh, yes. The pride of belonging and such." Byrd was nodding with total understanding. "Pray, do continue."

Greene bowed his head slightly to signify agreement and did so. "It took fifteen launches and cutters to carry us all ashore. Commander Franklin Buchanan, Skipper of the *Mississippi* received the honor of being the first American to set foot on Japanese soil. Our own Brevet Major Zeilin was next. It was his privilege to lead the procession to the meeting place." Greene straightened to his full height. "As we were disembarking from the launches and quietly falling into formation, I suddenly realized that we were probably outnumbered twenty to one. There had to have been five thousand Japanese soldiers in brigade formations lining the beach."

"That had to have been a moment of significant trepidation," interjected Byrd.

"Yes, it was," responded Greene. "But at the same time it was quite an adventure. When we saw the Japanese warriors up close, it was as though we had stepped back in time to the kingdom of King Arthur and his knights of the round table. Incredibly, their soldiers were actually clad in a type of armor!" Greene was getting excited as he spoke. He was looking out toward the darkened landscape passing by. He pointed with an outstretched hand to different locations as he described the scene. "There were pike men, and archers with eight-foot bows. There were even some companies of men carrying ancient matchlock muskets. Fierce looking two-sworded warriors were parading in front of the formations of soldiers. Lines of small-horsed cavalry were positioned behind the foot soldiers." He arced his arm across the horizon. "Huge heraldic banners made of bright colored silk were flying everywhere." He flashed his hands open and closed. "Pop, Pop, Pop. The noise the banners made in the wind sounded like gunfire. It all seemed unbelievable!"

"Wow!" was all that came out of Byrd's open mouth as he listened in total awe.

Greene lowered his crescendo. "Although the Japanese were physically smaller in size than us...they averaged maybe five feet tall...to a man they all glared at us with absolutely ugly scowls. Their faces reflected fear, hate, and suspicion. Some were even wearing ferocious-looking masks. Each warrior that I looked at seemed fiercer than the last." Greene shook his head. "They certainly didn't want us there and," he looked directly at Byrd, "what was worse, we didn't know what kind of fury they might turn loose on us at any moment."

Byrd gulped as his mind's eye pictured Greene's panorama of danger. "Now that had to be the epitome of true personal turmoil."

"Yes...Yes, it was," replied Greene somberly. "And with all sincere honesty, the farther we marched inland, the more my mind wanted my body to be somewhere else. If I could have followed my instinct, I would have scrambled back to the ship." He paused as the memory drifted past his consciousness. "Nevertheless, I was able to strengthen my resolve by remembering and repeating the Marine motto...Fortitudine." Greene placed his right hand over his heart. "That one word reminded me that I had sworn an oath to serve my country to the best of my ability and to faithfully lead other men in their service as well. My honor and the honor of the Marine Corps were on the line." He swallowed hard. "With an unexpected calmness and a warm feeling of inner peace, I accepted the idea of facing any ensuing danger 'with courage'." Greene again paused. He relaxed the fist he had made with his now upright forearm and lowered it to his side. "It was my duty, as well as my privilege. That was the reason I was there." He stopped and simply looked at his military companion with the warmth of an older brother passing on life's knowledge to a sibling.

Byrd returned Greene's look with a cordial smile and a facial expression of complete comprehension. He spoke slowly and passionately. "A rare and true gentleman you are, sir." He came to a position of Attention. "I genuinely appreciate your candor and honesty. I have taken your sentiment to heart." He tapped his chest twice with a closed hand. "I pray that I am able to emulate such steadfastness when my time presents itself before the Gates of Hell." He saluted. However, before Greene could return the salute, he cut it away and extended his hand.

"Thank you, my friend. My spirit is much lighter. And now, I must return to my Company. I sincerely hope that our paths shall meet again someday."

Smiling with satisfaction, Greene grasped the hand and pumped it warmly. "My pleasure, sir."

* * * * *

Corporal Gilbert had been watching Private Allen for several minutes. To the veteran's amusement, Allen presented a very laughable sight. With a look of deep concern on his face, Allen was slowly rummaging through his haversack. Occasionally he would grasp a food item, extract it from within, look at it carefully, and then return it to the bag. Absolute puzzlement was written all over his face. On his last extraction, Allen hefted the potato in his hand as though he was trying to guess its exact weight. He then rolled the potato around in his hands and examined it closely. With a look that conveyed that some mystery had yet to be solved, he shrugged his shoulders, sighed, and returned the potato to the bag.

"What seems to be the problem, Private?" asked Gilbert.

Allen was initially surprised by the question, but screwed up enough courage, found his voice, and replied, "I'mmm...not really sure what to do with these food items, Corporal." He paused, looked down at his haversack, and, with a low voice, continued, "My mother and sister were the cooks in the family. I was too busy swinging a pick to learn how to cook anything." He looked up and proudly said, "Except for roasting the salt pork on my ramrod and making coffee in my cup," his voice again lowered, "I'm not sure what else to do with these other food items except eat them raw." Allen gave a grimace to imply that he did not enjoy that idea at all.

"Well, then, lad. Let me give you a quick lesson in preparing a very noble dish the Naval folks call lobscouse." As he spoke, Gilbert shifted toward the edge of his seat and held out his hand to indicate that Allen should hand over his haversack.

"Lob-what?" asked Allen as he passed the haversack to Gilbert.

"Lobscouse, lad," responded Gilbert. He then added very

matter of factly, "An excellent delicacy that you will look forward to with true relish when you are assigned to shipboard duty." He opened the haversack, reached inside, pulled out the potato, and held it in front of Allen. "First, you slice off some of this potato." The Corporal eyed the potato carefully. "Maybe about this much." He indicated an amount equal to one third of the overall length. "Next, you cut that piece into real thin slices." Gilbert held the end of the potato up and made a cutting motion over it with his other hand. "Cut them as thin as you can. That will make them cook faster." He suddenly held the potato up close under Allen's nose. "And try not to cut your fingers off! Got that?"

Allen jumped back and stammered, "Ye...Yes, Corporal."

"Good." He dropped the potato into the haversack and withdrew a carrot. "You then do the same thing with about half of this carrot." Allen instinctively flinched as Gilbert moved to return the carrot to the bag.

The onion was the next item retrieved. "Now, this baby is handled a little bit differently." Gilbert was tossing it up and down slightly in his hand. "If handled wrong, this wee bit of vegetable will bring tears to a grown man's eyes." Propping it on the end of his fingertips, he circled the onion around so all three Privates could check it out. "About the best thing I can tell you about how to handle this onion is to make sure that you are near an open window, or, that you are outside when you cut it up." He fingered at the onion's skin. "Make sure you remove this part first. It's not eatable."

"Ha!" chortled Ruppert. "I'll tell you what's not eatable. It's those stinking lima beans that are served every Wednesday in the galley." He wrinkled his nose up and sputtered his tongue through his lips several times as though spitting something out. "For someone with a sweet tooth like me, those things are just plain vile!"

"Easy, lad," cautioned Corporal Gilbert. "Those lima beans are fast becoming a first-rate Marine eating tradition. He leaned back and flicked an index finger toward Ruppert. "And who do you suppose introduced those healthy green morsels to this country, AND, to the Marine Corps?"

Ruppert shrugged his shoulders as his face indicated a mournful look of 'I'm required to know this, too?'

"Think, Marine," continued Gilbert, "who do you know of at Head Quarters who is a right proper gentleman gardener?"

Ruppert was first puzzled by the question and then a look of surprised comprehension came over his face. He whispered, "You mean the Commandant?"

"That's right," confirmed Gilbert. "The Commandant, Colonel John B. Harris, himself, is the man responsible for introducing the lima bean to these United States. He brought some back from one of his earlier cruises to South America and first cultivated them near his home at Philadelphia.

"And, Private," Gilbert leaned closer to Ruppert and gave him the evil eye, "the next time the Commandant visits the galley during a Wednesday mid-day meal, he had better see your smiling face shoveling in those lima beans with absolute delight. Understood?"

Ruppert snapped back to Attention in his seat. "YES, CORPORAL!"

"Very well." Gilbert reverted to his smiling self and sat back in his seat.

"Excuse me, Corporal," said Allen tentatively, "but what about the rest of the lobcow recipe?"

"The what?" Gilbert had been distracted by his discussion with Ruppert and had absently forgotten to finish his lesson with Allen. He glanced at the onion still in his left hand. Recovering quickly, he said, "Oh, you mean lobscouse." He leaned forward. "Listen up, lad. The end of the word sounds like house." He leaned back. "Lob-scouse. Got it?" Allen nodded.

"All right, then. To continue." Gilbert leaned forward again and made some chopping motions with his hand. "You cut up some of the onion into small pieces." He held out his pinky finger, "about the size of your little fingernail. You then put the potato, carrot, and onion in your cup with enough water to cover it all. Add a little bit of salt and start it to boiling."

"Next, you take one of the six pieces of salt pork that Orderly Sergeant McDonough told you about and you cut it up into smaller pieces like the onion. You add the salt pork to the cup and you boil it all till it's soft." He looked at Allen's face for comprehension and found it.

"Well then, after everything has boiled itself real soft, you take two or three pieces of your hard bread and break it up into crumbs." Gilbert chuckled silently at an inner joke. "Here's where your bayonet socket will come in handy again. They don't call it hard bread for nothing."

"Dump the crumbs into the cup and let it boil for another minute or so. That way the hard bread will soften up some." Gilbert leaned back and continued, "Stir it all up with your spoon and you're ready to sample an exceptional Naval cookery delight. Any questions?" Allen shook his head. "Good. And don't worry, lad, you'll do just fine." He dropped the onion back into the haversack.

Gilbert turned to his right. "Ruppert, your turn to listen up. I'm going to tell you about a little dish you can cook up from these field rations for that sweet tooth of yours."

"Thank you, Corporal," responded Ruppert.

Gilbert sifted through Allen's haversack again and brought out an apple, the bag of sugar, and some ginger cookies. He held up the apple. "First you quarter and core the apple and then you slice up some of it like you did the potato." He looked around at all three Privates. "Real thin, so it'll cook faster, remember?" Everyone quickly nodded. "Next you put the slices and a sprinkle of sugar in a cup with just enough water to cover the slices. Stew the mix till its soft." He looked toward Allen. "Stew and boil mean the same thing, only stew uses less water. Got that?" Allen nodded. "Finally you add some crumbled ginger cookies and simmer awhile longer. When it's all done, it makes a mighty fine, sweet tooth satisfying, ginger-apple stew."

"Thank YOU, Corporal!" Ruppert was all toothy smile. "I think I'll try that one first."

Monday, October 17, 1859, 5:45 p.m.

"Ex..cuse me, sir." The hesitant voice came from behind Greene. He turned around from the edge of the car platform. Against the lighted door stood a darkened figure a little taller than himself. He knew he was a Marine right away because he could plainly make out the distinctive white belts in the dark. However, Greene was not sure of the person's identity. He thought the Marine to be young and rather on the lanky side.

"Yes, come forward," commanded Greene. As the figure did, so he could see that the individual was indeed a teenager. He assumed him to be one of his Musicians.

"Excuse me, sir. Orderly Sergeant McDonough sends his respects, sir. And he sends this food for the Lieutenant, sir." He was holding out a small tray with a plate, cup, and spoon on it.

"Thank you," said Greene as he accepted the tray. The cup had steam drifting away from the liquid inside. He tipped the tray slightly toward the door to catch a little light to see what the plate contained. "Ah, looks like a little lobscouse and coffee to chase away the evening chill. Please relay my compliments to the Orderly Sergeant."

"Aye, sir!" responded the teenager and he started to turn away.

"Hold on, lad," said Greene.

The boy snapped back to face the Lieutenant and queried, "Sir?"

"Have you eaten, lad?" interrogated Greene.

"Yes, sir, I have. Thank you, sir." The boy seemed confident in Greene's presence.

"What's your name?"

"Apprentice Musician Baxter, sir."

Greene did not recognize the name. "First name?" he asked.

"Richard, sir. Richard Jerome Baxter, sir." As he pronounced his full name, he seemed to stand even taller.

"You are not new to the Marines, are you Baxter?" Although he knew almost every man at the Head Quarters, Greene was sure he was familiar with the name, but he was just as certain that he did not know this boy. He was also confident that the lad's demeanor was the result of service experience.

The young fellow smiled and replied, "No, sir. My father enlisted me as a bound boy to learn music in July of Fifty-Five, sir. I currently hold the rating of Fifer, sir."

Greene spooned a bite of lobscouse off the plate. "And who is your father?"

"Woolsey Baxter, sir."

Greene swallowed the hot food quickly. "Emmm, yes.

Isn't he the blacksmith and armorer at Head Quarters?"

"Yes, sir."

Greene searched his memory. "Do I recall correctly that your father was a Marine at one time?"

"Yes, sir," replied Baxter with enthusiasm. "He served from Thirty-Six until Forty-Six, sir. He was with General Henderson in Georgia, Alabama, and Florida fighting the Creek and Seminole Indians. He was a Corporal when he discharged, sir."

Greene lowered the coffee cup from his lips and commented, "Very impressive service."

"Thank you, sir." Baxter was all grins.

Greene looked hard at the young Musician. "So, tell me, Baxter, where are you normally assigned, and how is it that you are with my Detachment on this particular expedition."

Baxter was suddenly shocked to silence.

"Come on, lad. Speak up. I run a tight ship and you are a bit of a loose end." Greene took another spoon of lobscouse while he waited patiently for the answer.

Baxter locked up at Attention. "Sir, I am assigned to the Marine Guard in the Sloop *Germantown*. We're homeported at Norfolk, Virginia. She's currently undergoing some minor repairs at the Gosport Naval Shipyard and I have been granted two weeks leave of absence to visit my parents, sir."

Greene continued to eat his meal. "Go on."

Baxter started to falter. "Aye, sir. Well, sir. It's like this, sir. Uhhh..."

Greene soothed the boy. "Calm down, lad. No one's going to shoot you." And he scooped up the last bite of food from the plate.

"Yes, sir. Thank you, sir." He paused briefly. "Your regular Fifer, sir, Jimmy Hogan, that is. Well, sir, he and I are old friends. And when I heard about this expedition..." He paused to phrase his words. "Anyway, sir, I sort of reminded Jimmy that he owed me a really big favor, and now was the time for him to pay me back." He gulped. "No harm intended, sir. And Jimmy is still at the Barracks, sir. He's not absent, sir, just not here. I'm here in his place."

Greene took a slow sip of coffee and eyed the boy over the rim of the cup. "Hmmm," he hummed. "Looking for a little action, are you?"

"Ye...Yes, sir," stammered the lad. "Ready to serve, sir."

"Are you up to the task?" inquired Greene with all due seriousness.

Baxter stood to his full height and sounded off. "Aye, sir. Fortitudine, sir."

Greene finished his coffee and placed the cup on the tray. He then handed the tray to Baxter who accepted it. "Very well, Apprentice Musician Baxter. Your service shall be monitored. If I find it lacking, you shall suffer the consequences of your folly."

"Yes, sir," moaned Baxter. His enthusiasm was deflating.

"However," continued Greene, "if your service is exemplary, you shall be allowed to return to the *Germantown* without reprimand or any mention of you being here. Is that understood?"

"YES, SIR!" His smile returned.

"All right, then. Kindly return the tray to the Orderly Sergeant. Dismiss." Greene shooed the boy off with the motion of his hand.

"Aye-Aye, sir! Thank you, sir!" exclaimed Baxter as he stepped back in preparation to turn about.

"Oh, and Baxter," Greene said in a fatherly tone. "Don't forget to convey my compliments to the Orderly Sergeant."

"Absolutely, sir!"

Monday, October 17, 1859, 6:15 p.m.

Allen had just returned from the 'head' and stopped in the aisle just outside of Corporal Gilbert's feet. "Pardon me, Corporal, but have you finished reading the newspaper?"

Gilbert reached between his hip and the armrest and extracted the paper. "Actually, no," he replied. "But you might as well have a look at it now." He started to hand it to Allen, but he suddenly stopped. His attention had been attracted toward the far end of the car. He stood up and absentmindedly pressed the folded paper against Allen's chest. He muttered under his breath, "Here...I have a few mess cooks to square away," and started to stomp away.

Allen was stunned. He grasped at the paper with both hands and looked where the Corporal was heading. He immediately recognized what was happening, or rather, what was going to happen. He ducked his head and scurried into his seat. He cautioned his seatmates in a low whisper. "Stand-by for heavy rolls, lads. Corporal Gilbert is on the war path!"

Both Quinn and Ruppert immediately stood up and looked toward the rear of the car to see what's what. Just as quickly, both returned to their seats. Quinn gasped, "I'm sure glad we're at this end of the car."

"That's for sure," agreed Ruppert.

As several rumbling expletives drifted through the air toward them, Quinn pointed to the paper in Allen's hands. "Why don't you read us some of the news until the storm passes."

"Great idea," responded Allen and he started to unfold the paper. When it was about half open, a brochure fell out onto the floor.

Quinn bent over and picked it up. "What's this?" he asked. He looked at both of the outside pages. There was a woodcut print on the front. "Looks like something to do with trains." He showed the representation to Ruppert.

"Yup," agreed Ruppert. "Something to do with trains."

An article about the insurrection had distracted Allen's attention. Although only half way through it, he stopped, neatly refolded the newspaper, and set it down on the Corporal's empty seat. Turning to Quinn, he reached out and said, "Let me see that." After quickly examining all of the pages, Allen exclaimed, "Hey, this is great!"

"What is it?" cried Quinn. Ruppert strained his neck to see more.

Allen pointed at the front page. "This is a pamphlet put out by the Baltimore and Ohio Railroad."

"Say," interrupted Ruppert, "where does this railroad go to in Ohio, anyway?"

Allen perused the first few paragraphs. "Interestingly enough, it doesn't go into the State of Ohio at all."

"What?" quizzed Ruppert.

"No," continued Allen rather matter of factly, "it actually stops at Wheeling, Virginia."

Ruppert was dumbfounded. "So, you're telling me that the B and O Railroad doesn't go into the State of Ohio whatsoever. It just stops at some town in Virginia?"

"Correct," said Allen. "According to this pamphlet, Wheeling, Virginia is actually ON the Ohio River. That's where the 'Ohio' comes from."

"Gee." Ruppert was still confused. "I always figured it went to some place special in Ohio, not just to the river."

Allen grinned. "That may be, but what's really special about this pamphlet, is that there's a lot in it about Harper's Ferry. That's where we're going!"

"Well come on man, read it to us!" Quinn leaned closer to Allen.

Allen quickly scanned more of the print. "Most of these words were apparently written by a man named Joseph Barry, a resident of the area." He started looking for facts about anything other than the railroad itself. "Okay, here's some good information,

> "Harper's Ferry is a town with a population of about three thousand – nine-tenths of whom are whites. The village is situated in Jefferson County, Virginia, at the confluence of the Potomac and the Shenandoah Rivers, at the base and in the very shadow of the Blue Ridge Mountains. The distance from Washington City is fifty-five miles, and from Baltimore eighty-one miles. The Baltimore and Ohio Railroad crosses the Potomac, at the place, on a magnificent bridge and the Winchester and Potomac Railroad has its northern terminus in the town. The Chesapeake and Ohio Canal, also, is in the immediate neighborhood.
> The scenery around the place is celebrated for its grandeur. On one side, the Maryland Heights, and, on the other, the Loudoun Heights rise majestically as guardian giants defending the portals of the noble Valley of Virginia. The Maryland Heights ascend in successive plateaus to a height of thirteen hundred feet above the surrounding country, and two thousand feet above the level of the sea. The Loudoun Heights are not as lofty, but they present an appearance of a more marked primeval wilderness than the Maryland mountain. Between these two ramparts, the lordly Potomac takes to his embrace the beautiful Shenandoah."

"What in the world does all of that mean?" asked Quinn with an absolute look of puzzlement.

"Well," mused Allen, "I think is means that Harper's Ferry is at the bottom of a mountain range and sticks out on a spit of land where two rivers meet, kind of like a pier. And, on the far sides of the rivers are some pretty tall mountains."

"What's all that lordly embracing about?" wondered Ruppert.

"I get the impression that the bigger river is the Potomac and the Shenandoah flows into it," answered Allen.

"Well, why didn't he just say so?" retorted Ruppert.

Allen chuckled. "I always wondered why the big words, too. My mother told me once that people who write books and such are paid by the page. I guess the bigger the words, the less you have to write to fill up a page." He looked back at the print. "One thing is for sure. Harper's Ferry is not in the flatlands. We might be looking at some pretty vigorous hill climbing once we get there."

"Oh, I sure hope this place isn't built on the top of a cliff," bemoaned Ruppert. "I hate high places like that."

Quinn warned, "You'd better keep that little fact to yourself when you go to sea."

Ruppert replied, "Okay," but he was not sure what about.

Allen reopened the pamphlet. "Well, here's some information about the Armory and Arsenal that might answer your question," he volunteered. "This section is written by a Mister Martin Conway."

> "Upon the insistence of George Washington, the Federal government, in 1798, established an Armory at Harper's Ferry. The availability of water power, the area's safe distance from the nation's capital, and a belief that the Potomac will be the main artery westward, were reasons that Washington insisted the gun factory be located at Harper's Ferry."

"That's a real good indication that the Armory is near the level of the water and not high up the mountain. They must use waterpower to run the machinery." Allen beamed with assurance as though he knew what he was talking about.

"Very interesting logic, Private." The voice flowed in from the aisle way. "What other information have you discovered about our destination?" Allen spun around to identify the speaker. It was Orderly Sergeant McDonough. Allen spun back around and froze. Quinn and Ruppert replicated his action. The Orderly Sergeant moved the newspaper aside and sat down in Gilbert's seat. "At ease, Private," he said softly to Allen. "I'd like to hear what else you have figured out by reading that little pamphlet."

"Ye...yes, sir, Orderly Sergeant!" stuttered Allen.

"You don't say 'sir' to me, Private. I'm not a commissioned officer." McDonough started to say something about 'working for a living', but thought better of it.

"Yes, sss...uh, Orderly Sergeant." Allen cursed himself for almost making the same mistake again. He quickly began to digest the information he had read. He formulated his words slowly. "It seems to me that Harper's Ferry is a pretty good sized town. There are over a thousand more people living there than in the village around the Navy Yard in Washington. That means a very large gun making industry. Assuming there is a supply of finished guns there, it would make sense for insurgents to want to take control of it."

"Interesting," commented McDonough.

Allen continued, "Since we headed North toward Baltimore before heading West, we'll probably be approaching Harper's Ferry from the Maryland side of the Potomac River. The pamphlet mentions a magnificent bridge over the river at that place. It must be right up against the Maryland Heights also mentioned." Allen thought seriously for a few seconds. "If the insurgents have control of the bridge, we may have to look for another place to cross over. The pamphlet also mentions a canal, but I'm not sure where it's at or where it goes."

"Good points," said an impressed McDonough. "What else?"

Allen pondered a little more. "Since the town has water on two of three sides, we might need to see about finding some boats of some kind."

"Hmm. Anything else?" queried McDonough.

Allen was starting to get into the swing of things but realized that there was not too much more he could contribute. "No, Orderly Sergeant. I guess that's about all I can come up with."

"Outstanding, Private!" exclaimed McDonough. You've just earned yourself a spot on the Skirmish Detail." He held out his hand and wiggled his fingertips, implying that he wanted the pamphlet.

Allen blinked. "Thank you, Orderly Sergeant." As he handed over the pamphlet, he thought to himself, *"I think!"*

At the same moment, Corporal Gilbert appeared upon the scene. "Any trouble here, Orderly Sergeant?" He gave Allen the once over quickly with his evil eye.

"No, Corporal," answered McDonough as he rose to his feet. "Just the opposite." He looked at Allen and back to Gilbert. "Take good care of Private Allen, here. He'll be part of any Skirmish Detail that we send out. He has a good head on his shoulders. He is able to think things out." He nodded his head. "He just might make a good Marine."

Gilbert snapped to Attention. "Yes, Orderly Sergeant."

As McDonough headed off toward 'Officer's Country', the Corporal sat down and asked, "What was that all about?" His dander was still up from dealing with the mess cooks and he did not need any further aggravation.

Allen replied calmly, "The Orderly Sergeant was merely asking me about what I had read in a pamphlet that was in the newspaper."

A relieved Gilbert said, "Oh." Then he added, "You must have impressed him good for him to put you on Skirmish Detail."

"I guess so," replied Allen absently. He had been watching the Orderly Sergeant who was now speaking with the Lieutenant who had just reentered the car. Allen gulped when the Orderly Sergeant brought out the pamphlet and pointed toward him. He instinctively dropped his gaze down to the floor. Dread passed over him and he thought, *"I sure hope and pray that I haven't killed myself with my big mouth."* He breathed a sigh of relief when he looked up again and saw that the Lieutenant and the Orderly Sergeant were seated and seemed to be talking pleasantly. Even Corporal Gilbert was smiling. *"Well, maybe the earth won't come crashing down on me after all."*

"Excuse me, Corporal," said Allen tentatively, "but what exactly is a Skirmish Detail?"

"Well, Fish," began Gilbert in textbook fashion, "skirmishers are the feelers with which the main body searches its way into the enemy's territory. Their mission is to clear the way for a large body of troops without committing the main force. They're deployed at specified intervals and direction, according to the location they are to cover."

Allen signified he was taking in all of this information by nodding.

Gilbert continued, "The smallest unit of skirmishers is four men. They're called Comrades-in-Arms. They move and act together as two pairs." He held out two fingers on each hand. Moving his left hand forward he said, "These are numbers one and two." Then he moved his right hand forward, "And these are three and four." He bent his middle fingers back 90 degrees toward his palms and left the index fingers pointing forward. "One from each of the pairs will aim at the enemy while the others wait. If they are ordered to fire, the partner of the pair," he raised first his left hand to indicate one with two, then the other hand to indicate three with four, "would take aim and cover them while they reload." He shifted his index fingers back and the middle fingers forward. "Once the first shooters are reloaded, they will signal that they are ready. Their partners could then be ordered to fire." Gilbert dropped his hands. "This fire and reload rotation enables the skirmish line to always present loaded weapons to the enemy. Got all that?"

"Yes, Corporal," replied Allen slowly. He pondered the information for a several quiet moments. Suddenly realizing the implications of what he had just heard, he stood up. "Pardon me," he said with a slight tremor, "I think I'm going to make another 'head' call."

Monday, October 17, 1859, 6:35 p.m.

"Yes, XO, I read the pamphlet earlier," nodded Greene. "I must have placed it inside the newspaper when I was finished. Have you had the opportunity to read it?"

"Not as yet, sir," responded McDonough. "But if you will allow me a few moments, I shall do so now."

"Please," offered Greene.

As the Orderly Sergeant was reading, Greene cast his gaze about the car. Most of the men seemed to be at ease and chatting amongst themselves. "Orderly Sergeant Mundell," he observed, "there seems to be a great deal of concentrated activity at the far end of the car. Any idea what is afoot down there?" It was more of a curiosity for him rather than a compelling perturbation.

Without even turning around, Mundell acknowledged, "Yes, sir. That would be some of the mess cooks cleaning up after their attempts at cookery. Corporal Gilbert is monitoring the situation, and has it well in hand, sir."

"Oh, very well," acquiesced Greene. "Thank you Orderly Sergeant." Everything was obviously under the control of the Non-Coms and subsequently required no further thought for him. He returned his attention to his XO.

McDonough finished reading and handed the pamphlet to Mundell. As Mundell began reading, McDonough and Greene began discussing the same points that Allen had mentioned earlier. They conferred about the geography for several minutes.

"It's ironic," concluded Greene. "I have traveled to Harper's Ferry several times by train in the past. And have always transferred to the Winchester and Potomac for continued transport toward Berryville." He shook his head. "Each time I was traveling at night and didn't pay any attention to the geography of the area. The only part of the town that I've actually seen is the lobby of the Wager Hotel, which is next to the station." He shook his head, again. "Any thoughts about Harper's Ferry, Orderly Sergeant?" He was addressing the question to Mundell.

"Yes, sir. Only one." Mundell handed the pamphlet back to the Lieutenant. "As it appears that the whole town is surrounded by elevated places, we may have to haul at least one of our cannon to the top of Maryland Heights to be effectively in command of the area." He held his two hands out in front of him, one higher than the other. He waggled the higher one. "Maryland Heights is the tallest and also on our side of the river."

"I concur, Orderly Sergeant," responded Greene. "Please make plans to execute such a strategy. We will decide whether to haul up one or both guns after we arrive at Weverton and reconnoiter the situation." He paused for a split second and continued. "Hopefully we may also find someone who knows about back roads or trails to the top." Both Orderly Sergeants indicated agreement.

"There is still another matter of pending precaution to consider." Greene looked to his XO. "Although Weverton is several miles away from the river crossing, we are not sure how far the insurgents may have extended out from Harper's Ferry." McDonough assented. "We shall have to ensure that the train is not ambushed as we approach."

"Yes, sir," introduced McDonough, "we can post four of our best sharpshooters as lookouts in the engine's cab or on the fuel car."

"We could also post some additional men on the forward platforms of the first two or three cars," interjected Mundell.

"Both are excellent tactics," agreed Greene. "However, I fear the Militia may take offense if we were to post sentries on 'their' cars." His eyes widened. "Not to mention the hubbub the Militiamen may raise as our armed men pass through their twelve cars en route to the cab."

"We might try the roof, sir," postured Mundell.

"Perhaps, but a little too dangerous in the dark, I think," observed Greene. "No." He smiled knowingly. "I believe I have something else in mind." To himself he contemplated, *"My dear Captain Byrd. It appears that our paths shall meet much sooner that you expected."* He absently tapped the pamphlet against his open palm. *"I need your help. And I sure hope that the good General Egerton is afraid of your father!"*

Monday, October 17, 1859, 6:45 p.m.

"Luke, what do you know about Orderly Sergeant McDonough?" queried Allen. They were taking their turn at getting some fresh air on the aft platform of the car.

Quinn laughed. "Besides the fact that he mess cooked for Noah on the Ark?"

"Yes, besides that," grimaced Allen. "I mean, what do you think of him?"

"Well, Bal, he has a reputation of being tough as nails, but at the same time fair and reasonable." He turned to face his companion. "For example, if you've deliberately done something wrong, he'll be all over you like feathers on a chicken." Quinn arced his arm over Allen for emphasis. "On the other hand, if you've done something wrong by accident or from the lack of knowing, he'll bend over backward to help you out." He cautioned with a shaking finger. "You might not like or appreciate his 'helping' methods, but you'll have to admit they'll be in your best interest." He also warned, "Oh, maybe it won't always seem like that right away, but they will be."

"I've noticed that, unlike some other NCOs, he's not always screaming in your face if you moved your eyeballs wrong or something." Allen shuttered at a flashing memory.

"Don't confuse training NCOs with staff NCOs, Bal." Quinn understood Allen's fear. "Since you're still a Fresh Fish, you haven't come to realize that training NCOs have a job to do." He poked Allen lightly in the chest. "They're responsible for turning YOU into a Marine. Once they see that you understand and live by the basic standards of the Corps, their attitude will change." He nodded his head. "And when that happens, it means that they've accepted you into the brotherhood."

Allen was perplexed. "What brotherhood?"

"Why, the Marine Corps' brotherhood of Comrades-in-Arms." Quinn curved his thumb over his shoulder and pointed toward their car. "Remember earlier when I said that I had found a home in the Marines and these shipmates are my family?" Allen affirmed the memory. "Well, we all value each other more than we do blood relatives. We've all been through the same sort of training, the trials and tribulations of shipboard duty, as well as all kinds of daily life experiences, together." He started to list them off. "We eat, sleep, work, stand guard, march, drink, carouse and such, together. We dress alike. We look alike. We speak the same confusing nautical language. We work things out together. We scheme together. We fight together." He laughed. "We'll even fight each other one minute and be the best of friends the next." He paused and turned serious. "But, I'll tell you one thing. When we go to places like we're going to now, it is very comforting to know that the Marines with you are just like you, and you can count on them. As they also know, they can count on you." He bobbed his head to signify assurance. "And another thing, once you really become a Marine, you're always a Marine. Even if you're not in the Corps anymore." He pointed again at Allen. "This brotherhood is bound together with something stronger than the world's best glue or any other kind of heavy duty fastener."

"Wow," whispered Allen, "that's a pretty solid bond of love."

"Easy, fella!" exclaimed Quinn. "We're not talking about THAT kind of brotherhood!"

Allen was shocked that his meaning was misunderstood. "Oh, no," he spluttered, "I meant an unbreakable, biblical kind of a love." It was his turn to point at Quinn. "You know, the kind of love that the Lord had for the children. Unconditional, without restrictions."

"Oh, okay," muttered Quinn sheepishly. "I guess you understand what I mean then."

"Yes, I think I do," confirmed Allen. "It's the kind of brotherhood where you would sacrifice your life for the lives or safety of the others."

Quinn brightened up. "YES! That's exactly what I mean. And, I can tell you a story to demonstrate it, too."

"Please, do!" returned Allen.

"Well, now," began Quinn as he shifted around on his feet to get comfortable. "It was the summer of Fifty-Seven. I was between ship assignments and temporarily assigned to Head Quarters. It was an election day in Washington City. And, apparently some thugs from Baltimore, called the Plug-Uglies, came down to disrupt the voting process. They had chased off the Washington Police and were just scaring the living daylights out of people who wanted to vote. So, naturally, the Marines were called out." He held up two fingers. "We formed up two Companies...one was led by Captain Zeilin and the other by Brevet Captain Maddox. Major Tyler...he was the Adjutant and Inspector...was in overall command." Allen nodded without really knowing about whom Quinn was talking. Quinn continued, "We marched to the Northern Liberties Market, near Fifth and K Streets, where a big voting place was located.

That's where we faced off against the Plug-Uglies. They were a mean looking bunch. They had muskets, pistols, revolvers, knives, billies, iron bar, slingshots, sledgehammers...all sorts of murderous instruments. One fellow was even carrying what looked like a sack half full of bricks."

Allen interrupted, "You said pistols AND revolvers. Aren't they the same?"

"No, Fish." Quinn shook his head slightly and gave Allen a 'Don't you know anything?' look. "Pistols are single shot weapons, while revolvers can shoot five or six times before reloading." For emphasis, he added, "Duals are usually fought with pistols." He chuckled. "Although if I was ever in one, I'd want a revolver." Both men laughed.

"Anyway, Major Tyler was having a tough time convincing those Plug-Uglies that they should stop their terrorizing and go back to Baltimore peaceably. Well, wouldn't you know it. They wheel out a brass cannon and aim it at us." Allen flinched.

"Well, sir, a tense few moments passed by, when, out of the crowd, steps this old man with a cane. And he walks right up in front of the muzzle of this cannon." Quinn shook his head as if he still did not believe the man's actions. "I didn't recognize him at first, because of his gentleman's clothes and all, but he turns out to be none other than General Henderson, our then Commandant." Quinn beams with pride. "He tells them that they had better think twice before they fire their cannon at the Marines."

Allen is amazed by the image.

"Naturally they disagree with him, so he comes back to the Marine line and tells his son, Lieutenant Henderson, "to take that gun". I guess about ten of us from the left of the line rushed forward with the Lieutenant and Orderly Sergeant McDonough, and we took the cannon. As we were dragging it back to our line, the Plug-Uglies charged us." Quinn beamed with pride once more. "Would you believe, General Henderson again steps out in front of us and tells those bullies to halt." Quinn held up his hand briefly in a 'stop' sign. "The closest fellow stopped about two feet away from the General, and raised his pistol. He was about to fire when Orderly Sergeant McDonough runs out and strikes this fellow's arm with his musket, causing the weapon to fall." Quinn tapped Allen on his forearm where the blow had occurred. "Maybe even broke his arm!"

Allen involuntarily cried out, "Ow!"

"Yes, sir," nodded Quinn. "Then the General calmly took a hold of this fellow by the collar, and he and the Orderly Sergeant marched him off behind our line." Allen looked toward McDonough and smiled with admiration.

"The Plug-Uglies got downright nasty after that. They started throwing rocks at us and anything else they could find that was loose." Quinn shook his head, again. "The officers kept telling us to hold our fire, even though some shots were coming our way. When one of our men was hit in the face by a bullet, some of the Marines on the right of the line started shooting back. Before long, a whole volley sort of rippled out from our line. As we were reloading, the Plug-Uglies turned tail and ran. I don't think they stopped until they got back to Baltimore."

Allen shook a slightly clenched fist. "All, right!"

Quinn settled back from his excitement. "Well, the long and the short of it is, from the General all the way down to the youngest Private, we all stood together. Moreover, when we were pushed, we pushed back, together. When one of us was hurt, we hurt back, together." Quinn nodded. "Guess you might say that if you meddle with one of us, you meddle with all of us." He nodded again in affirmation. "In your biblical sense, I suppose I'm saying that we're always faithful, one to the other."

After a contemplative pause, Quinn said, "You've really got to admire the General for bravely stepping out like that to help us. And even Orderly Sergeant McDonough for rushing out to protect the General, too." He pointed toward Allen. "That's what I mean about the Marine kind of brotherhood."

"Fortitudine!" exclaimed Allen.

"Yes, Fortitudine!" replied Quinn.

Monday, October 17, 1859, 7:00 p.m.

"You sent for me, Sir!"

Greene looked slowly toward the voice. It was Baxter. He

was standing at rigid Attention in the aisle outside of the Lieutenant's row of seats. His eyes were fixed at a spot somewhere on the window glass above everyone's head.

"Yes, Apprentice Musician Baxter," replied Greene as he leaned forward and looked at the boy. "Am I correct in assuming that, since you are rated as Fifer, that you possess a complete knowledge of all of the necessary tunes and calls?"

"Yes, sir."

"Good," resumed Greene. "Are you also familiar with any sea shanties?"

"Yes, sir," responded Baxter. "Quite a few, sir."

"And how about other tunes from the citizen community?" inquired Greene.

"Yes sir!" exclaimed Baxter as his gaze dropped to meet Greene's. "I have managed to pick up a great many, sir." He beamed with pride. "The Drum Major at Head Quarters has said that I have a natural ear for music, sir. And, if I may admit, sir, I only have to hear a tune maybe twice, and I know it well enough to play, sir."

"Marvelous," answered Greene. "I shall then ask you to teach the men a new tune. One that they have possibly never heard before. A catchy sort of a tune with a lively bounce to it. Can you do that?"

"Sir?...Uh..." Total bewilderment was evident on his face.

"Teach them to sing it, lad. To sing it!" added Greene for clarification.

"Uh...OH! YES, SIR!" Total relief swept through Baxter.

"Excellent." Greene checked his watch and continued. He was speaking to his Non-Coms as well as to the Fifer. "We have quite a while to go before we reach our destination. I want the men to relax and enjoy themselves before we arrive." He looked at the Fifer. "I'd like at least one Musician assigned to each car, so pick a tune that all three of you know. Is that clear?"

"Aye, sir," gulped Baxter.

"Very, well, Apprentice Musician Baxter." Greene smiled. "Carry on with your assignment."

"Aye-Aye, sir." Baxter almost saluted, but managed to refrain from doing so. He executed a smart Right Face and fairly sprinted to the 'music' end of the car.

Greene continued to speak to his NCOs. "We should be arriving at Weverton in approximately an hour and a half." Both men nodded. "We'll let the men relax and be comfortable for about an hour. The music should help them forget about what might be awaiting us."

He contemplated for a few seconds. "XO, the smoking lamp will be put out at Seven-fifty. You will please commence arrival preparations at that time. Have the men kit up with all accouterments. Then load the weapons, but do not cap."

"Aye, sir." McDonough reacted knowingly.

"Orderly Sergeant Mundell, after the smoking lamp is out, please muster your four sharpshooters on the forward platform as quickly as possible." Greene grinned slightly. "I have made arrangements with one of the Militia officers to escort them forward to the fuel car." Mundell nodded. "I have also made arrangements for the engineer to sound one long and one short blast twice on the whistle if the train should be required to stop for any reason before our scheduled arrival."

"Aye, sir." Mundell showed no reaction to his officer's last statements.

"At Eight O'clock, XO, we shall darken ship." Greene quickly looked at some of the lanterns mounted around the car. "No sense in illuminating ourselves to any possible riflemen on the outside."

Monday, October 17, 1859, 7:10 p.m.

A snappy drum roll commenced. After a spell, a fife twittered. Da Da Da DUT Ta Daaa. Everyone who had not already done so turned toward the end of the car. Baxter had jumped onto the seat just forward of the stove.

"GENTLEMEN, GENTLEMEN! MAY I HAVE YOUR ATTENTION, PLEASE?" Those closest to him began to laugh heartily. Both Baxter and the drummer had blackened their faces. Holding up both arms, Baxter continued his grand pronouncement. "IT IS WITH GREAT PLEASURE THAT I AM ABLE TO ANNOUNCE..." He paused. "THAT TONIGHT." He leaned over toward the men closest to him, "And fortunately, only tonight." A quick cheer arose from those who heard him.

Standing erect, he continued, "YOU WILL BE ENTERTAINED BY THE QUITE TEMPORARY," Again to those closest, "but hopefully unforgettable." This drew some good-hearted jeers. "THE FIRST EVER." Once more to the closest, "and maybe the last." Several jovial "No's" returned. "UNITED STATES MARINE RAILROAD MINSTREL SHOW." Baxter danced about as applause and cheers rang throughout the car. The men drew nearer to the 'stage'. Orderly Sergeant Mundell worked his way to the aft car door.

On cue, the Fifer and Drummer began playing a captivating tune. Quite a few of the men began singing the lyrics. Those who did not know the words clapped or swayed to the rhythm of the beat. The Musicians played several additional renditions of the chorus as more and more of the men caught on to the words and joined in.

As the last notes were fading into the air, Baxter was thinking, *"Well, it looks like Mister Foster's 'Camptown Races' is too well known."* He signaled to the Drummer and a second tune erupted. This time only a small number of the men joined in while the majority just listened and cheered. Because fewer were singing, the Musicians concluded the piece without additional choruses.

"*A little better*," thought Baxter. He raised his fife and played -- Tat Da Dut Dut Dadle Da Da Tut Dot Da Daa. Nearly every man in the front quarter of the crowd stopped what he was doing and turned to watch the Fifer. Baxter grinned broadly and signaled the Drummer. The two of them repeated the same sequence of notes twice more. Now the entire crowd was watching and totally silent.

"GENTLEMEN, I INTRODUCE TO YOU, 'DIXIE'." With great relish, the Musicians played through the first and second verses with special emphasis on the choruses. The catchy little tune was an instant hit. Men were nodding their heads to the rhythm, many were clapping their hands in time, and some were even swinging their arms as though conducting the music.

Baxter signaled for attention. "GENTLEMEN." He paused as his audience settled down. "Gentlemen, it is our pleasure this evening to offer to teach you the words to this catchy little tune."

"Yes," "All right," and "Let's do it," resounded back to him from different areas of the crowd.

"Very well, but first please allow me to provide you with a little history of this tune." Baxter was a natural entertainer and delighted in the response of the audience. "Although this is a song about life in the Deep South, it was actually written by a Northerner, a Mister Daniel Emmett from OHIO." A number of looks of disbelief reflected back at him. Undaunted, Baxter continued. "This song, 'Dixie', is just a month old, and was first played in New York City. It is the walkaround (finale) song for the famous Bryant's Minstrel Show." He raised his fife and played through the first verse. Cheerful delight returned to many faces.

"All right, gentlemen, the first verse." Both Musicians played briefly, and then Baxter began singing while the Drummer continued softly.

> "This world was made in just six days,
> And finished up in various ways;
> Look Away! Look Away! Look Away!
> Dixie Land.
> They then made Dixie trim and nice,
> But Adam called it "Paradise."
> Look Away! Look Away! Look Away!
> Dixie Land."

By the time he got to the second set of 'Look Away', a few of the men were already joining in. The blackface made Baxter's grin seem even bigger than it already was. "Gentlemen, the chorus."

> "I wish I was in Dixie! Hooray! Hooray!
> In Dixie's Land we'll take our stand,
> To live and die in Dixie,
> Away, away, away down South in Dixie.
> Away, away, away down South in Dixie."

Both Musicians played through the chorus again. Many of the Marines were totally captivated by the song and were adding their voices to the melodious din.

Baxter had to wait several moments for the enthusiasm to subside to a level that he could be heard. "GENTLEMEN

...gentlemen. The second verse!"

"I wish I was in the land of cotton,
Old times there are not forgotten,
Look Away! Look Away! Look Away!
Dixie Land.
In Dixie Land where I was born in,
Early on one frosty mornin',
Look Away! Look Away! Look Away!
Dixie Land."

Monday, October 17, 1859, 7:25 p.m.

Baxter was just about to introduce the third verse when a moanful whoooooooooooo, whooooop, whooooooooooo, whooooop could be clearly heard outside of the train. Mundell darted out the aft car door and into the next car. McDonough rose to his full height and bellowed, "ATTENTION ON DECK!" Each man froze. "RETURN TO YOUR SEATS, AT THE DOUBLE QUICK!" A wave of men rushed forward in the car. "DOUSE THOSE LIGHTS!"

One by one, the lights were extinguished. Almost as the last light went out, the shuffling of feet and the crashing of bodies into seats ceased. Except for the occasional heavy breath, a grave silence fell over the car. McDonough again barked. "LOAD YOUR WEAPONS, BUT DO...NOT...CAP!"

The train was beginning to slow down. Corporal Gilbert and Sergeant Buckley were pacing up and down their respective 'halves' of the car. "Quickly, boys, quickly!" Each NCO was driving the men on with a harshly whispered sense of urgency. At the same time, both were closely watching the men to ensure that no one accidentally capped his weapon in the excitement.

The Musicians jumped when the aft car door suddenly crashed open and, with a loud clatter, a number of darkened figures rushed in. The door slammed closed and five men continued forward. Weapons started pointing at them. A familiar voice bawled from the lead individual, "EASY, LADS, WE'RE FRIENDLY!" This caused a murmur to spread amongst the seated Marines.

"SILENCE!" bellowed McDonough. As the lead figure

approached him, he stood aside.

"Sharpshooters, ready and waiting, sir." It was Mundell reporting to Lieutenant Greene.

Greene was standing next to the open forward car door. His sword was drawn. He calmly replied, "Very well, Orderly Sergeant. Please post your men on the platform ahead of us." The train was continuing to slow down. "Be ready for anything," he warned as the men passed him. He exited the door behind the last man.

Outside Mundell had stopped in the center of the platform of the car ahead of them. A Marine was poised on each of the two steps on either side of the platform. "Fix, Bayonets," ordered Mundell in a whisper. The order was carried out smoothly and quietly.

Greene slowly oscillated from one side of his platform to the other. He was looking forward, trying to ascertain a possible attack side. The fact that the Militia cars were still brightly lit hindered his ability to see any great distance. He turned his head slightly and strained his hearing.

The train stopped. He leaned as far out as he could on the right side. After several anxious moments, he thought he heard the thumping sound of running feet coming towards them. He leaned back to center. "As Skirmishers, At Three Pace Intervals, On The Right," he whispered hoarsely. He leaned out and listened closely again. "Yes," he said half aloud, "they're coming down this side." Confident, he ordered, "MARCH!"

In rapid succession, the five men leapt from the platform. The first Marine hit the ground, ran out twelve paces into the dark, stopped, faced toward the front of the train, and knelt on his right knee. His weapon was half-cocked and at the ready. The second Marine did the same at nine paces. The third and fourth stopped at their appropriate intervals. Orderly Sergeant Mundell, with sword drawn, was also down on one knee between the second and third, and back about one pace. Lieutenant Greene was standing next to the car. All of their eyes were straining to see what was coming at them. The thumping sound was irregular and heavy. A group of men was coming!

"PRIME!" was Greene's next command. Each Marine unsnapped his cap box, fished out a copper-shelled fulminate of mercury cap, and placed it on the firing cone just under the half-cocked hammer. When finished capping, each man lowered the butt of his weapon to the ground while maintaining the barrel and bayonet at an upward forty-five degree angle.

They waited. The thumping sound grew louder. Instinctively, the riflemen hunkered down closer to the ground.

Greene willed his eyes to see into the dark. Finally, about three cars up, he could just make out moving images in the dim light emanating from within the cars. His breathing almost stopped. He could feel his heart pounding in his chest. *"Sit tight, Marine,"* he thought. *"Wait until you can see them clearly."*

At about one and a half cars distance, he could plainly see that the group consisted of four men. The front two were abreast, while the other two were beginning to straggle one behind the other.

"EVENS, AIM!" Greene yelled loud enough for all around to hear. Marines numbered two and four cocked their hammers fully back and raised the weapons to their shoulders.

All four of the approaching men stopped in their tracks. The man in the rear bent over, rested his hands on his knees, and was breathing heavily, trying to catch his breath. One of the pair in front raised both of his hands into the air. An unlit lantern was in one of them. The other man in front raised his right hand and hailed, "LIEUTENANT GREENE! HOLD YOUR FIRE!"

Greene recognized the voice and immediately commanded to his troops, "RECOVER!" The evens lowered their weapon butts back to the ground. "ADVANCE AND BE RECOGNIZED," he commanded to the panting group. The four men came forward at a walk.

When they were about five paces away, Greene called out, "Captain Byrd, who is with you, sir?"

"My dear Lieutenant, I am escorting the conductor, Mister McCurry," he indicated the man with the lantern next to him, "the train dispatcher from Monocacy," the man right behind them, "and the train's engineer," the heavyset man bringing up the rear. "We have an important message for you, sir!"

"Very well, please lower your hands and continue forward." As he was speaking, he was returning his sword to its scabbard. He looked to his right. "Stand Easy, Orderly Sergeant Mundell."

"Aye-Aye, sir," emanated from the unseen respondent.

As Byrd came closer, he commented, "I must admit, Lieutenant, this is quite a welcoming committee you have here." He swept his hand toward the skirmishers. He had been shocked at having weapons earnestly aimed at him, but he was not showing any fear.

"You don't know the half of it, Captain." Greene directed his attention to the conductor. "Why has the train stopped? We weren't scheduled to stop for almost another hour. Is there more trouble up ahead?"

"Yes...Uh...NO, NO! Well..," the conductor pointed to the heavyset man behind him. "The engineer spied a B and O lantern signal to stop as we were approaching the Frederick Junction," supplied the conductor. The engineer was nodding his head in the affirmative. "Mister Mantz, here," he waved at the man to come forward, "received an important message for the Commander of the Marines, and set up the signal to stop the train." The dispatcher stepped forward and extended a folded telegram sheet to Greene.

Greene opened the sheet and quickly read the message. He returned his attention back to the conductor. "How far is Sandy Hook from Harper's Ferry?" he queried.

"About a mile, maybe a mile and a quarter," replied McCurry.

"Closer than Weverton, then." verified Greene. The conductor nodded. "How far is Sandy Hook from where we are now?" continued Greene. "And how long will it take to get there?"

"Between nineteen and twenty miles." McCurry extracted his watch and stared at it. "At our present speed, I figure about an hour and ten, maybe fifteen, minutes." He looked to the engineer for confirmation.

"It's mostly downhill from here," volunteered the engineer, "and with the weight of sixteen cars pushing me, it'll most likely take less than an hour."

"Very well, engineer, please make your best time." Greene turned again to Mister Mantz. "Have you received any messages about Sandy Hook, recently? Are the insurgents out that far?"

"We set up a temporary telegrapher there after the line was cut at Harper's Ferry. About a half an hour ago, he keyed a message that all was quiet as far down the tracks as he could see or hear." Mantz was happy that he could contribute the information.

"One more question, Mister Mantz." Greene held up the telegram sheet he had been given. "Can you tell me from where and when this message was sent?"

The dispatcher bobbed his head several times and replied, "It came from Relay House, sir, about an hour ago."

Greene nodded. "Thank you." He looked around at the assembly, "Thank you, all, gentlemen. We shall reboard and continue on to Sandy Hook immediately." The engineer and dispatcher accepted the statement without question and started walking toward the front of the train. "Orderly Sergeant Mundell, you may secure your skirmishers and reboard the train."

"Aye-Aye, sir."

Although Greene could not see him in the murk, he knew that Mundell had saluted with his sword and reacted accordingly.

Smiling at the Captain, Greene offered, "Would you care to join me, sir?" The two men turned and walked toward the end of the train. The conductor took a moment to light his lantern and then rushed to catch up with the officers.

At about the middle of the car, Greene stopped and held his arm out to halt the Captain. "Orderly Sergeant McDonough?" he called out.

"SIR!" boomed back from the darkness ahead of them.

"You may secure your firing line and reboard the train." When an 'AYE-AYE, SIR' returned, he signaled Byrd and the conductor to continue.

Several more commands emanated from the dark. "FRONT RANK, RISE. UNCAP. MAKE YOUR WEAPON SAFE."

Byrd progressed about eight more paces and froze. He could not believe his eyes. At the edge of the lantern's light, he could just make out two ranks of armed Marines. Each line was made up of approximately twenty men, standing shoulder to shoulder. A standard space of about thirteen inches separated the two lines. Byrd's mind could only imagine what his eyes had not seen in the dark. One rank kneeling in front of a standing rank, and all forty weapons pointing forward. He looked at Greene and beamed appreciatively, "I declare, you ARE at all times ready!"

Monday, October 17, 1859, 7:45 p.m.

Leaning out as far as he could from the car platform, the conductor raised and lowered his lantern vertically. Momentarily, two long blasts sounded from the engine whistle. With a rush of steam from the drive pistons and belching black smoke from the stack, the engine started to jerkily pull its load down the tracks for the second time that night.

As their car banged to a start, Greene turned to McDonough. "Well Done, XO!" he expounded. "The members of your firing line were as quiet as gravestones in a churchyard. For a moment, there, I wasn't even sure that you had detrained."

"Yes, sir," replied McDonough kindly. "The men are quite eager and well instructed. Orderly Sergeant Mundell and his training NCOs have done an excellent job. A credit to the Corps, sir."

"Yes, indeed," agreed Greene. To Mundell he added, "And a 'Well Done' to you Orderly Sergeant. Are all the men up for the next challenge?"

"Without a doubt, sir. Without a doubt," retorted Mundell proudly.

"Excellent." Greene pointed toward the men. "Please relay a 'Well Done' to them for me. And try to calm them down a bit." He looked at the buzzing clusters of Marines in the aisles. "There's more work to be done and they will need to save their strength."

"Aye-Aye, sir." Mundell stood up. "And thank you, sir." He headed in the direction of the first cluster.

Greene pulled the telegram sheet from his inside coat pocket and opened it. "Well, XO," he said. "It looks like we now know who the Army has sent as overall commander." He handed the telegram to McDonough. "Brevet Colonel Robert E. Lee."

McDonough read the brief telegram. "Do you know anything of the officer, sir?"

"Actually, no," replied Greene regretfully. "However, we can assume that he's the best the Army has available in the Washington area." He paused. "And from the brevet rank, we can also assume that he has recently performed an unusual feat of courage or daring."

"Yes, sir," rejoined McDonough.

"One thing is for sure," supplied Greene. "He wants us to wait for him. So, we'll undoubtedly learn a great deal more about him and how he'll want to do things after he arrives at Sandy Hook."

Greene took out his watch and started talking to it. "Let's see...if Colonel Lee left Relay House immediately after sending that message, and if it takes him," he ran a quick calculation, "four hours to transit the distance as it will us..." He snapped the watch closed. "That means he'll be arriving around Ten-Thirty or so." He contemplated that fact briefly, and then exclaimed, "Perfect!"

Turning to McDonough, Greene smirked knowingly. "XO, we'll have to figure out some way to constructively 'wait' for maybe two hours." The Orderly Sergeant smiled broadly and nodded in agreement.

* * * * *

Allen and Quinn were at the heating stove trying to make some coffee. Allen could still feel the rush of excitement pulse through him. He turned to Quinn and asked, "Are all Marine Officers as calm as Lieutenant Greene?"

Quinn thought for a second or two. "It certainly seems like they are. At least when it comes to First Lieutenants and above. And especially the ones who have been in an action or two."

"It's nice to have him in command of this expedition," commented Allen distantly.

"Oh? And why is that?" queried Quinn.

"What? Oh...Well, think about it." Allen turned intently serious. "If you mix the bravery of the NCOs you've told me about," he surreptitiously pointed toward Corporal Gilbert, "the experience of the other NCOs and older Marines" he quickly jerked a thumb to indicate Orderly Sergeant Mundell, Sergeant Buckley and some of the 'old hands' who were clustered close by. "And the even-handed calmness of Lieutenant Greene." He manipulated his hands back and forth as though compressing a ball between them. "Put all that together with the eagerness the rest of us have, and it seems to me that we're just about ready to take on any kind of a problem."

Before Quinn could respond, a serene voice resonated from the aisle behind them. "Well, lads, all of that may indeed matter, but don't ever, EVER forget the two most basic rules for Privates." Both men immediately snapped to Attention. "What are they, you ask?" Orderly Sergeant McDonough spoke for them, as it was quite apparent that the cat had their tongues again. "Well now, they are..." he reached between them and held up an index finger for both to see, "Always do WHAT you are told," he raised another finger next to the first, "WHEN you are told." He placed a hand on Allen's shoulder and whispered to him, "Trust me, Private Allen, in a hot action those two rules can save your life." He patted the shoulder lightly and exited through the aft car door.

When they heard the door close, both men sighed, and relaxed. Quinn quickly commented, "Well, Bal, looks like you have a friend in Orderly Sergeant McDonough."

"That may well be." Allen shuttered, "but that man's hearing is much too good to suit me."

"Maybe it's not the hearing that scares you, but rather how he reacts to what he hears," offered Quinn.

Allen considered the idea for a spell and finally commented, "I think you're right, Luke. Every time he's talked to me today, he's been very soothing and agreeable. Sort of like...fatherly to me."

"Could be," replied Quinn, "that you remind him of someone." He shrugged his shoulders. "Maybe you're the son he never had, or would have liked to have had. He's..." Quinn searched for an appropriate phrase, "sort of becoming your 'sea-daddy' or something like that."

"Strange thoughts. I wonder if you're not right, though," mused Allen. All sorts of contemplations started to whirr through his mind. "A sea-daddy," he mumbled. An upsurge of introspection swept over him. He was caught up with unexpected memories about his own father. He stared absently into the cup as he slowly started stirring the boiling liquid. Thunk. Thunk. Thunk. The spoon resounded against the side of the metal cup, but Allen did not hear it. Quinn thought it best to leave his friend to his thoughts for the time being.

After a few minutes, Allen snapped himself out of his reverie. He looked around and realized he had been totally distracted. Not wanting to return to the previous topic, he decided to start a new subject of conversation. He asked, "Luke, what do you think about all of this abolition talk and this possible Negro insurrection at Harper's Ferry?" The subject had been playing on his mind off and on since he had briefly glanced at the article in the newspaper earlier.

Quinn finished a sip of coffee and sat the cup back down on the stove. "Well, me bucko, that's one hobbyhorse that I am NOT going to ride." He shook his head. "No, sir. There are men much smarter than me trying to solve that problem and I don't think my humble opinion will matter much to change things." He grinned at his cohort. "Besides," he continued, "I'm better off if I only concern myself with just two things." Mimicking Orderly Sergeant McDonough, he held up a finger, "Doing WHAT I'm told," he held up a second finger, "WHEN I'm told." He crisscrossed his open hands like fans in front of himself. "That's more than enough for me to worry about."

"Maybe," said Allen, "maybe. But I can't help but wonder about it." He drifted off into his own thoughts again.

Monday, October 17, 1859, 8:05 p.m.

Orderly Sergeant McDonough signaled Corporal Gilbert to attend him. A cheery Gilbert steadied himself by grasping the upper aisle corners of several seats as he made his way to the Orderly Sergeant's position. The car was rocking much harder than before.

"Our greater speed moves this car around like a rowboat in a wee storm at sea," he said as he approached McDonough.

The Orderly Sergeant grinned back, "Aye, that it does, shipmate." He pointed to the heating stove. "Watch yourself, there."

Gilbert deftly averted the hot obstacle. "What can I do for you, Orderly Sergeant?" he queried.

"I'd like you to collect Privates Allen and Quinn and bring them with yourself to the aft platform of this car in about ten minutes or so." He indicated the location with a tilt of his head. "Battle dress, Corporal. We're going for a little walk after the train stops."

"Outstanding," quipped Gilbert. "I could do with a bit of a stroll after five hours of being on this train."

"Exactly," agreed McDonough. "Get your men ready, now, and, when the train begins to slow down, make your way back here. We're stepping off as soon as the train comes to a complete stop."

"Aye-Aye, Orderly Sergeant." Gilbert fairly danced his way back to the other end of the car. Passing his row, he barked, "Allen, Quinn, start getting your gear on, NOW." He continued up the aisle and whispered something to Orderly Sergeant Mundell.

"What?" stammered Allen in a half daze, "why?"

Quinn hissed, "Bal, rules!" Allen looked up at him quizzically. Quinn leaned over and sternly held up first one finger and immediately a second.

"OH!" exclaimed Allen. He jumped up and started gathering his gear, all the while wishing that, maybe, Corporal Gilbert had not noticed his 'rules' indiscretion.

Gilbert returned and added, "No knapsacks or haversacks." He started to don his own accoutrements.

From the front of the car, Mundell commanded, "LIGHTS OUT. ALL HANDS, KIT UP! AT THE DOUBLE QUICK!"

Ruppert jumped to help his friends complete arranging their cross belts and waist belts over their greatcoats. Gilbert signaled them to sit down when they were finished. "Sit tight, Marines," he whispered, "I'll tell you when it's time to do something next."

After what seemed like an eternity, a short blast on the whistle could just be heard and the train started to slow down. When the hard rocking subsided, Gilbert ordered, "Rise and follow me."

Perceptible mumbling started to ascend from the seats as the three of them hustled down the aisle. Orderly Sergeant

Mundell sibilated harshly, "SILENCE ON DECK!"

Out on the platform, Allen counted five other men. Orderly Sergeant McDonough and the ones he thought had been skirmishers earlier.

The train slowed painfully. Brakes squealed as they were applied. The cars jostled fore and aft, as the momentum eased and then caught up with itself again. Allen and others grabbed onto platform uprights to steady themselves. Orderly Sergeant McDonough leaned out casually from the platform's right lower step for a better view

CHAPTER FIVE

"ARRIVAL"

Monday, October 17, 1859, 8:30 p.m.

When the train came to a complete stop, Lieutenant Greene rose and said to Mundell, "Orderly Sergeant, kindly post your sentries around our cars, if you please."

"Aye-Aye, sir." He made his way toward the rear of the car, stopped and spoke briefly to Sergeant Buckley, and then passed through the door toward the other car. The Sergeant rose and gave a few quick commands to a nearby group of eight men. As the men made their way out the aft car door, the Sergeant made his way forward to Lieutenant Greene.

"Sentries on their way, sir. Standing by for orders," reported Buckley.

"Thank you, Sergeant," replied Greene. "Please send a man to find the conductor and escort him back to this car."

"Aye-Aye, sir." Buckley turned, spotted Ruppert sitting alone in the dark, and decided he was the best candidate.

"Ruppert!" The Private rose. "Go forward and find the conductor." The Sergeant leaned closer. "Convey Lieutenant Greene's respects, and ask him to meet here with the Lieutenant at his earliest convenience. Got that?"

"Aye, Sergeant," whispered Ruppert in reply.

"He'll probably be up talking with the engineer by the time you get there," guided the Sergeant. Pointing toward the left side of train, he directed, "Go up this side." He looked Ruppert square in the eye and cautioned, "And stay clear of those Militiamen."

"Aye-Aye, Sergeant."

After Ruppert departed the car, Greene said to Buckley, "Sergeant, the rest of your men will remain on the car, but be ready to detrain at a moment's notice."

"Aye-Aye, sir."

* * * * *

The car had bucked one last time. Orderly Sergeant McDonough swung down to the ground, stepped out a few paces, turned about, and said, "Two ranks, right here." He indicated a line in front of him with a swing of his arm. "Smartly, now."

The men jumped off the platforms and fell in facing the Orderly Sergeant. Corporal Gilbert positioned himself to their right.

"Shoulder, Arms." It was done quickly and sharply. "Left, Face." McDonough nodded with satisfaction and stepped up beside the foremost file. "Forward, March."

As they advanced toward the front of the train, the Orderly Sergeant neither gave an additional command nor counted a cadence. The small Detail had the appearance of a well-disciplined and drilled unit. Their eyes were fixed and their faces were determined. Their footsteps sounded as one crunching the gravel. It was quite obvious they had somewhere to go, and going they were. Militia stragglers milling about and whole Companies attempting to form up hurried to get out of their way.

As they neared the first car of the train, McDonough correctly identified a group of men disembarking as the Militia Command Staff. He whispered, "Guide Right," to avoid passing too close to them.

"Orderly Sergeant, McDonough! Is that you?" The voice was familiar.

McDonough cursed his luck under his breath. "Detail, Halt." He executed a Right About Turn and started toward the end of the Detail. An officer was approaching. McDonough stopped at attention and snapped a salute. "Yes, sir," he said.

Major Russell returned the salute. "I thought it was you." He looked up and down the Detail of Marines. "Where are you off to, Orderly Sergeant?"

McDonough cut away his salute and responded, "Detailed to reconnoiter the approach to Harper's Ferry, sir."

"Ah, I see," said Russell as he continued to look about. "And where, pray tell, is the good Lieutenant Greene?"

"Preparing to disembark the Detachment and armament, sir. In anticipation of the arrival of the Army's Senior Officer." McDonough was anxious to resume his mission and did not like having to spend so much time providing information to this staff officer.

Russell nodded. "And how soon before the Army commander arrives?"

"Less than two hours, sir."

"Well, then, Orderly Sergeant," Russell unconsciously rocked on his heels, "since Lieutenant Greene is otherwise occupied, I see no reason why I shouldn't accompany you on this reconnoiter." He had chosen his word 'accompany' carefully. Russell knew that McDonough's last orders had been given to him by a line officer and that his own authority was still limited. *"And,"* he thought, *"who knows what additional information I may be able to amass for the arriving Army commander."* He smiled. "Carry On, Orderly Sergeant."

Monday, October 17, 1859, 8:40 p.m.

The conductor panted heavily as he entered the forward car door. He found Lieutenant Greene standing in the dark next to his usual seat. "Yes, sir," he puffed, "how may I assist you?"

Looking over the man's shoulder, Greene pointed down at the conductor's lantern. "Private Ruppert, kindly remove the lantern to the platform."

"Aye-Aye, sir."

"Sorry, sir," he apologized to the conductor. "But we're trying to accustom the men's eyes to the dark." The railroad man tipped his head quizzically to one side. Greene continued, "Men of the sea can take advantage of seeing great distances at night if we don't 'blind' them first with lantern light."

"Oh...certainly, sorry." He was a man who had always lived with lanterns at night and was not really sure what the explanation meant.

"Well, sir," continued Greene. "Is there an actual station, here?"

"No, sir, Sandy Hook is just a staging location for repair equipment and road supplies. There is just a work shack here, a water tower, and a few workmen's houses." He appeared apologetic for not having mentioned this information earlier. "The closest actual station is Weverton, about a mile and a half behind us."

Greene cursed to himself for not discovering this intelligence discrepancy earlier. He immediately determined he should regain a better footing. He graciously asked the conductor, "Are you aware of any roads or trails that might lead from here to the top of Maryland Heights?"

"From here?" He shook his head. "No, I don't think so. We're so close to the mountain side at this stretch, that there's barely enough room to pass by." He thought deeply. "There is probably something like you're looking for back at Weverton."

"Yes, continue," said an encouraged Greene.

"Well, sir, the route engineers have been surveying out a path for a possible branch line to run from Weverton, North to Hagerstown." He pointed past Greene. "They usually start by following existing roads and trails." He tentatively conjectured, "I'm sure that some of their plans or maps could be found at the Weverton Station. The route engineers and surveyors would be head quartered there." For quick explanation, the conductor added, "Somewhere near the main stem, I mean."

"Excellent!" exclaimed Greene. "Could you accompany my gunnery Sergeant to Weverton Station to help locate such information?"

The conductor was taken aback. "Uh...sir, I am unable to distance myself from my assigned train." He quickly offered, "However, there is a telegrapher temporarily set up here. I could have him send a message back to make them aware of your needs." He nodded. "That should allow a search to get started, or maybe even locate something useful before your Sergeant arrives there."

"Outstanding idea, sir. Please do so immediately." Greene liked the thought of expeditious communication to catch up on some lost time. "And, thank you."

Ruppert reentered the car after letting the conductor exit. "Private Ruppert." Greene stepped into the aisle. "Please request Sergeant Woodfield to report here immediately."

"Aye-Aye, sir!"

Monday, October 17, 1859, 8:50 p.m.

The Detail had continued along the right side of the train until they passed a small, poorly lighted railroad shack with an attached faded sign that ignominiously identified the location as Sandy Hook. There they merged onto the Harper's Ferry to Frederick Turnpike, a roadway carved out between the mountain slope and the North side of the railroad bed. On the other side of the railroad bed, between it and the river was the Chesapeake and Ohio (C&O) Canal and its towpath. All three of these enterprising ventures paralleled one another for over twelve miles. Their commercial jousting stretched from Point of Rocks, Maryland, upriver on a mere sliver of shoreline along this stretch of the Potomac to Harper's Ferry. From Weverton to Harper's Ferry they actually butted up against one another.

The Marines marched down the turnpike until McDonough spotted a small wooden footbridge crossing over the C&O. He commanded, "Detail, Halt." After a pause, he stepped in front of and past the first file of the Detail and peered toward the canal. Satisfied with what he could make out in the dark, he then stepped to the middle file of the formation. "Front." He then commanded, "Order Arms." Followed almost immediately by, "Rest."

"All right, lads, listen up." The men automatically leaned attentively toward the Orderly Sergeant. "Right now, we're roughly about a half a mile or so from the bridge to Harper's Ferry." He pointed off to his left into the darkness. "From here on we'll have to be especially watchful." Each man nodded total comprehension for the precaution.

"Greenhalgh, you and Tompkins." McDonough pointed to the men in the first file. "You two will cross over to the other side of the canal. The towpath is probably over there." He indicated the opposite side of the footbridge. They nodded.

"Wilson, Fisher." He pointed to the men in the third file. "You two will stay on this roadbed with Corporal Gilbert and Major Russell." The two men smiled and nodded. Corporal Gilbert, however, just looked up to heaven. All three knew their path would be the easiest on the feet.

McDonough turned to the middle file of Allen and Quinn. "You two will go with me down the railroad bed." While Quinn nodded, Allen grimaced. From his days in the mines, he knew that walking on railroad ties was going to be some tough going. They are never evenly spaced and the gravel in between them was always at different heights.

"We'll advance as skirmishers with fixed bayonets. Front rank odds, rear rank evens." He now looked directly at Allen as he spoke, but he explained for all. "That means that we go forward in a leap frog fashion. The odds will advance ten paces and stop." He moved his left hand out in front of his body. "Then the evens will advance past the odds by another ten paces and stop." He moved his right hand a distance in front of his left. "We'll continue this sort of movement until we encounter something or arrive at the bridge." He rotated his left and right hands over one another several times.

"By spreading out on all three of the approaching routes, we will widen our listening capabilities and decrease the possibility of being ambushed." Everyone nodded intently. "If someone sees or hears anything unusual or strange, stop and sing out the alarm." He cautioned, "Don't allow your file partner to pass by you if you are still trying to make out something you saw or heard. Sing out first." He looked around the group to ensure that all understood. "We'll all be close enough to hear anyone's alarm." He again circled around the faces in the group with his gaze. "Don't worry about warning the enemy. Since they're not moving, there's a good chance that they will likely hear one of us walking up on them before we see or hear them."

Besides preparing his men, McDonough also knew he had to calm his men. "Our advantage lays in the fact that they don't know we're coming, or who we are, or how many of us there are. In addition, it's also most likely that they're not as alert as we are." He paused. "Remember, they have been sitting still for quite some time. They have probably settled in for the night and are not attentive. If they hear us first, they'll be startled and will make more noise than your alarm will. Understood?"

Everyone whispered back, "Aye, Orderly Sergeant."

"Very well," McDonough nodded with confidence. "You're all here because of your experience or ability to think on your feet." To his right he could just hear the clamor the Militia was making while still trying to form up. He jerked a thumb in that direction and chuckled. "Don't be going Militia on me now!" Everyone in the Detail laughed. McDonough let the laughter die down naturally.

"I will maintain command and control from the center route." He glanced at Russell, but noticed that the Major did not seem to be paying attention.

"The alarm word will be 'CRACK', like 'crack in the

wall'." He looked around, noticed a couple of raised eyebrows, and added, "It's a good alarm word because, when you say it fast, it sounds more like a noise than a word." Allen soundlessly tested the word on his lips and nodded approvingly when he realized the Orderly Sergeant was correct.

"One last thing." He paused while everyone focused their attention. "If we don't encounter anything before then, we will all stop when one hundred yards from the foot of the bridge." All heads nodded in unison. "Any questions?" No one responded.

"Very well." He braced to full height. "Attention, Detail."

Monday, October 17, 1859, 9:00 p.m.

The night was thick and all enveloping. The sky was still heavily overcast. The chilled moisture in the air felt raw against face and hands. Eyes watered from strain as well as the cold.

Creeping along in the dark, ten paces at a time was nerve wracking. Especially when no one knew what was just ahead in the blackness. Allen's mind seemed to be playing tricks on him. He was not sure anymore what his eyes were seeing. Determining distance had quickly become a problem.

He had decided that ten paces were just a little too far. When Quinn was advancing, he could see him vaguely enough for about six paces or so and then he would just fade away. Quinn's greatcoat cape covered the white cross belts in the back and took away what little visual aid there was to be had.

Earlier, the Orderly Sergeant had helped him adjust to the pacing. "When he just ebbs out of sight, count to three slowly to yourself," McDonough had whispered. "When you get to three, you should hear his footsteps stop. Then it's time for you to move out. You should be able to see Quinn again after three or four paces."

What the Orderly Sergeant had not mentioned was the fact that when the eyes cannot see, the ears hear everything with greater intensity. Loudest of all was the crunching of the gravel bed under his feet. Each step sounded like a rapid rolling drum beat. He wondered, *"How can anyone not hear us coming?"*

Once, while stopped between advancements, Allen was

suddenly aware of a very different kind of noise. There was a lack of movement sounds to his left. The silence on that side screamed at him. He 'knew' the two skirmishers were still there and moving, but he wanted to make sure. After straining all his senses, he decided that he could actually feel, rather than hear, the even pacing of the two men on the towpath. As experienced Marines, they were very fluid and stealthy in their movements.

The noises to his right were another story. It took him some time to figure out how the four men on the road were moving. During one stop, he actually screwed up enough courage to ask his shadow partner, McDonough, for confirmation of his supposition.

"Orderly Sergeant?" he whispered. "The four men to our right." He pointed off in the dark, but still looked straight ahead. "Are they moving differently than we?" Allen and McDonough were moving together as one, opposite of Quinn.

"And how might that be, Private?" asked McDonough.

Before Allen could answer, he realized that Quinn had stopped. Without saying another word, he rose and cautiously advanced ten paces, then stopped, and squatted down again. As McDonough settled in next to him, Allen listened intently ahead of his location for several seconds. Satisfied there were no new sounds, he continued. "They seem to be moving as four rather than two like we are."

"Go on," prompted McDonough.

"It sounds like two are advancing in skirmish order, but the other two are walking some paces behind." It was time to move again.

After they settled in and listened, McDonough said, "What else?"

Allen listened intently with his right ear. "I'd say that the two in the back are making a steady pace. They are not stopping or slowing, but they are certainly not in matched cadence." A sudden realization hit him. Every time he moved, the Orderly Sergeant had been in step with him. They must have sounded like one man as they moved forward. He involuntarily gasped and started to turn toward his shadow.

"You're learning, Private Allen." McDonough patted him twice on the shoulder as an 'Atta Boy', but also as a signal to move again. "You're learning."

They had continued their advancement succession a few more times when McDonough suddenly grabbed Allen by the shoulders and twisted him gently toward the left. "Lights!" he whispered. Allen looked up from the pathway ahead of him. Sure enough, the nightlights of Harper's Ferry were starting to come into view.

The developing shape of the town looked odd. The higher up Allen looked, the more lights he saw. The lights seemed like a patterned blanket that only covered the upper part of an incline rather than the whole side of the mountain. Very few lights could be seen down near what he thought was the lower part of the town. He guessed that the lowest level, where there were no lights, had to be the water.

Allen was awed by the sight and said half aloud, "Certainly not the flatlands."

As they continued farther, the lights seemed to drift to the left. More lights had come into view with each passing footstep. Allen correctly surmised, *"We've been going around a bend to the right."*

With a sudden sense of panic, Allen's gaze left the lighted wonder and flashed back in front of him. What he saw paralyzed him. He instinctively dropped to one knee. He was just about to sing out 'crack' when a firm hand gripped his shoulder and McDonough breathed, "Easy, lad."

There, maybe 60 yards or so ahead of them was a well-lighted end of a bridge. Allen's eyes moved left along the dark and ominous structure. Its elongated shape went all the way across to the town. It looked to him like a big black snake with its head bent toward him and its mouth open. A lantern on either side of the opening gave the appearance of fangs.

Allen shook his head and blinked twice. He wanted to make sure he was seeing things correctly. He starred hard for a few seconds, then half whispered, half mouthed, "It's a covered bridge."

"So it is, lad. So it is," whispered McDonough back. He, too, had been surprised by this fact. However, McDonough's interest was not absorbed by the nature of the structure. He was carefully evaluating the manner of activity taking place near it.

"Looks like a small fire burning over there," he said in a

low tone to Allen. "To the right." He pointed. "Away from the bridge, on the far side of the opening." His eyes strained harder. "On the turnpike." He concluded, "Up against the mountain face."

"Looks like five, maybe six men," volunteered Allen.

"I'd say six," interjected Quinn. He had quietly advanced to a position next to them. "Three sitting and three standing."

McDonough was just about to agree when a figure moved into his view and blocked the image of the fire. "What the...?" he cursed. The figure was closer to him than the fire. The light from the fire partially silhouetted the figure. The Orderly Sergeant's fury raged when he recognized whose figure it was. Even more, when he realized that the figure was moving toward the fire.

McDonough signaled for Allen and Quinn to rise and follow him. He was moving quickly to his right. With just five bounding steps, he was next to a crouching Corporal Gilbert. "Is he out of his mind?" puffed out of his clenched teeth.

"Don't know," whispered the Corporal back. "Maybe just more brave than smart." Gilbert shook his head. "Couldn't stop him, Orderly Sergeant. It's like he's on his own mission."

"Very well," hissed McDonough. "Form up these men and move in quietly." He stood up. "If anything goes wrong, I'll try to get the Major out of the way. You fire as soon as we're clear." Bearing toward the Major's back, he took off in a crouching lope.

"Aye-Aye!" whispered Gilbert as he stood up. He looked at the four men kneeling near him. "You heard the man, form up in a single line." The men did so quietly. "Weapons At The Ready. Advance Step." He signaled with a sideways 'Forward' sign. The line moved excruciatingly slow. Each man 'advanced' with his left foot first, then brought his right foot up behind it. While not able to cover ground quickly, this crablike movement allowed the Marines to always be in the correct position to fire their weapons. Gilbert was concentrating on the group at the small fire and did not want to be hampered by whether his men had their left or right foot forward. Firing with the right foot forward is almost impossible and certainly precludes accurate aiming.

Major Russell was moving at an extended pace. It took

McDonough longer than expected to ease up beside him and fall into step. "Careful, Major," he warned, "we don't know who these men are."

"Nonsense, Orderly Sergeant," retorted Russell. "That's Captain Rowan there on the left." He pointed with an old Malacca (rattan) stick that was his constant companion. "He's an old Mexican War friend, and currently with the Jefferson Guard." He waved his right arm. "Ahoy, Captain Rowan!"

The three men seated at the fire stood up as the others turned around to identify the hailer. McDonough glanced around quickly to locate some cover. Gilbert called his Squad to a halt. The Major continued rapidly toward the fire.

"Captain Rowan," addressed Russell again. "It's Major Russell of the Marines."

"Russell?" questioned Rowan momentarily. Then his face showed recognition. "Oh, yes. Of course." He grinned. "I heard you boys might be on the way up here." He signaled a 'come in' sign several times. "Come on in by the fire, sir."

Gilbert watched patiently. He wanted to make sure that no one was moving toward any weapons. Satisfied, he motioned his men forward again. They advanced slowly toward the fire with an intensified alertness.

Monday, October 17, 1859, 9:10 p.m.

"Detail, Halt!" Gilbert had continued to bring his men in cautiously even after he saw the Major and the Militia officer walk off together toward the bridge. He was not going to let his guard down until the Orderly Sergeant told him to.

McDonough was standing close to the fire with the remaining five unknown men. Two young men were in uniform while the older men were dressed in daily clothing. One man had a bandage on his head. McDonough excused himself from the group and walked to Gilbert.

"You may stand the men down, Corporal." He was visibly relaxed. "This bridge," he pointed with his right hand, "was retaken around Noon today by the Jefferson Guard of the Charles Town Militia." He jerked his left thumb over his shoulder in the direction of the two Militiamen.

"Just those two?" queried Gilbert in all seriousness. The Militiamen were mere teenagers.

McDonough laughed. "No. They had a whole Company pressing forward at the time." He leaned closer to the Corporal and lowered his voice. "It appears, though, that there might have only been two or three insurgents guarding the bridge when they attacked.

"Ah," nodded Gilbert knowingly. He looked around the area quickly. "And where are those bridge snatching insurgents, now?" he asked.

"One dead, one captured and being held in town, maybe another wounded," replied McDonough.

Gilbert pursed his lips together and nodded with satisfaction. His demeanor changed to curiosity. "Have they left any for us?"

"I'm sure they have, Corporal. I'm sure they have." He clapped the junior NCO on the shoulder. "Come, there are some men here that you should meet." He pointed toward the townspeople. "They may be able to help us greatly."

Gilbert started to take a step, but stopped. He turned his head toward his men. "Detail, Rest," he commanded.

As they approached the fire, McDonough announced, "Gentlemen, this is Corporal Gilbert." All of the men nodded courteously. "Corporal Gilbert, I present to you Misters Higgins," he pointed with an open hand, first to the man with the bandage, then the others in turn, "Williams, and Whelan." Gilbert acknowledged each man.

"Misters Higgins and Williams, here," McDonough went on to say, "are employed as bridge watchmen by the B and O. They are responsible for preventing fires, as well as regulating the foot traffic across the bridge." Both men beamed with pride.

Turning to the third man, McDonough continued, "Mister Whelan, here, is a night guard for the Armory. It was during his watch last night that the insurgents attacked." McDonough smiled and looked at the older security guard. "They threatened him at gun point, but he refused to give them the key to the gate. So, they overpowered him and held him prisoner in the guardhouse. I'd say he's lucky to be alive to tell of it." Whelan grimaced fleetingly and looked down at the ground. It was hard to tell which part of the story embarrassed him.

"Mister Williams," McDonough pointed back to the man without the bandage, "was also captured and held prisoner for a period of time."

"I was the first one taken," volunteered Williams. "I thought they were joking when they first grabbed me." He shook his head. "Turns out that I've known one of those raider fellows, Cook's his name, for almost a year now. Among other things, he was a lock tender on the canal." He pointed upriver in the dark. "Lock number Thirty-Three over yonder." He shook his head, again, slowly. "He must have crossed over my bridge two or three times a day."

"They sure weren't joking when I met up with them," interjected Higgins. "I was looking for Bill, here," he pointed toward Williams, "to take over the fire patrol at midnight, when I ran up against those raider fellows. We tangled a bit near the middle of the bridge." He tossed a few punches into the air in front of him to indicate a fight. "I managed to break away and was running toward town when they started shooting at me." He touched his bandage gingerly with his fingers. "Luckily, all I got was a new part down my scalp and a verrry nasty headache."

"How is it," asked Gilbert, "that the two of you," indicating Whelan and Williams, "were able to escape?"

"We were rescued!" exclaimed Whelan.

"That's gospel!" declared Williams. "Captain Alburtis brought in his Militia boys around Three this afternoon." He smiled broadly with bragging rights. "Those fellows are mostly B and O railroad men, you know."

"They came in from the upper end of the Armory," continued Whelan as he pointed upriver. "They put down some heavy fire and forced the raiders back into the engine house." His tone was flat.

Williams nodded his head cheerily. "Some of those Martinsburg boys smashed in the guardhouse windows and helped us out." He looked to Whelan. "What do you figure, Dan, about forty or so of us being held in there?"

"Yes," agreed Whelan forlornly. "It was getting pretty crowded in there. No room to take cover when the shooting started." He shook his head at the thought.

"So," continued Williams, "we made good our escape. Then we snuck down the tracks on the river wall and popped into the Wager House." He pointed to Higgins. "That's where we found Pat, here. Doctor Starry had patched him up." He looked around at his companions. "We figured it would be a good idea for us to get over to this side of the river until all the shooting stopped. There's more than enough Militia over there to handle the problem."

McDonough had been taking in all of this information when he was distracted by a short burst of erratic gunfire coming from the town. He turned in that direction and listened. When he returned his gaze to the men around the fire, he had a rather scheming look about him. "Apparently the Militia has not wrapped up this problem, just yet."

Gilbert had seen McDonough's 'look' before. "What are you thinking, Orderly Sergeant?"

McDonough stood up to full height. "I'm thinking, Corporal, that we need the assistance of these brave watchmen here." He turned to the three men.

"Gentlemen," he resisted the urge to rub his hands together. "We need your help to get a very clear idea of what things look like over there." He pointed. "You know the lay of the land." The men nodded. "Our problem is, that in the dark, things look very different than normal, and a great many details are hidden from us." He shook his head slightly. "Not a good situation for us." Again, the men nodded.

"Now then, since all of you are undoubtedly the finest experts at what the town and Armory look like in the dark." He paused and held out his hand beseechingly. "I most respectfully request that you assist us tonight." The men stared at him blankly.

The Orderly Sergeant changed tack. "Gentlemen, the Marines will protect you." He arced his arm toward his men and added, "With their lives if necessary." Williams looked like he was starting to come around. McDonough slammed his right fist down on his open left hand. "This is your opportunity to pay back for some that you got earlier."

"I reckon I'll go," said Williams tentatively as he stepped forward. "I probably know the lower town better than anyone in the dark." He looked at Higgins. "Pat, you'd better stay here and keep an eye on the bridge." Higgins just nodded.

McDonough looked seriously at the older man. "Mister Whelan, I really need your help to learn more about the Armory."

"Well," began the man calculatingly. "It just doesn't seem right for them to scare us like they did." He was beginning to screw up a little courage.

"That's right, Mister Whelan." McDonough placed his left hand on the man's right shoulder and shook a clenched right fist in front of him. "Let's go figure out how to put some fear into THEM."

Whelan thought about that for a few seconds. Then with a hard nod, he said, "Let's do that!" His resolve set, Daniel Whelan started walking stoutly toward the bridge.

McDonough turned to Gilbert. "Corporal, take Mister Williams and Private Allen. Find the other two Marines and scout out the town between the bridge and the Armory." He motioned Gilbert to follow him. They stepped several paces away from the group. McDonough finished whispering to Gilbert. Gilbert nodded. The Orderly Sergeant bound into motion. "Privates Quinn, Wilson, Fisher. WITH ME!" He trotted off to intercept Mister Whelan. The Privates ran to catch up.

CHAPTER SIX

"RECONNAISSANCE"

Monday, October 17, 1859, 9:15 p.m.

"Excuse me, sir. Sergeant Woodfield and his Detail have returned." Orderly Sergeant Mundell was addressing Lieutenant Greene who was sitting in his usual seat. The car was still darkened.

"You may report, Orderly Sergeant." Greene had a feeling that he knew what was coming. He had been mentally reviewing everything that could possibly go wrong.

Mundell stated matter of factly, "Sergeant Woodfield has stated that he found the office and the maps that the conductor had discussed earlier, sir."

"And?" inquired Greene.

Mundell was disheartened. "Apparently, sir, according to the surveyors, there are no roads or trails to the top of Maryland Heights from this side of the mountain." He added, "Sergeant Woodfield also spoke with several of the town's people as well, sir." He shook his head. "Same results."

"Are there any roads at all to the top of Maryland Heights?" asked Greene, half-expecting to hear another negative report.

"Yes, sir, there are," piped Mundell. "Also according to Sergeant Woodfield, there are three or four trails that lead up to the top. They're farther up river, just past this end of the Harper's Ferry Bridge." He held out his left forearm and looped his right hand around the fingers of his left to demonstrate 'just past'.

Greene stood up. "Well, that is good news." He leaned into the aisle and called, "Private Ruppert?"

"SIR." Ruppert's boots clanged on the platform as he came to Attention.

"Any sign of Orderly Sergeant McDonough or any of his Detail?" queried the officer.

Some metallic footsteps, a brief pause, then, "No, sir."

Greene turned to Mundell, "We shall assume, then, that since we have not heard from Orderly Sergeant McDonough, he has not encountered any problems at the bridge," he nodded, "and has managed to slip into town as planned."

"Yes, sir," agreed Mundell optimistically.

Greene lightly ground his right fist into his open left palm as he thought about the next steps to the plan. Satisfied that all was going well after all, he thought to himself, "*Excellent*." Dropping both hands to his side and standing erect, he commanded, "You may detrain the artillery and horses, Orderly Sergeant."

"Aye-Aye, sir!"

* * * * *

Gilbert was just about to tell Allen to backtrack a ways and search for Greenhalgh and Tompkins, when the two Marines casually walked into the campfire light. They had come from the upriver side of the bridge and caused Gilbert to wonder out loud, "And just how the blazes did you two get back on this side of the canal?"

Greenhalgh hooked a thumb over his right shoulder and said, "There's a small wooden stairway going from the towpath up to the bridge over there." Gilbert's evil eye prompted him to continue. "The first bridge span crosses over the canal, Corporal. We climbed up the stairs there."

"Very, well," barked Gilbert. "Fall in behind Allen. Single file."

Gilbert turned to the bridge watchman and said politely, "If you care to lead the way, Mister Williams."

Williams looked down at the seated Higgins. "Take care of your head, Pat. I'll be back shortly."

Higgins waved without enthusiasm. "Keep your head down, Bill."

Williams smiled and stepped off to lead the group toward the bridge.

Allen observed that this bridge was very unusual. It literally came straight across from the river most point of land at Harper's Ferry and almost butted into the side of Maryland Heights. He estimated that, after negotiating the right-hand curve around the point of Maryland Heights, westbound trains had to make a better than thirty degree left turn in order to enter the structure.

Walking toward it, he could see that the first span indeed crossed over the C&O Canal. It was angled to accommodate the left turn. It was also distinctly built for two different traffic purposes -- the railroad on one side and conventional modes of transportation on the other.

The left half was trussed, wood covered, and had railroad tracks entering into it. Allen thought, *"This must be the head of the 'snake' I saw earlier."* The other half was not trussed or covered, and had a six-foot high protective sidewall on the right of it. He figured the turnpike entered into this side.

Looking ahead, he could just make out, that, beginning with the second span, the remainder of the bridge was trussed and covered. He estimated each truss to be about 15 feet high. He shuttered and thought, *"This is too much like going into a mine."*

Williams stopped at a storage box sitting against the outside right wall of the railroad half. He plucked out a kerosene lantern, lit it, and adjusted the flame. Raising the light to illuminate the whole structure, he beamed with obvious pride. "Quite a beauty, isn't she?" The Marines looked at it without wonder, but nodded politely.

"Only bridge like it in the whole United States." Williams headed down the turnpike side. "Specially built to handle both railroad and turnpike traffic."

He pointed toward the enclosed railroad side, which made up the left wall of the turnpike side. "This curved canal span and the first four river spans are all covered with horizontal clapboards and a metal roof."

Allen could not help himself. He was a little nervous and asked without thinking, "Why is this bridge covered?"

"Well, sonny," replied Williams, "that's because the trestle is made out of wood." He nodded. "The B and O covered it to cut down on any damage to the truss pieces caused by sun, rain, snow, and water spray from the river."

Williams stopped at the opening of the turnpike's first covered span and signaled the Marines to get inside. After they did so, he closed the two halves of a four-foot high gate behind them. "Crossing gate to stop the turnpike traffic," he said as he flipped the latch. "One at each end of the bridge."

This time Gilbert was curious. "What are they for," he asked.

"Part of my job," replied Williams, "is to stop all turnpike traffic as trains approach."

"But the train's over there," retorted Gilbert as he pointed over to the tracks on the left side of the span."

"Correct you are, Corporal," continued an undaunted Williams, "but there is no wall separating the two halves from here to the other end. If you were a farmer, in here on the turnpike side the same time that a train passed on the other side," he shook his head, "the noise would scare you and your animals. The steam spray would burn you, and the firebox smoke just might kill you before the air cleared." He grinned. "The B and O Railroad has me close the gates at both ends, before the trains come, to make sure that doesn't happen."

"Okay," said Gilbert speculatively, "but there are no trains running right now."

"I was caught by surprise on this turnpike side, once, last night, remember." Williams said ruefully. "Closing this gate is a little precaution that just might slow down anymore raiders long enough to warn us this time." Gilbert nodded understandingly.

Williams next stomped twice on the flooring they were all standing on. "Two inch thick planking on this side," he said, "all the way across the river. No gaps between the planks, either." He turned and started walking toward the town end of the bridge. "Yes, sir," he boasted again, "not another bridge like it in the whole United States."

After a short while, they came across a kerosene lantern mounted high on the outside wall. "This lantern marks the end of the shortest span," said Williams. "Only thirty-four paces from the crossing gate we closed to here." He pointed his arm toward the town end. "The rest of the spans are between a fifty-three and fifty-four paces long. There will be a lantern like this one marking the end of each span."

"How long is this bridge?" asked Allen.

"Well, an engineer from the B and O would tell you that the overall length is eight hundred and seventy-five feet." Williams, however, was not an educated man and always converted measurements into something that made suitable sense to him. "But I can tell you that it's about three hundred and fifty paces from one end to the other."

"Whew," whistled Gilbert. "That's pretty long. We'd have to moor seven or eight ships end to end to get something as long." The other Marines nodded complete wonderment at this fact.

"Well, it's long enough for me to have to walk from one end to the other every half hour to check it for fires and punch a mechanical clock at each end." Williams patted his stomach. "Keeps me moving enough that I don't get fat."

"How long is your watch?" asked Gilbert. When Williams looked at him blankly, he corrected himself. "Sorry," he said, "Navy term. I mean shift. How long is your shift?"

"Oh," he ruminated. "There are just two of us hired to patrol this bridge day and night. So Pat and I trade off every six hours."

Allen ran a quick sum. "So you walk the entire length of this bridge twenty-four times a day?"

"Sometimes even more, depending on how many trains run each day," responded Williams. "That's how I know how many paces there are between things."

As they continued to walk in silence, each man pondered the watchman's daily task. Most were thankful it was his monotonous job and not theirs.

When they reached the end of the third span, Allen asked, "Mister Williams, what can you tell us about the town, sir?"

"Like what, son?" asked the watchman.

"About the Negroes for one thing," said Allen. "I read in a pamphlet that there are about three hundred Negroes living here."

"Yes, that sounds about right," concurred Williams. "I'd say about half of them are free coloreds and the other half are slaves. And the ones that are slaves are mainly well kept house servants."

"What about plantation slaves?" queried Allen.

Williams laughed. "No plantations around here, son. The land's too hilly and rocky, and the climate's not hospitable."

Allen was confused. "Then why are insurgents here to free the slaves and start some kind of revolt with them?"

"I've been wondering that myself," replied Williams. "There are probably more Negroes living here in Harper's Ferry than there are male slaves in the vast six county area surrounding our little town." He shook his head. "Doesn't make too much sense, does it?" No one answered.

Allen was quiet for a few more paces, and then asked, "What is the general population like in Harper's Ferry and what do they do?"

"If you mean the people," surmised the watchman, "I suppose most of them are of Irish, English, and German descent." He deliberated for a few moments. "Maybe four hundred or so work for the Armory. They're skilled machinists and craftsmen. The rest of the people work at other factories along the Shenandoah River or in shops down in the lower town, where we're heading."

"Is the town prosperous," asked Allen.

"Like in well-off?" mulled Williams. "I'd say it is. We have six churches, five private girls' schools, seven dry goods stores, maybe four ready-made clothing stores, two railroads and a host of other businesses." He was surprised by his own comments and smiled. "Yes, I guess you could say that the town is pretty well-off."

They walked along in silence again until they reached the fourth kerosene lantern hanging on the wall. Williams stated, "This is the beginning of the Wyed span." He pointed ahead. "Your big Sergeant and the other fellows probably went off to the right where you see that next lantern."

Monday, October 17, 1859, 9:20 p.m.

"Well, Sergeant, we've reached the middle of the Wyed span." Whelan bowed his arm outward to his right. "We'll follow the main stem tracks from here, out along the river wall which borders the Armory."

McDonough looked down at the lighted flooring in front of him. The tracks had 'Y'd' and one set branched off to the right. They cut across the turnpike planking and curved off into a different span to ultimately complete a ninety-degree turn from the bridge. "I take it," he said, "that it's quicker to go off to the right."

"Quicker and safer," replied the security guard. "If we go this way, we'll stay out of a direct line of fire from the raiders." He pointed to the right, again. "Going this way will also give us the best view of the Armory from atop the river wall."

"Excellent!" exclaimed McDonough. "Please lead on."

"You boys," warned Whelan to all of them, "stay on the right side of the tracks from here, on." He shook his head. "This Wyed section wasn't made for turnpike traffic." He pointed at the tracks running ahead of them. "There's no planking between or to the left of the rails over here, just open ties." Everyone nodded and continued forward, carefully hugging the right wall.

After about two hundred feet, they emerged back into the evening air. Light from windows of several buildings off to their left cast an eerie glow over the area before them. Whelan extinguished the lantern he had been carrying and set it down next to a storage box.

As his eyes flexed to the differences in light and darkness, McDonough could see that the tracks ran down the right side of a wide platform area. He caught the glint of reflected light from a second set of tracks that were closer to the buildings. They were parallel to the ones his eyes had been following.

A short way up from him was a crossover between the adjacent sets that allowed trains coming from the bridge to use either set of tracks to continue upriver. Cautiously testing for a firm footing, he moved around to get an idea where the second set of tracks came from. Looking around the left end of the span, he saw the other set of tracks curve off to the right into the darkness. He figured that these rails had to be a connecting track to the Winchester & Potomac Railroad he had read about.

Walking a few steps away from the span, he discovered that the whole platform was planked. He could also make out a four-foot high, metal, double railed barrier running the entire length of the riverside of the platform.

From inside the closest building, came a loud, boisterous cheer. Within seconds, the middle of three large doors crashed open and about fifteen men with weapons spilled out onto the platform. They milled about leaderless for several moments, jabbering. A couple of men finally shushed the others and pointed them toward the Armory. As a group, they staggered away, crowding each other, pushing each other away, shushing, and whispering loudly to each other.

When the group had begun exiting the building, McDonough had quickly signaled his men back into the darkness of the span. He only had to observe the group's behavior briefly to determine, "They're drunk!" He leaned closer to Whelan and asked, "What is that place?" He was pointing to the three-story building with the now wide open door.

"That's the back half of the Wager House Hotel," responded the security guard. He pointed left to a three and a half story building that faced Potomac Street and said, "That's the front half." The 'front half' was a separate building behind the one next to the platform. From the higher roofline, McDonough could see that over a third of the front building overlapped the back building. Whelan continued, "The two are connected. Together they make up a very grand hotel and saloon."

More cheers and jeers came from the open door. The security guard shook his head. "Most of the Militia officers and many of the troops were holed up in there, earlier. Sounds like they still are."

Whelan next pointed a little farther down the platform to a building with a large portico. "That lit up building with the two large columns, to the right of the hotel, is the Potomac Restaurant." He could make out tables surrounded by customers through the windows. "Looks like they're still doing a booming business, too. That place is usually closed up and dark long before now."

Suddenly, from about twenty yards ahead of them, the sound of erratic gunfire erupted. Bright, reddish orange, muzzle flashes leapt into the night. Instinctively, the Marines had all dropped to one knee and hunkered down. McDonough had pulled Whelan down with him. As quickly as it started, it subsided.

"What are they firing at?" whispered McDonough into Whelan's ear.

"Probably the fire engine house," replied Whelan back in a whisper. "The raiders have barricaded themselves in there with some hostages."

The group of shooters started running back toward the hotel like a wild bunch of pranksters. One man was high stepping so dramatically that he appeared to be a clown dancing down the platform. Most were giggling, snickering, and poking each other. A few were shouting profanities into the night air. Several others were yelling a sort of Indian war cry. Ultimately, the unruly group crowded together, funneled into the hotel, and closed the large door.

McDonough just shook his head. "That's all we need. A drunk, out of control, rabble with weapons."

"It's been like this, off and on, since we were rescued out of the guardroom," volunteered Whelan. As he spoke, another erratic episode of gunfire occurred on the town side of the hotel.

Before McDonough could ask, Whelan offered, "Sounds like a group has come out of the Gault Saloon and is giving the engine house some 'what for' of their own."

McDonough was fuming. "It appears that these fine Militia units are attempting to make the insurgents disappear with indiscriminate musketry and loud yelling." He turned to Whelan and asked, "How far is it to the view point you mentioned?"

Whelan pointed up the platform. "It's the same place where the shooting took place. That tall black shadow is the B and O water tower. It's just inside the Armory wall."

"Very, well," muttered a determined Orderly Sergeant. He stood up. "Marines, rise. Single file. Fix bayonets." He placed the armory security guard in front of the first Marine. As a protective shield, McDonough stood between Whelan and the buildings. He withdrew his sword. "Arms, Port. Forward, March."

Since their immediate danger was potentially within the buildings, McDonough kept his Marines next to the double-railed barrier on the river wall. The barrels of their weapons all pointed toward the buildings. Everyone moved forward alertly and stealthily.

* * * * *

"Halt!" commanded Gilbert. His Detail was about seven paces away from the West end of the Wyed span when he heard the echo of distant gunfire. "Hard to tell where that came from," he whispered to Williams. "Maybe off to the right."

"Everything's off to the right up there," replied Williams as he pointed ahead of them. They could see one more span in front of them, but this one was an open framework and not covered. "Just to the left of the last span are three buildings in a row." Moving his hand away from himself, he successively pointed down at three spots in the air. "Behind them is the Shenandoah River," he added.

Suddenly a second flurry of gunfire erupted. "That's a lot closer," stated Gilbert.

"Yes," confirmed Williams, "maybe the middle of the Ferry Lot." He placed his lantern next to an upright truss, facing the wall to effectively dim its light.

"What's that?" asked Gilbert. "The Ferry Lot?"

Williams continued with his usual patience. "The whole six acre stretch of flatland from the bottom of the Bolivar Heights, and between the two rivers, is referred to as the lower town." He again indicated ahead of them. "The piece from here to the Armory gates," he pointed off to the right, "is about three quarters of an acre in size. It's called the 'Ferry Lot' by us old timers, and the 'Point' by the new folk." He shrugged his shoulders. "Guess it goes back to when there WAS a ferry across the Potomac."

Just as he finished, a pack of rowdy and loud men pushed and shoved their way past the opening to the last span and entered a brightly lit building to the left. "Hmmm," hummed Williams, "they're going into the Gault House."

Gilbert listened patiently for a few minutes. After hearing no additional gunfire, he ordered, "Fix bayonets."

While the Marines were mounting their bayonets, Gilbert asked the watchman, "Why isn't the last span covered?"

"We call it the Winchester Span. It's made of cast and wrought iron. No need to cover it." Smiling proudly he continued to explain, "Longest iron span in the country, too. Invented and built by a B and O engineer named Bollman."

"Great," commented Gilbert, more to himself than anyone, "just when we need cover, there isn't any." To Williams he asked, "Is the railroad side of that span planked as well?"

"Only on the far side of the rails," was the reply.

"Okay, let's use the lantern and cross over the ties to the far left of the railroad side, now." For explanation, the Corporal added, "No one will be watching that side for foot traffic."

Once all were across the rails, he said to Williams, "Better kill the light and follow behind us." He waited for the watchman to extinguish the lantern, and then commanded, "Marines, Forward, Route Step, March." The command 'route step' allowed each Marine to carry his weapon and make his footing as best he could for the existing conditions.

The wind caught most of them by surprise when they stepped out onto the open truss. It was wet, chilly, and seemed to swirl around them from all directions. For Gilbert the veteran, it was just like being on a ship's fighting foretop again. He smiled. For Allen the novice, it was a little unnerving. The wind had sucked the breath right out of him. He gasped for air, closed his mouth tight, and tucked his neck down into his coat collar.

When they neared the middle of the span, Allen noticed the increasingly constricting crisscross pattern of the suspension diagonals next to him. Looking at the other side of the span to see a broader image, his mind struck a comparison. "Spider web," he whispered to himself. He reached out and touched one of the diagonals. It felt surprisingly cold and rusty to his touch. "Oh," he said half aloud, "not what I expected." Rubbing the unanticipated residue between his thumb and his fingertips, he thought, *"It's a good thing ships aren't made out of iron. Too harsh and impersonal. Feels dead and decayed."* He wiped the rust grit from his fingers onto his coat.

Gilbert signaled a halt. He whispered to Allen, "Pass it back, 'Mister Williams to the front'." The message quickly relayed down the line and the watchman came forward.

"Mister Williams," asked Gilbert as he pointed, "what are each of those buildings on the left?"

Williams pointed to each building in turn. "Well, the first one is the toll house for the turnpike." It was dark. "The second is the B and O office that I work out of." It was also dark. "The lit up one is the Gault House." He turned to the Corporal and added, "That's a large saloon. And from the look of things, there are quite a few Militiamen in there." He looked back at the buildings. "The one down a ways from the saloon is the Winchester and Potomac Railroad depot." With the exception of three platform lanterns, the depot was dark.

"How far is the Armory from here?" asked Gilbert.

Williams calculated for a moment, and then said, "Maybe

fifty or fifty-five paces to the gate. Another fifteen or twenty paces from there to the engine house."

"All right," said Gilbert. "What we'd like to do is move out from here, and get a good feel for what's between here and the Armory gate."

"We should go across Potomac Street, then," Williams pointed down at the macadamized surface, "and move forward, down the far side of the street." He nodded. "We can see everything from that side, and the Armory fence will keep us hidden."

"Excellent," agreed the Corporal. "The three of you," he indicated the Marines, "go with Mister Williams, across the street to that first building over there." He pointed to indicate which building. "Wait on the left side, out of sight. I will be with you shortly." He looked around the area ahead of them for movement. Finding none, he commanded, "Move Out, quietly."

Gilbert watched the four men start in the direction of the designated building. He then proceeded toward the saloon. When he arrived there, he stepped up onto the long porch and stopped just outside the edge of the first window. He peered in furtively. The place was indeed crowded with Militiamen and their weapons. Scanning the interior quickly, he decided, *"These boys are roaring drunk!"* The din from within subsided and the sounds of a melodious Irish tune being sung enthusiastically by several harmonizing voices vibrated against the window glass. He listened for a second or two, *"Well, maybe not all of them."*

Gilbert quickly made his way to the door. Above it hung a shingle, which announced in bold letters, "The Gault House, Geo. W. Chambers, Proprietor." A small chalkboard attached to the door, proclaimed, "Redeye Whiskey – 5¢ a shot," and below that, "Irish Whiskey – 10¢ a shot." Gilbert shook his head and mused, "And me with a reconnoiter to conduct!"

Moving silently, he placed three chairs from the porch, close together, at odd angles, in front of the door. Then he placed a fourth chair on top of the three. Bounding off of the porch, he hustled to catch up with his Detail.

When he caught up to them, Williams was the one who asked Gilbert, "What was that for, Corporal?"

Gilbert flashed his toothy grin. "A little trapfall to slow them down if they decide to come running out for a shooting spree, again." Everyone agreed with a nod and a smile.

Monday, October 17, 1859, 9:30 p.m.

Once well past the Potomac restaurant, the Marines started angling left toward the tall black shadow Whelan had pointed to earlier. Just before they reached it, they encountered another four-foot high double-railed barrier like the one along the river wall. Looking down over it, McDonough could see that this rail was a protective measure to prevent anyone from falling the twelve or so feet to the ground below.

The Orderly Sergeant waited until all of his men were protected by the water tower before he called for a halt. He moved to the end and whispered to Quinn, "Keep a watchful eye out toward the buildings we passed." Quinn nodded and turned around to face the direction he was pointed in.

Moving back to the front of the line, McDonough said, "Mister Whelan," he gestured at the structure next to them, "you sure this is a water tower?" It didn't look like any water tower he had ever seen. This one was about eighteen feet square and measured maybe forty feet from the ground up to the bottom of the roof rafters. With what looked like windows on the upper level, it appeared to be just another building.

Whelan laughed softly. "It was designed to blend in with the other Armory buildings." Indicating the tower, he added, "Inside the exterior facade, from the bottom to the top, is a 17 by 17 foot, square brick water tank. Besides water for the engines, it also provides fire protection for the bridge and the trestle we're on."

McDonough shook his head and looked up at the top of the tower. "Humph. Who would have guessed?"

Whelan slowly edged up to the corner of the tower and pointed to a dark stain on the platform. "This is where they killed Mayor Beckham." He was quiet for a moment. "Someone in the engine house shot him in the right breast. They say he died instantly." Still looking down at the spot, Whelan shook his head, "Strange thing happened right then, too. Just about the same time he was hit, it started to rain a heavy downpour." He looked up at McDonough. "It had been showering and drizzling off and on all day, but that was the first hard rain." He looked down again and shook his head. "No sir," he said prophetically, "not a good omen for the town."

McDonough placed a comforting hand on the man's shoulder and said softly, "Mister Whelan, can you show me where the engine house is located?"

The security guard came out of his reverie sluggishly. When his eyes focused, he swung around the corner of the water tower and pointed. "See that little building on the other side of the compound?" His hand shook slightly. "That's it." He rolled back behind the safety of the water tower.

McDonough stared hard across the Armory and could make out a one-story brick building with a slate roof. A white, bell cupola centered the roof. There were three arched doorways. Facing Whelan, he stated, "Looks to be maybe thirty-five feet across and twenty-five feet deep. What's behind the doors?"

Whelan answered rapidly. "The one on the right, with the narrow windows along either side the door, is the guardroom. The two double doors on the left are the engine house."

"You said earlier that you were rescued when the Martinsburg men smashed in some windows and helped you out." Whelan only nodded, so McDonough continued, "Are the windows you exited on the side of the building?"

"Yes," breathed Whelan.

"Are there any windows like those on the side or on the back of the engine house?" asked McDonough.

Whelan shook his head and barely whispered, "No."

McDonough felt he needed to calm the man down. "Okay, Mister Whelan, please relax. We are perfectly safe up here. And you're doing a great job," wheedled McDonough. "Can you tell me what equipment is inside the engine house?"

The security guard took a deep breath and exhaled slowly several times. "Nothing out of the ordinary," he finally said. "Two hand fire engines, two hose carts and the usual fire appliances...buckets, axes, picks...things like that."

"Please tell me about the engines," coaxed McDonough.

"One is an old style bucket machine. We call it *Rough and*

Ready. It's usually on the left side of the engine house." He started to smile. "The other is a modern double deck suction engine with reciprocating pump handles on both sides. We call her *Liberty.*" He had reached a state of calmness that was visible.

"Excellent," praised McDonough. "What else can you show me about the Armory?"

The security guard eased around the corner of the water tower, and, this time, stayed there. "Off to the right of the engine house is the Armory office building." He pointed to each building in turn. "On our side, right over there, is a warehouse. Just beyond that, the one with the real tall (90 ft) chimney is the Smith and Forging Shop."

"How long is the Armory compound?" interjected McDonough. He only needed the immediate area identified.

"Close to six hundred yards," guessed Whelan.

"Can we enter from this side?" asked McDonough.

"Sure," said the older man, "there's a ladder that goes from the trestle into the compound just on the other side of the Smith and Forging Shop." He smiled. "That's how Bill Williams and I got out of there."

"I see," acknowledged McDonough. Continuing, he started to put things into prospective for containment. "So, we have the river wall on this side. It's about fifteen feet high." He pointed to the main Armory entrance to the left. "That entry wall seems to be about eight feet high, half stone and half iron rod." He looked back to his guide. "Is that a wall behind the engine house?"

"Yes," replied Whelan. "It's a solid wall, eight feet tall. Runs all along Potomac Street to where the Armory canal meets it." He calculated, "Maybe sixty yards, maybe more."

"Good," remarked McDonough. "Are there any other ways in or out in this area that I should know about?" He indicated from the warehouse, across to the office building, down past the engine house, and around to where they were.

"Well, there is the boatway," supplied Whelan.

"You mean there is an access ramp to the river?" McDonough was surprised. "Where?"

"About thirty feet from here." Whelan pointed up river. "Just before the warehouse. It's about twenty feet wide."

McDonough looked along the platform to gauge where the boatway was located.

The security guard continued, "Right after the Militia chased the raiders back to the Armory, one of them, a young fellow, ran out the boatway and tried to swim across the Potomac." He shook his head. "He was killed." Whelan pointed out to the darkened river. "His body is still out there on an islet." He said shamefully, "I think the Militia boys have been using it for target practice."

Before McDonough could comment, he was alerted by, "Halt, who comes there?" As he rushed toward Quinn, he also heard, "Friend" in the distance. When he arrived at the end of the line, Quinn, who was aiming at the sound of the voice, finished saying, "Advance, friend, and be recognized."

Moving toward them was a man in a uniform and wearing a military style revolver holster. His arms were slightly raised out and upward. At about a four pace distance, the man spoke. "I am Captain Sinn, of the Frederick Militia." He spoke with a tenor of authority and confidence.

McDonough recognized the man's attitude and demeanor as those of an experienced officer. He whispered to Quinn, "Stand easy." He also sheathed his sword. When the man was close enough to see his uniform clearly, McDonough clicked to Attention and snapped a salute. "Orderly Sergeant McDonough, United States Marines, sir."

The Captain returned the salute. "Good evening, Orderly Sergeant. Are you four the only Marines coming?"

"No, sir, we're part of a reconnoiter Detail. The main body is still at Sandy Hook." To explain the delay, McDonough added, "We were ordered to await the arrival of Colonel Lee from the Army. Once he arrives, the whole Detachment will march over, sir."

"Well, then," started the Captain, "we shall all have to wait, won't we." He cracked an infectious smile. "In the meantime," he pointed toward the Armory, "I just came out of the engine house a little while ago. Perhaps I can help you with your reconnoiter."

McDonough was not sure he had heard correctly. "Are you an escaped hostage, sir?"

"No, Orderly Sergeant, just a concerned humanitarian of

sorts." Sinn shrugged his shoulders slightly. "Since an earlier written demand for surrender had failed, I went down there on my own to see if I couldn't talk them out peaceably. Spent almost an hour conversing with their leader." He shook his head. "No luck. He's a stubborn man." He pointed back toward the hotel. "I was just going to fetch our surgeon from the Wager House when I saw you pass down the platform."

"Then you know how many insurgents are in the engine house, sir!" McDonough could not believe this fortuitous meeting. Most of all, he couldn't believe how lucky the Captain was to still be walking around, free and alive.

"Yes...let's see," Sinn pondered. "There were a total of eight insurgents, but that number includes one dead and two badly wounded." He interposed, "That's why I was looking for our surgeon." Continuing, he added, "There were also between ten and twelve hostages, and maybe half a dozen slaves." He shook his head, "Hard to tell exactly how many hostages, though. They were all huddled together against the back wall."

McDonough was impressed with the Captain's attention to detail. "Any other information you can provide, sir?"

"The insurgents all have Sharps rifles." Sinn nodded his head. "That's probably why they've been able to hold off the Militia."

McDonough also nodded with understanding. A good man with a Sharps rifle could fire up to five rounds per minute, while someone with a musket could get off maybe two or three in the same period of time. The insurgents were indeed well armed.

Sinn continued, "They have cut loopholes in several places. At least one in each door and one in the center abutment." (A loophole is an opening just large enough to poke a rifle barrel through without exposing the shooter to opposing fire.)

"Any idea how many insurgents attacked originally, sir?" asked McDonough.

"First reports were around twenty," said Sinn. "We can account for fifteen so far." He pointed toward the engine house. "Eight in there." He pointed back at the hotel. "One wounded captive, there." He next pointed toward the upper town. "One held captive in the town jail." He circled his hand around to nowhere in particular. "And five known dead at various places." He shrugged his shoulders. "If there are more, they haven't shown themselves."

McDonough speculated, "Probably made good their escape."

"They won't get far!" declared Whelan.

McDonough clicked to Attention and saluted. "Thank you, Captain. I shall relay this information to my Commanding Officer."

"Glad to be of help." Sinn returned the salute. "Good luck, Orderly Sergeant. I am off to finish my errand of mercy."

McDonough watched the Captain walk back toward the hotel. He looked over at Quinn and said, "Now that is one brave fellow. Too bad he's not a Marine."

* * * * *

While his men waited in the dark shadows next to the building, Corporal Gilbert looked around its front corner. He saw no one on the street and beckoned the watchman to his side.

"Okay, Mister Williams, what are we looking at out here?" he asked.

Both men looked around the corner together. "Well," started Williams, "that big building just across the street from us is the B and O depot, although you'd hardly know it tonight." He pointed to the left of the darkened depot, across a broad walkway to a large, well-lit building. "That's the Wager Hotel. Most everyone who is someone waits in the hotel lobby for the train." He chuckled. "Much more comfortable for the fancy folk."

"Okay," said Gilbert as he carefully noted the two buildings. He checked again for activity on the street. Seeing none, he signaled everyone forward. "Let's go," he whispered and stepped around the corner.

The building they had been standing next to turned out to be a jewelry store. Gilbert peered intently into the darkened shop behind the windows. He saw no movement. After testing the door to ensure it was locked, he continued on to the next building. This smaller structure was a barbershop. It was also locked and darkened.

Around the corner of the barbershop was an open area. It continued back, away from the street, to a stone wall and large iron gate. Gilbert stepped out from the corner and signaled his men to come around. As each man passed between the corner and him, he whispered, "All the way to the gate." He checked the street once more and then brought up the rear.

Once at the gate, Gilbert asked the watchman, "What's in this compound?"

Williams replied, "This is the Arsenal Square. It's where they store the finished guns from the Armory."

Off to his left, Gilbert could see a narrow end of a large, rectangular, two story building. His seaman's eye estimated its size to be about 30 feet wide and 125 feet long. He pointed at it and asked, "Is that where they keep all of the weapons?"

"No, actually, this building used to house the guns, but it's old and in disrepair. They just keep supplies and such things in there now." The watchman pointed off to the right and farther into the compound to the wide side of another two-story building. It was about 70 feet long and 35 feet wide. "That's where they keep all of the guns. Maybe twelve thousand of them in there."

Gilbert moved over to his veterans. "Greenhalgh, Tompkins. The two of you head over to the smaller building over there." He pointed to the Small Arsenal. "Check it out. Make sure it's secure and report back here." The two Marines nodded and hustled off.

Gilbert continued to look around the Arsenal compound. In the corner closest to the Armory, he spotted a small, one story dwelling. He pointed to it. "Mister Williams, pray tell, what is that little building over here?"

Williams responded matter of factly, "That used to be a house, but back in the early Thirties it was converted into an office for the Armory Superintendent. Now the town leases it, and uses it as a Town Hall."

"Thank you," replied Gilbert to the watchman. He turned to the remaining Marine and said, "Allen, go over to that small building and check it out." He pointed first to the building, then directly down at the ground. "Return here when you're done."

"Aye-Aye, Corporal," whispered Allen.

"Mister Williams," pressed Gilbert, "come with me back to the street." They quietly moved back to the front corner of the barbershop.

"Okay, sir," started Gilbert. "Please tell me about the three other buildings," he pointed across the street, "that are between the hotel and the Armory gate."

"Actually," supplied Williams, "there are five more buildings on that side of the street." He pointed across the street. "You know about the Wager House." He moved his arm a little to the left. "Now," he continued, "there is a small building just to the left of it that is a ready-made clothing store. It look's kind of tiny next to the hotel." He looked at Gilbert to make sure he could see it. When Gilbert nodded, he continued. "The next two buildings are right against one another, and look like one big building. The first one, the closest one, is a drug store. The second one is a dry goods store." He again looked at Gilbert, and then continued. "There's a building behind the drug store that you can't see from here. It faces the train platform. That's the Potomac Restaurant. Good eating, there." He nodded. "And behind the dry goods store is a two story house." He dropped his arm down to his side. "That's about it for that side of the street.

"Thank you," started Gilbert. However, before he could ask about the buildings on their side of the street, he heard the alarm, "Crack," coming from the gate. He spun around and darted toward it.

When Gilbert got closer to the gate, he saw Allen crouched down on one knee, pointing his weapon at a figure moving toward them. His first instinct was danger, but when he sighted white cross belts on the figure, he said to Allen, "Stand easy, Private. He's one of ours." Allen breathed a sigh of relief.

Greenhalgh was returning at a trot. When he could see the gate clearly, he sped up and closed the remaining gap quickly. "Corporal!" He puffed several times to get his wind back, and then continued. "The main door of that building has been broken into." He puffed a few more times. "We checked the bottom floor. There are signs that things like desks and cabinets have been gone through, but the crates and stacks of weapons don't seem to be disturbed." He puffed one last time. "We didn't see anyone inside, but I told Tompkins to stay outside and keep an eye on the place."

Gilbert grinned. "Well done, Private." He patted the man once on his upper arm. "Catch your breath for a few moments."

Gilbert looked to Allen. "Report."

"The Town Hall is locked and dark, Corporal," stated Allen. "And no sign of movement inside."

Gilbert nodded. "Very well, Private." To the watchman he queried, "Mister Williams, have you heard about any insurgents being rousted out of the Arsenal?"

Williams thought for a while. "I seem to remember their leader sending a couple of men over here right after they took Dan and me, and forced the Armory gate open." He thought for few more moments. "Guess they must have departed when Colonel Gibson and his irregulars took this end of the bridge and the Ferry Lot around Noon today."

"Nonetheless there's still the possibility that someone remains in the building," worried Gilbert. He considered his options for a few moments. When his course of action was clear, he said, "Greenhalgh, rejoin Tompkins. Post yourselves so each of you can see one long and one short side of that building. Challenge anyone coming out or entering the building." He looked hard into the Private's eyes. "If anyone fails to halt, shoot to kill. Got that?"

Greenhalgh blinked once and replied calmly, "Aye, Corporal."

Gilbert nodded with satisfaction. "Very well, Post." Without another word, the Private started back to the Small Arsenal.

"All right." Gilbert spun on his heel, signaled, and started back toward the street. "Let's finish looking at the rest of this Ferry Lot." Williams and Allen fell in behind him.

Cutting diagonally across the open area, they made their way to the front corner of the next building on their side of the street. Peering around the corner, Gilbert first saw the beginning of a flagstone sidewalk. It continued in the direction of the Armory. He next noticed that the building had no porch like the ones across the street.

A hint of movement caught his attention. Down the street and about four feet out from the sidewalk, was a lumpy mound of something dark. It was barely moving. He ducked back around the corner and said to Williams, "I think there's something laying in the street about half way to the corner."

"Probably one of those drunk Militia boys," offered

Williams.

"Maybe," retorted the alert Corporal, "but we need to check it out. Before moving, he indicated the structure they were leaning against. "What is this long building, here?"

"There's two between here and the corner," said Williams. "This one houses a tobacco shop." He looped his hand up and over. "The next one is big enough to have two shops in it. A clothing store and a shoe store." To be helpful, he added, "They're all probably locked up and dark, too."

Gilbert nodded acknowledgement and leaned around the watchman. "Allen, Fix Bayonet," he whispered, then affixed his own. "Mister Williams," Gilbert held up his hand in a 'halt' sign, "please wait here while we check it out." He signaled Allen to move out with him. "Be ready for anything," he cautioned to the Private.

The pair moved cautiously down the sidewalk, hugging the storefront. Their weapons were at the ready. As they neared the mysterious object, both still took the time to check the door and windows of the first building. Satisfied, they continued.

While not quite able to clearly make out what the dark lump might be, Gilbert thought, "*It looks like three, maybe four figures lying there.*" He began to hear grunting noises. He signaled a halt. Squatting down and looking as hard as he could, he realized, "*They're hogs...feeding.*" He watched them for a few more moments. "*But what are they eating?*" he wondered. He rose and took a few more steps.

Finally he was close enough to recognize what the fourth figure was. "*My God!*" With a suddenness that surprised Allen, Gilbert charged forward wordlessly and poked the closest hog hard in the rump with his bayonet. The animal screamed and bolted, causing a stampede of the others.

Allen rushed up behind his Corporal. "What is it?" he asked.

Gilbert stepped aside and said, "It's a man."

Allen leaned forward. "Is he dead?"

"Worse," replied the little Corporal as he looked around intently to see what the squealing hogs might have stirred up.

In an instant, Allen took in everything before him. The dead man was an older Negro with graying hair. His throat was nothing more than a nasty, ragged gash. His ears and nose had been cut off. Sticks had been jammed into all of his facial openings. The hogs had gnawed at his head and various other parts of his body.

Allen whirled away, took two steps, and vomited.

Gilbert waved his arm to catch Williams' eye. He signaled him to them. Upon arriving, the watchman looked down at the body, and grimaced.

Gilbert asked, "Is there something around here to cover him up with?"

"Sure," replied Williams, "I'll go get the piece of canvas off of the baggage cart behind the depot." He looked back briefly at the ghastly scene, and then trotted of across the street.

Gilbert went to the still bent over Allen and patted him kindly on the shoulder. "All right, lad," he whispered soothingly, "time to straighten up. We've got work to do."

Allen stood erect, spat, and wiped his mouth on his coat sleeve. "Who would do such a thing?" he asked.

"That I don't know, lad," said the Corporal slowly as he looked around the street again. "That, I don't know."

Allen pointed back to the body. "Was his throat cut?"

"No," replied Gilbert, "it's not a clean cut." He looked again at the wide wound. "Something big ripped through him." He shook his head. "But, the devil take me if I know what it was." He looked around the street, again. "I'd like to get my hands on the yellowbelly that did the rest of that to him, though." His anger was evident.

Williams came running up with a folded piece of canvas under his arm.

"Let's spread that out next to the body and wrap him up in it." Gilbert looked back at the dead man. "It's the least we can do for him."

As they were beginning their task, a voice boomed out of the deeply recessed doorway of the second building. "HEY, WHAT DO YOU THINK YOU'RE DOING?" Gilbert indicated to the other two that they should continue and he moved to meet the approaching man.

"I SAID, 'WHAT ARE YOU DOING'." He gestured angrily toward the men at the body. "LEAVE THAT THING ALONE!"

Gilbert stopped the man with his weapon at Arms Port.

"That thing, as you call him, is a man. And we're removing him from the street."

The untidily dressed man in front of Gilbert was taller than the Corporal and heavier by about 60 pounds. He also reeked of alcohol. "That THING was one of the raiders. It deserved to die." He attempted to move around Gilbert.

The Corporal extended his weapon to the side and blocked the man's advance. "To die as a warrior, maybe," he said. "But to be cut up like that and fed to the hogs is downright criminal."

"THAT THING'S JUST A BLACKBIRD!" shouted the man. "If it had a thousand lives, I'd kill it a thousand times!"

Gilbert pressed his weapon across the man's chest and shoved him backwards against the building front.

The man bounced off the wall, staggered forward, and sputtered in his drunken state. "And I'd cut off its ears a thousand times again, too!" He was grinning.

Gilbert drew the butt of his weapon back with his right hand. With the deft, swift movement of a twenty-two year service veteran, he pivoted his body and swung the butt around and up. The flat of the stock caught the man alongside his head. With a dull thud, the man dropped like a heavy sack of potatoes. Gilbert stood over the drunk for a few seconds with the point of his bayonet poised just above the man's heart. He shook his head, relaxed his stance, and then returned to the street.

"Mister Williams, do you know the man I just hit?" Williams shook his head 'no'. "Do you have any objections to my actions, sir?" asked Gilbert as he lowered the butt of his weapon to the street's surface.

Williams had just finished rolling the dead Negro's body up in the canvas. He was still on his knees. Looking around Gilbert's legs, he asked, "Did you kill him?"

"As much as I'd like to...No." Gilbert glanced over at the crumpled drunk. "However, I hit him with enough force to knock him out for a long spell." He looked back at the watchman. "He'll have a terrible headache for about a week. Maybe even a good sized knot to go along with it."

Williams shook his head, "That's not enough punishment for the likes of him." Signaling Allen to pick up the wrapped body by the shoulders, the watchman took the feet. "Let's lay this fellow over next to the Arsenal wall."

Gilbert accepted Allen's weapon. He stopped at the drunk's body to double check that he was still breathing. Satisfied that he was, the Corporal stepped nonchalantly over his deserving casualty.

Taking his weapon back from Gilbert, Allen asked, "Why'd you do it, Corporal?"

Gilbert looked down and pointed at the wrapped body. "Black, white, yellow or brown. It makes no difference." He looked back at Allen. "After you've been at sea for a dozen or so years, you'll have a chance to see a lot of the world's different people." He looked up to the darkened clouds above and swallowed hard. "I spent a couple of hard years off the coast of Africa in the Slave Interdiction Squadron." He looked back at Allen again. "Maybe, like I have, you'll come to realize that, although some men have a different coloring than you, they are all still men. Maybe some are better off than others and maybe some worse, but each one is trying to eke out an existence like the rest of us." He paused briefly, looked down at the body again, and shook his head. "Insurgent or not, he didn't deserve to be butchered up that way."

He looked back up at Allen and placed a hand on his shoulder. "Sea duty will give you a whole different outlook on the value of life, lad. Pay close attention to the lessons your ocean travels will teach you."

"I will, Corporal," stammered Allen.

"Good." Gilbert jerked his weapon up vertically and caught it near the middle. "Let's go finish this reconnoiter."

Monday, October 17, 1859, 9:40 p.m.

Orderly Sergeant McDonough looked around the whole platform and Armory area carefully. *"What is it,"* he thought, *"that is so strange, here?"* He peered around again, slowly. Then it suddenly hit him. *"No one's out here watching the engine house!"*

He asked the security guard, "Where are the Militia sentries?"

Whelan looked around quickly. "I guess they're all in the saloons, strengthening their courage."

"My thoughts, exactly," agreed McDonough. He moved near his veterans. "Wilson, Fisher. The two of you will be posted here as sentries." He pointed upriver. "One of you move up the tracks near the corner of the warehouse." He then pointed downriver. "The other will stay near the corner of the restaurant closest to the double handrail."

He cautioned both. "Stay out of sight. Your assignment will be to observe the engine house and give the alarm if anyone in there tries to make a break for it." He looked at both Marines. "And stay away from the Militia. Most of them are drunk. If they come out again, just melt into the shadows. Got that?" Each Marine nodded understanding. "Good," he continued, "now unship your capes and bring the front edge around to cover your cross belts, then post."

"Aye-Aye, Orderly Sergeant," whispered both men. First, one unbuttoned the other's cape button in the back and flipped the 'wings' forward, then the other reciprocated.

McDonough pointed first at Mr. Whelan and then at Quinn, signaled them to follow him, and said, "Let's go see if we can find the good Corporal Gilbert."

* * * * *

Gilbert led Mr. Williams and Private Allen past the tobacco shop, the clothing shop, the still unconscious drunk, and the shoe shop. They stopped at the far corner of the shoe shop. Another street ran between them and the Armory. It intersected Potomac Street. Across this new street was the entry wall and main gate to the Armory.

Gilbert looked to the watchman and asked, "Okay, Mister Williams, what can you tell me about this entry wall?"

Williams eased up next to Gilbert. "There's one long fence across the front of the Armory." He pointed to the far right. "The fence piece over there by the dry goods store is just like the fence piece you see to the left of the gate. You can't see it, but it goes all the way down to the stone river wall under the train trestle."

Gilbert nodded. The 'fence' Mr. Williams was referring to was about eight feet high. Tall pillars were evenly spaced about every ten feet or so. The lower half of the area between the pillars was solidly built, while the upper half was made of evenly spaced sets of vertical bars filling the gap to the top of the pillars. He looked around a little more then said, "Looks like the gate is farther away from us than the walls."

"That's right," agreed Williams, "the fence curves inward on both sides to the gate area. That entrance is set back about ten or twelve feet from the main line of the fence." He pointed toward the gate. "If you look real close, you'll see a small gate for the workers, just to the left of the large wagon gate." All of the gates were wide open.

Gilbert nodded. "What's that building just inside the gate to the left?" he asked.

"That's the engine house," replied Williams. "The guardroom is on the other end of the same building. That's where most of us were held captive."

Gilbert looked intently at the building. "So, that's where the insurgents are holed up with some hostages?" Williams nodded. "We need to get a closer look. You can stay here if you like, Mister Williams."

"Nope," disagreed the watchman, "I've come this far with you. Might as well go all the way."

"Excellent!" said a smiling Gilbert. "Allen, you go across to a pillar where you can still see the front of the engine house." He indicated off to the left. "Keep a good aim on the doors, but don't fire unless I do. Mister Williams and I are going to the worker's gate." He signaled them all forward. "Go, go, go!"

The Corporal and the watchman ran straight to the left pillar of the worker's gate. Right next to it was the first pillar of the 'fence'. Both were about two feet square and provided excellent cover for the two men.

Once safely protected behind the gate pillar, Gilbert leaned against it to steady himself after their brief run. He could feel the coolness of it near his cheek. He instinctively touched the pillar with his hand. "Feels cold, like stone," he commented.

"All the gate pillars are made of stone, but the fence is made of brick and iron," supplied Williams.

Gilbert bent down on his right knee. He held his weapon vertically, at the ready, in front of him. He shifted his left foot out about twelve inches into the gate opening. Next, he leaned forward over his foot and twisted his body to the left.

Simultaneously, he aimed his weapon toward the engine house.

Sighting down his barrel, Gilbert could see the three arched doorways of the engine house. The two sets of double doors to the left were closed tight. The single door of the guardhouse was wide open. He looked for light under and around all the doors, but found none. He shifted back behind the pillar and stood up.

"Don't see any light around the doors," he said to the watchman.

Williams took a quick peek around the pillar and popped back. "There's no light in the engine house whatsoever," he said.

"How can you tell?" asked Gilbert.

"The arches above the doors are glass windows," replied Williams. "If there was any light in there, you'd see the glow through the windows. They'd look like golden arches."

Gilbert took a careful look around the pillar. "You're right," he said. "How many window arches are there on the engine house?"

Williams ticked off a quick count with his finger in the air. "Six," he declared. "Two in the front, two on the side and two in the back."

Gilbert asked, "Are they all the same height above the ground?" Williams nodded. "And how tall are the doors?"

"Maybe eight feet," was the reply.

"So," said Gilbert, "there are four other ways out of the building other than the doors and windows in front. They may possibly want to try escaping out one of the back windows."

"That might be so," retorted Williams, "but if they use the ladders inside to get up and out the back windows, they still have to get over the back wall. It's solid brick and eight feet tall, too." He was pointing to the back of the engine house.

"Let's take a look," said Gilbert. Both men bent over to stay below the top of the lower half of the entry wall. When they neared Allen, Gilbert whispered, "Follow us." The three of them made their way quickly to the corner of the Armory.

As Williams had said, the back wall was solid and tall. Gilbert looked down the street behind it. "How far does this wall go?" he asked as he pointed.

"It goes as far as the street goes," replied Williams. "You

run out of flat land about a quarter of a mile down there. The street and the wall end at the stone face of the bluff."

Peering down the street to see if he could distinguish the end of it or the wall, Gilbert asked, "What's the name of this street?"

"This is another part of Potomac Street," answered the watchman. "It kind of zigzags around the front of the Armory compound."

Gilbert looked to his left and saw that the street that intersected Potomac Street in front of the Armory and where they were standing, also went off towards more dark buildings. Looking back to Williams, he asked, "And what's the name of this street?"

"This one's called Shenandoah Street," he replied. "There's about four more acres of flat land going off that way." He pointed away from the Armory and Ferry Lot

"What's out that way?" asked Gilbert.

"Well," began Williams, "there's the rest of the lower town. A block down from here is High Street." He pointed off to the right and upward. "It runs up the slope to Bolivar Heights." He shrugged his shoulders. "Guess you might consider the buildings on the slope as the upper town. Although we don't call it by that name." He paused, then pointed down Shenandoah Street again. "And about a half a mile or so down that way, there's the Rifle Works."

"Oh?" queried Gilbert. His interest was aroused.

"Not to worry, Corporal," assured Williams. "The Militia chased three raiders out of there." He nodded his head several times. "Yep, killed two and captured one."

"So, as far as you know," stated Gilbert, "the only remaining insurgents are boxed up in the engine house."

"Yes, sir," assured Williams, "that seems to be the looks of it."

Gilbert nodded, then signaled for the others to wait for a minute. He made his way across Shenandoah Street to the section of the Arsenal wall that was in front of the Town Hall. It was a good vantage point. He knelt there, slowly and quietly looking around for several minutes. He was sorting out the situation as he understood it.

The other two men waited for the Corporal in different

ways. Williams eased his way over to the first commercial building outside of the Ferry Lot. It was a dry goods store with rocking chairs on the porch. He lowered himself softly into one and silently rocked back and forth.

Allen had cautiously moved back to the place where the rear wall and entry wall of the Armory met. He was down low, but still high enough to see and aim his weapon through the iron bars. From there he was keeping a watchful eye on the back of the engine house.

Gilbert returned to Allen's side. "Allen," he said, "I want you to make your way to the back of the B and O Depot. Do you remember where it is?" Allen looked off toward the Ferry Lot and nodded. "Good." Gilbert continued, "Go there and look for Orderly Sergeant McDonough. If he's not there already, wait for him. He will be there shortly. Got that?"

"Yes, Corporal," replied Allen.

Gilbert instructed, "Tell him that the rest of us are checking out the Small Arsenal and will rejoin him at the Depot as soon as possible. Got that?"

"Yes, Corporal," said Allen again.

"Cross over here and go back the same way we came. Keep to the shadows as much as possible. And," he warned, "stay away from the Militia." He squinted. "They're dangerous."

Allen started to grin for a second, but decided it wasn't a good idea since Corporal Gilbert wasn't grinning. Instead he squinted, too, grasped his weapon firmly, and started making his way toward the Arsenal wall.

Gilbert met the approaching watchman in the middle of the street. "Mister Williams, is there another way into the Arsenal Square?"

"Sure," replied Williams, "there's an entrance over by the Small Arsenal." The two men headed that way.

<u>Monday, October 17, 1859, 9:55 p.m.</u>

The Corporal and the watchman made their way from the Arsenal gate to the corner of the barbershop. After checking the Ferry Lot for any activity, they crossed over to the B&O Depot.

They found McDonough and the others behind the building, in the shadows near the baggage cart.

"Ahoy, Orderly Sergeant," whispered Gilbert just loud enough to be heard clearly.

"Ahoy, Corporal," replied McDonough in the same manner.

"Mission accomplished," announced Gilbert as they drew within touching distance.

"Very well," said McDonough. "Where are your other two men?"

"There seemed to be a lack of Militia sentries in the area, so I posted my veterans to keep an eye on things from two different vantage points." Gilbert pointed back toward the Armory. "They're watching the near side and back of the engine house."

"Well done," beamed McDonough. "And what of the Arsenal?"

"Looks like at least two men had been in the Small Arsenal building," Gilbert shook his head, "but they're gone now."

McDonough shook his head slightly and commented, "Didn't amount to be much of a revolt after all, did it?"

"Sure doesn't seem that way," replied Gilbert. He hooked his thumb toward the Armory and added, "Whatever's left of it is holed up in the engine house."

McDonough nodded agreement. "Let's get back to the train and report all of this to Lieutenant Greene." He turned to Whelan and Williams. "Gentlemen, I can't tell you how much we appreciate your services, tonight." He shook both men's hands. "If you'll light two lanterns for us, we'll be scout stepping back to Sandy Hook." The watchman and security guard both nodded and headed for the Winchester span.

Allen whispered to Quinn, "What's scout stepping?"

Quinn whispered back, "That's where we trot for fifty paces, then walk for fifty paces, and then trot fifty paces again. We keep switching like that until we get to where we're going."

Allen looked dumbfounded. "What?"

Quinn explained. "It's a way to cover ground quickly without wearing ourselves out." He slapped Allen on the shoulder and started walking behind the NCOs, "Come on, Fish, you look a little peaked. Maybe you need the exercise."

Monday, October 17, 1859, 10:15 p.m.

As they exited the bridge on the Maryland side, Quinn asked a quiet Allen if anything exciting had happened on his side of the town. "Exciting, no. Disturbing, yes," replied Allen. His tone was melancholic. "Maybe we can talk about it later," he added. Quinn looked at his friend with curiosity, but accepted Allen's reluctance to talk. The remainder of their transit was made in silence.

During the walk phases of the return trip, Gilbert briefed McDonough about the lower town, the Arsenal, and what he knew about the engine house. McDonough reciprocated with what he knew about the people inside the engine house.

"What about Major Russell?" asked Gilbert.

"Never met up with him again," replied a relieved McDonough. "I would think that he's still 'reconnoitering' with the Militia commanders at the Wager House."

Gilbert just nodded and grinned. He, too, was aware of the Major's preference for strong drink.

* * * * *

"Sir! Orderly Sergeant McDonough and his Detail are returning," announced the sentry posted at the car platform.

"Thank you, Private," replied Greene. "Please pass the word for Orderly Sergeant Mundell to report to me as soon as possible." He stood up, slipped his scabbard into his sliding frog, and exited the car. As he reached the ground, McDonough was calling his Detail to a halt. Greene waited as the men were dismissed.

"Good evening, sir," said McDonough as he stepped up and saluted. "Pleased to report the reconnoiter is completed," he announced loudly. He lowered his voice and added, "And that things are not as bad as feared."

Greene returned the salute and said, "Excellent, Orderly Sergeant." Mundell approached quietly and fell in next to McDonough.

Greene signaled both men to follow him. The three headed off toward the railroad line shack. At about five paces from the structure and out of earshot of anyone else, they stopped. McDonough reported his findings freely.

Monday, October 17, 1859, 10:55 p.m.

"So," concluded Greene after McDonough finished. He was speaking to Mundell. "It appears that we can reboard the howitzers and horses. I doubt we'll be needing them at this time."

"Yes, sir," agreed Mundell. "Shall I make arrangements with the conductor to ship them back to Washington City immediately, sir?"

Greene pondered this idea over for a few moments. "Yes, Orderly Sergeant, that sounds like an excellent idea." He looked to McDonough. "I believe we can also send back all of Section D as well."

"Yes, sir," piped McDonough, "I agree, sir."

"Very well, then." He nodded. "We shall prepare for such transport now, and make it so if Colonel Lee concurs." Greene was pleased with the decision and was also sure that the Army officer would agree.

He said to McDonough, "We stripped the Head Quarters to the bare bones when we left. Sending back one Sergeant and fourteen Privates would significantly help support the few watch standers left there until this Detachment returns."

"Yes, sir," replied the Orderly Sergeant. He, too, did not anticipate being in Harper's Ferry too much longer.

Off in the distance a train whistle screeched into the night. All three men looked to the East.

"Looks like the good Colonel is about to arrive, sir," smiled McDonough.

"It appears so, XO," granted Greene. "Shall we go to meet him then?" The three men headed for the end of their train.

As they approached from an angle, they intersected with two men passing down the side of the cars. They were also heading to the end of the train. One was the conductor, Mr. McCurry. He held a lantern in his left hand. The man to his right was in the shadows and not readily identifiable until he spoke.

"Well, Lieutenant," the voice began. "It appears that the Army's overall commander is about to finally arrive." It was Major Russell.

"Yes, Major," said Greene civilly, "Colonel Lee should be

here any minute."

"Ahhh, they've sent a Virginian," beamed Russell. "Governor Wise and Colonel Baylor shall indeed be pleased." He grinned with pride at his insider knowledge. "I look forward to discussing with him the complete Militia situation here at Harper's Ferry.

The party stopped at the end of the last car while the conductor continued forward. McCurry began raising and lowering his lantern vertically to signal the oncoming engineer to stop. In acknowledgement, the engine's whistle gave one last night piercing screech and steam began escaping from the drive pistons as the engineer opened the bleeder valves and applied the brakes. The engine slowed and finally stopped with a voluminous whoosh of steam. The engineer rang the bell several times to signal all clear to the conductor.

Upon hearing the bell, McDonough could not help but smile as he thought, "*Ding, ding. Ding, ding. Brevet Colonel, United States Army, Arriving.*" His many years aboard Naval ships had deeply engrained into his psyche the Navy's ceremonial protocol for ringing aboard a senior officer.

The party of Marines approached the almost visibly panting engine. All were undoubtedly surprised to see that, except for the fuel car, no other cars were trailing behind the locomotive

Monday, October 17, 1859, 11:05 p.m.

Mark Hess, the engineer, double-checked his gauges and valve settings while the military men finished their saluting and handshaking. When they had finished with their introductions and headed off toward the parked train ahead, he climbed down from the cab of Engine 22 to speak to the waiting conductor. Once on the ground, he removed his hat, extracted a large red bandanna from the rear pocket of his grimy coveralls, and mopped his brow. "I tell you, Mister McCurry," he said slowly, "if I never go that fast again, it will be much too soon for me!"

"Oh?" asked the conductor. "Just how fast were you steaming to get here?"

"Well, sir," started the engineer, half with genuine fear and half with enthusiastic pride, "with the throttle wide open, mind you, it only took us two hours to get here from Relay House!"

"Mercy!" exclaimed the conductor. "That's unheard of." Using his fingers to tabulate with, he started some quick calculations. "Let's see...you arrived here in half the normal time." He suddenly looked up and exclaimed, "That means you were running between thirty-two and thirty-three miles per hour!" He sputtered a little. "Why, over that terrain, that's absolutely hazardous!"

The engineer quickly added, "And in the dark, too!"

The conductor withdrew a small flask from an interior coat pocket and handed it to the engineer. "Here, man," he said, "you could probably use a bit of this."

"Thank you, sir," smiled the engineer. He unscrewed the cap and took a long pull on the contents. When he finished, he reaffixed the cap and returned the flask.

"Whatever possessed you to push so hard?" inquired the conductor.

"It's all because of my older passenger in the gentleman's clothes." Hess stabbed over his shoulder with his thumb. "He is apparently a Colonel in the Regular Army. And according to my younger passenger in the uniform, sent here by President Buchanan, himself."

"And that's reason enough to hazard your engine and all of your lives?" puzzled McCurry.

"No, sir," retorted Hess, "but a direct order from B and O president Garrett, sure is!" The engineer was shaking his upheld right hand with the index finger pointing toward heaven, as though he were referring to the Almighty, himself.

"Oh...," commented the conductor slowly.

"Yes, sir," continued the engineer, "from what president Garrett told me, that Colonel was apparently having a little trouble catching trains on time."

McCurry settled his weight on one foot in preparation for a long story.

Hess continued. "It seems as though he missed the Three-Twenty out of Washington City." He leaned closer to the conductor. "As you know, that meant at least a two and a half hour delay leaving Washington."

The conductor nodded knowing agreement.

"Well, sir, that delay also caused him to miss your special Military train heading West from Washington Junction." Hess shook his head. "Apparently he spent over an hour at Relay House before president Garrett found out he was still there." McCurry shook his head slowly and "Tsked" several times.

Hess stretched to his full height and beamed with pride. "Since number twenty-two was all fired up and ready to make the run back down to Washington City, president Garrett personally directed me to unhook the cars and high ball it to Relay House." He rocked on his feet. "Upon arrival there, I was to pick up this military fellow and then," he quickly swung his right arm out to its fullest extension and pointed toward the town, "melt the rails all the way to Harper's Ferry."

"And melt them you must have," concluded the conductor with a smile. "By my calculations, you actually cut the Colonel's four hour en route delay down to just two hours." He reached out and patted the engineer on the shoulder. "Well, done, Hess, well, done! I'm sure that president Garrett will appreciate your efforts most heartedly." He reached into his interior pocket again. "Here, sir, finish this off. You most certainly deserve it!"

Monday, October 17, 1859, 11:20 p.m.

"Thank you, Lieutenant Greene," said Colonel Lee with a slight bow of his head, "I have a very clear image of the tactical situation as it now stands." He handed the rudimentary map back to the Marine officer seated to his right. "I concur that we shall not require the artillery pieces." Greene smiled.

Lee turned toward a drowsy Major Russell seated across from him. Because the background field of the Major's rank-straps was black and not blue, Lee understood that, although the Major was senior in rank, he was a staff officer, and, therefore, Greene's input of operational information had been requested first. "Now then, Major," said Lee cordially, "you mentioned earlier that you had information concerning the responding Militia units."

Russell jolted upright. He had presupposed Greene's information to be tedious and had been lulled toward sleepiness.

He flashed his best political smile. "Yes, Colonel, that is correct." He was overjoyed to be the focus of attention and leaned closer toward Lee as if he were about to impart significant secrets. "I have met, personally, with each of the Militia commanders and have a detailed accounting of which units are present, how many men are mustered in each, and how they have participated in today's action." He was dripping with self-importance.

Without a noticeable change of expression or demeanor, Colonel Lee moved back and to his left slightly to escape the Major's acrid alcohol breath.

Russell was heedless of the Colonel's positional adjustment and continued. "Yes, sir, the first to respond to the crisis were two Companies of the Charles Town Militia, commanded by Colonel Gibson. They arrived around Noon and managed to retake the bridge and drive the insurgents into the engine house." He checked his handful of papers. "The next unit to appear was a Company of the Martinsburg Militia. They arrived around Three O'clock. This group, commanded by Captain Alburtis, had a running gun battle with the insurgents in the engine house and managed to rescue the hostages held in the guardroom."

"Were there any Militia casualties resulting from either of those two encounters?" inquired Lee.

Russell was surprised by the interjection. "Uhh," his eyes quickly scanned his notes, "yes, sir, the Martinsburg Militia incurred minor wounds to eight men."

Lee nodded. "Thank you, please continue."

Russell visibly stirred with excitement at having the Colonel express an interest in his verbal report. "Yes, well," he looked furtively at the members of the group, "uhh, shortly after the rescue of the hostages, a Company of the Hamtramck Guards, as well as a Company of the Shepherdstown dismounted cavalry troop arrived. In addition, a Captain Washington arrived with one Company from Winchester in the late evening."

He lowered his papers. "Those six Companies make up the current Virginia response." Aware that Lee was a Virginian, he added, "And Governor Wise has placed Colonel Baylor in charge of all the Virginia troops."

Lee closed his eyes momentarily. Misinterpreting Lee's prolonged blink as displeasure or distain, Russell quickly added, "And, by the way, sir, uhh, Governor Wise is currently enroute from Richmond with two additional Companies of Militia."

"Yes, thank you." Lee blinked again from fatigue, this time more quickly. "And," he asked softly, "what of the Maryland Militia units present?"

"Yes, uhh, let's see." Russell referred back to his papers. "Colonel Shriver arrived around dusk with three Companies from Frederick. And, of course, Brigadier General Egerton arrived with four Companies of Maryland Volunteers from Baltimore, along with our Detachment of Marines, earlier tonight."

Lee nodded. "Is the Brigadier General in overall command of the Maryland troops?"

"No, sir," replied Russell. "General Egerton is under strict orders from the Governor of Maryland to remain on Maryland soil. Colonel Shriver commands the Maryland troops in Harper's Ferry."

Russell opened his mouth to provide additional information. Lee, however, raised his right hand and again spoke softly, "Thank you, Major. I believe I have an adequate image of the manpower situation." The Colonel had made a quick mental computation and realized that approximately six hundred Militiamen were now amassed in and around Harper's Ferry, and more were still coming.

A dejected Russell momentarily held out his handful of papers and said, "But I have more important..." He quickly reclaimed his deportment, smiled deliberately, and added slowly as he leaned back into his seat, "Certainly, Colonel, perhaps later." His mind raced ahead, *"Later, yes, but without a doubt, before you fill out your after action report."*

From within his breast pocket, Colonel Lee could feel a particularly heavy piece of paper crinkle against his chest as he turned to address the officers around him. He reached within his coat, touched the paper surreptitiously, and prospectively thought, *"I shall, thankfully, not have to invoke President Buchanan's proclamation of Martial Law."*

Withdrawing his hand, he said, "Well, gentlemen, it appears that we do not have as horrible a crisis as first reported to Secretary Floyd." All nodded agreement. Satisfied, Lee continued to his audience, "I propose that we advance Lieutenant Greene's Marines onto the Armory grounds to reestablish control over government property, and to surround the remaining insurgents within the engine house." Looking particularly at Major Russell, he added, "I shall request the Militia commanders to position their men outside of the Armory walls to prevent any possible escape, as well as to prepare for deflection of any reinforcement to the insurgents." A glow of success flickered within Russell's eyes.

As Lee rose, the others followed suit. He turned to Greene. "At your convenience, Lieutenant, kindly prepare your men to march into Harper's Ferry.

"Aye-Aye, sir!" replied Greene, with a smile, as he snapped to Attention.

Lee involuntarily winced at the unusual verbal response, recovered, and added, "I shall join you, momentarily. However, I must first draft two telegrams. One to stop the advance of the Regular troops from Fort Monroe, and one to Secretary Floyd to apprise him of the situation as it currently stands." He again closed his eyes, and, with several diminutive nods, said half to himself, "I am of a mind to end this thing as quickly as possible."

CHAPTER SEVEN

"ENTRY"

Tuesday, October 18, 1859, 12:10 a.m.

Colonel Lee held up his right hand and slowed his pace. Lieutenant Greene immediately commanded, "Detachment ...Halt!" The Colonel continued forward for several more paces, stopped, turned his head slightly, and strained his left ear toward the darkness beyond the covered bridge ahead of him. Everyone else stood still and quiet in the dim light of the four lanterns illuminating their procession. The three officers at the front of the column were also straining their hearing.

Lee turned around and called, "First..." He caught himself and said softly, "Sorry." He coughed as though clearing his throat and continued, "Orderly Sergeant McDonough."

"Sir!" barked McDonough as he stepped out from behind the officers and took four quick paces to the senior Army officer. The Marine Non-Com was smiling broadly. It was a common mistake for most Army officers to address him as First Sergeant. McDonough was appreciative that this cavalry officer had remembered the proper Marine title and had corrected himself. "Yes, Colonel," he said as he stopped before the man, "how may I assist, sir?"

"Lieutenant Greene," began Lee, "had reported that, during your reconnoiter of the town, you encountered Militiamen minimally, and, that on sporadic occasion, they fired irregularly upon the engine house."

"Yes, sir," replied McDonough, "that's correct."

"Interesting," commented Lee as he turned back toward the lower town. "There seems to be a great amount of musketry rattle coming from that direction now." Lee had just explained why he had stopped the Detachment near the Maryland end of the bridge. He turned back to McDonough. "Can you hear the report of any Sharps rifles amongst that firing?"

McDonough listened a few moments for the distinctively harsher and louder explosive 'boom' or report made by a Sharps rifle. "No, sir," he declared, "just the unorganized rattle of various calibers of musket. I don't believe the insurgents are responding."

"I wonder why the sudden increase in erratic weapons

fire?" puzzled Lee.

"With your permission, sir?" requested McDonough. Lee nodded. "My military guess, sir," continued the Orderly Sergeant as he pointed, "is that the Militiamen over there have just come awake, sir."

"Continue," directed an inquisitive Lee.

"Yes, sir." McDonough paused and looked toward the darkness to listen to a new flurry of musketry. Failing to discover a Sharps report, he shook his head negatively, and then continued. "Apparently everything had been fought to a standstill by sunset. At that time, the majority probably wandered off," McDonough quickly changed tack, "or, uhh, ...were dismissed...to search for food and drink." Lee indicated agreement discretely so as to convey his understanding of the Orderly Sergeant's meaning. "As you know, sir, a heavy meal and more than a little alcohol would make many a weary man sleepy."

"Hmm, yes," reasoned Lee, "that could explain the paucity of Militiamen earlier and, if they're now refreshed, the apparent resurgence of activity." He thought for a few more seconds then said, "Very well, Orderly Sergeant," a small smile cracked under his moustache, "shall we mount'em up and move'em out?"

McDonough grinned widely at the little joke. "Aye, sir!"

Tuesday, October 18, 1859, 12:20 a.m.

Colonel Lee signaled another halt. This time at the town end of the Winchester span. The door to the Gault House had crashed opened briefly and then closed. The din inside the saloon had been tremendous. With a start, he first surmised that a skirmish had begun. The melodious resonance of loud singing quickly dispelled that notion. In a search for updated strategic information, he swung his gaze slowly from left to right.

In the brightly lit area in front of the saloon he could clearly see several small groups of five and six men with muskets milling about on or near the porch. Most of them seemed to be reloading their weapons. A few were resting their hands or forearms on the upright barrels of their weapons. One brilliant individual was actually leaning across the butt of his weapon while the barrel was grinding into the street surface. Here and there he could see bottles being passed from man to man. Laughter and loud, but indistinct, conversations were prominent.

In the darkness of the street, he could just make out some of the buildings. Large groups of shadowy figures seemed to float about in the thoroughfare. He could vaguely make out the murmur of whispered conversations. There seemed to be as much shushing being bandied about as there was muffled chitchat.

Outraged at the lack of any semblance of proper military comportment anywhere within view, he swung about and called out, "MAJOR RUSSELL, LIEUTENANT STUART!" The two men quickly stepped up to the Colonel. Before either officer could utter a word, Lee pointed forcefully and continued, "Lieutenant, you will close THAT saloon, IMMEDIATELY." He was trying hard to control his anger. "And any other saloons that are open as well. Is that understood?"

"Yes, sir!" echoed back the young cavalry officer.

Lee's demeanor returned to a more gentlemanly state. "Major, kindly ask each State's senior Militia officer to report to me as soon as they have regained control of their forces."

"I shall see to it immediately, Colonel." Russell felt a sudden trepidation that he was unaccustomed to.

"Very well, then." He momentarily glanced back at the saloon. "Lieutenant Greene and I shall continue on to assume possession of the Armory." He turned back to Russell and Stuart and said evenly, "You may carry on." The two officers saluted quickly and departed. Stuart hastily beelined toward the Gault House as Russell strolled toward the Wager House.

Lee turned to Greene. "All right, Lieutenant," he said with an invitational gesture, "Shall we find the back door to this Armory?"

Tuesday, October 18, 1859, 12:35 a.m.

"Skirmishers, Forward, March." Two sets of Comrades-in-Arms had been posted as the Detachment prepared to advance down the Armory grounds toward the front gate. Ruppert, Quinn, and Allen were three of the four that had been numbered as 'Twos'. They waited patiently as the 'Ones' advanced their first ten slow paces.

Orderly Sergeant McDonough was just one pace behind the center of the 'Twos'. "Easy, lads," he whispered. "This is just a simple walk in the park. It's scarcely over a hundred yards to our halting point." He had advised them earlier to stop when they were abreast of the near end of the second building on their left. "The first one," he had said, "is a long building with a large smoke stack near the middle." He also added that the "second one is a two story warehouse," and cautioned, "we don't want to advance beyond the corner of the second building, just yet."

Allen was near the center of the skirmish line. He looked down the direction of their advance. To his right was another long building. It appeared to be as long as the one on his left. In the darkness, the parallel walls of the two buildings seemed to be narrowing toward each other at the far end. He suddenly felt closed in. He shuddered, involuntarily, and thought, "*Another mine shaft!*" Just ahead was the dim light of the Gault House. "*Light at the end of the tunnel!*" flashed through his mind.

"Private! Move!" hissed McDonough softly.

Allen was startled into motion. His momentary lapse of attention had caused him to miss the fact that his 'One' had stopped. As he stepped off, he shook his head to clear the previous imagery.

After several paces, his eyes were inadvertently drawn to the distant light. The softness of it was mesmerizing. It seemed to flicker like the flame of a candle. He absently wondered why it did that.

"Bal!" hissed Quinn from his left.

Allen stopped and looked around. He was amazed to see that he was almost two paces ahead of the rest of the 'Twos'. He immediately dropped to one knee as they had. With a grimace, he silently scolded himself for not paying closer attention.

During his next rotation of advancement, he noticed that the distant light was now steady and brighter. Suddenly, he was struck with revelation. Apparently an irregular, but continuous line of men exiting the saloon's door had caused the flickering phenomenon, and now, the door was wide open.

"Dangerous," softly escaped his lips as Corporal Gilbert's previous warning about Militiamen flashed through his head. He was instantly awake and alert. Allen began focusing on the details of his surroundings.

Greenhalgh was to his immediate right. The sign beyond him, above the large door near the center of the building, identified it as a multipurpose structure. "Boring Mill, Polishing, and Finishing Shops," read Allen half aloud. Looking ahead, along the side of the building, he thought, "*High windows, no lights.*" With a sudden stirring of apprehension, his eyes flashed back down the row of large windows. "*Good*," he thought, "*none are open.*"

Unexpectedly, as Greenhalgh was taking a step forward, his foot slipped away from under him. Half way through the slide, his boot heel established purchase on a dry spot and scrapped along the walking surface. The sound echoed loudly off the wall.

Watching Greenhalgh regain his balance, Allen immediately figured out that the surface next to the building was different than the surface he was treading upon just a few feet away. He surmised, "*There must be a flagstone sidewalk over there, like the one by the Arsenal Square.*" He nodded affirmation. "*Have to remember to be careful on flagstone. It's mighty slippery when wet.*"

After several more rotations of advancement, the 'Twos' arrived and stopped in a line between the ends of the two long buildings. The area that lay beyond them seemed wide open compared to the confining path they had just traversed. To their left, just beyond an open gap of about ten yards, was the warehouse that Orderly Sergeant McDonough had mentioned earlier. To their right was another gap of almost equal distance. Beyond it, and still further off to the right, was a one story building. It was almost as long as the warehouse. Because of the numerous windows facing the street, most correctly surmised this structure to be an office building. This conjecture was reinforced as they could also make out four or five shade trees implanted in front of the building. The only odd features noted were a couple of dark mounds amongst the trees at the far end of the building. One mound was compact and squarish in appearance, while the other was more like a large pile. Neither was moving.

The 'Ones' advanced slowly past the 'Twos' and automatically spread out to compensate for the wider front. When their line spanned the near corners of the opposing warehouse and office buildings, they stopped and dropped to one knee, weapons aimed forward. The 'Twos' advanced forward and assumed the same aiming position in the spaces between the 'Ones'.

Behind them they could hear the steadily advancing cadence of the Detachment. Crunch, crunch, crunch. Allen experienced an uncontrollable urge to look back over his shoulder, but willed himself to resist.

"Detachment...Halt!" commanded Orderly Sergeant McDonough in a lower than normal tone. Crunch, crunch ...echoed back, then silence. No one seemed to be breathing.

Three erect figures unhurriedly advanced to a spot behind the left end of the skirmish line near the warehouse. They stood quietly for several moments. Each of them was assessing the engine house up ahead and to their right, just past the office building on the opposite side of the street.

Lee broke the silence. "It is curious," he said, "that the insurgent's 'fort' stands peacefully dark and quiet."

"Aye, Colonel," replied Greene. "Perhaps, with the exception of a sentry or two, most are asleep."

"I, too, am hoping the same," confided Lee. "By now they

have been intensely active for more than twenty-four hours." He nodded in the dark. "Their fatigue will certainly work to our advantage." He returned his contemplations to the engine house.

After an uncounted number of seconds, Lee slammed a fist into his other palm and spun about. "Very well, Lieutenant," he said with determination, "let's get this done!" He stepped off briskly toward the Detachment. At a spot almost half way between the skirmish line and the Detachment, he suddenly stopped, and spun about again. "Lieutenant," he said calmly after waiting for Greene to catch up to him, "I believe that we shall require a means to force our entry past those doors."

"Aye, sir," replied Greene. "My thoughts exactly." To McDonough beside him, he added, "XO, I believe the Smith Shop we just passed may well provide us with the tools necessary to break in a few doors." He pointed to the near end of the long building with the tall smoke stack. "Please see what you can find.

"Aye-Aye, sir," returned McDonough and stepped off toward the indicated building. As he traversed the Detachment in the darkness, he hissed, "Section C. With Me."

In the distance Greene could hear Sergeant Davis quickly order, "Countermarch, By Files, Left...March." He returned his attention to the Army officer and said, "Just a few minutes, Colonel, and we shall have what we need."

"Excellent," rejoined Lee. "Excellent."

Almost immediately, Greene heard footsteps approaching from the direction of the Smith Shop. *"Much too quick,"* he thought. Then he realized that the footsteps were irregular and hurried. He turned around to Lee and said, "A small group approaching at a near run, sir!"

"Thank you, Lieutenant." He looked toward the sound of the clumping footsteps. "You may stand easy. I believe I know who they are." As Greene saluted and turned to go back to the skirmish line, Lee slowly crossed his arms in front of him and patiently awaited the approaching men. "Even by Militia standards," he said softly to himself, "they have made unusually good time.

Tuesday, October 18, 1859, 12:50 a.m.

Rain started to fall as a steady drizzle. Lieutenant Greene continued to intently focus his attention toward the two dark mounds amongst the trees at the end of the office building. *"Odd,"* he thought, *"the squarish one is taller, but the roundish one is larger in breadth, as well as haphazardly defined."* Shaking his head in wonder, he queried himself barely out loud, "What are they?" He squinted into the darkness in an attempt to see more clearly. "Is that a pole resting against the building?" He bent forward even farther. "I wish this cloud cover wasn't blocking the moonlight," he whispered with regret. At that moment, a hand reached out from behind him and clapped him firmly on the shoulder. "Oh!" exclaimed Greene with a flinch.

"Sorry to startle you, Lieutenant," said Lee as he lowered his hand, "however, we have been requested to delay our assault on the 'fort'."

"Sir?" puzzled Greene.

"It appears," continued Lee in a low tone, "that the Militia commanders are expressing severe trepidation that some of the hostages may be inadvertently harmed if we attack the insurgents in the dark." He looked back momentarily at the group of men that he had been conferring with. "Apparently there are some very prestigious citizens among the hostages. Both Militia commanders, as well as a few accompanying townspeople, are adamant about protecting their lives." He nodded his head. "Tactically, surprise is on our side if we attack now." He paused for a moment of inner reflection and continued with apparent regret, "Nonetheless, in light of a name just provided to me, I am inclined to acquiesce to them." He steeled himself and stood erect. "Lieutenant, we shall attack at first light. Kindly mount a tight sentry patrol around the 'fort'." He looked up briefly into the rain. "And, pray, secure a Head Quarters location to use for the remainder of this beastly night."

Aye-Aye, sir." replied Greene to the receding Lee. He was about to call for Mundell when McDonough approached out of the darkness. As Greene returned the Orderly Sergeant's salute, he said, "Well, XO, from the grin on your face, I assume that you have secured some suitable tools."

"Aye, sir," responded McDonough, "three of the finest millwright sledgehammers you have ever seen." He pointed around his shoulder toward Section C, which had just come to a halt. "Truth be told, sir," he smiled broadly, "they're almost big enough to require two men to handle just one of them!" Each head of the sledgehammers he was referring to had been made from a seven-inch long block of solid steel. The hammer face was four inches in diameter. The heel of the sledgehammer tapered about three inches to a rounded wedge shape that was perpendicular to the metal handle. The whole tool weighed more than thirty-five pounds.

"Excellent," acknowledged Greene as he leaned closer. "However," he whispered, "there has been a situational development that requires us to adjust our immediate operational plan."

McDonough became intently serious and also leaned forward. "Yes, sir," he whispered back.

Greene continued, "We shall be delaying an assault on the engine house until first light."

"I take it the hostages have become a factor, sir?" offered McDonough.

"Apparently, so," said Greene. He straightened up as he turned around and moved closer to the skirmish line. "And that means that we will post a watch around the insurgent's 'fort', as the Colonel called it." Pointing at the engine house, he looped his hand around in a counter-clockwise circle. Next, he looked to his left at the warehouse. "I anticipate that we will be able to use that structure to shelter the men until morning."

"Aye, sir," nodded McDonough.

Greene then pointed at the office building on his right. "We shall establish a Head Quarters in this structure if it proves to be suitable." McDonough again nodded and the Lieutenant returned his gaze to the 'fort'.

"Post the watch standers in pairs, XO," decided Greene as he looked around. He gestured with two fingers toward the broken windows of the guardroom. "Two men to patrol this side wall of the engine house. They can also check the back wall from the aft corner." He then smoothly curved his fingers up and then down to indicate 'over'. "Two outside the front fence." And added, "At the location where the rear Armory wall and fence meet. They can easily view the rear wall and the far side wall." He lowered his arm as he pondered the open area in front of the engine house doors.

"I recommend, sir," supplied McDonough, "that one pair patrol between the water tank and the main gates." He shifted his position to imitate a spot between the tower and engine house. "If we open the worker's gate and the half of the main gate closest to the engine house," he swung his horizontal left forearm away from his body, "toward the engine house, the overlap of the gates will provide some cover."

"A bully proposal," agreed Greene. "They will be able to view the far wall and the front." His eyes affixed on the dark gap between the water tower and warehouse. "Two men will also have to patrol the boat ramp." He pointed intently in that direction. "That's the only likely avenue for escape." He nodded. "The gate-tower patrol will add two more muskets for that zone as well."

"Yes, sir," agreed McDonough. "And if we split up a fifth pair to guard the entrances to the office building and the warehouse, that will give us at least six pairs of eyes always watching the front doors of the engine house."

"Outstanding, XO!" Greene smiled. "We've managed to double cover all four sides of the engine house as well as concentrate observation on the only way in or out."

"Aye, sir," said McDonough as he looked up into the drizzle for several quiet moments. "It appears that the temperature, as well as the rain, is falling, sir." He tipped his head down and wiped the dangling droplets of water from the edge of his cap's visor. "This is going to be a bitter night. I recommend, sir, that we rotate the watch standers every hour." Before his superior could respond, he added, "Ten men on watch with a roving NCO will split each section into equal sized forces. Six watch-standing teams and hourly rotation will not overtax any one group of men."

"Excellent scheduling, XO," complimented Greene. "Make it so."

Tuesday, October 18, 1859, 1:10 a.m.

"Skirmishers, Rise," hissed McDonough. "Weapons At The Ready. As A Single Line, Advance Step, March." The line of eight men progressed slowly forward.

In the meantime, Sergeant Buckley repositioned the remaining twelve men of his section from a two abreast column into a line of battle. When finished, Section A stood as two ranks facing the same direction as the skirmish line. Six men in each rank, standing shoulder to shoulder. Sergeant Buckley stood at the right end of the front rank, while Corporal Gilbert was positioned at the left end. Sections B and C each replicated the lead section's formation with their full complement of men.

Lieutenant Greene stepped to a spot two paces in front of the center of the Detachment's new formation. "Section A, Forward, March," he commanded quietly over his shoulder. All fifteen men stepped off together at the standard twenty-eight inch pace.

By the time they reached the middle of the office building, the skirmish line had stopped at the far end of the same structure and had dropped to one knee. "Halt," ordered Greene. He executed a flawless right about turn. "NCOs, To Your Assignments, Post."

Sergeant Buckley whispered in rapid succession, "First Squad, Right Face, Forward, At The Double Quick, March." The six closest men turned and moved out behind him toward the entryway of the office building. Corporal Gilbert's Second Squad executed his similar commands and followed him toward the entryway of the warehouse. Each group quickly entered their respective building in a single file.

Sections B and C automatically advanced when Section A split in two different directions. At Lieutenant Greene's signal, they halted. Several quiet minutes passed by.

Greene took full advantage of the time. He moved forward several paces. From this nearer position, he systematically scrutinized the mysterious dark mounds. Once he could clearly see the objects, and the area around them, sudden realization struck him. "*Ahh*," he thought, "*now it all makes sense!*" The round mound was a pile of old slate shingles that had been removed from the roof. While the tall, square mound was a pallet of new shingles waiting to be installed. In addition, the 'pole' he had seen earlier was actually a heavy-duty roofer's ladder leaning against the eave. He nodded understandingly. "*A sturdy ladder would be necessary to support the weight of a man and a roofer's trough full of slate shingles he'd be carrying.*" His attention was suddenly drawn to the sound of moving feet.

As if by coordinated timing, both Details were exiting their structures simultaneously and reforming into their Section positions. Buckley and Gilbert continued to a spot between the Lieutenant and the front rank. They stopped one pace apart. Without a word, they smartly faced their OinC (Officer-in-Charge).

"Report," said Greene.

Buckley spoke first. "The office building is all secure, sir." Greene nodded. "The first office to the right is the superintendent's, sir. It is the largest and, by far, the best furnished."

"Thank, you, Sergeant," said Greene. He then looked at Gilbert.

The Corporal immediately spoke up. "The warehouse is all secure, sir." Greene nodded. "Plenty of room for the Detachment, sir. Nice and comfy dry, too. And there's even an old heating stove back by the rear wall, sir." He flashed his toothy grin in typical fashion.

"Thank, you, Corporal," said Greene with a suppressed smile. He pointed toward the ladder, "After dismissal, kindly assign several men to lower that ladder to the ground. In the event of a skirmish later, we don't need that sort of thing crashing down on us accidentally."

"Aye-Aye, sir. Certainly not, sir." Gilbert beamed with excitement at the thought of such a surprise happening.

Greene returned his attention to Buckley. "Sergeant, you

will kindly take two men and join Orderly Sergeant McDonough and the skirmishers. The honor of posting the first security watch is yours."

"Aye-Aye, sir. Thank you, sir." Buckley was all business. The Sergeant's twenty-four years in the Corps assured Greene that a tight watch would, indeed, be established.

"Very well, then," said Greene as he stretched to his full height. "Detachment," he whispered as strongly as he could, "Dismiss." Immediately, quiet salutes were made and returned. Buckley indicated for two men to follow him and departed. Gilbert ordered three men to handle the ladder. He then directed the remainder of Section A to follow him into the warehouse. Sections B and C would silently follow in proper turn.

Greene sought out Colonel Lee and found him standing behind the formation with his aide, Major Russell and the Musicians. The Marine OinC saluted the SOPIC (Senior Officer Present In Charge) and said, "Colonel, if you will follow me, sir, we have identified a suitable Head Quarters location."

CHAPTER EIGHT

"WAITING"

Tuesday, October 18, 1859, 1:30 a.m.

"Thank you, Baxter. That will do nicely." Greene was addressing the Fifer. The teenager's fire making skills were again being put to good use in the superintendent's office. He had a roaring blaze going in the fireplace.

Baxter threw on one last piece of wood and stood up at Attention. "Yes, sir," he said. "Will you require anything else, sir?"

Greene leaned close to the boy's shoulder and whispered, "You certainly might have another go around with the soap and water." He grinned. "You're showing a bad example to the Army." With a look and a nod, he directed the boy's attention to the Colonel sitting at the Armory executive's desk, conferring with his standing aide.

Baxter's teeth flashed bright white inside the uneven dark gray smudge covering most of his face. "Yes, sir, no more blackened face without proper cleaning articles." He turned slightly to hide his face. "I'll apply a good scrub right away, sir."

"Very well, lad," said Greene. "Carry On." Baxter hurriedly crabbed sideways out of the room to prevent the Colonel seeing his face. Greene struggled to suppress a smile.

Lee finished his conversation with Stuart, arose, and walked over to the fireplace. He stood before the flames for several minutes. He was absorbed in thought and absently made hand and arm movements to warm himself with the radiant heat.

In due course he snapped out of his reverie. "My apologies, gentlemen," he said sincerely. His arm stretched out in invitation. "Please, warm yourselves." He returned to the desk. Only Major Russell stepped toward the fireplace. The two Lieutenants moved to the front of the desk.

Lee looked around the room and assured himself that there were adequate chairs available. With a nod, he said, "Please, be seated." Everyone took a chair closest to his own position. All were quiet for two long minutes.

Slowly, Lee started. "Gentlemen, we appear to have a significant dilemma that may have even perplexed King Solomon." He shook his head. "We have an unknown enemy with an unknown purpose." He leaned back in the chair and paused for several more moments. "We only have three recognized pieces of information about these insurgents." He leaned forward again, propped his left elbow on the desktop and extended his thumb from his closed hand. "We have a fair approximation of how many initially started this raid." He next extended his index finger. "How many have been killed or captured." He extended his next finger. "And how many await us inside the 'fort'." He then retracted his fingers back into a clenched fist and dropped it down quietly onto the desktop. "What we need to know, is who their leader is and why is he doing what he's doing."

Lieutenant Stuart spoke to no one in particular. "Know thine enemy."

"Perhaps I can be of some assistance, Colonel," volunteered Russell. He rose from his chair and pulled at his lapel to retrieve the stash of previously referenced papers from his inside coat pocket.

"Yes, Major, please do," said Lee.

Russell shuffled through the papers. "Ahh, here we are," he said as he shifted the object of his search to the top. "Several townspeople who have seen the leader of this raid have identified him as a local resident, Isaac Smith." Russell looked up momentarily. "Apparently, he rented a farm about five miles north of here, sometime in July of this year." He double-checked his notes. "There are conflicting accounts as to whether he is a farmer planning to fatten stock for market or a prospector looking for minerals in the local hills." Russell looked up at his audience, again. "Whichever he is, everyone agrees that he pretty much kept to himself."

"Interesting," commented Lee. "A recent arrival with no clear presentation of what he does." He was about to make another comment when Russell continued.

"There is, however, Colonel, another identity that he has claimed in writing."

"In writing?" quizzed an amazed Lee.

Russell was encouraged by Lee's sudden reaction of interest. "Yes, Colonel," continued Russell with a twisted smile. "Around Six O'clock this evening, there was an exchange of messages between Colonel Baylor and the insurgent leader." He stood taller as he delivered this new tactical bombshell.

Lee leaned forward over the desk. "And you have information concerning those communiqués?"

"Better, still," smirked Russell. "I have the actual response the leader wrote!" Beaming with pride at his intelligence coup, he approached the desk and handed over the message to Lee. "This is his reply to Colonel Baylor's demand for surrender."

Lee accepted the piece of paper and read out loud for all to hear.

> "Captain John Brown answers
> In consideration for all my men, whether living or dead, or wounded, being soon safely in and delivered up to me at this point, with all their arms and ammunition, we will then take our prisoners and cross the Potomac Bridge, a little beyond which we will set them at liberty; after which we can negotiate about the Government property as may be best. Also we will require the delivery of our horse and harness at the hotel.
> John Brown"

Before Lee could put the note down, Stuart jumped up and remarked, "John Brown? Is this possibly the abolitionist from Kansas?" He looked around at the others. "Osawatomie Brown they call him."

"Quite possibly the same man," replied Russell. "He told his early captives of this raid that he was here to free all the Negroes in this State." He nodded his head. "According to what I've read in the newspapers, that's certainly the sort of abolitionist threat he is known for." The Major shrugged and said pretentiously, "Although Virginia is the largest slaveholding State in the Union, no one around here seems to know what the Kansas John Brown looks like."

Stuart took a heavy step toward Russell and jerked a pointed thumb back at his own chest. "I do!" he exclaimed and angrily stabbed a finger at the papers in Russell's hand. "Where's THAT in your precious notes?" He looked as though he was going to attack the Major.

Lee stolidly rose to his feet and extended a hand toward the chair Stuart had vacated. "Lieutenant," he directed, "please sit down, and calm yourself."

Stuart was frozen in place. His facial expression was one of disdain. Slowly he moved back and sat down in his chair, but did not settle back into it. He leaned forward toward the edge of Lee's desk. Excitement was dancing in his eyes.

Russell swallowed hard. With visible vacillation, he reluctantly sat down. He realized that he might have gone too far and had just been upstaged.

"My apologies, Major," said Lee flatly, "for the behavior of my young aide. His Virginian blood has undoubtedly been raised by the tension of these unusual events."

Russell looked quickly at the Lieutenant and then back at the Colonel. Within the blink of an eye, he realized that the Colonel was also referring to his own Virginian blood. Choosing not to further antagonize the SOPIC, Russell discreetly bowed his head and blinked his eyes as a sign of acceptance.

Lee regained his seat. "Now then, Lieutenant," he said warmly, "kindly relate to us how you know what this John Brown might look like."

"My apologies, sir," started Stuart. Lee nodded ever so slightly. "Well, sir, as you know," continued Stuart, "after graduation from West Point, I was posted to the First Cavalry at Fort Leavenworth, Kansas." He leaned back until he was sitting straight up. "I was under the command of Colonel 'Bull' Sumner."

"Bull??" Greene couldn't help himself. "Oh, excuse me," he pleaded. "That just slipped out of my mouth."

Stuart looked toward his Marine rank equivalent. "Unusual, yes," he agreed. "However, Lieutenant, I assure you it is a nickname of endearment. It refers to his booming voice on the parade field."

"Actually, gentlemen," interjected Lee, "the sobriquet was originally 'Bull Head'." He chuckled. "The story I remember from my Academy days was that a spent musket ball had bounced off of his head during a battle long ago." His audience smiled with amusement. Normally Lee would not have engaged in such gossip, however he thought the recent friction seemed to require it. He continued with proper decorum. "I should also tell you that the good Colonel has been in military service since Eighteen-Nineteen and possesses an outstanding record for performance and innovation." He looked back to his aide. "Please continue, Lieutenant."

"Yes, sir." Stuart leaned back into his chair. "Colonel Sumner was under orders from the President to break up any and all armed bands he could find in Southeastern Kansas." He thought for a few seconds. "Shortly after the Pottowatomie massacre in Fifty-Six, we found out that a band of Free-Soilers led by John Brown had attacked a force of Militia from Missouri at Black Jack Creek and had captured some of them." Stuart shifted in his chair. "We went out on patrol and soon came across their camp." He leaned forward and grasped the air. "In rapid order, we had that gang of cut-throats bottled up good and tight." He unclenched his hand and leaned back again. "After about an hour, Brown himself came out and tried to negotiate terms with Colonel Sumner." He shook his head. "That man haggled long and hard, but Colonel Sumner refused to bargain, as he said, 'with lawless and armed men'." He beamed with pride. "Finally, the Colonel ordered us into the camp." Stuart sliced the air with a forward thrust of his hand. "We charged in, freed the Militiamen, and dispersed Brown and his men." His hand concluded its fanning motion and descended to his lap.

"Do you believe you can identify Brown if you saw him again?" queried Lee.

"Yes, sir!" replied the energized Stuart. His face suddenly moderated as he explained. "I'll never forget his eyes." His voice took on a haunted tone. "They were cold steel gray in color, yet burned with rage at the same time." He paused several moments, nodded, and said with his usual confidence. "Absolutely, sir, I will know him when I see him."

"Excellent," said Lee. He picked up the insurgent's note again and reread it carefully to himself. "It appears that our Mister Brown has a propensity for being long winded and demanding as well." He nodded twice. "I agree with Colonel Sumner's refusal to bargain." He became very quiet and meditative.

"Excuse me," interrupted Russell. "With your permission, Colonel, I shall endeavor to discover if there are any additional details that the Militia commanders may have recently discovered and will possibly be relevant to dealing with John

Brown." He had risen and was anxious to return to the Wager House for his own reasons as well.

"Good idea, Major," said Lee absently, but then was struck by a pressing thought. Holding his hand up in a halt sign, he directed, "And, Major, please inspect the new strategic positions of the Militia. We must ensure that the commanders have adequately positioned their men outside of the Armory walls."

"Aye-Aye, Colonel," said Russell without conviction as he rushed out of the room before any additional requests could be made of him.

Lee smiled and said to his aide. "Lieutenant Stuart, will you kindly check to make sure that the saloons remain closed?"

"Yes, sir!" said Stuart with a wide grin. He jumped up and strode with pleasure to the door.

Greene stood up ramrod straight. "With your permission, sir, I would like to check on my men."

"Yes, of course," said Lee as he rose from his chair. "Dismiss."

Tuesday, October 18, 1859, 2:05 a.m.

The warehouse door suddenly swung open with a loud, grating groan. It rushed up against several crates, stopping with a dull thud and the clank of the pull ring against its metal mounting plate. The wind tumbled in with a whoosh, bringing with it a blast of vision obscuring rain and fog. Many of the veteran Marines jumped up with weapons at the ready, waiting to face a potential danger. Some of the more awake 'Fresh Fish' mimicked their actions.

Startled, Baxter strained to see who or what was at the door. His heart was pounding in his chest. The flickering firelight from the open stove door next to him added surrealistic lighting to the scene.

A bent over figure slowly drifted in through the doorway. It was tall, dark, and hooded. A shadowy opening in the limp shroud oscillated where a face should have been. The specter carried a long object by its right side with a seemingly curved, glinting blade at its end. Baxter whispered solemnly, "Death!"

A hand clapped Baxter on his left shoulder from behind.

The boy almost jumped out of his skin. "No lad, not quite," whispered Gilbert into Baxter's ear. He then shouted to the poised Marines. "STAND EASY! HE'S ONE OF US."

Almost in sync with Gilbert's shout, the specter raised its left arm and, with one deft movement, pushed back the hood. Instant recognition swept through the combat primed Marines. A few breathed sighs of relief. All relaxed and started to return to their previous positions of rest.

"Greenhalgh?" breathed Baxter. He was still frozen in position.

"Aye, lad," said Gilbert as he gently shook the young Musician. "None other than our own Private Greenhalgh." The Corporal was grinning broadly and shaking his head slightly. "A little devilish he might be, but 'Death' he is not."

"But...but," stammered Baxter, "wha...where'd the hood come from?" He was still frozen and staring at his specter.

"Oh, that," said Gilbert matter of factly. "You can make your own hood by first buttoning up your cape, and then flipping it up and over the back of your head." He nodded. "It's an old seagoing trick. We sometimes use the 'hood' to keep snow and rain from running down our necks when we don't have rubber slickers." He chuckled. "I always thought it made us look like monks."

As Gilbert spoke, Baxter watched the rest of the hooded watch standers file into the warehouse. He suddenly relaxed and grinned broadly. "You're right," he observed, "they do look like monks!" He signaled with his arm and called out, "Over here, fellows! There's room for you near the heating stove." Gilbert calmly held his hand up to further attract the attention of the 'monks'.

Tuesday, October 18, 1859, 2:30 a.m.

Just a few moments earlier, Greene had finished checking on the last of his posted men near the Armory's main gate. Now, standing at the Wager Hotel's front doorway, he was intent on not stopping to engage in conversation with any Militiamen inside. He opened the door quickly and made determined strides through the hotel toward the river. It turned out to be an easy task as only a few members of the Militia were standing about. They quickly and wordlessly stepped aside to let him pass.

Once outside, he proceeded to a location on the trestle near the water tower. He intended to observe the engine house from this elevated prospective. Unfortunately, the fog was starting to drift in heavier from the river and his view was obscured. Turning to continue toward the rear entrance of the Armory, he was stopped by a familiar voice coming from behind him.

"Lieutenant Greene, may I accompany you back into the Armory?" It was Stuart.

"Certainly, Lieutenant," replied Greene. Permission granted to come alongside." He indicated a position to his right. "Glad to have your company."

"Come alongside!" chuckled Stuart as he caught up with Greene. "A nautical phrase for 'Walk with me' I take it.

"Yes, something like that," grinned Greene in return. "I apologize for my use of Naval expressions. A force of habit that is not easily changed."

"Quite all right, sir," agreed Stuart. "I am sure that I, too, make occasional use of the unusual Cavalry expression as well."

They walked quietly for several paces. Unnoticed by either of them, they were 'in step' with one another. This manner of 'walking in unison' is a subconscious, yet reflexive, mannerism that is readily apparent when observing professional military men outside of a training environment.

Finally Greene spoke. "Pardon me for asking, Lieutenant, but can you tell me more of this Pottawatomie Massacre you mentioned earlier. I am afraid that I am not familiar with the event."

"Certainly, sir," replied Stuart. He laughed. "You were undoubtedly engaged in one of your great sea adventures when it occurred."

Greene laughed, too. "Yes, quite possibly."

"Well, sir," started Stuart, "in the latter part of May of Fifty-Six, the Free-Stater town of Lawrence, Kansas was ransacked by a band of pro-slavery ruffians. Although the attack was destructive," he flicked his outstretched hand waist high to the right, palm down, "it was bloodless...several buildings were burned and newspaper presses destroyed."

Greene nodded understanding and Stuart continued. "However, this act of opposition to a free-soil Kansas somehow gave the abolitionist Brown sufficient reason to retaliate with a vengeance."

"How so?" queried Greene.

"Two days after the Lawrence Raid, during the middle of the night, Brown, with four of his sons, a son-in-law, and two other followers, descended upon a small settlement on the banks of the muddy Pottawatomie Creek, which is about thirty miles South of Lawrence." Stuart raised his right hand with a pointed index finger. "Although the residents of this settlement were pro-slavery sympathizers," he wagged the finger back and forth slightly for emphasis of a denunciation, "none owned slaves, and, not one of them was known to have participated in the Lawrence raid." He lowered his hand as his voice suddenly changed to a reflective tone of dread. "It quickly became a night of unmoral terror." He became very quiet and stared at the wooden planking ahead of them.

"Go on," prodded Greene softly.

Stuart brushed away his personal thoughts and began reporting mechanically. "The worst of it is that five unarmed men were dragged a few yards from their cabin doors and summarily murdered in full view of their families." He looked up to Greene. "Supposedly, Brown started the killing himself by putting a pistol to the head of a farmer named Doyle and pulling the trigger." Stuart again looked back down at the planking. "The other men were brutally hacked into bloody pieces with short broadswords. They had been bound and couldn't defend themselves."

Greene was so stunned that he stopped walking. "Why were those men killed?" he asked incredulously.

Stuart shrugged his shoulders. "No obvious reasons." He signaled Greene to start walking again. "The investigation report revealed that the murdered men weren't all killed at the same time. It was also discovered that, in the course of the killings, Brown's mob had rousted other men from their homes as well. They were apparently bedeviled and threatened, but released."

Greene was still in a state of disbelief. "So the five killings weren't random?"

"Possibly not," postulated Stuart. He again shook his head. "No one understands Brown's actions that night. He is known to be a fervently religious man, perhaps even a zealot. He spouted scripture throughout the night, and often professed to be an instrument of God's wrath." He looked momentarily up toward the dark sky. "Maybe only God knows what Brown was in the hunt for, or possibly what he might have found to identify his victims." Sweeping his arm in front and away from himself, he continued. "All in all, Brown's leadership and moral judgment had debased to an extraordinarily low point." Stuart slammed his right fist into his left open hand. "It must have!" The fist ground into the palm. "How else could he have allowed and participated in such a demonstration of cruel and inhuman butchery?" He again used a pointed forefinger for emphasis. "Rest assured, my friend, as soon as the terror of this massacre became known, John Brown became a hunted outlaw." They continued on quietly for a while.

Greene reluctantly broke the silence. "How is it, then, that he is referred to as Osawatomie Brown rather than Pottawatomie Brown?"

Stuart assumed that he understood his companion's inquisitiveness. "I see," he said, "you strive to better 'know thine enemy' as well."

Greene almost whispered, "More or less."

"Well, sir," started Stuart in his familiar story telling manner, "Brown and several members of his family lived around the small settlement of Osawatomie, Kansas." He pointed off into the distance, "about twenty miles from the Missouri border." He nodded knowingly. "That area was also the operational Head Quarters of the Free-State forces." Greene nodded acceptingly. "In August of that same year, a heated battle took place between the Free-Staters and an assault group of pro-slavery Missourians." Stuart held out his left hand with all the fingers extended. "Five of Brown's men were killed, including one of his sons." The open hand dropped. "Although Osawatomie was burned to the ground, Brown's bellicose actions to defend the community earned him the nickname 'Osawatomie'." Stuart held up his hand again. This time only a couple of fingers were extended. "Two wagonloads of dead Missourians were collected from around his stronghold."

Greene nodded his head slightly, indicating that he understood the military implication of Stuart's last statement -- Brown had been in possession of Sharps rifles at Osawatomie.

After several moments of reflection, Greene bemused, "This Brown seems to be a man on opposite ends of the scale at the same time." He held out his left hand, "By one side he's reportedly a murdering extremist...a terrorist." He held out his right hand. "And by the other, he's heralded as a protecting hero...almost a saint."

"True," agreed a reluctant Stuart. "But based on his current actions here in Harper's Ferry, it appears that he is here as the former, but this time he is armed as the latter." He nodded pensively. "Indeed, a very dangerous man to contend with."

Greene nodded pensively, also. "Whatever his reasons or rationalizations for being here, he apparently believes that, to achieve his objectives, the end justifies the means...and that makes him doubly dangerous."

They finished their walk in silence. Each man strategically contemplated the opponent as well as the next day's possibilities and potential problems.

* * * * *

Baxter was seated on the floor of the warehouse. His upright knee functioned as a tabletop as he finished scribbling another line on a scrap of paper. As he looked up toward the warehouse wall, his eyes half closed, his head bobbed rhythmically, and his pencil hand swayed dreamily in the air. He stopped, silently mouthed several words, nodded approvingly, and again continued the bobbing and swaying.

"Fifer Baxter!" Gilbert maintained a somber face as the Musician startled out of his reverie and spun around on his knees to face him.

"Yes, Corporal?"

"What kind of skylarking are you so involved in as to neglect your duties as fireman?" Gilbert jerked a thumb toward the stove. Only a faint red glow emanated from inside its open door. "There's hot work to be done by all in the morning, but it's YOUR responsibility to keep everyone warm tonight." He leaned closer toward the lad. His right eye narrowed to a mere slit, as his 'evil' left one seemed to expand and bulge forward as its eyebrow rose formidably. His mouth pursed into a crooked sneer. He stabbed his finger at the Musician and hissed, "Or do you need extra instruction about keeping a tight watch?"

After a hard gulp, Baxter stammered, "N-no, Corporal!" He jumped to his feet. His two hands fumbled agitatedly to shove the paper and pencil into his trouser pockets. Dropping to his knees, again, he quickly dumped several pieces of broken wooden slats into the stove, feverishly blew on the coals enough to regain a flame, and then, after an initial misstep at obtaining traction, scurried off to retrieve more wood for the fire.

While other men near the stove laughed out loud at Baxter's plight, Gilbert did not. He didn't personally believe in the 'old school' of physical abuse or meaningless and laborious tasks for minor misconduct. He just figured that the occasional 'evil eye' or more traditional 'dressing down' was his best way of reminding a young subordinate of a Marine's two most important virtues -- his sense of duty and his word of honor. He shook his head. He thoroughly understood that everyone who undergoes Marine basic training is ultimately structured with the same ideals. He thought, *"It's good to know that only a few knot heads actually fail to understand or live by our fundamental code."*

He looked around at the men nearest him -- Quinn, Ruppert, Allen, and Greenhalgh. *"Not a bad apple in this bunch."* His customary wide grin returned. *"If these boys ever figure out that my bark is worse than my bite..."* He didn't finish the thought. He just pulled the cape of his greatcoat a little closer around him.

In between his trips in and out, Baxter stoked the heating stove amply to ensure it didn't burn down too far while he was out. He had managed to locate a stockpile of lightweight crates and pallets under the trestle behind the warehouse. The stack of wooden slats next to the stove had grown to an appreciable height. As he was breaking up another crate, he was approached by one of the Drummers.

"I've been sent by Corporal Gilbert to relieve you as fireman." The boy spoke as he rubbed the sleep from his eyes.

Baxter pointed at the supply of crates. "I've been propping them up and jumping on them to break them apart." The

Drummer looked around and nodded. "And, don't allow the fire to burn down too low," he warned. Again the Drummer nodded.

Baxter picked up an armful of wooden slats and headed toward the warehouse entrance. After he had added his last load to the pile of firewood, he stood before Corporal Gilbert and reported, "I have been properly relieved as fireman by Drummer Schultz, Corporal."

"Very well, Baxter." Gilbert smiled and nodded his approval. "You may join your shipmates."

The Musician picked up his greatcoat and moved to the side of the stove opposite the woodpile. He plopped down near Quinn and Allen. His mood was doleful.

In an effort to cheer him up, Quinn said, "So, Fifer. What was it you were writing on so hard?"

"Oh, just some words to a tune." Baxter was barely auditable.

"Well, now," quipped Quinn cheerily, "would those be new words for an old tune, or old words for a new tune?"

Baxter turned to look squarely at Quinn. "What?"

"All I heard," remarked Quinn, "was 'words' and 'tune'. You'll have to say again all around 'mumble'." His smile was broad and fetching.

Baxter half smiled in return. He leaned back and withdrew the scrap of paper from his pocket. As he straightened out the crumpled page, he said, "I was working on some new lyrics to the tune of 'Dixie'."

"You mean the catchy little ditty about the 'Land of Cotton'?" Quinn's interest was genuine.

"Yes, that's the one!" The Musician's melancholy was quickly forgotten. "Only my lyrics are about the Fresh Fish when they first report for training."

Allen's curiosity was peaked. "Now those I'd like to hear."

"As would I," piped in Ruppert.

Baxter quickly cleared his fife from its sheath. "Do you remember this?" So as not to disturb others, he played very softly. Tat Da Dut Dut Dadle Da Da Tut Dot Da Daa. The three men all nodded. "Well, then, here's the first verse." He leaned closer to the trio. He was a little nervous.

"Oh, when they first join up, their clothes are sodden.

Some do stink, but others smell rotten." He waved both hands in a shooing motion. "Get away! Get away! Get away! You stinky Fish." The members of the trio grinned.

"So, we'll get some soap, and we'll get some water. Then they'll bathe, like we know they oughter." He waggled his index finger in a 'draw near' sign. "Come this way! Come this way! Come this way!" His listeners joined in. "You stinky Fish." Baxter beamed, "There you go." His excitement could hardly be contained.

"Now the chorus." His hands began swaying as though he was directing a choir.

"Oh, I'm glad I'm in the U S M! Today! Today! In the USM we've made our pledge, to live and die in glory. Away, away, away at sea forever." He started to wave his right hand in a 'goodbye' sign. "Away, away, away at sea forever." By the time he had gotten to second 'away', his audience was chiming in.

"All right, now. The second verse." Baxter held up an oscillating hand. "But I warn you, this one still needs a little work." The trio pleaded with 'come on' signals.

"Well, we'll brush them down, till they're bright 'n pink. That's how we know, that they won't stink." His moved his hand back and forth across his opposite forearm. "Scrub away! Scrub away! Scrub Away! The stinky Fish."

Ruppert reflexively yelped, "OW!" and rubbed his own forearm as though a bad memory had surfaced.

"Soon, we'll take their clothes, and burn them proper. Give 'um a uniform and a brand new topper." He adjusted his cap evenly on his head. "Squared away! Squared away! Squared away!" Next he held up a 'hold it' sign as the trio prepared to chime in again. "The Privates Fish." Baxter grinned widely as his audience laughed at the unexpected change is the fish status.

"Ho, ho," huffed Gilbert as he stepped to the edge of their little ring. "Well done, lad. Well done, indeed." He patted the Musician gently on the shoulder. "As much as we'd all like to hear more." He looked around at each man. "I'm going to recommend, instead, that we all try to get a little shut eye. Reveille will be coming soon enough, and you've all had a tolerably busy day as it is." His tone softened as he patted

Baxter on the shoulder again. "The entire Detachment will enjoy the whole of your little tune on the train ride back." The lad returned the Corporal's warm smile, lowered himself to the floor, and wrapped up in his greatcoat. Within moments he was deep into the sleep if the innocent.

Tuesday, October 18, 1859, 2:45 a.m.

As Greene and Stuart entered the 'Head Quarters' office, they found Lee standing in front of the fire. He turned to greet them. "Ah, gentlemen. It is good to see you again." He motioned to the chairs near the fireplace. "Lieutenant Greene, please warm yourself while I borrow Lieutenant Stuart for a few moments." He indicated the desk to Stuart and both men headed toward it.

Greene removed his boat cloak and draped it over the back of the chair farthest from the desk. He stood in front of the fire and extended his hands. The warmth was a welcome relief from the cold, misty rain and fog outside. As the skin stopped stinging and his fingers began functioning properly, he mused, *"I shall definitely retrieve my gloves from my valise before sailing into this weather again."*

He eased himself into the chair and extended his brogans toward the fire. *"And after these soles dry out a bit, I shall also retrieve a fresh pair of socks."* He smiled to himself at the thought of the warm woolen threads snuggling around his toes. He shook his head slightly. *"Ahh, the simplest of things can add so much to the quality of life when out of home port."*

The two Army officers concluded their conference at the desk. The junior officer departed the room and the senior approached the fire. Before Greene could rise from his chair, Lee gestured for him to remain seated.

"I beg your pardon," began Lee as he eased himself into the other chair. "I hope you do not anticipate that the Army is conspiring against you." He was genial in nature.

"No, sir. Not in the least," responded Greene.

"Excellent," smiled Lee. He was sitting upright in the chair with his left leg crossed over his right knee. "While you were both out, I had written a surrender demand for the insurgents in the 'fort'." Greene nodded. "I have asked Lieutenant Stuart to deliver that message to their leader at first light." He was reflective. "It will be a great deal simpler if they resign the 'fort' without a fight."

"Aye, sir. A great deal simpler," agreed Greene in return.

Suddenly breaking from his abstraction, Lee turned to Greene, smiled, and thumped the chair arm lightly. It was a clear indication that he wanted to change the mood of the early morning hours. "Tell me, Lieutenant," he started with unexpected animation, "is there a difference between your service's use of one eye and two eyes?" He pointed vaguely to his right eye.

Greene was bewildered at first, but then realized what the Colonel was referring to. "Oh," he said. "Uh...,yes, sir, there is." He sat forward and leaned closer. In a soft tone he continued. "The word we use, sir, is 'aye', spelled A..Y..E." He paused until Lee nodded for him to go on. "It actually has two meanings." He held up one finger. "When one 'aye' is used, as in 'Aye, sir' it is a reply of concurrence to a question or statement, much like 'Yes, sir, I agree, sir'." He next held up two fingers. "When two 'ayes' are used, it is in response to an order or command. The man receiving the order is acknowledging the order. By saying 'Aye-Aye, sir' the junior is informing his senior of two things: 'I understand the order and I will obey the order'." Greene held out both palms with a slight shrug. "It is a means of abbreviated but concise communication, much the same as our use of signal flags." He looked carefully at the Colonel for comprehension.

"Ahhhh," said Lee slowly. "Thank you, Lieutenant. Your explanation has been most instructive."

"My pleasure, sir," replied Greene with relief as he sat back in his chair.

Several quiet minutes passed before Greene leaned forward again. "Excuse me, Colonel," he said cautiously, "but may I ask a question?"

"Certainly, Lieutenant." Lee's manner remained genial.

"Well, sir," began Greene tentatively. "When we first surveyed the engine house up close, an immediate attack was planned." He paused, indicating that a potentially touchy subject was forthcoming. Lee simultaneously blinked and nodded slowly to authorize continuance. Greene did so.

"I was wondering, sir," he hesitated slightly, hoping that he was not overstepping his bounds. "That is, sir..." He wanted to get this over with quickly, so he braced up within and pushed on. "Concerning the hostages in the engine house, sir. We know how many and I assume the Militia commanders provided some of their names." He swallowed hard. "Who..."

It had become obvious to the senior officer that the junior officer wanted to know why he had changed his mind about attacking the darkened 'fort'. Fortunately, as Stuart had likewise reported to him, Lee was beginning to take a liking to the tenacious Marine officer and decided to let him off the hook.

"It's quite all right, Lieutenant," he smiled, "you're not going to step on your sword." Lee had used a figurative expression depicting a walking or marching officer whose legs become entangled with the sword scabbard hanging from his sword belt and, as a result, falls humiliatingly on his face. It is actually a military euphemism for literally doing oneself irreparable damage to reputation and career.

Greene felt a heavy weight lift from his shoulders. "Thank you, sir."

"It appears," continued Lee, "that the most prestigious hostage in the 'fort' is none other than Colonel Lewis Washington. He's..."

"The great grandnephew of George Washington!" blurted out Greene. "I know him!"

Lee was taken aback. "You know Colonel Washington?"

"Yes, sir." Greene expounded, "I've actually been to his home on several social occasions."

"Indeed." Lee was still incredulous.

"Why, Colonel," sputtered Greene with the exuberance of a Navy Midshipman, "on my last visit to Beall-Air, I actually held the pistol presented to General Washington by the Marquis de Lafayette, and...and even the sword presented by the Prussian King, Frederick the Great!"

Lee smiled broadly. It was one thing to possibly know about Colonel Washington's possession of these items, but to be enthusiastically energized by having actually held them...that was exactly how Lee had felt, too. "I guess you do know the good Colonel Washington." He nodded acceptance.

"Oh, yes, sir!" Greene's face beamed with assurance. "I can see why we're waiting until morning. It's important to safeguard the lineage and history of our first President. Kind of like protecting the American aristocracy."

"Well, actually Lieutenant," cautioned Lee softly. "It's a little different than that."

It was Greene's turn to be taken aback. "Sir?"

"There is a familial connection between my house and the house of Colonel Washington." Lee wasn't bragging. He was merely providing information.

"And how, sir, are the two of you related?" Greene was indeed curious.

"Actually it is a circumstance of marriage," continued Lee. "My wife, Mary, is the great granddaughter of Martha Washington." He quickly interjected, "Something we don't make a great ado about, of course." Greene nodded and Lee continued, "and Colonel Washington is the great grandson of Charles Washington, General Washington's younger brother." What he did not mentioned was that his father, 'Light Horse Harry' Lee, had been a close friend of George Washington's.

Greene tried some quick mental calculations. "I approximate that would make your wife and the Colonel something like third or fourth cousins, then."

"I believe third is correct," stated Lee without emotion. "A distant relation, but nevertheless a relation." He closed his eyes and thought, *"I fear the fatigue of this long day has lowered my usual defenses."* He reopened them and gave Greene a serious look. "I would appreciate it if you would keep this information to yourself."

"Absolutely, sir," replied Greene in a hushed tone. "My word of honor."

"Thank you, Lieutenant." Lee adjusted himself in his chair so as to look more directly at Greene. "Please tell me, then, how is it that you know Colonel Washington."

"As in your case, sir, it is a circumstance of marriage." Both men smiled. "My wife, Edmonia, is the daughter of a Doctor Samuel Taylor." Greene now adjusted himself in his chair. "My father-in-law initiated his medical training with an established doctor in Alexandria, a Doctor Craik, who," he pointed upward, "it turns out, was the personal physician of the Washington family at Mount Vernon."

"Ah!" exclaimed Lee. "It is indeed a small world after all."

"Yes, indeed" agreed Greene as he moved to the fireplace to add another piece of wood to the faltering flames. Sitting back down, he continued, "Following the completion of his formal medical education, my father-in-law relocated to Berryville, Virginia," he pointed over his left shoulder, "about twenty miles South of here. He has maintained social contact with Colonel Washington and others in his family over the years." The good Colonel had purchased his own home from the Beall estate near Halltown, not five miles west of Harper's Ferry.

After several moments, Greene queried, "I've often wondered how Colonel Washington acquired his rank?"

"Colonel Washington was initially awarded his military title by President Jackson, and again by the Governor of Maryland. Both times because he was a distinguished member of their political support staffs." Again Lee was being matter of fact. He chuckled, "I sometimes think that way is much harder than on the drill field or battle ground."

Realizing his defense was again slipping, Lee quickly changed the subject. "So, tell me, Lieutenant, what of your own lineage?" True to the military adage that the best defense is a good offense, he would now rely on asking the questions rather than answering potentially revealing ones himself.

"Well, sir," began Greene, "on my father's side of the family, I guess the only notable in our family tree is Major General Nathanael Greene."

"You mean General Washington's Quartermaster General?" asked Lee.

"Yes, sir, he's the one." Greene stared at the fire as he thought. "Let's see, now." With his left hand, he deliberately counted upward across the tips of his fingers with his thumb. Then pointing toward the ceiling, he said, "If you go up my family tree five generations above me," he drew a small horizontal line in the air with his finger, "shift over to my ancestor's brother," he then represented a line toward the floor, "and come down three generations," you will be at General Greene." He smiled widely. "Sorry, Colonel, other than that I couldn't begin to describe the familial relationship."

Lee smiled. "Quite all right, Lieutenant, I get the picture. It appears that General Greene was in the same generation as your grandfather." He thought for a second then laughed. "It is fittingly ironic that your grandfather and General Greene were third cousins as well."

Greene shook his head. "Well, I'll be. Isn't that interesting?" He smiled. "My grandfather's first name is the same as mine, Israel." Lee nodded and smiled at this new information.

"Any notables on your mother's side of the family?" Lee was again on the defense.

"Well, sort of," replied Greene. "Her maiden name was Platt. Her father, my grandfather, founded Plattsburgh, New York." He grinned. "That's where I was born."

"Were you raised there as well?" asked Lee.

"No, sir," answered Greene. My parents soon moved to Wisconsin where my father helped establish a little community along a long, narrow bay on Lake Michigan." Childhood memories flooded past his mind's eye. "On a map, the lake sort of looks like a mitten hanging finger pocket down, and the bay is a thumb sticking out from it on the top left."

Having never learned anything about Lake Michigan, Lee had a little trouble imagining the image. He just nodded and did not respond. Both men stared at the fire as the moment passed.

Finally Greene continued. "I guess the only other notable in my family is on my wife's side."

"A relation of your father-in-law's?" pressed Lee.

"Not directly, sir." Greene held out his two hands with their palms facing each other. "My wife's younger sister," he shook his left hand, "is married to Edward Marshall." He shook his right hand. "Edward Marshall is the grandson of Chief Justice John Marshall." He rested his hands on the arms of the chair.

Both of Lee's eyebrows rose involuntarily when he heard this last bit of information. "Fascinating," passed his lips before he could recover himself. Embarrassed by his own reaction, Lee fished out his pocket watch and said, "Lieutenant, I am most impressed with your ancestry. You have a fine family tree to be proud of." He stood up from the chair. "I thank you very much for your candor and sociability." He paused, "but," he bowed slightly to the junior officer, "if you will excuse me, I have a few more things to contemplate regarding our daylight activities."

Greene had also risen when Lee had. "Thank you, sir." He bowed slightly in return. "I apologize if my babblings have detained you from your duties."

"Quite the contrary, Lieutenant, I am most grateful to have been able to relax my mind with such pleasant conversation." He patted Greene lightly on the upper arm and slowly turned toward the desk.

Greene waited until Lee was seated at the desk before he stoked up the fireplace with more wood. As he did so, he, too, started to contemplate the coming daylight activities.

* * * * *

Allen gently shook Quinn's shoulder and whispered, "Luke, are you awake?"

Quinn pushed his cap up from his eyes. "I am now," he whispered back jovially and rolled on his side to face his friend. When he saw the expression on Allen's face, he asked, "What's up?"

"I'm not really sure," began Allen, "I just feel rather strange and can't quite tell you why."

"Are you ill?" queried Quinn as he propped himself up on his elbow.

Allen paused briefly and stared blankly downward as he mentally checked his physical well-being. He looked back at Quinn. "No, I don't think so." He shrugged. "I just feel rather queer...unsettled."

"Well," reminded Quinn, "I did say you were looking a little peaked earlier."

"No, this is different," he countered as he shook his head. "I was peaked then," he whisked his hand in front of his face as if trying to wipe the thought away, "because I threw up when I saw something bad during the reconnoiter."

"You were rather gloomy about whatever that 'something bad' was." Quinn popped the cork from his canteen and took a swallow of water. "Maybe, if you tell me about it, you'll strike upon what's bothering you now." He offered the canteen to Allen.

Allen pondered ruefully as he took a sip of water and handed the canteen back. His thoughts began to verbalize slowly. "I've seen death in the mines." He idly played with one of the buttons on his greatcoat. "Down in the hole, death by accident happens often enough. It could be a result of nature against man," he paused, "or machine against man." He unconsciously tugged at the button. "But, today, I saw death caused by man against man." The thread holding the button suddenly popped due to his tight strain. The release startled Allen and his eyes stared dumbly at the button in his hand. His mind raced.

Struck by a sudden realization, he closed his hand around the button and shook his fist toward Quinn. "No!" he hissed. "What I saw today went beyond man against man warfare." He shook his head. "What I saw today was the senseless and wanton mutilation of a dead man for no other reason than his color." He shook his fist again. "That's wrong! Absolutely wrong!" He smashed his fist into his other palm. "This abusive slavery must be stopped!"

Quinn reached up and gently grasped Allen's fist. "Easy, Bal," he soothed. "You clearly saw a pretty gruesome sight today, but you're working up a heavy lather about something that was well beyond your control." He patted the fist with his other hand. "You've got to settle down." He waited several seconds before continuing. "It's okay to be angry. Slavery angers a lot of people. But you can't be so blinded by your anger that you go off half-cocked or fret yourself into knots." Slowly as Allen's grip on the button relaxed, so did his whole body. Quinn let go of Allen's hand.

Allen's eyes bespoke internal anguish. "Are you saying that fighting the inhuman wrongs of slavery is above our station in life?"

Quinn shook his head slightly. "No, what I'm saying is that you had your first encounter with the evils of slavery, today." He pointed at Allen's chest, "But YOU can't fix something that is so badly broken." He leaned closer. "Just maybe, when the right time comes, you WILL be able to prevent some bad things from happening around you...like you want to."

"Personal victories, but not the big problem, huh?" questioned Allen. "Some things I can affect the outcome of, and some things I can't. Is that what you mean?"

"Aye." Quinn unexpectedly sat up and crossed his legs Indian style in front of himself. "And I have an example of what NOT to do." He thumbed in the direction of the engine house. "Take those insurgents over there." Allen's eyes followed the movement. "From what I can gather, those fellows are supposedly fighting to free the slaves. They're attacking the big problem, right?" He held his hands out wide. "A magnificently noble idea," he retracted his arms and shook his head, "but if you ask me, they've gone about it all wrong."

"How's that?" asked Allen.

Quinn held out one finger. "Well, for one thing, they attack here where there aren't a great many slaves." He held out two fingers. "For another thing, the first person killed was a free Negro." He closed both hands together tightly. "And finally, they've gotten themselves trapped in a box." He then opened his hands, held them out and shrugged his shoulders. "They kind of got off to a bad start, wouldn't you say?" Allen nodded an affirmative.

Quinn spun his cap around in his hand by its sweatband. "No, Bal, as I figure it, one man, or a small group of men, can't fix the big problem." He prophesied, "It's going to take a much larger fracas than this one to change half of this country's mind about slavery."

"And what makes you so sure about that?" challenged Allen.

"Ah, lad, have you forgotten that I'm from Ireland?" joked Quinn as he tossed his cap at Allen's chest.

"No," replied Allen sheepishly as he flipped the cap back.

"Then it's Irish history that you know nothing about!" Quinn admonished his friend with a waggle of his pointing forefinger. "The Irish have been 'hit and run' fighting the English seemingly forever. They want to rid their Emerald Isle of the overbearing Protestant landlords and their brand of 'land slavery'." He shook his head. "But sadly, the undersized Irish tactics haven't worked to achieve their grand desires...and probably never will."

Before Allen could speak, "And it's quite clear," he thumbed outward again, "that the undersized tactics of those insurgents haven't worked either." He pursed his lips and shook his head to indicate a serious negative. "No, I'm sure of it." He kicked his legs out and repositioned to lean on his arm again. "It's going to take a really great effort to end slavery in this country."

Allen thought for a long while before he spoke again. "I guess even the Bible speaks about the oppressions of the strong over the weak in many different books." He nodded with revelation. "And it finally took God's angel of death and the parting of the Red Sea to release the enslaved Hebrews from Egypt."

"Well now, if THAT was the case, there," interjected Quinn, "then about the best that you and I can do, here," he pointed down toward the space between them, "is make sure that we do our duty and do it honorably."

He reached out and grabbed Allen on the arm. "You're going to see different kinds of abuse as time goes on, Bal." He shook Allen's arm slightly. "You've got to learn to honestly recognize when your efforts or arguments can change something and when they can't." He released his grip and admonished, "But don't be afraid to speak up when you should, either. Silence is as bad as inaction." Allen nodded understanding.

"Now remember," Quinn held out a pointed index finger, "there are too many big problems going on out there for you to be battling or getting upset about." He winked. "So, as in all things in life, take satisfaction and pride in the victories you can accomplish," he held his thumb and forefinger close together, "in the wee bit of world around you."

Allen said hesitantly, "Do our duty and do it honorably."

"That's all the Marines have asked of us." Quinn smiled knowingly. He lay back down as his friend continued to mull over things for a while.

Allen was quiet for another long time. Finally he spoke. "Luke?"

Quinn replied through the cap covering his face. "Yes."

"Thanks. I feel much better, now." He grinned and poked his friend. "Say, how did you get to be so smart for your age?"

Quinn raised the cap up slightly and said, "Simple, Fish. I've been a Marine for four years." He let the cap drop back over his face. They both started to snicker.

"Pipe down, you two." hissed Gilbert. "And get some rest!"

With the exception of the occasional crackle in the wood stove, silence enveloped the room. Without looking around, the veteran Corporal instinctively knew that many eyes were still open and many different thoughts were still being sorted out.

Tuesday, October 18, 1859, 4:45 a.m.

The unmistakable sound of a musket butt thumping twice on the doorjamb brought Greene to his feet. He quickly moved toward the office door.

Lee leaned forward from his chair behind the desk. "Is there a problem?" he asked.

"No, sir," replied Greene. "The sentry outside has merely signaled that someone friendly is approaching."

"Oh?" Lee was puzzled.

"Yes, sir," explained Greene, "it is a courtesy gesture used by Marines at sea to advise the Captain of a ship that he is about to have a visitor."

"Most ingenious," stated Lee as he, too, rose to his feet. "You never let your commander be caught off guard while he's billeted."

There were two quick taps on the door before it began to slowly open. Several sets of footsteps could also be heard continuing down the hallway.

Orderly Sergeant McDonough's smiling face entered the room. He held a tin cup of steaming liquid in each hand. He looked first to Greene who was closest. "Good morning, Lieutenant." Then to Lee, "Good morning, Colonel." He handed each man a cup as he greeted him. "I thought you might like some coffee, sirs."

"Thank you, Orderly Sergeant," beamed Lee. "That is most kind of you." He blew the steam away and sipped gingerly.

As an announcement to both officers, McDonough said, "I

have taken the liberty, sirs, to persuade the hotel owner to provide some hot water, basin and towels." Footsteps were now heard returning from the far end of the hall. "They have been set up in the next office down the hall." He pointed toward the back of the building.

Greene turned to Lee. "Colonel, please accept the loan of my razor." He half pointed toward his valise. "I expect that you were unable to bring any personal equipment with you."

"Thank you, Lieutenant." He felt the stubble on his chin. "A wash and a shave would do wonders to improve my well-traveled appearance." He was smiling.

Greene fished out a small canvas bag containing his shaving gear and presented it to Lee. As the Colonel withdrew to the rear office, Greene whispered to McDonough, "XO, please see what you can do about having someone brush out the Colonel's coat. It should be dry enough now that the cinders from the engine smoke can be removed."

"Aye-Aye, Skipper," grinned McDonough as he followed after Lee. "He'll soon be as squared away as we can make him."

Greene walked to the entrance of the office building and peered outside. It was still dark. The false dawn had yet to start. The rain had stopped. However, the air was heavy with the mist of the river fog. *"Cool and damp,"* he thought. *"Easier to concentrate in this weather than in hot and humid. The chill sharpens the senses."*

Ten minutes passed before Lee returned to the office. "I apologize for appearing before you without my coat, Lieutenant." He set an empty tin cup and Greene's 'ditty' bag on the corner of the desk. "Your Orderly Sergeant McDonough has assured me that he will return it posthaste." Lee felt embarrassed. A gentleman was considered to be undressed if he was exposing his shirtsleeves.

He rubbed his chin briefly. "And I most certainly thank you for the loan of your personal gear." He placed his hand on his stomach. "All I would need now to be in top form would be some jerky and trail bread."

"I believe we can do a little better than that, Colonel." Corporal Gilbert was standing in the office doorway. He was carrying a couple of plates of food on a two-foot piece of board.

"Cooked salt pork, sir, sliced thin, and hard bread soaked in warm gravy." He was solid grin from ear to ear. He placed his cargo on the desk and signaled a Private behind him to enter. "More coffee, Colonel?" he asked.

Tuesday, October 18, 1859, 5:20 a.m.

Greene had finished his morning toilet, changed his shirt and socks, and was about to return to the front office when McDonough entered the room. "How are the men doing, XO?" he queried as he slipped into his frock coat.

"The posted sentries are all secure, Skipper." He shook his head minutely. "Nary a sound or movement detected in the engine house all night." He smiled. "Quiet as any church on Monday." He gestured toward the warehouse. "The remainder of the Detachment is well rested, completing their morning meal, and will be ready to fall out in about fifteen minutes." He paused. "Or sooner, if necessary."

Greene retrieved his watch from his pocket and checked it. "No, sooner won't be necessary." He closed and replaced the timepiece. "Dawn won't be for another hour and a quarter. We'll fall in at Five-Forty-Five as originally planned."

"Anything else, Skipper?" asked McDonough.

"Yes," began Greene meditatively, "With all of this rain and fog, the possibility of rust is very good. I think it would be a good idea that each and every cap cone be replaced with a spare from the cartridge boxes." The cap cones screws into an area near the bottom of the barrel called the breech. The fulminate of mercury cap fits onto the cone. When the hammer strikes the cap, a small explosion occurs and the resultant blast of heat and flame channels down the hole through the center of the cone into the breech area. The hole is of such a size that just the smallest buildup of rust could prevent the desired effect. "In addition," he continued, "each breech should be picked to ensure that the powder has not caked." A screw on the side of the cone mount allows a pinhole access to the powder in the breech. By pushing a sharp needle pick into this hole, the powder can be loosened. Loose powder is more likely to flash to its explosive capability when exposed to the detonation of the cap. "It may be necessary," he cautioned, "to have the Section Sergeants assist the new men with this procedure."

* * * * *

"Luke?" queried Allen as he fished out a 'housewife' from his knapsack. "Is it possible to feel excitement and fear at the same time?" He opened the sewing kit and picked out one of the larger needles.

"You're not worrying about the big problem, again. Are you?" shot back Quinn.

"No," said Allen. "I feel excited by all the events that have happened so far." He searched through his supply of available threads. "And certainly excited about what might happen this morning." He picked out the thickest and longest one. "At the same time, I'm also fearful." He paused as he attempted to pass the thread through the eye of the needle. Once he got the thread started, he continued. "Fearful of not doing something right," he pulled the thread through the eye, "you know...messing up and doing something stupid." He matched the two ends of the thread, tied a quick knot, then whispered, "And maybe even a little fearful about getting hurt."

Quinn gave his friend a light shove. "Fish," he laughed, "what you've got is called the 'jitters'." Allen pierced the greatcoat with the needle. "Everyone gets them before going into action. You wouldn't be normal if you didn't."

Allen pulled the thread through the material and stopped. "What's it like...facing an armed opponent?"

"You mean the thrill of action?" asked Quinn.

Allen nodded as he passed the needle through the metal loop on the back of the button. "I guess so," he speculated as he let the button drop down the thread to the material.

"Well now," evoked Quinn, "when things are going hot and heavy." He held his hands up as though carrying a musket across his chest. "And you're in the middle of it all." He thrust his imaginary musket outward. "You get such a feeling of super strength, it's unbelievable!"

Quinn was becoming so animated that Allen stopped his sewing. "Your heart pounds!" He grabbed his chest. "Your head pounds!" He placed his hands on either side of his head.

"Your eyes move so fast, everything seems to be at half speed." His hand made a slow oscillating motion across the air in front of him. "You feel like you could move mountains!" He flexed his bicep, then collapsed backwards. "And when it's all over," he propped up on his arm, "you're as weak as a kitten for quite a while."

"Does everyone feel all of that?" asked Allen seriously.

"Can't rightly say," replied Quinn as he sat back up, "but that's how I've felt the few times I've been in harm's way."

"I...I'll let you know if anything like that happens to me, today." Allen tried to concentrate on his sewing as he made several more passes through the loop and material with the needle. His mind nevertheless wrestled with the uncertainty of his 'jitters'.

"ALL RIGHT, KIT UP!" bawled Orderly Sergeant Mundell. "NO HAVERSACKS OR KNAPSACKS!" He waited a few seconds. "WEAPONS INSPECTION IN FIVE MINUTES."

CHAPTER NINE

"ACTION"

Tuesday, October 18, 1859, 5:45 a.m.

Orderly Sergeant Mundell signaled Sergeant Buckley and Corporal Gilbert to join him outside. Once there, he instructed, "Place yourselves in such positions so as to create a line facing the Armory gates. Sergeant," he pointed away from the gates, "the end of this warehouse." He pointed across the compound to the structure opposite them. "And, Corporal, the far end of the 'Head Quarters' building." Both men nodded. "We shall form up on you."

As the two men walked to their posts, Mundell opened the warehouse door and took a step back toward the Armory gate. "MARINE DETACHMENT." He sang. "FALLLL IN." He directed the first man out toward the assembly area with a quick movement of his eyes. The rest followed without prompting.

Silently, and with the minimum of commotion, each Section fell into its proper position. Every man automatically aligned himself with his file partners. They all stood ramrod straight with their weapons along their right sides in the Order Arms position.

As the Orderly Sergeant slowly walked to his place in front of the formation, he could hear a few cheers and whistles, as well as some complimentary remarks, coming from outside the Armory walls. Mundell thought to himself, *"You should marvel at this, you Militia rabble. One command and my boys are parade perfect."*

He stopped at the appropriate position and surveyed the front line. His broad smile told every man before him that they had done well. "SHOULDER, ARMS." He executed a smart Right About Turn.

Greene and McDonough stepped out of the office doorway and headed toward Mundell. When they were within six paces, Mundell ordered, "PRESENNNT, ARMS." The Commanding Officer came to a stop before the Orderly Sergeant. Mundell saluted and reported, "Detachment all present, sir." When Greene finished his return salute, Mundell sang, "SHOULDERRR, ARMS." He was about to give the next command when the Lieutenant unexpectedly looked left, then right, as if he were checking something.

Greene was surveying the muzzles of the muskets as they

stuck up above everyone's heads. "Good," he said, "I see that the tompions have been used." He was referring to a uniquely shaped wooden 'plug' that could be inserted into the end of the barrel to prevent moisture from collecting on the inside of the barrel and saturating the powder in the breech. "Carry on, Orderly Sergeant."

"ORDERRRRR, ARMS." The sounds of the hands smacking the upper stocks in unison and the following single dull thud of the musket butts striking the ground resonated throughout the whole compound. Again "Ohh's" and "Ahh's" could be heard from outside the walls.

"Please open ranks for inspection, Orderly Sergeant," said Greene calmly.

Mundell executed a Right About Turn. He inhaled deeply. "TO THE REAR IN OPEN ORDER." A slight pause while the Sergeants and Corporals from Sections B and C stepped backward their respective preparatory paces. "OPEN RANKS." He measured a quiet two count. "MARCH."

At 'March', Section A, the front rank, stood fast. Sections B and C all took one pace backward. Section B stopped while Section C continued one more pace backward.

When each man stopped he checked to his left to align on his Sergeant and to his right on his Corporal. The only sounds made were the scrunch of boots and the light tap of musket butts on the macadam surface.

Mundell turned about again and reported to Greene. "Detachment standing by for inspection, sir."

Greene proceeded to Sergeant Buckley. "Are your men prepared, Sergeant?" he asked when he stopped in front of the Section Leader.

"Aye, sir," reported Buckley, "In all respects."

Greene turned and passed down the line. He checked each man from toe to head. He briefly looked into every man's eyes before he continued on to the next man. Each Marine met his gaze. No one faltered. Everyone was resolute.

When finished with Section A, Greene proceeded through the other sections the same way. Section C was the smallest because of its ten men still on sentry duty. Satisfied that his men were prepared mentally as well as militarily, the Marine Officer-in-Charge returned to his position in front of the formation.

Mundell stepped forward and commanded, "Close Ranks, March." The Detachment contracted to its original formation. "In Place, Rest."

Tuesday, October 18, 1859, 6:00 a.m.

When Lee exited the office building, he paused momentarily to observe the weather above him. Seemingly satisfied, he walked several paces and stopped on the flagstone sidewalk. He looked toward the Marine Detachment and nodded. It was a prearranged signal for Greene to join him.

Greene stopped before the senior officer and saluted. "United States Marine Detachment standing by for orders, Colonel."

Lee bowed slightly. "Thank you, Lieutenant." He pointed toward the entrance of the compound. "Please join me for a stroll to the Armory gates."

The pair crossed over to the warehouse. As they turned right to proceed to the gate, Greene positioned himself between the Colonel and the 'fort'. In step, they walked purposefully, yet calmly. Neither man looked toward the engine house. If anyone in the 'fort' was watching, there was no indication of it.

As they neared the gate, comments could be clearly heard.

"Did you see that?"

"Bravest thing I ever saw."

"Those men have ice in their veins."

"Boy, talk about grit."

The two men didn't seem to hear or be distracted by the comments.

Just outside the gate, a Squad of Militia was barely managing to keep an area clear of spectators. In the middle of the small clearing stood Lieutenant Stuart and Major Russell.

As Lee walked through the gates, Stuart and Russell both saluted. Stuart spoke. "Good morning, Colonel. As per your orders, sir, the volunteer troops have been paraded on the lines assigned to them outside the Armory."

"Thank you, Lieutenant," replied Lee. He looked around at the Militia in formations outside of the Armory wall and along the trestle between the water tower and warehouse. He was surprised at the number of townspeople already gathered throughout the lower town area as well. "Would you please ask Colonel Shriver of the Maryland Volunteers to join me?"

As they waited, Lee continued to look about at the citizenry. They were perched in windows, atop the roofs, and vying for any other vantage point. The size of the crowd seemed to be increasing rapidly.

"You sent for me, Colonel?" Lee turned to observe an average looking man bedecked in a fancy dress uniform.

"Ah, yes," said Lee, "Colonel Shriver." He pointed toward the engine house. "Although this insurgency has involved Federal Government property," he looked back to the Militia commander, "I believe that the raid has been chiefly aimed against State authority." He paused. Shriver looked at him blankly. "As you are the commander of the State troops first on the scene and currently the largest force in attendance." He paused again. Shriver's expression hadn't changed. Lee said plainly, "I am offering the men from Maryland the honor of the opening attack."

Realization suddenly flashed across Shriver's face. He pointed out toward the parading Militia nearby. "These men of mine," he stammered, "have wives and children at home. I will not expose them to such risks." He stabbed a finger at Lee. "You are paid for doing this kind of work!"

Lee could not help but be personally affronted by the response. As much as he wanted to say something in retort, he did not. He merely bowed slightly to Shriver and turned to Stuart. "Please ask Colonel Baylor of the Virginia Militia to join me." He turned his back to the Maryland Militia commander and again surveyed the crowd. Shriver stormed off to sulk.

After several minutes, the Virginia Colonel appeared. "Yes, Colonel," he said cheerily, "how may I be of service?"

Without mentioning his proposal to Shriver, Lee explained the assault against State authority premise and offered the fellow Virginian the same invitation as before. To his horror, the Virginia Militia commander also expressed his unwillingness to attack.

"I will not send my men against the murderers in that

engine house." Baylor protested vehemently. "They have not been trained for such close action." He ended his refusal by pointing at Greene and saying, "Let the Marines do it. They're the mercenaries!"

Lee was seething with internal rage. In order to maintain his composure, he closed his eyes and turned his back to the Virginia Militia commander. Several seconds passed before he opened them again. When he did so, Greene was standing before him. The Marine did not display any sort of discomfort or humiliation suffered by either of the two Militiamen's comments. Lee smiled at the Northerner who had made Virginia his adopted home.

Lee spoke with increased volume so those around him may hear. "Lieutenant Greene," he held his arm out, rigidly pointing toward the engine house, "do you wish the honor of taking those men out?"

Greene snapped to attention. While simultaneously starting to bow, he grasped the bill of his cap with his right hand and swept the cover off in a wide, flowing arc until his arm was across his waist and the cap was suspended off to his left side. His movements were quite majestic. "Colonel Lee," he said dramatically, "on behalf of the United States Marines, it is with great pleasure that I accept the honor." He straightened from the bow. "Thank you, sir!" He was smiling widely.

Lee turned around to Baylor and gave him such a look as to say, *"A mercenary, maybe, but a brave one."* Instead, he said, "Thank you, Colonel. I have no further requirements of you."

Baylor stammered, "Well, I never!" and departed in a huff.

Lee returned his attention back to Greene. "Lieutenant, please prepare your Storming Party." He held up his hand as a caution. "In order to preclude accidentally wounding or killing any of the hostages," he dropped his hand, "I shall request that you go in with cold steel."

Greene nodded. He understood the Colonel meant that there would be absolutely no weapons firing by the Storming Party. Even after one round is fired from a musket, the barrel is immediately warm to the touch. After several rounds, it would be absolutely hot. Contrary to popular belief, 'Cold Steel' means no firing.

"Yes, sir, bayonets, then?" The bayonet was primarily a

weapon of intimidation. The sight of a soldier bearing down on you with a long, gleaming bayonet was usually enough to change your mind about staying put and continuing to fight. The Storming Party's muskets would now become a means of thrusting the bayonet outward, or for use as a club.

"Yes," acquiesced Lee. "And please be mindful of the safety of the hostages." Lee further added, "The Negroes will also bear close attention."

"Yes, sir." Greene was in a festive mood. "Any other instructions, sir?"

"Not at the moment," replied Lee. "Kindly report back to me when you are ready."

Greene drew to Attention and snapped his best salute. "Aye-Aye, Colonel." He turned to make his way to the gates.

Tuesday, October 18, 1859, 6:25 a.m.

Lee couldn't help but smile as he watched Greene calmly traverse the distance back to his Detachment. The Lieutenant strode smoothly with an aura of dignity and determined military bearing. Lee then looked up at the clouds above. They were lighter in color. He commented to no one in particular. "It appears the sun has crested the horizon."

As Greene approached his men, he was positively beaming with enthusiasm. Had he responded to the little boy feeling inside of him, he would have skipped back across the compound. He was that excited.

Orderly Sergeants McDonough and Mundell walked out several paces to meet their Lieutenant. They knew from experience that something was up and, most probably, immediate work to be done.

Greene returned their salutes as he came to a stop before them. "Gentlemen," he started, "we have been given the honor of taking those men out!" He vaguely pointed over his shoulder toward the engine house. "It appears the bravado of our local brethren in arms has disappeared along with the alcoholic vapors." As he was speaking, he was starting to unhook the top button of his boat cloak. "And you would be horrified to know how they refer to us soldiers of the sea."

Once his cloak was removed and draped over his left forearm, he said, "Now, to work." He shifted slightly to his left so as to see the Detachment clearly. "We shall make up a main Storming Party from Section A." He looked to Mundell. "Twelve good men, I believe. Veterans preferably, but not mandatory."

Mundell looked the men of Section A over. "Aye, sir," he nodded, "easily done."

"Good," said Greene with satisfaction. "We'll also make up a second party of twelve from Section B." He looked around to McDonough. "And we'll need three strong men to handle the millwright sledgehammers you 'liberated' earlier this morning."

McDonough grinned. "I've already picked out the men, sir. They're standing ready with their new 'weapons', now."

"Excellent." He said this partially to McDonough and partially to Gilbert who had come from the ranks to relieve him of the boat cloak. No longer encumbered, Greene continued. "Orderly Sergeant Mundell, please assign the men to the Storming Parties and have them assemble," he pointed in the desired direction, "behind our 'Head Quarters' building."

After Mundell saluted and turned to address the Detachment, Greene continued to McDonough. "XO, the storming parties will attack with cold weapons." McDonough nodded. "Just have them leave their leather caps in place and fix bayonets." A leather cap is a piece of leather approximately one half-inch square. In wet weather, it is placed between the cap cone and hammer. When the hammer is pressed hard against the leather cap, it makes a slight impression in the leather that will maintain a seal against moisture. "Have both parties remove their greatcoats. They'll need freedom of movement."

"If I may suggest, Skipper," said McDonough with a knowing look. "We might want to have the men take their cross belts off and just wear their waist belts."

"Right," agreed Greene. "Don't want them snagging on anything inside." He pondered several other preparation thoughts.

"The only other thing that I can think of applies to Colonel Lee's words of warning." Greene leaned closer to McDonough so there would be no mistake. He held up a pointed index finger for emphasis. "We shall assume that the insurgents are armed and the hostages are not." He waved the finger lightly. "And, we will disregard any Negro unless he is armed or showing signs of a fight."

McDonough nodded. "Aye, sir, understood. I shall pass the word carefully." He searched Greene's eyes. "Anything else, Skipper?"

"I think that's it, XO," he finally said. "Kindly take charge of the storming parties and quietly move them along the back of the office building to the space between it and the engine house." Greene looked toward the Armory gates. "I shall join you there after I report to Colonel Lee we are ready."

"Aye-Aye, Skipper." The two men saluted each other.

As Greene approached the remainder of his Detachment, he performed a quick count. Sections A and B now contained one Sergeant and nine Privates each. Section C had one Sergeant and ten Privates. He thought approvingly, *"I see Mundell has sent a Corporal with each of the Storming Parties."* He already knew that Section C's Non-Com was still posted as Corporal of the Guard for the sentries around the engine house.

"Orderly Sergeant Mundell," said Greene coolly, "have the men fix bayonets and then prime their weapons." As the commands were given and executed, he worked his way over to a position beside the Section C leader.

"Sergeant Davis," he said quietly, "after the Detachment concludes the forthcoming forward movement, you will bring your Section around to accompany me." He gestured to indicate how he wanted the Section to move out from behind the formation and along the warehouse side of the compound. "We shall form a single firing line opposite the engine house." Greene had selected Section C because it had the only remaining veterans.

"Aye-Aye, sir," replied Davis.

As Greene moved to the front of the Detachment he pulled out the leather gloves that were tucked into his sword belt. He hadn't put them on earlier because Colonel Lee wasn't wearing gloves. As he finished slipping the second one on, he nodded to Mundell.

"DETACHMENT, SHOULDERRR, ARMS," barked the

Orderly Sergeant. "FORRRWARD, MARCH." The Detachment stepped out.

When they neared the end of the office building closest to the engine house, Mundell ordered, "DETACHMENT, HALT."

Greene waited as Davis moved his Section out and around. At the appropriate time, he stepped off at an angle to intersect with Sergeant Davis. As they continued forward, Greene said to Davis, "Keep your men 'At Rest' until such time it becomes plain that you should go to the 'Ready' position."

"Aye-Aye, sir," responded Davis without hesitation.

Greene eyeballed their approach. "Now!" he whispered and continued toward the gate.

Davis calmly ordered, "Section, Halt." He waited a two count, and then said in paced sequence, "Right, Face. Order, Arms. In Place, Rest."

Greene approached Lee and saluted. "Colonel," he said, "the Marines are ready." He quickly started ticking off information. "The primary Storming Party is made up of twelve men. A secondary Party of twelve is also standing by. All have been told about the hostages and the Negroes. We will attempt to breach the doors with sledgehammers. The remainder of my Detachment is in position to take on any possible reaction from the engine house."

"Excellent, Lieutenant." He gestured toward his Aide. "Lieutenant Stuart shall execute delivery of the surrender ultimatum." He shook his head and added pensively, "However, if their leader is indeed the man we suspect, I am doubtful he will surrender." He mentally shook himself out of his downhearted mood. "If he will not capitulate, I have instructed Lieutenant Stuart to wave his hat to signal the Marines to start the attack."

"If I may suggest, Colonel," interjected Greene, "we might add one additional signal for Lieutenant Stuart to give." Both Army officers concentrated on Greene. "A signal that would indicate that the leader is indeed John Brown of Kansas." He looked at Stuart. "Lieutenant," he suggested, "I recommend you remove your hat if the leader is Brown." He looked at Lee. "I doubt the leader would think anything of it, and you and I will know for sure who we are dealing with."

"An outstanding idea, Lieutenant!" Lee beamed and

looked at Stuart. "We shall make it so." Stuart nodded concurrence.

"If there is nothing else, Colonel," he gestured at Stuart and himself, "we shall begin the task at hand."

"No, nothing further to add." Lee looked at both men with affection. "Good luck, gentlemen."

The two lieutenants saluted and stepped off toward their destinies. They passed through the Armory gates and stopped near the mid-point of Section C's line. They faced each other and Greene removed his right glove.

"Good luck, Lieutenant," he wished as he extended his right hand.

"Good luck, Lieutenant," rejoined Stuart as he grasped the proffered hand.

They shook hands solemnly.

Tuesday, October 18, 1859, 7:00 a.m.

As Greene made his way to the guardroom end of the engine house, he realized that the morning light was getting stronger. *"Good,"* he thought, *"there should be adequate light in the engine house, now."*

Stuart waited patiently as he watched Greene move to his position. He took a moment to gaze about his surroundings. The number of people gathered around surprised him. "Why," he said softly, "there must be at least two thousand people out there."

"All set," whispered McDonough as Greene arrived. The primary Storming Party was positioned in a row along the sidewall of the engine house. Outboard of them, in their own file, were the three men with sledgehammers. The Second Storming Party was in a single line formation about three paces away, closer to the end of the office building. Everyone was back from the street and out of view from inside the engine house.

"Excellent," whispered Greene in return as he made his way past the hammer men to the Northwest corner of the engine house. He leaned against the cold brick abutment and peered around the corner. All was still quiet inside the building. He withdrew back around the corner and extracted his sword from its scabbard.

Sergeant Davis ordered his Section to Attention. "Shoulder, Arms," came next, then, "Ready." At this last command each man shifted his right foot ninety degrees outward and a little behind his left to form what's referred to as a firing 'T'. In unison, their muskets fell forward and were stopped at a forty-five degree angle by their left hands. Their right thumbs rested atop the weapons' hammers in preparation for cocking and aiming or advancing with bayonets.

Stuart unfurled a white flag from the three-foot stick he was carrying. *"Time for a little parley,"* he thought and stepped determinedly toward the engine house. After he had moved several paces, everyone realized that 'it' had started and a sudden hush fell over the compound and the surrounding area.

Lee removed his watch from a vest pocket and noted the time.

Stuart stopped about half a pace in front of the two doors under the center arch. Since the guardroom was behind the door mounted below the brick arch to the right, he was actually in front of the right hand entrance of the engine house. He reached out and banged on the door with the butt end of his flagstick. "In the engine house," he called, "I have a message for your leader from Colonel Lee, Commanding United States Troops."

Greene positioned himself so he could see Stuart clearly, but hopefully not be seen by anyone inside. The right hand door started to open. Greene pulled back reflexively. He edged his head back out so he could just see Stuart. He could barely hear voices. He eased his head out farther. Stuart was covered two ways. His hat was still on and the muzzle of a rifle was pointing at his abdomen.

Greene watched as Stuart took a piece of paper out of his inside coat pocket and hand it to whoever was holding the weapon on him. The door was only open about four inches. He wasn't able to ascertain anything else without exposing himself.

Stuart began speaking again. He looked as though he was having a conversation with a neighbor. Quite casually, he reached up and removed his hat.

"It is Brown!" breathed Lee.

Greene nodded acknowledgement, leaned back, and hissed to the hammer men, "Get ready!"

As one of the hammer men, Allen had been standing with the head of his hammer resting on the ground while he steadied the upright handle with his left hand. He quickly bent down and, with his right hand, grasped the other end of the handle just below the head. With a grunt he raised the head up and rested it on his shoulder.

Greene kept waiting for Stuart's second signal. He watched impatiently as Stuart continued to converse with Brown. Their communications seemed to be rather one sided. Stuart would listen for quite a while, shake his head 'no', speak briefly, and then listen for another long while. *"Come on, Stuart,"* thought Greene, *"you yourself said the man has a reputation for haggling long and hard. Let's get on with it."*

Lee checked his watch for seemingly the hundredth time. "This is taking much too long," he said to himself. He wanted to shout across the compound what he had told Stuart earlier, *"Remember, Lieutenant, do not get involved with the insurgents. They must not have time to harm the hostages or use them as shields."*

Suddenly, as though he had just heard his Colonel's admonition, Stuart jumped back to his left, away from the door. With his back against the center abutment, he began to wave his hat spectacularly in a figure eight above his head. The door closed with a bang.

"NOW!" exclaimed Lee in a harsh whisper. He involuntarily checked the time again.

Tuesday, October 18, 1859, 7:20 a.m.

Greene sprang away from the corner abutment and yelled, "HAMMER MEN, ADVANCE!" He then rushed toward the abutment between the guardroom and the doorway Stuart had been parleying at. With his sword arm outstretched, he braced the sword's protective cross guard against the left doorframe of the guardroom. His back was against the door. He leaned out to make sure the engine house door was still closed. When he saw that it was, he made an overhead, sweeping motion with his left arm. "COME ON, BOYS," he shouted, "LET'S HIT IT!"

As Allen, the first hammer man, approached the engine house doorway, Greene moved closer and pointed with his sword toward the middle where the two doors met. "AIM FOR THE CENTER...BREAK THE STRONGBACK!" As he moved back to the abutment to give the hammers swinging room, he signaled his first Squad of attackers to move forward to the guardroom door.

Allen stopped in front of the left side door and swung the heavy hammer. ***THUD.*** He caught the door just at the center edge. A second later, another hammer man stopped in front of the right side door and swung as well. ***THUD.*** Allen, his feet better planted, swung a second time with earnest intensity. ***THUD. CRACK!*** The 2 by 4 strongback used to bar the doors closed was starting to break. Allen heard it and quickly swung accurately again at the same spot. ***THUD. CRACK! CRUNCH!*** The strongback parted. The doors moved inward, but failed to open. He swung again and the doors retreated under his blow, but repositioned themselves when he drew back for another go. The former miner rotated his hammerhead around to use the wedge end against the door. *"Maybe I can bust up the wood,"* he thought. He continued to swing as fast and as hard as he could.

The hammer man on the right was striking the doors when he could without interrupting Allen's rhythm. After several ineffective blows of his own, he leaned toward Greene. "SIR, THE DOORS MUST BE TIED OFF WITH A ROPE. THEY JUST KEEP SPRINGING BACK!"

"KEEP AT IT." replied Greene, "WE'LL TRY SOMETHING ELSE."

Greene started to turn, but immediately bumped into someone. He hadn't expected anyone to be that close to him and instinctively pushed the other person back. Suddenly he focused on the face in front of him. "MAJOR RUSSELL!" exclaimed Greene. He wanted to ask 'what in the blazes are you doing here', and a dozen other questions that raced through his mind. Instead, he dodged around him and leapt past the First Storming Party whose formation bent around the corner of the building.

The third hammer man had been standing slightly behind

and out of swinging range of the other two. Allen signaled him to take his place. Fortunately Orderly Sergeant McDonough had been foresighted enough to tell them to use the third man as a relief. He had figured correctly that there wasn't enough room for the three of them to wield their hammers at the same time. He also knew that any activity with those behemoth tools would wear a man out quickly. He had been right.

Allen's arms felt like rubber. He dragged his hammer with him as he backed up past Lieutenant Stuart, who was still standing against the middle abutment. They exchanged glances. "Spent," was all Allen could say between gasps for breath. Stuart nodded knowingly.

"SECOND STORMING PARTY," Ordered Greene, "GROUND ARMS AND PICK UP THAT LADDER." He pointed to the ladder behind them, leaning lengthways against the office building. It was the heavy roofer's ladder that had been lowered there earlier that morning. "WE'LL USE IT AS A BATTERING RAM!"

"Quickly, lads," said McDonough as he bound towards the ladder. "Quickly."

Without the usual precision of practiced drill, each man in the Second Storming Party hurriedly lay his weapon down on the ground. In several cases, the muskets were actually dropped the final ten or so inches and landed with a clatter. McDonough cringed when he heard the sound, but ignored it for the time being.

The first man to arrive at the ladder yanked it outward. It rotated away from the building and fell flat on the ground. "Right, lads," ordered McDonough, "six men on each side. Facing the street. Let's go." His voice was calm, yet determined. He worked his way to the 'front' of the ladder.

As each man grabbed the ladder, he hoisted it waist high. Even before all of the men had a firm grip, McDonough signaled with a 'Forward' motion and commanded, "Follow Me!" He started out at a trot as he made a wide sweeping arc toward the door. The ladder movement was a little jerky until all of the men got into the rhythm of the run.

THUD. THUD. The hammer men at the doorway continued their slow but steady pounding. Each man was pacing himself. Their objective now was to damage the doors as much as possible, rather than force entry.

Through a loophole in the abutment behind Stuart, a rifle barrel gradually poked its way out. Initially it pointed skywards, but after it extended to its full length, it slowly came down. Stuart was unable to see the danger because it was behind him.

Allen, who was bending over with his hands resting on his knees, heard a faint scrape of metal on the brick and mortar above his head. As he looked up, the barrel was angling to the right. Instinctively, Allen looked in that direction. "The Colonel!" he mouthed with surprise.

Lee had moved from behind the gates to a slightly elevated position inside the gates. He was across the street from the engine house, perhaps forty feet away. He appeared stately as he stood erect and coolly observed the assault. However, he was clearly a target.

Allen shuffled backwards to a point where he could stand up without being in front of the gun barrel. He shouted to Stuart. "LIEUTENANT, DUCK!" Stuart startled and spun around. As soon as the barrel was within his peripheral vision, he impulsively dropped down.

Allen raised his sledgehammer as though it were a lightweight bat. Both of his hands were low on the handle, the hammerhead poised in mid-air. He took aim at the end of the barrel, stepped forward on his left foot, and swung the hammer with all his might. The hammerhead swept around in a smooth, wide arc until it struck the small muzzle opening squarely. The two instruments collided with a solid, metal to metal, ***CLINK!*** The force of the blow drove the barrel back inside the loophole. A scream of pain could be heard from within the engine house. Allen dropped the hammerhead back to the ground. He grinned broadly at Stuart, but kept an eye on the loophole.

When Greene saw McDonough leading the ladder men around toward the door, he thought, *"Good, he's sweeping wide to line up on the door. Won't have to waste time adjusting the angle of attack when they get here."* He signaled the First Storming Party to come out from around the corner. They'd have room to maneuver, now. Greene held out his left arm and made a chopping motion with his hand to indicate that he wanted the Party to form in a diagonal line out from him.

Gilbert was the first one to make a move. He danced out backwards, holding his musket out horizontal to his chest. "Step Out, boys," he ordered. "Form On Me." The line of twelve men snaked out from around the corner and guided up to an imaginary line extending from the ends of Gilbert's weapon. The Corporal stopped the formation when he achieved the positioning Greene desired.

McDonough stopped his ladder party about six paces away from the double door. "All right, lads," he called out, "inboard hands on a ladder rung." He pointed to the interior of the ladder. "And your outboard hands on the side rail." He nodded approval as each flank obtained their handholds accordingly. "When we go," he warned with a pointed finger, "everyone start on their outboard foot." Several men quickly shifted their feet around. McDonough raised his right arm to signal his crew was ready.

When Greene saw the Orderly Sergeant's raised arm, he waved the hammer men off. He moved forward and pointed at the right half of the left door with his sword. He indicated an area approximately one third of the way up from the ground. "Here!" he mouthed to McDonough.

Greene had chosen the spot to be rammed carefully. The doors were strongly made. But most significantly, they were double battened. Meaning that they were made with two layers of boards, held together with heavy wrought-iron nails. The outside layer was vertical. The inside layer was mounted behind the outside layer at a forty-five degree angle from the center edge, downward to the hinge edge.

McDonough nodded. To the men at the front of the ladder he said, "There's your spot, lads." He twisted around for all to hear, "READY!" He swung his arm toward the doors. "CHARGE!"

By the third step, the ladder crew was at full speed. The two lead men aimed for the 'spot'. As they neared their objective, the crew shifted the ladder backward with their hands. When they took the final step, they brought the ladder forward with extra force for the impact. **WHAMMM!** The shock vibrated the door and the ladder with tremendous energy.

Before the tremor of the impact had stopped resonating, weapons fire from within the engine house started. Allen quickly checked the loophole. Nothing. Apparently the insurgents inside were shooting at the doors the Marines were attempting to breach. Two, maybe three, loud reports had sporadically occurred. They had no obvious affect on the men outside.

McDonough had run forward with the ladder crew. Upon seeing no visible damage to the door, he immediately ordered, "BACK, LADS! WE'LL RAM IT AGAIN!" With equal speed they withdrew about five paces and turned to face the door again.

Without wasting any additional time, McDonough raised his arm and checked his crew. Once satisfied, he ordered, "CHARGE!" Again the crew bound forward and thrust the ladder at the door with explosive intensity. ***WHAMMM! CRACK! CRUNCH!***

When the ladder was pulled back, there it was! The lower right corner of the left door was slanting part way into the building. The exterior boards had cracked and broken while the left ends of the inside diagonals still held the damaged segment in place, but the door had been breached.

Immediately another round of erratic firing occurred from within the building. Undaunted, Greene rushed forward. He spun around and squatted down. He placed his left shoulder against the inclining corner and extended his opposite leg. He dug his right foot into the dirt to gain leverage. Pushing as hard as he could, he managed to finish what the ladder had started. With a loud ***CRACK!***, the lower corner gave way to the left allowing a ragged hole big enough for a man to enter.

From all the pressure he had been exerting, Greene fell forward into the opening. Quickly recovering, he scrambled in on all fours. A fire engine loomed just inside of the doors. He twisted to his right and made every effort to regain his feet.

Private Quinn was next in line to enter the engine house, but before he could drop down to make his entrance, Major Russell jumped in front of him. Armed only with his rattan 'swagger' stick, Russell crawled into the opening. Quinn made sure he was next and followed close behind.

Inside, the room was filled with acrid smoke from the recently discharged weapons. Visibility was minimal. Greene had successfully stood up and taken just one long stride when he encountered one of the insurgents in the corner. That individual was attempting to reload his Sharps rifle. Greene body slammed into him, forcing the insurgent up against the brick wall. A blow to the face from the hilt of Greene's sword stunned the opponent enough that he dropped his weapon.

As Greene made his way along the side wall to the rear of the engine house, he heard another bodily impact and a loud "UMPPH". He figured the next Marine had also made contact with the insurgent in the corner. He was unaware that Russell was the Marine behind him.

* * * * *

Quinn hustled through the door opening as fast as he could. Crawling forward through a tight space with a bayoneted musket is difficult at best. He was just inside the door and about three quarters of the way to making it to his feet when, **KABOOM!** An insurgent, skulking under the engine, had fired upward and point blank at Quinn. The bullet struck him in the lower abdomen and knocked him backward against the right door. His musket dropped with a clatter to the floor. Without uttering a sound, Quinn staggered forward and dropped unconscious, headfirst toward the gunman. He lay face down. A stream of blood slowly flowed from under his body.

Ruppert was kneeling down to enter the opening. He heard the gunshot. He knew it was close because it was so loud. Anticipating that other insurgents had also reloaded their weapons since firing when the breach was achieved, he made every effort to scramble in and get to his feet as quickly as he could. Once erect, he started to turn to his right. Another loud, **KABOOM!** resonated from his left. The bullet felt like a hot poker had burnt him on the face. Striking just below the cheek and moving upward past the bottom of the nose, it creased the moustache line on his upper lip and broke the incisor just in front of his left canine tooth. He was fortunate to have been turning his head when the bullet was fired. Ruppert instinctively clutched the wound with his left hand. Blood oozed between his fingers. Dragging his musket, he staggered to the corner.

* * * * *

Greene passed to the back of the engine house without further incident. Clearing the left rear corner of the first engine, he stopped to assess the situation. Through all the smoke, he could barely make out the shapes of men huddled together near the rear wall behind the second engine. *"Must be the hostages,"* he thought.

"Hello, Greene," brought the Lieutenant's attention to the aisle between the engines. There, just a pace away, was Colonel Washington standing near a hose cart. He was acting as though he were greeting his friend at a fall social. Exhibiting a great deal of dignity and calmness, he graciously offered his right hand out to Greene. The Marine grasped it with his left hand, since his sword was uplifted in his right. The Colonel pointed his left hand toward a kneeling figure near the front of the engine house. The man had just swung the breech lever forward to reload his weapon. "There is Osawatomie," said Washington without animosity.

* * * * *

Worried about the two gunshots heard after his men had entered the breach, Corporal Gilbert stopped the Marine behind Ruppert and scrambled through the hole himself. Inside he saw Quinn. He crawled to the downed Marine who was more than half under the engine. As he drew nearer, his left hand discovered a pool of thick, sticky liquid. Gilbert brought his hand close to his face. The fluid was warm and smelled like copper. "Blood!" he gasped.

At the same moment, a metallic clicking sound farther under the engine attracted Gilbert's attention. The insurgent was fumbling to reload his rifle. The Corporal yanked his weapon up from his side and thrust it at the man as best he could with one hand. Unfortunately, the strike was ineffective. The man had scurried backward like a frightened animal.

Before he could thrust again, Gilbert heard a macabre moan from the corner. He looked over and could clearly see the white waist belt of a Marine. He immediately scrambled to this other shipmate and knelt next to him. "Are you badly hurt?" he asked.

Ruppert removed his left hand for his Corporal to see. Gilbert evaluated the laceration and quickly put Ruppert's hand back over the wound. "Hold on," he said as he gripped the man briefly on the shoulder.

Gilbert stood up. *"Two good men down,"* he thought. *"And Quinn is probably dead or dying."* He jerked his weapon up to the ready position. Anger boiled up inside him to a full rage. With his bayonet point at chest height, he advanced down the smoky aisle next to the wall.

*****

Greene stepped off toward Brown. As he did so, Russell emerged from the smoke and herded Washington back to the group of hostages. The Major stood facing the small group with his arms outstretched. "Gentlemen," he said, "please remain behind me." He looked over his right shoulder. "There are more Marines coming and I don't want you to be accidentally hurt." He wanted to appear as a protective shield for them. He hoped that his act of 'heroism' would be duly noted to certain officials.

Brown was still kneeling. He was holding the Sharps rifle in his left hand while starting to insert another round into its breech with his right. Suddenly he looked up and saw Greene advancing upon him. They briefly made eye contact. Greene could see the fury in Brown's eyes. The Marine raised his sword higher and charged at the insurgent leader. "YAHHHHHHH!" yelled Greene as he advanced the remaining distance to his target.

When he was nearly on top of Brown, he struck downward mightily with his sword. At that instant, Brown instinctively raised his weapon high to deflect the blow. Greene's sword crashed down on the rifle's breech lever with a loud, resonating **KALANG!** The combination of the colliding angles of the rifle and the sword, along with the thrusting motion of Brown's protective movement, resulted in Greene's sword being deflected outward to the right. When his arm reached the extremity of its warded off direction, Greene instantly reversed its course and swung back at Brown. This time he strategically aimed under Brown's extended arm, at his now exposed left side.

Unbeknownst to Greene, however, the intense blow against the breech lever had caused his sword to bend. The lightweight sword had not been intended for this sort of heavy assault. A little forward of its center point, the blade was bent to the right more than forty-five degrees.

When Greene's newest swing struck Brown, the forward half of the blade doubled back toward the hilt, but did not break. The blow was sufficient to wound Brown, but the laceration was not deep or deadly. Brown dropped his weapon, grabbed his side, and attempted to rise to his feet.

The instant it struck, Greene was astonished by the 'softness' of his blow. He expected Brown's body to stop the blade completely. By chance, he had managed to catch a glimpse of the damaged blade as his swing continued past Brown. Without hesitation, Greene reached out with his gloved left hand and grasped the bent over blade. He released the sword's grip with his right hand and slipped out of the wrist strap. He grabbed atop the fingers of his left hand and squeezed the bent blade halves together. He intended to use the doubled over sword as a club. He raised his 'new' weapon above his head. With the same ferocity as his first blow, he commenced to beat down upon Brown's head and shoulders with the sword's hilt, grip, and cross guard.

* * * * *

Just as Gilbert started advancing, he heard the harsh scraping of boots, first on wood, then on the stone floor. It had come from somewhere ahead of him. Suddenly, in the dissipating smoke, not another two paces away, was a man. He was facing the engine with his arms reaching up toward it. One of his feet was pumping the air, trying to gain purchase on a wheel spoke. Gilbert realized the man was attempting to climb aboard the engine. Looking him over quickly, he spotted a cartridge belt slung over the man's shoulder. Then he noticed a rifle already positioned on the engine. "A Shooter!" he hissed.

The man heard him and turned around. He was startled when he saw the bayonet brandishing Marine. He started backing up quickly.

Gilbert followed purposefully, but guardedly. He was wary of a trap. He no longer flashed his usual grin, but rather the distorted mouth and clenched teeth of a man furiously determined to kill if he had to.

The man unexpectedly backed hard into the rear wall. Momentarily panicked, he looked around. He had nowhere to go. His eyes suddenly glowered resolutely as he braced for the Marine to come at him. His hand started to reach for the hunting knife in the sheath hanging from his belt.

Gilbert recognized the stubborn look of resistance on the man's face and saw him go for the knife. He leveled his bayonet and drew his weapon back slightly. Yelling as he did so, he charged.

Thrusting his weapon forward at the last second, he caught the man just below his sternum and shoved upward with all his strength and pent up anger. The bayonet pierced completely through its victim and stuck into the brick wall behind him. Gilbert continued to yell and bear down firmly against his weapon. It was as if he wanted to push the bayonet through the wall itself.

The victim dangled there for a moment. He attempted to cry out, but only gurgling passed out of his throat. He flailed about violently. When the kicking stopped, his body rotated, gradually and hideously, until it hung, lifeless, with its head downward. Only then did Gilbert extract his bayonet.

A horrible shriek from behind caused Gilbert to spin about and crouch low, expecting more trouble. The opposite was true. Two additional Marines from the Storming Party had bayoneted the gunman under the engine. The scream was his death knell. Gilbert flashed a momentary hairline grin of satisfaction. *"Two of 'them' down,"* he thought. With his pulse still pounding in his ears, he spun back around and dashed to the end of the engine.

* * * * *

Greene continued to pummel blow after blow upon Brown. He had knocked the man down and finally into unconsciousness. When Brown slumped over, Greene stopped.

He held his 'club' aloft with his right hand and shook Brown to check for muscle resistance. He wanted to make sure Brown wasn't faking. He wasn't.

From his slightly stooped stance, Greene looked all around to survey the general situation. Except for Marines, he could see no one exhibiting a willingness to fight. He relaxed his defense, stood up straight, and allowed the 'club' to dangle at the end of his limp arm. He took in a deep breath and called out, "MARINES. AVAST FIGHTING."

The Lieutenant looked down at the prostrate Brown. Typical of most superficial head wounds, blood seemed to be flowing profusely. It was also beginning to dry in Brown's hair, on his face, and on his shirt collar. It was difficult to distinguish between the actual wounds and the coagulating rivulets of blood.

Greene quickly glanced around the engine house one more time. In that sweeping movement, he caught sight of a number of seemingly lifeless bodies lying on the floor throughout the engine house. Conclusively, he said to no one in particular, "Enough blood has been spilt at this place. We shall spill no more."

CHAPTER TEN

"AFTERMATH"

Tuesday, October 18, 1859, 7:23 a.m.

Outside, the seventh Marine in the Storming Party was about to crawl into the breach when he heard the command to stop. He relaxed and stood up. "It's over," he said to the men behind him.

Stuart jumped away from the abutment and waved his hat back and forth above his head. "IT'S OVER," he yelled for all to hear. "IT'S OVER!"

Lee looked at his gold watch for the last time. "Hmm," he mused. "Only three minutes...start to finish."

Beneath the cheers of the crowd, McDonough chided the remainder of the First Storming Party. "All Right!" he hissed under his breath. "Let's go, you Jack Tar rejects. This isn't Rope Yarn Sunday." (Rope Yarn Sunday refers to a casual afternoon, usually mid-week, allowed to a ship's crew for personal equipment and clothing construction or mending.) He waved the first man in line toward the breach. "There's still work to be done." He signaled the rest of the Storming Party forward. "The Lieutenant undoubtedly needs more help in there."

When the second man finished crawling into the breach, McDonough knelt down and peered through the opening into the engine house. He could just make out that the engine was almost up against the doors. A cloud suddenly moved away from the rising sun and a ray of light illuminated the opening. McDonough caught a glimpse of an unmistakable pair of sky-blue trouser legs, motionless beneath the engine. He jumped up. To the Marines at the front of the line he barked, "LEAVE YOUR WEAPONS!" He signaled them to hustle. "GET IN THERE AND MOVE THAT ENGINE BACK!" He banged his fist against the door. "AND GET THESE BLASTED DOORS OPEN...AT THE DOUBLE QUICK!"

* * * * *

In a rush, Gilbert arrived at the middle of the engine house. His eyes, glaring through the rapidly thinning gun smoke, darted from side to side. His fast breathing exhaled loudly through his mouth. He spotted Major Russell pushing back against a small pack of men. Gilbert's first reaction was "*He's under attack*" and leveled his bayonet in that direction.

"CORPORAL!"

The shout stopped Gilbert. He blinked and stared at the 'attackers'. Their actions were not hostile. He blinked again. *"Hostages?"* he wondered. Suddenly he realized what was going on and that the Major was not in danger. *"He's keeping them out of the way,"* he thought.

"Corporal," repeated the voice. "Over here."

Gilbert turned quickly to his left. There stood Lieutenant Greene signaling to him. The sight of his favorite Lieutenant was a welcome relief. The fact that the officer was alive and seemingly unharmed brought Gilbert's trademark wide grin back to his face. He hurried over.

As Gilbert moved toward him, Greene first saw the blood on his bayonet. Another step closer and he could make out blood splatter on the Corporal's fatigue coat. The final step brought him close enough to see dried blood on the fingers and back of his left hand.

"Are you...?" inquired Greene as he gestured toward the bloodied hand.

"No, sir," replied Gilbert with a shake of his head. He denoted the doorway with a slight thrust of his bayonet. "But we have two men down."

"Seriously wounded?" queried Greene as he looked to see if he could make out anything in the direction Gilbert indicated.

Gilbert nodded his head and said softly, "I fear one mortally, if not already gone, Lieutenant."

"Blast!" exclaimed Greene.

Gilbert continued. "The Storming Party has killed at least two insurgents." He pointed at Brown with the butt of his weapon. "Is this one dead, sir?"

Greene looked down to make sure Brown was still breathing. "I don't think so," he finally said. He looked up to see four Marines advancing cautiously around the rear of the fire engine. "Let's put a guard on him." He signaled the others over. "He's their leader." He remembered Lee's comments. "I think the State of Virginia will want to put him on trial.

"Stand guard over this man," ordered Greene as he pointed first to the lead Marine and then at Brown. He next motioned his hand about with a sweeping movement. "Two of you start collecting the insurgents' weapons and ammunition." He looked back toward the hostages. Russell was still holding them back. "The last man assist Major Russell with the hostages." The Marines immediately moved to perform their assigned duties.

"Come with me, Corporal," said Greene as he moved to check out several horizontal bodies he had seen earlier.

Gilbert first leaned toward the Marine standing guard over Brown. "If this one even twitches a muscle," he snarled, "knock him out again." He nodded decisively, and then started after his C.O.

Greene was carefully making his way between the front of the second engine and the other set of doors. After stepping over several strewn pieces of firefighting equipment he arrived at the side wall. A vigilant Gilbert was now right behind him.

* * * * *

The third Marine into the engine house after McDonough's impassioned orders yelled to those ahead of him, "STAND BY TO MOVE THIS ENGINE BACK FROM THE DOORS." His two predecessors rushed to the back end of the engine. They quickly checked for chocks or other obstructions under the wheels. Finding none, they leaned their weapons against the closest wall and grasped the spokes of the rear wheels.

One of the hostages wiggled out between Russell and the wall, quickly stepped over to the side of the engine, and released the brake. Major Russell said to the remaining hostages, "Gentlemen. Please remain calm and stay behind me." It seemed to be a wasted speech as none of his 'charges' were exhibiting hysteria. After nearly thirty-six hours of captivity, they were probably more tired and hungry than anything.

The 'third' Marine began untying the rope that held the doors closed as still another Marine crawled in. When the piece of rope fell to the floor, the 'third' braced himself up against the front of the engine, as did the 'fourth'. "GIVE WAY, ALL," he shouted. Each man pushed or pulled vigorously.

After a second, the resting inertia was broken and the engine rolled with increasing speed away from the doors. It struck the rear wall with a thump. When it did so, the 'brakeman' serenely stepped back over to it and reset the apparatus. Smiling broadly he returned to his group. He was received with back slaps and cheers from most, but a subtle sneer from Russell.

*****

When Greene was able to clearly look down the side wall, he was capable of seeing the scene that had been partially blocked by the second engine earlier. In the far corner was a group of five or six black men. He scanned them immediately for weapons. After seeing none, he gestured with a nod of his head and said quietly to Gilbert, "Slaves."

Along the wall were four white men, three horizontal and one kneeling next to the closest, tending to the prone man. Greene assumed the two other bodies were dead men. He indicated for Gilbert to first check them out and then the slaves. He would take care of the other two.

As the Corporal worked his way toward the bodies, Greene repositioned the 'club' in his right hand. Cautiously, he approached the kneeling figure. He raised his weapon, bent down, and grabbed a hold of the shoulder material of the man's coat. "Are you wounded?" he asked?

"No," responded the man, "I have surrendered." He sounded tired and worn out. The other man moaned. The kneeler comforted the man and said to Greene, "He is hurt bad and needs a doctor."

"One will be forthcoming," said Greene. He looked around

both men for weapons. He didn't strongly suspect hand guns because none of the other insurgents had been using them, but he wasn't ruling them out either. "Are you armed?" he asked.

"No," replied the kneeler. "I threw down my gun some time ago."

Greene released his grip on the coat and asked, "What is your name, sir?" He stood up straight.

"Coppoc, Edwin Coppoc from Springdale, Iowa." It wasn't a boast, just a statement of fact.

"And who is this wounded man?" continued Greene.

Coppoc mopped perspiration from the suffering man's brow with a dirty bandanna. "This is Watson Brown," he said.

"Any relation to John Brown, your leader?" Unseen by Coppoc, Greene had pointed to the center of the engine house as he asked the question.

"Yes," said Coppoc. "His son." He gestured toward the dead men. "Over there are Oliver Brown, Watson's younger brother, and Stewart Taylor."

While Greene was looking in that direction, he saw Gilbert herding a black man toward him at the point of his bayonet. "What have we here, Corporal?" he asked.

"Not rightly sure, sir," said Gilbert. "He claims to be one of the slaves." He thumbed back toward the corner. "But those fellows back there are standoffish from this one and don't seem to know anything about him." He pressed his bayonet point slightly against the man's back to remind him that it was still there. "And another thing, Lieutenant," continued Gilbert, "this individual has a badly bruised or broken right shoulder."

"Oh?" puzzled Greene. "And why is that significant, Corporal?"

"Well, sir," he began with a smile, "just before the ladder was positioned in front of the doors, I saw Private Allen take a swing at what looked, maybe, like a rifle barrel, sticking out a loophole." He grinned wide and nodded. "He hit it pretty hard, too."

Greene looked to Coppoc. "Is this man one of yours?" he asked.

"Yes," nodded Coppoc. "His name is Shields Green, but

he calls himself 'Emperor'."

* * * * *

Outside, McDonough was busy. He had signaled Orderly Sergeant Mundell to him at the double quick. When his peer arrived, he began rattling off instructions.

"We have a man down...maybe more!" He shook his head to Mundell's questioning eyes. "No, we don't know who." He pointed toward the Wager House. "Send for a doctor right away." He looked to make sure the Musicians were still behind Mundell's formation. "Have the Musicians make up two field litters." (Musicians were also trained as the stretcher-bearers of the era.) He contemplated the office building that had been Head Quarters. "We'll take our wounded to the Clerk's office. It's the small office down the hall and to the left." He thrust his arm out toward the building and then bent his hand at the wrist to the left. "The door is clearly marked." Mundell nodded. "We can use the desk tops for surgery if necessary." McDonough quickly scanned the loud crowd by the gate. People were pressing inward closer and closer. "Take enough men to establish a tight half circle perimeter in front of the engine house." He arced his arm around to demonstrate his meaning. "Keep the townspeople back." He paused for a second. "...and the Militia, too!" He suddenly spotted Lee who was approaching slowly. "No one allowed in except the Colonel and his Lieutenant." Mundell nodded again. "And one last thing. Have Sergeant Davis get the Second Storming Party back under arms with his Section. They'll be our reserve troops." He gave Mundell a sharp nod to indicate he was done.

"Aye-Aye, Orderly Sergeant," replied Mundell in practiced military fashion as he snapped a salute.

McDonough returned the salute and turned back toward the engine house doors.

Mundell waved toward Section C, held two fingers up high in clear view for several seconds, and then placed them across his outward extended left forearm. He next signaled 'To Me'. Sergeant Davis responded at the Double Quick.

Tuesday, October 18, 1859, 7:30 a.m.

Greene and Gilbert were returning to the center aisle with their two prisoners when the doors were finally pushed fully open. Muted sunlight flooded the space within. It seemed bright compared to the gloom of the shadowy interior. The remaining gun smoke started to swirl upward on a freshening current of air.

Greene turned to Gilbert. "Have several men take these prisoners outside and sit them down on the ground." Without looking down, he gestured at Brown. "Carry him out and lay him next to the prisoners." Pointing toward Watson Brown, he added, "And him, too." He glanced toward the men still being restrained at the rear wall by Major Russell. "After this aisle way is clear, you can allow the hostages and slaves to exit." Without looking in their direction, he said, "When everyone else is out, you can remove the dead."

* * * * *

McDonough ran in and knelt down beside the downed Marine and gently raised the man's left shoulder up to see who it was. "Quinn!" he gasped when he saw the pale, passive face. A wave of emotional dread swept over him. Unexpectedly, Quinn moaned faintly and McDonough realized the Private was still alive.

Next to McDonough was Sergeant Buckley. The Orderly Sergeant indicated for him to straighten out Quinn's legs. While the Sergeant was doing so, McDonough slowly rolled Quinn over on his back. Thick, sticky blood had soaked through the majority of Quinn's uniform from his upper chest down to the middle of his thighs. With total disregard to staining his own hands, McDonough unhooked Quinn's waist belt and then unbuttoned his coat. He lifted the coat halves apart and moved his hands carefully over the blood soaked uniform to locate the entry wound. Finally he found it, a hole in the trouser material, about two inches below the waistband, a little left of the fly. McDonough grimaced and looked to Buckley. The expression on the Sergeant's face clearly indicated his mutual understanding of the wound's location.

In response to a hand on his shoulder, McDonough looked back to find Greene standing behind him. He stood up and accepted the handkerchief his C.O. was offering. As he started wiping his hands, he said softly, "Gut shot." Greene nodded his head solemnly. (It was common knowledge of the day that any lower abdominal wound was assuredly fatal.)

* * * * *

Allen was standing fast where he had been when the breach was made. He figured that he'd stay put until ordered to do otherwise. *"Sit tight,"* he had thought. *"Not a good idea to get in the way when not told to."*

He had witnessed the removal and seating of the prisoners on what had been the Marine's staging ground between the engine house and the office building. Allen flinched when they laid the first bloodied figure next to the prisoners. *"That was none too gentle,"* he thought. A few moments later, he watched with admiration as Lieutenant Greene exited the structure and strode over to Colonel Lee's location.

Allen didn't think anything of it when the Musicians ran to the opening carrying blankets. It wasn't until Baxter laid out a blanket and asked for two muskets, that he began to watch with increased curiosity. He carefully observed the Fifer lay the muskets parallel to one another on top of the lengthwise blanket, dividing the blanket into three almost equal parts. As Baxter began folding the left outer third of the blanket over one musket toward the other musket, Allen realized, *"He's making a litter."* At each end of what would become the litter, one musket butt was opposite of the other's barrel. This allowed the weapons' hammers to face toward the outer edges and away from the patient.

As the Musician folded the other outer third over the now layered two thirds, Allen started moving toward the opening.

"Strange," he mused, *"they didn't carry that injured insurgent out on a litter."* He moved closer and peered between the shoulders of several Marines watching the activity just inside the opening. Seeing only the lower legs and boots of the downed Marine, he asked, "Who's hurt?" His heart stopped when he heard, "I think it's Quinn."

* * * * *

When the Marines began ushering the hostages toward the open doors, Lewis Washington seemed to be holding back. Hovering beside him was the ever-calculating Major Russell. After the last of his fellow hostages departed, the Colonel began fussing with his attire. As soon as he finished straightening out his cravat and vest, he continued by brushing dust from his frock coat sleeves and skirt. He withdrew a monogrammed handkerchief from his pocket and stroked it across his forehead and around his neck. A quick flick outward on each cheek concluded his cleaning. He then inspected his hands and commented to Russell, "I do wish I had a pair of gloves. I should hate for my good neighbors to see my soiled hands."

"Please, Colonel," solicited Russell as he began removing his own gloves, "may I offer you mine?" He smiled wryly. "They are made from the finest kid leather. A supple hide worthy of a gentleman such as yourself."

"Why, thank you, Major," rejoined Washington. "That is most kind of you."

They started toward the doors. Major Russell beamed as he proposed, "And if I may, Colonel, please allow me to escort you to the Wager House. You must be famished." He smirked shrewdly. "And undoubtedly thirsty, after your long and harrowing ordeal."

"Indeed I am." Washington nodded his concurrence ardently. "It seems years since I have had anything." As he exited the engine house, the crowd cheered him uproariously. Ignoring the throng, he looked back to Russell and said, "It had been a most trying night."

* * * * *

Corporal Gilbert arrived at Quinn's feet just half a step before Allen did. He had seen the Private rushing forward, the anguish on his face clearly visible. With his left arm across Allen's chest, Gilbert reached out and grabbed his shoulders to stop him. Before Allen could say anything, he leaned close and spoke softly into his ear. "Easy, lad. Quinn's hurt bad, but we're giving him the best help we can." Allen stopped struggling forward and stared down at his unconscious friend. He felt helpless as he watched them finish moving him onto the litter. Gilbert released Allen and said, "Why don't you help the Musicians carry him out of here." Allen stared back at Gilbert dumbly. "You can stay with him," said the Corporal with a smile. "He'll need to see a friendly face when he comes to." Allen attempted a smile in return. Holding back his tears, he bent down to grasp the butt end of the closest litter musket.

As Quinn was being rushed off, McDonough stepped up behind Gilbert. "I fear he's going to take this pretty hard," he said, referring to Allen.

"Aye, that he is," replied Gilbert. "I'll keep a close eye on him, though."

"Excuse me," interrupted Baxter. "Will we need the second litter?"

McDonough was about to answer 'no', but Gilbert looked toward the interior of the engine house and said, "Wait!" He finished a quick scan and asked, "Where's Ruppert?" He rushed to the right hand door. "He was in the corner!"

Gilbert swung the door away from the wall. There, still slumped against the inside of the brick abutment, was Ruppert. The fully opened door had concealed him from view. His face was ashen, but his chin and left hand were brilliant with dried blood. His right hand still maintained a firm grip on his weapon.

McDonough checked him over quickly. "He's alive," he pronounced. Ruppert's eyelids sprang open as McDonough tried to peel back the bloodied hand. "Easy, Private," soothed the Orderly Sergeant. "I just need to see the scratch you've got here." Ruppert relaxed as McDonough checked out the wound.

"Well, now," grinned McDonough, "you're definitely going to live." He staunched the wound with the handkerchief that Greene had given to him earlier. As he began to help Ruppert to his feet, he joked, "One thing is for sure, you're shaving time is going to be greatly reduced." Ruppert started to grin, but stopped when he realized it hurt to do so.

"Baxter," said Gilbert as he handed him Ruppert's weapon, "kindly escort our 'vanishing' Private to the 'sick bay'."

Tuesday, October 18, 1859, 7:35 a.m.

Lee listened intently as Greene took his time reporting the situation he had encountered in the engine house. The Colonel nodded occasionally during the narration. He seemed to be pleased with everything he heard.

"You and your Marines have performed quite admirably, Lieutenant." Lee smiled. "My congratulations for a job well done." He was momentarily distracted by the shouts of the crowd. "Lynch...lynch...lynch!" seemed to be the chant of the hour and the volume was increasing steadily.

"Now Lieutenant, I fear that I must ask you to protect the men you so valiantly assaulted and captured." Lee was not of the same mind as the mob. "Unlike the local townspeople and the Militia, I am sure that you will treat the prisoners with kindness and decency."

"Yes, sir," replied Greene. He indicated the semi-circle of Marines on guard duty. "The orders have already been given." He next pointed to the Musician running across the compound with an armload of blankets. "In addition to the blankets, one of the Militia doctors will be requested to minister to them." He looked up to the sky, "And, if the weather turns foul again, the prisoners will be taken inside."

"Thank you, Lieutenant." Lee looked pleased. "If you will excuse me," he continued, "Governor Wise is expected to arrive on the Noon train." He signaled for Stuart to attend him. "And I must see what I can do to settle this mob down and restore some semblance of civil obedience."

Greene saluted. "Good luck, sir."

* * * * *

Sergeant Buckley quickly shoved a desk and several chairs toward the outer walls of the office. He then signaled the litter bearers to bring their precious cargo into the room. With the utmost of care, Quinn was placed gently on the floor. He moaned briefly when his body straightened out against the hard boards. Buckley snatched a seat pillow off of one of the chairs and placed it under Quinn's head.

To the Drummer Shultz, he said, "Run down to the hotel and get some sheets, towels and a bucket or bowel of hot water if they have some." He pointed at the youngster. "Cold water, if they don't." The boy bolted from the room. "Aye-Aye, Sergeant." was vaguely heard over the pounding of his boots receding down the hall.

Buckley turned to another Marine who had helped with the litter. "Jump over to the warehouse and bring back a couple more blankets." He, too, was gone in a flash.

To Allen, Buckley said, "Start taking off his brogans." He softened his tone of voice. "We'll need to undress him and clean him up some so the doctor can see how badly he's hurt." Allen nodded and started tugging at one of the leather bootlaces.

Baxter and Ruppert suddenly appeared at the door. The Fifer guided his charge around the men working on the floor and into one of the chairs. He propped Ruppert's musket into a corner where the Private could see it. Returning to the chair, he asked, "Will you be all right?" Ruppert nodded.

Baxter placed the blanket he was still carrying within Buckley's reach and continued toward the heating stove. "I'll have a fire going here lickety-split," he said cheerily.

Tuesday, October 18, 1859, 7:45 a.m.

Orderly Sergeant Mundell appeared at the door. He stepped in and to the side. "This way, doctor," he said to a tall man following him. Behind this stranger was Corporal Gilbert.

The man, who appeared to be about thirty-five, entered the room, carrying a traditional black medical bag. Mundell introduced him to all in the room simultaneously. "This is Doctor Starry. He is the local doctor here at Harper's Ferry." He leaned toward Allen. "He's highly recommended. Knows his stuff and is very thorough."

Buckley finished a last couple of strokes with a damp towel. He had managed to clean the majority of the blood off of Quinn. Earlier he had torn one of the hotel sheets into three pieces. One of the pieces was used to cover Quinn from his shoulders down to his belly button. Another piece covered him from just below the wound down to his toes. The third, and smallest, piece had been folded and placed over the wound to curb the flow of blood.

"One second, Doctor," said Buckley as he signaled Allen to pick up Quinn's legs. When Allen was in position, he whispered, "Ready...Now." Together, they lifted Quinn up and placed him onto a blanket that had been spread over the closest desktop. Quinn moaned pitifully, but remained unconscious.

Buckley lingered near Quinn's shoulders while Allen stayed at his feet. Gilbert positioned himself to Allen's right. Mundell and the doctor moved up to the side of the 'examination' table. Doctor Starry leaned slightly over Quinn's left side and slowly raised the dressing from the wound.

The Doctor spread the wound apart. To no one in particular, he said, "Hmm, there are powder burns inside the wound." He looked to his right at Buckley, and, half as a question and half as a statement, he said, "This was inflicted at very close range." Buckley nodded affirmative. The Doctor then asked, "Did you find an exit wound on his back?" Buckley shook his head negative.

Doctor Starry reached into his bag and extracted a thin, twelve-inch long, shiny metal rod. He probed gently into the wound for several long minutes. Ultimately satisfied that he had discovered as much as he could, he retracted his instrument.

Turning to Mundell, he shook his head and said solemnly, "I'm afraid it's not good." He contemplated his words as he wiped off the rod. "The bullet is still in there." He paused. "It has lodged against his spine. From what I could feel, it has functioned like a typical soft lead bullet was designed to do." He gathered the tips of his fingers together on one hand and then spread his fingers and hand out wide. "It has mushroomed out quite a bit. It's now wider than it is long and I think some pieces have broken off of the flattened end." He paused again. "His insides are all torn up." With true sadness in his eyes as well as in his voice, he continued, "I'm sorry...but there is nothing that can be done."

Allen gasped and his legs went rubbery under him. Gilbert jabbed a beefy hand under Allen's right armpit and braced him up. "Steady, lad," he whispered. "Breathe deeply." As Allen did so, his legs regained their strength. "Come on, Allen," coaxed Gilbert, "Let's go outside for a little bit."

Doctor Starry moved over to Ruppert and began tending to his wound. When he was finished, Ruppert sported a bandage that encircled his head. The main part of the bandage passed around the back of his neck, under his ears and under his nose. His lips seemed to be covered, but if he opened his jaw, the lower lip was exposed. To keep this bandage from falling down toward his chin, an additional piece of bandage crossed the crown of his head and attached to the circular bandage on both sides, just in front of his ears.

"You'll be just fine," said the Doctor. "Make sure you keep the bandage clean and report to your military surgeon when you return to Washington." He returned to his first patient.

Buckley had covered Quinn with a sheet as well as a blanket. He had also placed the pillow back under his head. On Quinn's forehead was a strip of moist towel.

"Ahh," said Doctor Starry. "I see you've handled this kind of a case before."

"Unfortunately, yes," replied Buckley.

"Then you remember," admonished the Doctor, "that the patient is not to be given any water to drink."

"Only enough to wet his lips and his tongue," rejoined Barkley. The good Doctor nodded approval and turned to

Mundell.

"Thank you for your time, Doctor," said Mundell, "You have been most kind."

"I wish I could do more." He shrugged his shoulders and turned to leave.

Mundell held up his hand. "If you don't mind, Doctor, there are a couple more things you could help with."

"Yes?" said the puzzled physician.

"Yes, sir," continued Mundell, "Could you please tell me where we can find a Catholic Priest and a good laundress in your town?"

"Oh...yes," said the surprised Doctor. "Saint Peter's Church is just up the hill from us." He pointed upward toward the seam where the back wall and the ceiling met. "If you stand in the middle of the Armory compound, you can see its white steeple clearly." He played with his chin slightly. "But as to the laundress." He shook his head. "I don't understand why..."

"It's quite simple, Doctor," explained Mundell. "If we are to bury Private Quinn, we'd like to have his uniform cleaned, first."

"Ahh, I see!" exclaimed the Doctor. "In that case, I most heartily recommend Mistress Wagner. She is an outstanding seamstress, as well as an excellent laundress." He thought for a second. "Her shop is just a little ways up High Street, perhaps the second building on the left. I believe it's called the Havener House."

"Thank you, again, Doctor." Mundell extended an arm toward the door. "Your information is most helpful." The two men exited the room.

Baxter jumped away from the fire he had been tending. He disassembled the litter and propped up the muskets. "I'll take care of both of those errands right away," he said as he wrapped Quinn's uniform inside the litter blanket.

Buckley smiled broadly and said to the unconscious Quinn, "He's a bright lad, that one."

* * * * *

Outside, Gilbert guided Allen around to the side of the office building away from the engine house. He positioned him so he could lean up against a section of the wall between two windows. He waited quite a while before he spoke. "How are you feeling," he finally asked.

Allen come back with, "None too good." He looked away from Gilbert and blinked hard, twice. He was doing his best to fight back the tears. "Why did it have to be Luke?"

"It could have been any one of us," replied Gilbert. "It just happened to be Luke." He shook his head. "If I had my way, no one would be lying on that tabletop."

"But he's dying...for nothing," stammered Allen.

"No, you're wrong," retorted Gilbert. "Luke is a Marine. A Marine in the service of his country, and he's dying because he was doing his duty as any Marine should." He wanted to pace back and forth, but, instead, stood directly in front of Allen. "Many a good Marine has died doing his duty in the past, and I imagine that many more good Marines will die doing their duty in the future."

He stabbed a finger at Allen's chest. "It's what we're here for." He made an 'X' on his left palm with his right index finger. "We made our marks and swore to put our lives on the line for our country. We fight, and maybe die." He shook his index finger back and forth. "Not for the glory of fighting...but to make sure that the good folks we call 'neighbor' don't have to live in constant fear that death or destruction are just a moment away." He lowered his voice. "Maybe that sounds like a fancy, glorified idea, but if you think about it, that's what it all boils down to." He pointed down at the ground. "We're here because not every man alive has the desire or the ability to do what we're called on to do." He gestured toward the front of the Armory. "The Militiamen we've encountered at this place are a good example of what the average citizen has the ability to do." He pointed at the window to Allen's left, toward the 'sick bay' on the other side of the building. "And Luke's courage is a fine example of what a few good men can do."

He grasped Allen squarely on both shoulders and looked

him straight in the eye. "Don't feel sorry for yourself, Bal. Be proud that you could call a Marine like Luke Quinn your shipmate and friend." He leaned back and thumbed toward his chest. "I certainly am."

Allen nodded faintly. "But I wish he would live..." He struggled to get the words out.

"Aye, lad," replied Gilbert solemnly, "we all do." He moved to Allen's side and put an arm around his shoulders. "But remember, Bal, if you're faithful to his memory, your friend will always live in you." He gently tapped Allen's chest, just outside of his heart.

They were quiet for a long time. Finally, Allen spoke. The words came out slowly, but positively. "It's better to remember his life, rather than mourn his death." As each word passed from his lips, his sorrow diminished more and more.

Gilbert nodded and grinned. "Now you're catching on to the whole idea behind a good Irish wake."

Allen grinned briefly as he leaned away from the wall. "I feel a little better now." He wiped his nose on the back of his hand and sniffed. Standing tall, he said, "Let's go back in."

CHAPTER ELEVEN

"CLEAN-UP"

Tuesday, October 18, 1859, 10:00 a.m.

"Excuse me, Colonel," begged Greene as he forced his way past the pressing townspeople.

"Yes, Lieutenant," replied a harried Lee.

Stuart, always the vigilant aide, made every effort to keep the exasperating crowd of journalists, Militiamen, and well-wishing citizens away from their conversation. The two officers were able to step a few paces away from the crowd.

"Yes, sir," said Greene, "I'd like to give you an updated report on the prisoner situation."

"Very well, please continue," replied Lee as he turned his back to the beckoning horde.

"I am sorry to report," Greene began, "that Watson Brown has died." He quickly added, "The attending doctor had anticipated as much. Apparently he had lost too much blood." Lee only nodded acceptance.

"Because of the press of gawkers," continued Greene, "and the continuing potential of riotous acts against him, John Brown has been removed to the Paymaster's office." Lee's puzzled look caused Greene to add, "That's the office where we shaved this morning." Again, Lee wordlessly nodded acceptance. "The doctor's initial evaluation is that Brown's wounds are not life threatening and may only be flesh wounds." Greene chuckled slightly. "If that is the case, then he is a first-rate actor. To hear him howl when he was moved, you'd have thought he was being murdered."

Lee's non-reaction triggered Greene to go on with his report. "We have also removed an injured insurgent from the Wager Hotel and carried him to the Paymaster's office." Lee nodded as usual. "In addition to the two uninjured insurgents we captured in the engine house, we have also assumed responsibility for one more of their kind. He had been caught, yesterday, and imprisoned in the local jail." He gestured over his shoulder. "The three of them are now under guard and out of sight in the engine house."

Greene next pointed to the grassy area between the office building and the engine house. "We have, so far, collected a total of eight dead insurgents." He turned to Lee to indicate that he had finished his report.

"Thank you, Lieutenant," said Lee. "Please keep up the good work."

Tuesday, October 18, 1859, 10:30 a.m.

Major Russell made his way down the office building's hallway. The Marine sentry at the far end snapped to Attention at his approach. Russell said, "At Ease, Private," and, without knocking, opened the door to the right and entered the room. When only a single pace inside, he was surprised into motionlessness by the sight before him.

There was the 'dying' Brown. He was standing perfectly upright in the middle of the room. In view of the fact that he wasn't using any furniture or other convenience to stabilize himself, he seemed quite strong and capable. His shirt and trousers were unfastened. His head and shoulders were twisted around to his left. With his hands, he was calmly examining the wound on his side.

Brown suddenly looked up and saw Russell. Without saying a word, the grizzled old man resumed his former position on the floor and covered himself with a blanket.

"Excuse me." The voice coming from behind Russell was soft and unassuming. "Are the injured Marines in here?"

Russell turned around to see a Priest standing at the threshold. Before he could respond to the cleric, Brown began shouting, "GET HIM OUT OF HERE! I DON'T WANT HIM ABOUT ME! GET HIM OUT!" Both men in the doorway were stunned by the hatred and malice Brown was demonstrating toward the Catholic man of God.

Russell quickly ushered the Priest into the hallway and closed the office door behind them. Brown's ranting voice could still be heard through the door's glass pane. Russell said to the sentry, "You'd best assume a position inside the room with the prisoner."

To the Priest, Russell said, "I believe the men you seek are inside this room." He opened the door to the clerk's office.

Inside they found the injured Marines, as well as Corporal Gilbert and Private Allen. The two attendants came to Attention when they sighted the Major. "As you were," said

Russell to the men as he guided the Priest over to Quinn. "This Marine may be best served by your comfortings, Father," he said softly.

While the Priest made the sign of the cross and began praying, Russell moved over to Gilbert and Ruppert. Please, tell me, Corporal," he began as he pointed to the bandaged Ruppert, "how is this Private fairing?

"He's doing quite well, Major," replied Gilbert. He has a nasty gash on his upper lip," He indicated the position of the wound on his own face with his index finger, "and one of his teeth has been broken off." Gilbert grinned widely. "However, Private Ruppert appears to be getting along famously." He laughed lightly. "Why, just a few moments ago, sir, he was telling me that he 'thinks he may have truly lost his sweet tooth'."

Although Allen snickered, the humor of Ruppert's statement was lost on Russell. The Major gestured toward Quinn. "And how is he doing?" he asked.

"The doctor has confirmed that Private Quinn's wound is fatal, sir," said Gilbert with all seriousness. "We're doing our best to make him comfortable." He leaned closer to the Major. "Quinn is Roman Catholic, sir."

Russell walked back to the Priest and tapped him gently on the shoulder. When the cleric looked up, Russell said, "A moment, please, Father." He stepped toward the window and the Priest followed.

In a whisper, Russell said, "Apparently Private Quinn is indeed a Roman Catholic," he shook his head, "and his injury is unfortunately mortal." The Priest quickly crossed himself. "Father," continued Russell, "will you please make arrangements for a coffin to be made as quickly as possible." The cleric bowed his head solemnly. "As the Paymaster for the United States Marines," added Russell, "I assure you that the undertaker will be compensated for his labor."

"Thank you, my son," said the Priest. "I shall make all of the necessary arrangements." He turned back toward Quinn and began making preparations to administer the last rites.

Tuesday, October 18, 1859, 11:55 a.m.

The four 'Regular' officers had assembled at the train platform just behind the Wager Hotel. Russell, Stuart, and Greene were standing close together as they awaited the arrival of the train carrying Henry Wise, the Governor of Virginia. Lee had stepped several paces away and was patiently listening to an agitated townsman.

"It shall be good to see the Governor, again," stated Stuart as he rocked back and forth on his toes.

Russell was astutely curious, but forced himself to remain quiet. It was Greene who asked, "You are acquainted with Governor Wise?"

"Yes, indeed," beamed Stuart. "I have probably known the good Governor," he thought briefly, "well, longer than I can remember right now." His smile enlarged. "Why, in my younger days, I used to refer to him as 'Uncle Henry'." He held up a hand. "Although he isn't, really."

Russell's curiosity had the best of him. "How is it, then, that you are so close?" Considering his previous run-in with Stuart, he asked as diplomatically as he could.

"Oh," said Stuart matter of factly to Russell, "the Governor and my father have been old political allies since my father's term in the U.S. House of Representatives, starting back in Thirty-Seven." He looked to Greene and chuckled. "I guess that means I would have been just four years old, then."

Before the conversation could continue, Lee returned to their group with the townsman following behind him. "Lieutenant Greene," he began, "this is Mister Unseld." He gestured around to the man. "He has a farm close to where Brown was living before his attack here." Unseld's head bobbed up and down as Lee spoke. "I believe it would be prudent to investigate this place."

"Aye, Colonel," injected Greene. "Uh, I concur, sir," he rephrased.

"Excellent, Lieutenant," smiled Lee. "Would you kindly take a Squad of your Marines and follow Mister Unseld to its location." He turned to the farmer. "I am sure that he will pilot you there." Unseld bobbed heartily.

"Aye-Aye, Colonel," said Greene with a salute.

Before Greene could depart, Russell proposed, "Perhaps you would care to join them, Lieutenant Stuart?"

With a roguish look, Stuart replied, "I believe Lieutenant Greene to be an excellent officer." He smiled. "It would be a disservice to encumber him with an awkward marching, horse soldier such as myself." Unseen by Russell, he winked to Greene. "I shall remain here, and continue to assist Colonel Lee as necessary.

"Yes, of course," conceded Russell dejectedly. Greene smiled and took Russell's answer as his cue to escort Unseld back into the Armory.

An engine's whistle resonated inside the covered bridge. "Gentlemen," said Lee to the remaining two officers as he looked toward the Maryland side of the river, "I believe the Governor's train is arriving."

Tuesday, October 18, 1859, 12:33 p.m.

Allen had not left his friend's side at all during the morning. He had dampened the compress on Quinn's forehead regularly. In addition, he had changed the dressing over his wound whenever it was entirely soaked with blood. On one occasion, when Quinn's breathing was very minimal, Allen, in a panic, had asked Gilbert to check Quinn because he wasn't sure if he was still breathing.

Shortly after that momentary scare, Allen had commented to Gilbert that he wished that 'Luke would regain consciousness'. Gilbert had replied, "It's probably best that he doesn't. The pain from such a wound tends to hit a man something fierce." From then on, they both had started holding their breath whenever Quinn moaned or grimaced. Gilbert had also advised that Allen talk to his friend whenever he seemed to be in discomfort. "It'll help settle him down," he had said.

Now, while Allen was removing the compress, Quinn suddenly became restless. His limbs moved about slightly. His body quickly tensed and then relaxed several times. His breathing became labored.

Allen placed his hand gently above his friend's brow. It was very cool to his touch. With the one hand still on Quinn's forehead, he placed his other hand on Quinn's forearm and gave a slight squeeze. "Easy, Luke," he said softly. "It's okay. I'm here with you."

Quinn's movements started to subside. He gasped a shallow lungful of air and then exhaled long and slowly. As the last of the breath escaped, his body relaxed completely.

Gilbert placed a comforting hand on Allen's shoulder. "He's no longer in pain, Bal," was all he could say.

Silent, uncontrollable tears streamed down both of Allen's cheeks.

Tuesday, October 18, 1859, 1:30 p.m.

Greene had called upon Sergeant Callahan and his Section B for the trip to Brown's hideout on the Maryland side of the Potomac. Mister Unseld led the way for the Marines with his wagon and team of two horses. "It's only about five or six miles up the road," the farmer had said. What he hadn't said was that this little trip was going to be over a dusty, winding, and mostly, uphill country road.

As the trip progressed, Greene had called for several rest stops along the way. His men had to be as tired as he was. With a shake of his head, he, at one time, thought, *"I think I understand why Lieutenant Stuart declined to make this trip."*

Finally, Unseld brought his team to a stop. He turned around on the bench seat and pointed off to the left of the road. "The farm house is just over there, Lieutenant," he said.

Greene walked up beside the wagon and peered off toward the location his 'pilot' was indicating. At first, besides a narrow dirt path, all he could see were woods and underbrush. He moved about to get a better view. "There," he said as he aimed his finger at what appeared to be a large two story log structure. It was well over one hundred yards away from the main road and efficiently hidden. "An excellent choice of location," he said admirably. "A perfect place to hide a group of men and supplies from nosy neighbors."

Suddenly, Greene heard the sounds of voices and banging objects coming from the direction of the house. He signaled Callahan forward. "Have the men Fix Bayonets and Prime their weapons," he ordered. "We shall advance slowly," he pointed up the lane, "until we know who we're dealing with up there."

When the ready-for-action Marines broke out into the open and formed a battle line facing the house, the scene before them was surreal. Frantic men, women, and children were ransacking the place. All sorts of items were strewn about on the ground and more was being thrown out doors and windows. Some of the people were carrying armloads of objects off to nearby wagons or horses.

At Greene's signal, Sergeant Callahan discharged his weapon high into the air. At first everyone ducked low, frozen in place. The diminishing muzzle report was the only sound to be heard for several seconds. Slowly the foragers regained their wits and began turning about to see who had fired the shot. Unexpectedly, a man dressed in bib overalls bolted out onto the second floor porch and pointed at the Marines. He shouted and everyone scurried away like scared rabbits.

"I think they're all locals," stated Greene.

"Aye, sir," agreed Callahan. "I didn't see anyone with a weapon, either."

"Sergeant, take a third of the men," commanded Greene, "and search the lower floor. I shall take the rest of the men and search the remainder of the house." With just the minimum of hand signals, the two groups moved out quickly and silently.

On the upper level, Greene found a living room, two small bedrooms and a narrow stairway leading to an attic above. He detailed several men to check out the attic. As he looked around the living room, Greene was amazed at the disarray of furniture, clothing, and personal possessions within. *"The locals were having a grand old time in here,"* he thought. It didn't appear that much of anything had been left untouched.

Callahan appeared with several of his men. "Down below," he reported, "is a kitchen and a couple of storerooms." He pointed toward his feet. "The storerooms are filled with wooden crates. Looks like cases of blankets, tents, shoes, and other military accouterments for a campaign."

At that time a Private approached. "Lieutenant," he said, "I found this in a corner of one of the bedrooms." He was toting a two-foot by two-foot carpetbag. "It's full of papers, sir."

"Very well," responded Greene. "Leave it here with me."

As he placed the carpetbag next to Greene's foot, the Private continued, "The other bedroom is full of long handled pikes, too, sir."

Greene went to investigate. After scrutinizing the second bedroom, he figured, "There must be a thousand pikes in here."

"There are more pikes below, Lieutenant," added Callahan.

Greene asked his Sergeant to hold onto the carpetbag and went below to evaluate the cache of supplies. When he reappeared outside after his inspection, he sighted Unseld. The farmer had brought his wagon close to the house. "Mister Unseld," Greene said, "I would like to use your wagon to carry anything of military value back to Harper's Ferry." Unseld merely bobbed his head.

Greene called up to Sergeant Callahan. "With the exception of adequate sentries, have the men stack arms," he pointed to the storerooms, "and start loading these crates onto the wagon."

"Aye-aye, sir," acknowledged Callahan as he held the carpetbag over the porch rail. When Greene nodded, he dropped the bag to the ground. Greene picked it up and moved closer to the wagon.

"What's in that?" queried Unseld.

"I'm about to find out," replied Greene. He opened the bag and was truly surprised to find that it was, indeed, full of papers.

On top were folded maps. As he sorted through them, he realized they were individual maps of all the Southern States. He unfolded one at random. It was a map of Alabama, and it was heavily marked over. There were colored lines indicating different routes for attack and escape, as well as circles delineating safe hiding places. On the margins were numbers labeled as white and slave populations. Greene shook his head and half whispered, "Wow!"

He next picked out a handful of letters and scanned through them. "Hmm," he mused, "here's one from Gerrit Smith. He's the Abolition Presidential candidate." He checked out another one. "And this one is from Frederick Douglass." Greene's excitement was beginning to build as he thumbed through more of the letters. "There are also several letters from Frank Sanborn and Thomas Higginson." He looked up to Unseld. "They're both prominent Northern abolitionists." Unseld merely shrugged his shoulders. Greene decided to ignore him for the time being and wrestled through more of the letters and papers.

After an intense period of silent reading, Greene started putting the papers back into the bag. He looked back to Unseld and said, "Besides a number of letters from other abolitionists such as Theodore Parker, George Stearns, and Samuel Howe, there are also some printed pamphlets." He held one of them up. "They seem to be a constitution for a provisional government that Captain John Brown was going to create for the liberated slaves."

"Isn't that treason?" asked a serious Unseld.

"It would certainly seem so," replied Greene as he dropped the pamphlet into the bag. A loud scrap of wood against wood attracted his attention. He looked around and noticed that the last of the crates had been loaded onto the wagon.

As the Marines started bringing some of the pikes out from the storeroom, someone yelled, "Hey! Can we have some of those?" Many of the locals had sufficiently stiffened their nerve and were pressing closer to the house.

"Why would you want them?" asked Greene.

"Those handles are made of fine ash wood," retorted one obvious farmer. "We can use them for hayforks, rakes, shovels, and the like."

Greene quickly surveyed the load on the wagon and realized that there wasn't enough room left to accommodate all of the pikes. He called over to Callahan, "Sergeant, take the men upstairs and throw some of the pikes out to the ground." After several armloads had been jettisoned over the porch rail, Greene yelled to the farmers, "Each of you may take five pikes."

The eager farmers retrieved their allotted number. Remembering how many pikes he had seen upstairs, Greene realized that five apiece would hardly make a dent in the insurgent's stash. He signaled the Marines above to continue dropping the pikes. "All right," he said to the farmers, "each of you can have ten." Even with more locals emerging from the surrounding woods to claim their share of the treasure, it didn't take long for Greene to again recognize the need to increase the allowance. In desperation, he upped the ante to fifty apiece.

The Marines on the second floor were rushing as fast as they could to unload the pikes. It had become a game to them. They were dropping the pikes and gleefully watching the frenzied locals first jump out of the way, then scamper back to capture their prizes.

When the pile on the ground started to grow in size, Greene relented completely and, with a wave of his arms, shouted, "Take as many as you want!"

When the locals' hunger for booty was finally satiated, the Marines loaded the remaining pikes onto Unseld's wagon and began the downhill march back to Harper's Ferry.

Tuesday, October 18, 1859, 6:00 p.m.

It was already beginning to get dark when the Marines arrived back inside the Armory. Stuart and McDonough approached Greene after he had finished giving orders for the material to be offloaded from the wagon into the warehouse.

"Welcome back, Lieutenant," greeted a smiling Stuart. "It appears that you have produced a successful scavenger hunt after all." As a former quartermaster, he eyed the boxes carefully.

"It was interesting, to say the least," was Greene's limited response. His fatigue was evident in his voice.

"Obviously a most tiring excursion," acknowledged Stuart. "However, I do have some news that will cheer you up."

"Pray continue," said Greene hopefully.

"Well, sir," began Stuart. "It appears that the good Major Russell has vacated the field."

Greene was taken aback. "Oh?" was all he could manage to say.

"Yes," smiled Stuart. "For some reason or another, except for a formal introduction, he was unable to ingratiate himself to the good Governor Wise." Stuart was absolutely pleased with the telling of his tale. "Apparently your Major finally recognized the impossibility of such a personal undertaking. He later advised Colonel Lee that, since his advisory role to you was completed, his orders had been fulfilled." Stuart made a wriggling snake motion with his hand. "In the company of the

B and O Transportation Master, Mister Smith, he made his way out of here on the early afternoon train for Baltimore."

Greene looked to McDonough for confirmation. The Orderly Sergeant nodded and smiled discretely.

"Well, sir," rejoined a perked up Greene to Stuart. "Such a favorable report deserves a reward." He held up the carpetbag. "In this bag are enough documents to possibly charge Brown with treason or rebellion." He patted the bag. "In addition, there are plenty of letters that will implicate a number of prominent abolitionists from the North and West." He nodded his head. "Those men were well aware of Brown's efforts here. In addition, they financed him." He bowed to Stuart. "Will you ensure that Colonel Lee and Governor Wise are made aware of its contents?"

Stuart snatched the bag's handles. "With great pleasure, sir." He bowed in return. "If you will excuse me, I shall do so immediately."

To prevent Stuart from bolting away, Greene placed a gentle hand on the Lieutenant's upper arm and stated, "With regards to my recent expedition." He released his grasp. "Please advise Colonel Lee that I will be available to brief him fully, at his convenience." Stuart smiled, nodded, and departed jubilantly.

Greene turned to McDonough. "Well, XO," he asked, "any other items of interest?"

Yes, sir, there are several," frowned McDonough. "First, I regret to report that Private Quinn has died."

"A shame," said Greene sadly. "He was a good Marine."

Yes, sir. He will be missed." McDonough paused briefly, then continued. "Before he left, Major Russell settled financial accounts with the local undertaker, the Catholic Priest, and a laundress for all things concerning Quinn's burial.

"Excellent," said a mildly astonished Greene.

"To change the subject for a moment, sir," interjected McDonough. "The Governor, Colonel Lee, and several other distinguished gentlemen interviewed Brown for almost three hours while you were gone." He looked around to see who might be near. "The Governor has declared that the Commonwealth of Virginia will try Brown and his men for crimes against the State."

"I expected as much," said Greene.

"Yes, sir," continued McDonough, "and as a result of the Governor's decision, Colonel Lee has requested that we escort the prisoners to the Charles Town jail tomorrow morning."

"I assume some arrangements have been made?" queried Greene.

"Yes, sir," nodded McDonough. "Because they fear that some of his confederates may attempt to free Brown if we take him overland, a train has been arranged to take us there. The scheduled departure is at Eight O'clock."

Greene knew that the train referred to belonged to the Winchester and Potomac line. Charles Town, Virginia was just ten miles away via their tracks. He nodded an understanding of McDonough's comments.

"If all goes well in the morning," continued McDonough, "then we shall be able to bury Quinn at about One O'clock tomorrow."

"Yes, indeed," replied a weary Greene, "One O'clock."

"Just a few more items, Skipper," said McDonough. "You should know that one of the first things that Governor Wise did when he arrived was to reopen the saloons."

Greene's attention was instantly aroused. "That means we'll have to be extra vigilant tonight."

"Yes, sir," added McDonough, "and the Governor also had the Militia impress all of the horses in town." He scratched his temple. "As to the why of it, we're not sure."

Greene pondered the 'why' for several moments. Subsequently, he could only hazard a guess. "Probably to make sure that, if any of Brown's associates are still in town, they cannot free him and escape on horseback." He started circling around, taking an evaluative look about the Armory yard. "Another reason to be vigilant."

"Aye, sir," agreed McDonough. "We're in for another long night."

Greene ended his survey when he espied the farmer's now empty wagon. Still feeling the ache in his feet and legs from the recent march, he thought, *"I fear our 'pilot' will have a long walk home without his accustomed transport."* He turned back to McDonough. "XO, Mister Unseld has provided us with an invaluable service, today. Please ensure that he and his wagon are escorted safely across the river and onto the westbound road." He winked. "I'd like to make sure that his horses are not impressed by any overeager Militiamen."

"Aye-aye, sir," chimed McDonough with a salute and a grin. Unseld just nodded.

Wednesday, October 19, 1859, 7:45 a.m.

"We're ready, Lieutenant," said McDonough after a salute.
"Very well," replied Greene. "You may bring them out."
McDonough signaled to the doorway of the office building. Almost immediately, Marines filed out of the building carrying a wooden stretcher with a mattress on it. Lying on the mattress was the 'wounded' Brown. He was not silent as his 'cot' was mounted aboard a large wagon. He complained angrily at the slightest bump or jostle. After Brown was aboard, another stretcher bearing the other injured insurgent was brought out. This man, suffering from four bullet wounds, was awake and lucid. Although he raised his head to see what was going on about him, he remained silent.

As the tailgate of the wagon was being raised to its closed position, Governor Wise, Senator Mason, and several other dignitaries stepped into place at the rear the wagon. Behind them, the three other prisoners were formed up in a line abreast. Overall, this little assemblage had the somber look of a funeral procession.

However, surrounding the whole convoy was a double filed, square of protective Marines. Each man's weapon was loaded, primed and had a bayonet affixed atop of it. They meant business and they wanted the onlookers to know it

Greene was positioned at the head of the formation. Behind him were Lee and Stuart. McDonough and Mundell were carefully placed outboard of the square, each one near the middle of a side. When Greene gave the command, "Forward, March." the organized gathering moved slowly toward the Armory gate.

Earlier that morning, Lee had said to Greene, "We shall undoubtedly require your whole Detachment to keep a close guard over the prisoners when we move them to the train."

Greene had also noticed the gathering crowd outside the Armory gates. Shortly after Seven O'clock, they had begun to line both sides of the fifty-yard long street to the W&P train depot. He was especially wary of this motley group and had replied to Lee, "Aye, Colonel, this crowd is more ugly than noisy. If they're all as hung-over as I think they might be, they could easily turn into a mob." Consequently, he had spent a good twenty minutes with his Orderly Sergeants figuring out the best way to keep potential trouble at bay.

Now underway, the procession moved forward to the DUMP, DUMP, THADUMP of the Drummers. The wagon driver had one Drummer sitting on either side of him on the bench seat. Their drums were held securely between their knees. Baxter had been relegated to watching over the 'patients' on the cots because his fife might sound too cheery.

As the gates were opened to allow the procession out, the crowd started jeering and booing. Greene ordered, "Arms, Port." The snappy movement of the Marines' weapons stunned most of the crowd into silence. DUMP, DUMP, THADUMP. The procession moved on.

As they neared the depot, the crowd started to become boisterous again. Shortly after Greene commanded, "Detachment, Halt," a rhythmic chant of "Lynch them! Lynch them! Lynch them, now!" reached riotous proportions.

McDonough moved quickly to the forward end of the line. His side of the square was nearest to the largest and rowdiest part of the crowd. He commanded his Squad to face them.

In the meantime, Governor Wise had unexpectedly walked up upon the deport platform to address the crowd. He held out his right arm dramatically toward the chanters and, with dignity, called out to them, "Oh, it would be cowardly to lynch them now!"

As if this were a cue, McDonough commanded, "On Guard!" In a fraction of an instant, the Marines on the outer rank simultaneously assumed the first position of their bayonet drill. Their weapons flashed forward. Their right arms held the musket stocks down near their waists while the left arms held the bayonet tips up about chest high. They lunged forward half a pace with their left feet, thus distributing their weight evenly on both feet. At the same time, they yelled as one,

"AHHHHH!" The effect was immediate. The crowd hushed and hastily started to disperse. Some even ran to get away. McDonough looked to Greene and smiled. Their planning had worked out perfectly.

The rest of the trip was anticlimactic. Greene had only asked for Sergeant Davis' Section C to board the train with him. He was so confident that Brown and his men would be delivered to the Charles Town jail without further ado that none of the prisoners were even restrained. The watchful eyes of twenty prepared Marines were assurance enough.

Wednesday, October 19, 1859, 11:30 a.m.

Baxter caught up with Gilbert, as he was about to enter the undertaker's shop. Holding out the brown paper wrapped bundle of clothes he was carrying, he said with pleasure, "Mistress Wagner did a number one job on Quinn's uniform, Corporal." He lowered the bundle and finished in a subtle tone. "It's ready in all respects for his final inspection.

"As well it should be," replied Gilbert as he removed his cap. He opened the shop door and indicated for the other to uncover and enter. Inside, Mister Ferko, the ever smiling, but seemingly nervous, undertaker, arrived from a back room to meet them. "Good day, sir," said Gilbert.

"Ahh, good day," responded Ferko as he finished slipping on his black frock coat. "You, umm, gentlemen are undoubtedly here about your fellow soldier." He started to bow respectfully, but stopped when he saw Gilbert cringe slightly. "Oh," he said worriedly, "we've said something wrong."

"Yes sir. Uh, no sir," stammered an embarrassed Gilbert. "What I mean, sir, is, uh." He hadn't expected his reaction to be so evident. Swallowing hard, he pressed on. "Yes sir, we're here to see about Private Quinn." He flashed his best disarming grin. "And, uh, no sir, he's, uh, not a soldier, sir," he stood tall, "he's a Marine."

"Yes, of course," said the undertaker, politely. He pondered the difference for a quick moment. When he couldn't make out what it all meant, he flashed his hands about in an anxious, but dismissive, manner. "Be that as it is, how may we help you?"

"Well, sir," replied Gilbert. "We have brought Private Quinn's uniform." He indicated Baxter's bundle. "We would like him to be buried in it."

The undertaker accepted the package Baxter was offering forward. "Yes, of course," he said. "Is there anything else your 'private' might require?"

"Yes, sir," offered Gilbert. "These are his socks and boots." He held up the well-blackened brogans and pointed inside one of them. "His waist belt is also in here."

Ferko placed the uniform bundle onto a chair and accepted the boots. "As we are not familiar with the proper wearing of your uniforms," he passed his hand up and down in front of Gilbert, "may we ask that one of you assist us to ensure that it is done correctly?"

Baxter immediately piped up, "I will." Gilbert nodded approval.

"Excellent," remarked the pleased undertaker. He looked to Gilbert. "The dearly departed has already been prepared." He glanced up at a clock on the wall. "It shall take a while to dress him." He looked back, a saddened look on his face. "However, we are afraid we have not been able to finish the casket."

"Oh?" queried Gilbert in a slightly incredulous tone. Expecting a setback, he leaned closer, his affable grin gone.

"Oh, we do beg your pardon," countered the intimidated undertaker, "We merely meant that the finishing touches have not been completed." He fished a handkerchief from his black coat. "That is to say that we are unable to provide iron handles for the casket." He wiped his brow. "This raid has caused the unexpected demise of five of our citizens, and," he wiped his brow, again, "has, unfortunately, depleted our supply of handles."

"Well, that's quite all right, sir," said a relaxed Gilbert. "We'll be able to manage without them."

"Oh," sighed a relieved Ferko, "wonderful." He looked back at the clock. "In that case, we shall indeed be ready at One O'clock." He looked to Gilbert again. "We expect, then, that we shall meet you at the final resting place?"

"I've been told about a cemetery at the top of the hill,"

stated Gilbert as he pointed in that general direction. "You mean there?"

"Oh, no!" protested Ferko. "That's the Protestant cemetery." He looked about nervously. "We thought we understood from Father John, that your friend was a Roman Catholic."

"That is correct," said Gilbert.

"Well, then," said a self-righteous Ferko, "the Catholic cemetery is in an entirely different location."

"Then, just how do we get there?" demanded an impatient, non-grinning Gilbert. Without him realizing it, his 'evil eye' had manifested itself.

Ferko was absolutely taken aback. In a panic, he faltered over the words. "It's a-actually about a mile and a q-q-quarter away from here." He struggled with how best to give the directions. "Since you are not familiar with this c-community," he shook his head several times as he spoke, "it will be rather d-difficult to d-describe how to get there." His hands wrung the handkerchief nervously as he strained to remedy the situation.

Gilbert was stymied by the reaction of the undertaker, but then he questioned himself, *"Is this poor fellow afraid of military men?"* He looked the quivering Ferko over carefully. *"Yes, he is! And he thinks I'm going to blame him for something, or injure him in some way."*

He held up his hand in a halt sign. "Please calm yourself, sir," he said with an assuring grin, "I apologize for any misunderstanding." He rolled his cap around in his hands. "You must recognize that we've been rather, uh, busy and haven't had a great deal of time to organize all the particulars for this funeral." When Ferko nodded, Gilbert patted the man on the arm. "Please believe me, sir, when I say that the Marines are most appreciative of your assistance and professional capabilities."

Ferko smiled meekly. As he settled down, an idea formulated. "Perhaps it would be best if we were to meet you at the bottom of High Street," he proposed, "then we could lead you the rest of the way."

"That would be an excellent solution," said Gilbert, wondering just who the often referred to 'we' actually were. "There is, however, just one request," he added, "that I would like to make concerning the casket."

"Yes, yes, anything," said the placating Ferko.

"I would like to ask that the lid of the casket not be nailed down until sometime after we arrive at the cemetery."

"C-cer-certainly," spluttered the perplexed undertaker.

Wednesday, October 19, 1859, 1:00 p.m.

"The Funeral Parade is ready, Lieutenant," said McDonough with a salute.

"Very well," replied Greene as he returned the military courtesy. "Assume your position."

After McDonough had done so, Greene commanded, "Detachment, Fix Bayonets." The metallic clatter, clink, and thud sounds of bayonets and musket butts resonated against the warehouse wall. When silence reclaimed the air, he ordered, "Shoulder, Arms." The muskets elevated swiftly. Glints of sunlight danced off the bayonets while the muskets were settled into their familiar positions.

"Forward, March," brought the column into motion. At the Armory gate, "Column Right, March," initiated the turn as well as prompted the Musicians to begin playing their slow funeral dirge.

The overall appearance of the Detachment was stately. Each man was neatly dressed in his freshly brushed coat and trousers. The immaculate white cross belts and waist belts were highlighted by their highly polished brass breastplates and belt buckles. The brass letters on the front of their caps were also shining brightly. In the chinstraps, resting above the glossy black cap visors, each man displayed a sprig of boxwood. This special gesture was for Quinn. It symbolized the 'wearing of the green' for their Irish comrade.

Only a few spectators were present to witness the majesty and dignity of the occasion. Most of the townspeople had resumed their daily concerns. As for the Militia, all, except one small Company, had departed earlier for their homes. To a man, the absence of gawkers suited the Marines just fine, as this funeral was not meant to be a public affair.

Up ahead, Greene could see the undertaker's hearse.

Although its purpose was foreboding in nature, it was a magnificent vehicle. The body and roof of the wagon were matte black in color; while the undercarriage and wheels were contrastingly gloss black. Two pairs of matched black horses waited patiently in the traces. Seated on a black velvet cushion sat Mr. Ferko, dressed in his black suit and stovepipe hat.

Inside the hearse, billowy black curtains draped down and were tied back to the sides of the large viewing apertures. The platform that constituted the bed of the wagon was covered with white silk. Centered on this angelic stage was Quinn's casket.

Even at a distance, Greene could make out the casket clearly. It was made of fine oak lumber and polished to a notable luster. *"Good,"* he thought, *"I'm happy to see that Major Russell didn't order a plain pine box."*

Six Marines stood at Attention, without weapons, outboard of the hearse. Three were stationed on each side. Allen stood near the right rear wheel. He and the five others were the designated sideboys. A civilian onlooker would have called them pallbearers.

As the column neared the intersection, Ferko released the foot brake. With a snap of the reins and a soft "Git up," he pressed his team into service. The horses, long accustomed to a steady pull, began their climb up the hill.

"Column Right, March," directed Greene when the head of the column was at the appropriate location. As he executed his turn, he noticed a street sign at the far corner. The marker identified the street they had just turned onto as High Street. Greene's eyes followed the macadamized surface up, and up, and up toward the top of the hill. *"Oh, yes,"* he thought, *"this street is suitably named. High is right!"*

A sudden realization hit him. *"Harper's Ferry is a simple little place,"* he mused. *"There are only three streets in the lower town."* He shook his head and grinned. *"The one behind the Armory and paralleling the Potomac River is aptly called Potomac Street. The one paralleling the Shenandoah River is, of course, called Shenandoah Street."* He looked up again to the top of the hill in front of him. *"And this one going up to the heights is perfectly named High Street."* He nodded and smiled to several townsmen who had stopped and removed their hats. "Simple, but nice," he said aloud.

An urge to turn and look over his Detachment waved through him. But, realizing the difficulty of marching backwards while traversing uphill, he allowed the feeling to pass. *"Besides,"* he thought, *"I know this formation by heart."*

Behind the hearse and its six sideboys, followed the three Musicians. The Fifer was first, behind whom were the two Drummers. Lieutenant Greene constituted the third row by himself. The two Orderly Sergeants made up the fourth row, and in the fifth row were Sergeants Callahan and Davis. A consecutive file of twenty-one Privates followed behind each of the Sergeants.

Bringing up the rear was a special Detail made up of ten men in two files. Nine had been selected as the Honor Guard to render full military tribute. Sergeant Buckley, Quinn's Section leader, commanded them.

The slow march up High Street while in formation was long and demanding. Normally such a trek would have elicited a wide range of comments from the ranks. However, not one syllable was uttered. A tribute to the caliber of the men involved, as well as to the man being escorted.

Traveling along relatively level terrain at the top of the hill was short lived. About twenty-five yards past a Lutheran Church, the hearse started negotiating a left turn onto a side street. Greene quickly commanded, "Column Left, March." In a matter of three paces in this new direction, the street surface gave way to a packed dirt lane, and started downhill. *"We're heading back toward the Shenandoah River,"* thought Greene.

The remainder of the lane meandered through heavy tree growth and, as a result, the journey seemed to be longer than it actually was. Eventually the hearse passed through a wide wrought iron arch mounted across two tall stone pillars. The iron letters on the arch proclaimed the place beyond to be "St. Peter's Cemetery".

The lane proceeded to a large circle near the center of the cemetery. Standing off to the right, near the outer edge of the circle, was the Catholic Priest. He was dressed in a black cassock with a short, large-sleeved, white linen surplice over it. A large crucifix was suspended from a long chain about his neck. He signaled the hearse toward his location.

Greene halted the Detachment a good ten paces before the

hearse came to a stop. After the command, "Order, Arms," was given, the two Orderly Sergeants moved smartly from their positions. McDonough headed toward the Priest, Mundell to take command of the Musicians.

Mundell waited as his counterpart spoke with the Priest. When the priest pointed up the grassy slope toward the tree line, he ordered, "Music, Forward, March." He paraded them five paces toward the hearse and then executed a Right Turn onto the leaf-covered landscape. High up the slope, near the last few tombstones just before the trees, he could make out a mound of freshly dug earth. He guided the Musicians toward that target. About a third of the way up the slope, he halted his Detail. "Right About, Turn." The four men faced the Funeral Parade.

At the hearse, McDonough had directed the sideboys with the offloading of the casket. Until such time that the lid was secured, they would carefully carry the container snugly between their chests. Each man's hands clasping their opposite partner's underneath the bottom. McDonough guided them toward the Musicians. When they arrived at the appropriate spot, McDonough halted the sideboys and assisted them with lowering the casket to the ground.

With the three pairs still facing each other on either side, he ordered, "Uncover." Each man bent down and grasped the edge of the casket lid with his fingertips. "Rise." Now they stood up together, the lid rising with them. "Three Sidesteps To The End." All six men turned their heads toward the 'foot' of the casket. "March." As they slowly sidestepped, the uniformed Quinn was gradually exposed to the bright light of the day. At the conclusion of the third step, they each faced Front. "Lower." The sideboys bent down to position the lid. When they stood back up, the 'head' of the lid rested against the 'foot' of the casket, and the 'foot' of the lid was on the ground. Satisfied, McDonough commanded, "Three Paces To The Rear, March."

When he saw the sideboys step backward, Greene raised his right arm and commanded slowly and precisely, "In Half Time, At The trail, Pass In Review." He dropped his arm. "March."

The Musicians began to softly play another funeral tune. Each man in the Parade, without stooping or leaning toward his weapon, firmly grasped the musket at his side with his right hand. With sheer strength, they all pressed the barrels forward so that the butts raised about three inches off the ground in the opposite direction. Simultaneously, the Detachment stepped forward at the prescribed slow cadence. Mr. Ferko fell in behind them with his bag of nails and hammer. The Priest walked in prayer beside him.

As they neared the lid, the two files parted slightly to facilitate each line passing between a side of the casket and the sideboys. The pace enabled each man to view their comrade one last time, as well as afforded them the opportunity to whisper or mentally pass on any last words or wishes to the deceased. A few of the Irishmen tossed in sprigs of boxwood as well.

The two files continued up the slope to the gravesite. Mr. Ferko and the Priest stopped quietly at the 'foot' of the lid. McDonough ordered the sideboys forward. In due order, the lid was replaced to its proper position. McDonough then ordered the sideboys back and signaled to the undertaker that he could now conclude his work.

With swift, sure strokes, the nails were driven home. When he finished, Ferko slowly circled the casket one more time, checking every feature. Satisfied, he nodded to McDonough and stepped out of the way.

The sideboys approached the sides again. This time, when the casket was raised, it was positioned upon their shoulders. Facing uphill, they additionally braced their burden with one hand against the bottom and the other hand against the side. At McDonough's command, the Detail proceeded slowly up the hill, followed by Mundell and the Musicians.

As they approached Quinn's final resting place, Allen could see more and more of the gravesite. First, he could see the mound of earth with two shovels laying neatly on top of the mass. Just beyond the mound was the opening to the grave. Two sturdy planks lay across the width of the opening. On top of the planks were lengths of rope, the ends of which were coiled neatly.

Using the grave as the focal point, the Funeral Parade was converting into a formation. About five paces on either side of the grave stood the parallel files of Marines, facing inboard.

Lieutenant Greene was positioned three paces above the center of the 'head' of the grave.

Farther up the hillside was the Honor Guard. They were facing downhill and distinctly grouped into three sets of three. Each group consisted of two Privates on the flanks and a Corporal in the center. Allen couldn't help but smile when he spotted Gilbert in the center of the middle group. Buckley stood a pace behind his favorite Corporal.

The sideboys carefully straddled the mound of earth and edged up along the opening. McDonough called a halt when the casket was centered. At the command, "Lower, One," the two files of sideboys shifted the casket from their shoulders and in one easy motion, twisted their bodies inboard to hold it in a position between them, against their chests. "Lower, Two," brought the casket down atop the planks and ropes.

Mundell had halted the Musicians just downhill of the mound. The Priest had made his way to the 'head' of the grave by passing behind the right file of Marines. When the cleric arrived at the appropriate spot, McDonough assumed his position just to the left of the 'head' of the grave. "Sideboys, Post," resulted in the six men marching downhill to form two lines behind the Musicians.

The Officer-in-Charge and the Executive Officer faced each other. McDonough saluted and said, "Sir, the Funeral Square is formed."

"Very well," replied Greene as he returned the salute. He turned and bowed slightly to the Priest and said, "You may proceed, Father."

The Priest nodded acknowledgement. He kissed his ritual stole and placed it around his neck. While making the sign of the cross, he began, "In nomine Patris..."

At the end of the Latin service, the six sideboys were again posted alongside the casket. The man in the center of each sideboy line prepared to remove one of the planks, while the other four took hold of the ropes. When so ordered, the planks were removed and Quinn's casket was lowered carefully into the ground. The sideboys maintained their positions when the undertaking was completed.

After the Latin benediction, the Priest offered Greene the opportunity to say a few words. Greene accepted. He took a pace toward the grave and removed his cap. Looking down at the casket, he paused for a long moment. He lifted his eyes skyward and prayed, "Dear Heavenly Father, we commend to you the body and soul of our comrade in arms, Private Luke Quinn." He held his arm slightly out toward Quinn's resting place. "He was one, who, at a time of trial, accepted his duty without question and with courage." He looked around at the men in formation. "We highly recommend him, Lord, for sentry duty on the streets of Heaven." He looked out over the cemetery below them. "We know he will always be faithful to such a responsibility, and you, too, will be proud to call him 'Shipmate'." He bowed his head. "Amen." Greene remained with his head lowered for several moments before covering with his cap and stepping back.

Through the silence surrounding the formation, Sergeant Buckley's voice could be clearly heard. "Honor Guard, Shoulder, Arms." He waited for three seconds. "Honor Guard, Ready." All nine men assumed the firing 'T' position.

With parade field volume, McDonough ordered, "Marine Detachment, Aaaten...Shun. Preeesent...Arms."

With his own measured tone, Buckley commanded, "Honor Guard, In The Name Of The Father, At Extreme Elevation, Aim." The center triad raised their muskets straight ahead and high to the sky. "Fire." The report of the three shots boomed loudly.

"In The Name Of The Son, Left Oblique, At Extreme Elevation, Aim." The trio on the left of the line (their left) raised their muskets to the left and high to the sky. "Fire." Another report boomed.

"And In The Name Of The Holy Spirit, Right Oblique, At Extreme Elevation, Aim." The threesome on the right of the line raised their muskets to the right and high to the sky. "Fire." The last report boomed and slowly faded to silence.

McDonough waited for the Honor Guard to recover to the Ready position before he ordered everyone to "Order, Arms". After the Priest had departed from the Square, he then ordered, "Detachment, Right About, Turn." The next command to follow was "Ground, Arms." He quickly ordered the men to "Recover", and then, in quick succession, accomplish directional movements so that they were all facing downhill.

What came next was a command that had been developed just for this occasion. "Countermarch By Files To Bury The Dead, March." The sideboys each stepped back two paces. The man on the lower end of each file took one pace forward, turned inboard, took four more paces, and turned up toward the grave. The remainder of the file followed behind their 'leader'. As they neared the mound, the 'leader' picked up a shovel, filled it with earth, and tossed the contents onto the casket. When he concluded this act, he passed the shovel to the next man in line, and moved on to reform the file behind his Sergeant. As the process continued, the formation looked like two large ovals on either side of the grave, rotating around the sideboys in the centers.

By the time each of the forty-four men had their turn with a shovel, the grave had nearly been filled. The sideboys finished the task as the files retrieved their weapons. McDonough next called the Detachment to Attention and placed everyone at Shoulder Arms before facing everyone uphill. Mundell turned his little Detail around to face in the opposite direction.

Bracketing the finished grave, Greene and McDonough marched straight ahead, downhill. While Greene continued to his post in front of the Musicians, McDonough stopped at a position next to Mundell. Greene gave the next command over his shoulder. "Countermarch By Files, March." Each of the Sergeants turned outboard and proceeded down along his following file. When the appropriate time arrived, half of the sideboys fell in behind each file, and the Honor Guard fell in behind them.

The Sergeants halted their files just behind the Staff's position. Ten seconds later Greene ordered, "Detachment, Forward, March." As a unit, the Marines proceeded first to the lane and then back to Harper's Ferry.

The only exceptions were Gilbert and Allen. Allen had earlier requested time to stay with Quinn. Gilbert had assured both Orderly Sergeants that the 'visit' would be short and they would return to duty as quickly as possible.

Both men watched the Detachment exit the cemetery. As the cadence beat of the drums faded into the woods, the area around them became very silent. Gilbert reluctantly broke the spell. "Grab one of those shovels, lad," he said to Allen. "And

I'll fetch the cross."

He was referring to a freshly painted, white wooden cross leaning against one of the stone markers close by. When he returned, he explained, "This morning, the good Father had assured me that it would be up here." He held the cross steady so Allen could tamp it down with the shovel. "And Father John said this was only a temporary marker. Later on, Quinn will be receiving proper head and foot stones."

"That's comforting to know," said Allen as he moved to view the black letters bedecked on the front of the cross. "Private Luke Quinn, USM," he read out loud. He looked to Gilbert and lamented, "It just doesn't seem right, somehow."

Gilbert shook his head and replied softly, "Aye, lad. It certainly doesn't." He stooped down to retrieve his weapon. "Take your time, Bal," he said as he picked up the other shovel. "I'll be down by the lane when you're ready." He gestured toward the shovel in Allen's hand. "Bring that with you when you come down."

"Thank you, Corporal," respond Allen. "I will." He sat down next to the grave.

Looking about slowly, he really took in the surroundings for the first time. Following several minutes of silence, he said to the cross, "Well, one thing's for sure, Luke. You've got a really nice view to look upon every day." He pointed down the slope. "Down there, just above the tops of those trees, is the Shenandoah River." He looked up at the sun. "It maybe bears East North East from here, about half a mile away." He looked around at the trees behind him. "Looks like you'll get the morning sun every day, and the trees will shade you in the afternoons. He double-checked the tombstones to the left of the grave. "It's not too crowded where you're at, either. So it should be nice and peaceful all the time, too."

Several silent tears ran down his cheeks. "I'm going to miss you, Luke." He wiped the back of his hand across one cheek. "We didn't know each other very long, but I feel as though we've been friends for years." He picked up a small dirt clod. "You taught me a lot about doing well in the Marines and I'll try to remember everything you said." He crushed the clod between his fingers. "I guess the most important thing you taught me was that my attitude can make or break my experience in the Marines." He picked up another dirt clod. "In your own way, you were very clear that I should always be upbeat and confident, no matter how difficult things may be." With his thumb, he flipped the dirt clod high into the air. It landed near the center of the grave. "I tell you what, my friend, if it's okay with you, I'll probably be checking in with you for some guidance about that, now and again." He sat still, almost half expecting a retort to his statement from Quinn.

Allen looked down the slope and saw Gilbert standing patiently by the lane. Brushing his hands on his trouser legs, he concluded, "Well, I suppose it's time for me to go." He stood up. "I promise I'll stop by to visit as often as I can." He smiled. "Duty permitting, of course." He rendered a salute toward the cross and held it. "Fortitudine, Luke. Keep a tight watch while on your sentry duty."

He cut away the salute and picked up the shovel. Holding the handle close to his chest with both hands, he reread the black letters on the cross, one more time, to himself. After a last few quiet moments, he hefted the implement to his shoulder and started down the slope toward Gilbert.

Wednesday, October 19, 1859, 4:00 p.m.

"Corporal Gilbert," began a smiling McDonough, "it's time to send you out on a Foraging Detail."

"Yes, Orderly Sergeant," replied Gilbert, "and what is the desired target, if I may ask?"

"Well now," said McDonough, trying to contain himself, "would it help if I told you that the Lieutenant has authorized us to 'splice the main brace'?"

"Aye, that it would, Orderly Sergeant. That it would." Gilbert was all grin and nearly dancing with delight.

"I figured as much," said McDonough. He pointed toward the quiet figure seated a little distance away by the heating stove. "Take Private Allen with you. He could probably use a bit of fresh air." As a precaution, he added, "And try to return at the Double Quick."

Gilbert wasted no time. "Private Allen," he yelled. "With Me." He signaled a repeated 'down' motion. "Leave your weapon here." He was nearly at the warehouse door before the last syllable left his lips.

Allen ran to catch up with Gilbert. "What's the hurry, Corporal?" he asked.

Slowing outside the door, Gilbert pointed toward the Gault Saloon beyond the Armory gates. "We're on a Foraging Detail to obtain the fixings for grog."

"That's the second time I've heard you mention grog," puffed Allen. He took another long stride to catch up with the little Corporal. "What exactly is that?"

Gilbert halted abruptly and spun around. Allen almost crashed into him. After a moment of sizing up the Private, the 'evil' eye subsided and Gilbert said, "Yes, I reckon you wouldn't know." He beamed. "It's a fine 'at sea' tradition." He then said, "Ah, but you haven't been to sea, yet, have you, lad?"

"N-no, Corporal, I haven't," stammered Allen.

Gilbert reinitiated the march with a wave of his hand, but the pace was much slower. "Grog is an old Naval tradition that we inherited from the Brits." He thought for a second. "I seem to remember that it gets its name from one of their famous Admirals named Vernon, I think." He scratched his temple. "Apparently his sailors used to call him 'Old Grog' because of the grogram cloak he usually wore at sea when the weather was foul."

"What's grogram?" asked Allen.

"Hmm," thought Gilbert again, "I guess you don't see it much anymore. It's a rough-hewn fabric of mohair and silk."

"Sounds rather harsh," said Allen with an urge to sympathetically rub his neck.

"Probably like their old Admiral," laughed Gilbert. "Hence the nickname." They walked on a few more paces, "Anyway," he continued, "the Brits used to receive a half-pint of rum every day. They drank their spirits neat, that is without water." Gilbert licked his lips at the thought of it. "Well, this caused a lot of drunkenness and disobedience on board their ships. For which many men were brutally disciplined, flogging being the usual method back then." He involuntarily shuttered. "In order to cut down on the drunkenness, Admiral Vernon ordered that the rum issue be diluted with water to reduce its effects on the men." He wagged his index finger in the air. "The British sailors didn't like this diluted ration much and scornfully named it 'grog' from the name they had given Vernon."

"What's it made of?" queried Allen.

Gilbert stopped just outside the Armory gates. "The traditional mix calls for one part rum, two parts water, with cane sugar and lime added for taste." He nodded. "But we usually added cinnamon or nutmeg to spice it up a little."

The Corporal looked down Shenandoah Street, away from the Armory. "Tell you what I want you to do, Private." He pointed off toward the lower town. "There's bound to be a grocer's shop out there somewhere." Allen followed Gilbert's arm toward the shops. "Find one, and get the following items." He held out a finger. "A pound of sugar." A second finger was extended. "A quarter pound of cinnamon sticks." With a third finger, he added, "And if they have any, half a dozen or so limes or lemons. Limes are the first choice." He touched Allen lightly on the forearm. "If they don't have fresh ones, see if they have a small container of lime or lemon juice."

Allen nodded as each item was listed to indicate that he understood. "What about payment?" he asked innocently.

"Ask for credit and pledge to the grocer that the Marines will most assuredly pay him." Gilbert pointed toward the Gault Saloon. "When you have those three items, meet me over there." He grinned broadly. "I shall make arrangements for the main ingredient and await your arrival."

About twenty minutes passed before Allen was able to meet back up with Gilbert. He found the Corporal sitting in a chair on the porch of the saloon. In his lap he was gently cradling a one-gallon cask. Next to him was five-gallon scuttled butt (a simple cask with a lid). Allen held up a small cloth sack to indicate that he had acquired the requested items.

"Excellent," said Gilbert as he rose to his feet. He hefted the small cask upon his shoulder. "Just put those items inside that big cask, there," he said pointing to the lid, "and bring it with you."

Allen was surprised at the size of the larger cask. "Are we going to make this much grog?" he asked.

"Unfortunately, no," replied Gilbert, "but we need a container large enough to mix up three gallons of it."

"Three gallons!" exclaimed Allen. "Why so much?"

"Well, lad," explained Gilbert as they started back toward the warehouse. "A ration of grog is four ounces. We call that a 'gill' and even have a dipping cup just that size." He smiled. "Trust me when I say there are exactly thirty-two gills in a gallon of rum." He softly patted the cask on his shoulder as though it were a baby's behind. "Now then," he continued, "the quickest mixing measure would be three gallons of grog, made up of one gallon of rum and two gallons of water. That's enough for ninety-six gills." He did some quick arithmetic in the air with his finger. "Since we have about seventy men total, and" he held up an admonishing finger, "because we don't want to throw any extra out as required by regulation." He grinned widely. "We simply won't water down the rum so much." Another quick calculation in the air. "We'll just mix the rum with one and a half gallons of water." He nodded. "That should mix up just the right amount to issue." He licked his lips generously. "And it won't hurt the taste none, either."

Wednesday, October 19, 1859, 5:00 p.m.

McDonough stepped inside the warehouse door and called out, "Attention On Deck." The members of the Detachment were already standing by and merely snapped to. At his side, each man was carefully holding his cup upright by the handle with his right hand. Their issued gill of grog waited patiently within.

Lieutenant Greene strode into the space. Behind him were Colonel Lee and Lieutenant Stuart. The three of them proceeded to the front of the assembly. A makeshift table with the scuttled butt on it was behind them against the wall.

"At Ease, men," addressed Greene. He waited for all movement to stop, then said, "We have gathered to 'splice the main brace' (have a drink) for two reasons." He shifted his feet slightly. "Our primary reason is to celebrate our fallen shipmate." He turned to look at Lee. "In addition, Colonel Lee has requested the opportunity to say a few words to you."

Gilbert presented each officer with a cup. Greene held his up high and the Marines silently came to Attention. Several quiet moments passed. "To Private Quinn," he said respectfully. "Fortitudine."

Each man also held up his cup in salute. As one, they all said, "Quinn. Fortitudine." Everyone took a generous sip from his cup.

Greene motioned to Lee that he may have the floor. Lee graciously nodded and stepped forward. "It is with great pleasure," he said resolutely, "that I thank all of you for your steadfast dedication to duty and your unwavering service to your country during this time of trial." He held his cup up high. "To the United States Marines."

The Marines raised their cups. "United States Marines. Fortitudine." Most took a very long pull from their cups.

Lee and Greene exchanged places. "I have just one more bit of information to pass on," said Greene. The Marines listened intently. He held up a piece of paper. "I have received a telegram from Secretary of the Navy Toucey. We have been ordered back to Washington." He couldn't help but smile, again, at the news himself. "We shall be departing on the next train East."

Most of the Marines raised their cups once more and sang out, "FORTITUDINE!" The veterans drained their cups and held the empty vessels upside down. This was the normal practice aboard ship to indicate to the issuing officer that they had finished their grog and were ready to resume work.

The officers placed their cups on the table and Greene escorted them back through the door. Once outside, Lee commented, "A most unusual tasting beverage, Lieutenant." He smiled warmly. "Please allow me to impose upon you during our return train ride for an explanation about slicing your main space."

"Certainly, Colonel," grinned an amused Greene. "It shall be my pleasure." He realized that Lee had probably been without sleep for as long as he had.

Thursday, October 20, 1859, 1:25 a.m.

Lieutenant Greene plopped down exhausted onto the seat of the B&O passenger car. He had been on the move for well over sixty-five hours without any significant sleep. A couple of twenty-minute catnaps while the adrenaline was flowing had been enough to sustain him, but now his body was rebelling against any activity at all. The tumultuous alarm at Nine O'clock concerning an 'attack' at Pleasant Valley, Maryland drained the last of his energy. Deep sleep was now claiming the Marine leader. His Non-Commissioned Officers would ensure he would be undisturbed, at least until they reached the Relay House.

* * * * *

Earlier, upon their return from the little village of Pleasant Valley around Eleven-Thirty, Sergeant Buckley had lamented, "Well, Orderly Sergeant." He started to unlace his boots. "That forced march was a complete waste of time."

"I take it, then," offered Mundell, "that our Lieutenant's intuition was correct.

"Yes," rejoined Buckley, with one boot off, "the Lieutenant was pretty skeptical about the whole story all along." Greene had been unconvinced when a farmer named Moore had ridden in, claiming that raiders had just attacked the home of one of the local settlers and massacred the whole family. Buckley shook his head. "It didn't seem likely to Colonel Lee, either, that any more insurgents were in the vicinity."

"You will have to admit, though," presented Mundell, "the folks who scrambled in from Sandy Hook were panicked by the rumors and were causing quite a disturbance here for something to be done."

"That's the main reason," continued Buckley, "that the Colonel, Lieutenant Greene, and I took Section A up there to check out the situation." He closed his eyes and shuddered. "I mean to tell you, it was a tough march."

"Aye," nodded Mundell. "Corporal Gilbert mentioned to me that it was a very taxing five mile hike both there and back. "Uphill all the way" were his exact words, I believe."

Buckley nodded agreement as he dropped his second boot onto the warehouse floor. "And when we got there," he pointed out, "we found the 'massacred' Gennett family all fast asleep and comfortable in their beds." He shook his head. "Colonel

Lee didn't say much of anything to that fellow Moore about the wild goose chase." He rubbed his calf muscle. "The Colonel was mighty quiet on the hike back here, too."

"Uh huh," agreed Mundell. "Lieutenant Greene didn't have much to say about the whole thing when he got back, either."

* * * * *

Now, two hours later, the Marines had finished boarding two of the cars making up the Eastbound Wheeling to Baltimore Express. Just seventy-two hours beforehand, at the start of the incident, the same train had been flagged down because the insurgents had taken the bridge and it was feared that they had mined or disabled it somehow. Ironically, when the train whistle blew and the Marines' cars lurched forward, the B&O railroad was back on schedule again.

Allen had claimed a seat by a window on the town side of the car when they embarked. He watched the settlement's lights quickly disappear as the train entered the covered bridge. On the other side, as the last visible light of Harper's Ferry flickered and disappeared around the corner of the Maryland Heights, he whispered, "Rest in peace, Luke."

CHAPTER TWELVE

"REWARDS"

Wednesday, December 7, 1859, 10:30 a.m.

Lieutenant Greene looked up from his desk in response to three quick knocks at his office door. "Enter," he said to the figure standing just outside the opening.

An almost healed and smiling Ruppert stepped before the desk and stood at Attention. "Sir," he said, "I have seen the elderly gentleman you have been looking for."

"Excellent," said a jubilant Greene. "Where did you locate him?" He had been worried that something serious had happened to the older Marine. After not finding him at 'his bench' on several occasions, Greene had asked the men of the Marine Barracks to keep an eye out for him.

"I just saw him at the omnibus pickup stop on Pennsylvania Avenue, sir." Ruppert was glad that he was the one to have made this discovery for the Lieutenant. "Not more than five minutes ago," he added.

Greene stood up. "Thank you, Corporal Ruppert. You may carry on with your new duties." He withdrew a flat, rectangular box from the bottom drawer of his desk. Tucking the package securely under his arm, he snatched his cap and boat cloak off the hat rack and hurried out the door.

Nearing Pennsylvania Avenue, Greene could see that the gentleman was all bundled up and sitting on the bench below the now leafless tree. He waved to attract his attention. The man signaled back with his cane.

"Good morning, sir," said a smiling Greene. "It is good to see you again."

"And I am happy to see you again, Lieutenant" responded the man. "Please sit down, if you have a moment." He gestured to the vacant bench seat beside him. "You seem to be in a bit of a hurry."

"Only to get here," said Greene as he settled onto the seat. "I have been looking for you, but have not been able catch you here."

"My apologies, Lieutenant," he said with a bow of his head, "I have been ill of late and unable to enjoy my outings as before."

"Oh, I'm sorry to hear that," sympathized Greene. "I trust that you have made a complete recovery?"

The man nodded. "As complete as anyone my age can get," he said.

Greene wasn't sure how to respond. He managed to say, "I hope that your good health continues, then."

"Thank you, Lieutenant." He turned to face Greene. "And, pray tell, why were you looking for me?" he asked.

"Well, sir," began Greene, "the last time we met, I was preparing to take a Detachment of Marines into harm's way. We were soon off to Harper's Ferry to deal with a bit of an insurrection." He adjusted the box on his lap. "I greatly appreciated your advice then, and I wanted to give you a full report of what happened there."

The man held up his hand and said, "That won't be necessary, Lieutenant." He smiled. "I have already enjoyed a detailed account of your adventures at Harper's Ferry."

Greene was completely puzzled. "And...and how is that possible, sir?" he stammered.

The man laughed out loud. "I guess you might say that I had a spy in your camp!" He was enjoying the drama of keeping Greene on the hook.

"Oh?" queried Greene.

"Oh, yes," continued the man. "At supper, on the day of your return, I received a very enthusiastic, verbal description of everything that everyone had done at the Armory and the engine house."

Greene was dumbfounded. "How?" was all he could say.

The man couldn't keep it to himself any longer. He chuckled again and said, "Perhaps I should formally introduce myself." He tipped his hat. "I am James Baxter, former Sergeant of Marines. Your Fifer, Richard Baxter, is my grandson."

Greene shook his head and grinned. "Well, I'll be. ."

Baxter continued. "And Woolsey Baxter, your armorer, is my son."

Greene shook his head and chuckled. "It's no wonder that you know everything about the events at Harper's Ferry." He coughed apprehensively. "Are there, perhaps, any details that you may have questions about?"

"Yes, actually, there is one," smiled Baxter. "Richard was unable to give me a description of this John Brown." He shrugged. "He said that he was only able to espy Brown after he was bandaged, and, then, not able to see him clearly." Baxter held out an open hand. "Perhaps you can recall his appearance inside the engine house?"

"There isn't much to tell, really," pleaded Greene. "Although taller than me, he was not a large man." He pondered for a second. "Perhaps five feet eight inches tall and rather gaunt looking." Greene's thoughts drifted back to his first encounter with the insurgent leader. Staring blankly, he started listing off Brown's characteristics as he could recollect them. "His hair was graying...He had a beard, only about two or three inches long...His eyes..." He turned to Baxter. "The look of his eyes is difficult to describe, but believe me when I say that you wouldn't forget such a look if you ever saw it." Greene looked away. After a few moments he continued. "I don't remember his dress distinctly. I should say that he had his trouser legs tucked into his boots, and that he wore clothes of gray." He thought for another moment. "Probably no more than trousers and shirt." He looked back to Baxter. "I suppose the last thing I can add is that I don't remember a hat upon his head."

"Did he ever tell you why he did it?" inquired Baxter.

"No," replied Greene. "I had little conversation with the man, and spent very little time around him."

"I read in the paper, that he was hung this past Friday," said Baxter.

"Yes," agreed Greene. "December Second, at around Eleven-Thirty in the morning."

"Were you there for the hanging?" asked Baxter.

"No," replied Greene matter of factly. "I had been summoned to Charles Town to testify for the Commonwealth of Virginia." He shook his head. "I remained there for two weeks, but was not called."

Baxter felt it was time to change the subject. "And what of any future assignments for you, Lieutenant?" he asked.

"Well," said Greene modestly, "I suppose I have received a reward posting for my actions at Harper's Ferry."

"Do tell!" exclaimed Baxter.

"Yes," beamed Greene in response to his company's excitement. "I shall be the Officer-in-Command of the Marine

Guard aboard the Stream Frigate *Niagara*." He smiled broadly. "She has been assigned to an around the world cruise and departs this coming Spring."

"That's wonderful," affirmed Baxter.

"It should prove to be a marvelous journey." Greene was energized. "We will be escorting the first emissaries of the Japanese Emperor back to their native land."

"Ah, yes," commented Baxter, "that should prove to be most exciting." He held an index finger to his lips as he thought. "The *Niagara*. Was she the steam frigate that was just here at the Navy Yard?"

"Not exactly, sir," replied Greene. "You are undoubtedly thinking of the *Merrimack*. The *Niagara* is one of her sister ships. She also is a forty gun Frigate with a propeller extending through the hull near the keel, just forward of the rudder." He beamed. "The *Niagara*, however, is the largest ship in our Navy."

"Well, then!" exclaimed Baxter. "There you have the sum of it!" He was animated. "Command duty aboard our most magnificent ship, sailing around the world, and escorting the intriguing Japaners is indeed a grand reward." He slapped Greene on the knee. "You should feel most proud, Lieutenant."

Greene was embarrassed. "I shall just continue to do my duty, sir."

"You are much too modest, sir," said Baxter with a wink. "I don't doubt that you will always live up to the Marine motto to the best of your ability."

Greene hastened to change the subject away from himself. "Speaking of rewards, sir." He handed the box to Baxter. "I have brought one of sorts for you."

It was Baxter's turn to be embarrassed. "Why, thank you, Lieutenant." He started to open the box. "You are most kind."

Inside, wrapped in newspaper, was a weapon made of iron. It was a broad two-edged blade about ten inches long. Below the sturdy four inch guard, a three inch handle shaped ferrule was attached. The ferrule was conical and open at the end. A small hole had been drilled into the side of the ferrule about three quarters of an inch from the opening.

Baxter lifted the object and examined it closely.

"This is a head from one of the pikes that Brown had stored

at his hideout," said Greene. "A six foot long ash handle was originally inserted here," he pointed first to the ferrule and then to the small hole, "and fastened here with a screw." Greene removed his hand. "We think he intended to arm the freed slaves with them."

"Fascinating," remarked Baxter.

"I brought this back for you," explained Greene, "as a remembrance of the 'pointed'," he touched the tip of the blade, "leadership secrets that you imparted to me during our carriage ride."

"Thank you, again, Lieutenant," expressed a grateful Baxter. "I shall display it with distinction in my home."

"You honor me by doing so," maintained Greene.

As Baxter began rewrapping the blade in the newspaper, Greene checked his watch. "I am afraid, sir," he said with regret, "that I must return to my duties at the Barracks."

He turned to face Baxter again. "Before I go, though, I would like to commend Fifer Baxter to you." He smiled tenderly. "He was a busy little bee the whole trip." His demeanor became thoughtful. "When called upon, he performed his duty to the utmost of his ability." He nodded knowingly. "In fact, there were several occasions where he unhesitatingly performed tasks that would humble most men. His actions were well above the call of duty." He placed his hand gently on Baxter's forearm. Sincerely, he said, "I find him to be a credit to the Marine Corps. I don't doubt he will continue to make you proud." Baxter smiled. Moisture welled up in his eyes.

Greene stood up. With a salute, he said, "With your permission, then, I shall say 'Good day'." He bowed toward the gentleman and concluded politely as he held out his right hand, "Sergeant of Marines Baxter, I look forward to many more meetings and friendly discussions with you."

"As do I," rejoined Baxter, "As do I." They shook hands warmly.

When Greene was across Pennsylvania Avenue, he stopped and looked back. The elderly man waved and called out, "Fair winds and following seas, Lieutenant."

Greene smiled, returned the wave, and replied cheerily, "Fortitudine!"

In Place, Rest.

APPENDIX

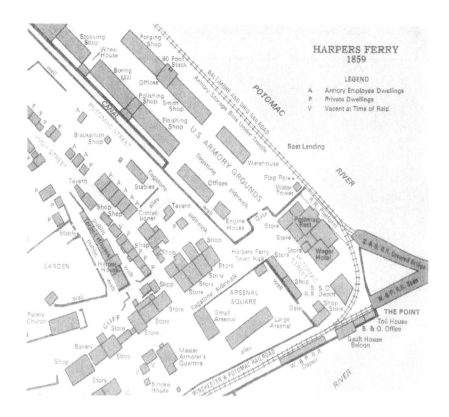

Harper's Ferry in 1859

Sadly, except for the relocated engine house, all of the structures of the Armory Grounds, Arsenal Square, and the Ferry Lot (the Point) are non-existent today

[United States National Park Service History Series]

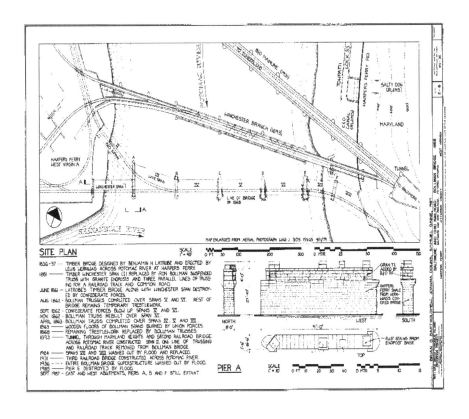

This B&O Site Plan depicts the original bridge, as well as the two 'modern' bridges that are still in use today

[Library of Congress Prints and Photographs Division]

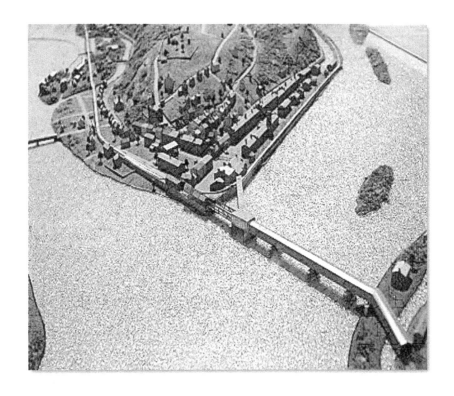

Model of Harper's Ferry (1859).

(NHP model located inside the Master Armorer's House at Harpers Ferry)

Potomac River and Maryland Heights to the right
Shenandoah River and Loudoun Heights to the left

[Photo by Author]

Artist's depiction of 1859 Harper's Ferry

[Historic Photo Collection, Harpers Ferry NHP]

Lithograph of B&O Bridge at Harper's Ferry
(Viewed from Maryland Side)

Train shown on wrong side of bridge
(Seen here on the turnpike side)

[Library of Congress Prints and Photographs Division]

Lithograph of Armory (1857)

Clearly demonstrates the path of the B&O Railroad along the River Wall between the Armory and the Potomac River

[Historic Photo Collection, Harpers Ferry NHP]

B&O Bridge (1859) - viewed from Maryland side of Potomac River

St. Peter's Catholic Church and steeple in the center
The Wager House, Potomac Restaurant, Armory water tower
and warehouse can be clearly seen atop of the river wall
The boat landing is hidden from view by the shack on the right

[Historic Photo Collection, Harpers Ferry NHP]

B&O Bridge, Ferry Lot / The Point, and Lower Town (1859)
(Viewed from Upper Town)

The Water Tower is the tall, square structure just left of center

[Historic Photo Collection, Harpers Ferry NHP]

B&O RR Wyed Span opening onto the
River Wall Platform (1859)

Wager House Hotel, Potomac Restaurant (with columns),
and Water Tower on the right.

[West Virginia & Regional History Collection, WVU]

Opposite View from Wyed Span onto River Wall Platform (1859)

[West Virginia & Regional History Collection, WVU]

The Main Gate(s) to the Armory (as photographed in 1862)

Pedestrian Gate (left) and Wagon Gate (Right)
The Engine House is the first structure on the left
The Office Building is to the left of the trees near the center
The Warehouse is the first structure on the right.

[Historic Photo Collection, Harpers Ferry NHP]

Today's view of 'The Point' from the
footbridge along the Winchester Branch

Pier A is to the left

Behind the trees are the attachment points
of the Winchester Span and B&O Span

What is left of the River Wall continues off to the right

[Photo by Author]

The engine house as it exists at Harpers Ferry, today

After being dismantled and rebuilt twice, it is smaller than the original, as well as backwards

The Guard Room is on the 'wrong' side

[Photo by Author]

This photo has been 'flipped' to show the view
of the engine house as it existed in October 1859

The open door is the one the Marines breached

[Photo by Author]

Inside the Engine House when the Marines attack

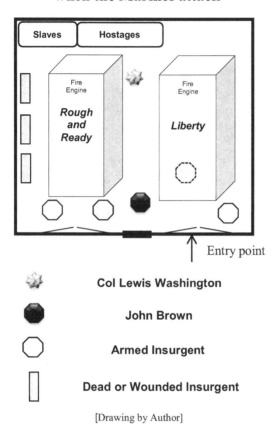

[Drawing by Author]

1850's style Hand Pump Fire "Engine"

[Aurora Regional Fire Museum, Aurora, IL]

The following is from www.nps.gov/archive/hafe/jbfort.htm.
Author: David T. Gilbert

The Armory's fire engine and guard house was erected in 1848 and described in an Armory report the same year as: "An engine and guard-house, 35½ x 24 feet, one story brick, covered with slate, and having copper gutters and down spouts, has been constructed, and is now occupied."

John Brown's Fort, as the structure became known, was the only Armory building to escape destruction during the Civil War.

The engine house has been dismantled and rebuild 2 times, as well as moved a total of 4 times:

In 1891, the fort was sold, dismantled, and transported to Chicago where it was displayed a short distance from The World's Columbian Exposition. The building, attracting only 11 visitors in ten days, was closed, dismantled again, and its materials left on a vacant lot.

In 1894, Washington, D.C. journalist Kate Field, who had a keen interest in preserving memorabilia of John Brown, spearheaded a campaign to return the fort to Harpers Ferry. Local resident Alexander Murphy made five acres available to Miss Field, and the Baltimore & Ohio Railroad offered to ship the disassembled fort to Harpers Ferry free of charge. In 1895, John Brown's Fort was rebuilt on the Murphy Farm about three miles outside of town on a bluff overlooking the Shenandoah River. (It was, unfortunately, reassembled backwards.)

In 1903, Storer College began their own fundraising drive to acquire the structure. In 1909, on the occasion of the 50th Anniversary of John Brown's Raid, the building was purchased and moved to the Storer College campus on Camp Hill in Harpers Ferry. (Storer College was a historically black college located in Harpers Ferry. It operated from 1865 until 1955.)

Acquired by the National Park Service in 1960, the building was moved back to the Lower Town in 1968. Because the fort's original site was covered with a railroad embankment in 1894, the building now sits about 150 feet east of its original location.

MARINE DETACHMENT

A complete list of the Marines from the Marine Barracks, Washington D.C., who took part in the John Brown insurrection a Harper's Ferry, October 17 to 20, 1859.

1st Lieutenant	Israel Greene	
Orderly Sergeant	James McDonough	
	Joseph Mundell	
Sergeant	Thomas A. Buckley	1 Officer
	Eugene Callahan	2 Orderly Sergeants
	William Davis	4 Sergeants
	Benjamin Woodfield	3 Corporals
		2 Drummers
Corporal	Aaron D. Gilbert	1 Fifer
	Alexander McLeod	<u>74</u> Privates
	George A. Pollock	87 TOTAL
Drummer	Robert Cushluf	
	John Shultz	
Fifer	James Hogan	

Private:

Robert Achuff	Amos Hill
John Badent	Thomas Howard
James Banney	William Jones
Alfred Beck	John A. Kennedy
Edward G. Bendlow	Charles Kleiber
John B. Bentley	Albert Koch
Frederick Black	Milton Kukens
William Bowran	Henry Loop
James Buchanan	John McCaffery
David Cambpell	John McNally
John Casay	Peter Miller
William H. Conklin	James Mullen
William Cook	William Murphy
John B. Crater	Anthony Nahouse
Richard Cripps	Michael O'Brien
Louis Croneghk	William Phillips
Richard Dalton	Luke Quinn
John Davis	Ethelbert Reese
Samuel Day	Joseph S. Robinson
W. Freak Eckhardt	Albert Roe
Andrew J. Edsall	Elijah Rose
Charles Ferkler	Samuel Rothchild
Charles Fisher	Joseph Roy
George W. Fox	Mathew Ruppert
John S. Fraser	Nicholas J. Ryan
Hugh Gallagher	John M. Sherry
James Gibbons	Charles Snyder
Albert Graw	Thomas Tompkins
Gustavus Greenhalgh	John Tonshaerdt
Henry Grogan	Thomas J. Trainer
John S. Gross	James Walker
Frederick Grott	Aaron Walmsley
George W. Harris	Charles Warren
Enoch S. Hawkins	Herman Weitlase
Jacob D. Hencke	Christian Whalen
Enoch S. Hewith	Joseph E. Wilson
Edward Hicks	Samuel Williamson

[List provided by David M. Sullivan]

Luke Quinn

Very little is actually known about Luke Quinn. He was born in Ireland in 1835. At the age of nine, in 1844, during the height of the Irish Potato Famine, he emigrated to the United States. An examination of his enlistment document reveals that, like most people of the time, he was unable to read or write. He signed his name with an "X". He was twenty when he enlisted at the Brooklyn Navy Yard on November 23, 1855. According to Marine enlistment records he was five feet six and a half inches tall, had hazel eyes, dark hair and a fair complexion. His profession was listed as Stone Cutter.

Examination of his service record shows a solid, basic service, typical of Marines between the Mexican War and the Civil War. On December 4, 1855 he was transferred to Marine Barracks, Washington, DC. He was later detached to the Gosport Navy Yard, (Norfolk, VA) on September 19, 1856. The next day he was transferred to the Marine Guard on board the US Frigate *St. Lawrence*. He spent the bulk of his career aboard the *St. Lawrence*, except for a brief one-month temporary tour aboard the US Brig *Perry* (December 31, 1858 to February 3, 1859). On May 27, 1859, Quinn was transferred back to Marine Barracks, Washington, DC. On July 8, 1859, he was assigned to the Marine Detachment, Washington Navy Yard.

Luke Quinn was just twenty-four when he died at Harper's Ferry. He alone is the only non-resident casualty of the raid who is still buried there. (The ten raiders who were killed were reburied at John Brown's farm at North Elba, New York in 1899.)

[Researched by Robert O. Wagner, Jr.]

The following is the epitaph on his current tombstone:

Luke Quinn

Private U.S. Marine Corps

Born in Ireland in the year 1835.
Came to the United States of America
At the age of nine years.
Enlisted in the U.S. Marine Corps
November 13, 1855; was mortally
Wounded October 18, 1859 while
Participating in the storming of
The engine house, one of the
Buildings of the U.S. Armory
And now known as John Brown's Fort
During the John Brown Raid
At Harpers Ferry.

Erected by the Western Section
Of the Richmond Diocese Union
Of the Holy Name Society

Best information indicates that this
tombstone was erected sometime around 1930

[Photo by Author]

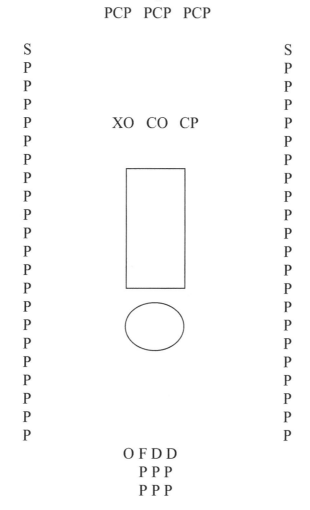

The Funeral Square

Legend: CO – Commanding Officer
XO – Executive Officer
CP – Catholic Priest
O - Orderly Sergeant   P - Private
S - Sergeant   F - Fifer
C - Corporal   D - Drummer

[Drawing by Author]

What Happened to Them?

The following information is from David M. Sullivan's two volumes *"The United States Marine Corps in the Civil War - The First Year and Second Year"*

Private Mathew Ruppert -- Had only been in the Corps just over a month when he was wounded at Harper's Ferry. As a reward for his bravery, he was promoted to Corporal. He would have been promoted to Sergeant but for his inability to read and write. He received an Honorable Discharge from the Marine Corps at Philadelphia on October 10, 1863.

Major William Russell -- Was a charming and cultivated man of great coolness. He was about thirty-five years old when he jumped through the door behind Greene. Why he did so is not really known. In late 1861, an additional position with the rank of Colonel was established for the Marine Corps. Subsequently, there followed a great deal of political maneuvering to appoint Paymaster Russell to the newly created Colonelcy, thus making him heir apparent to the post of Commandant. The favoritism and political interference earned him the enmity of his fellow senior officers, many of whom would have been superseded had he been appointed. When Congress failed to appoint him to the position, Russell took a leave of absence and served on the staff of Major General McClellan as an aide-de-camp during the Peninsula Campaign of 1862. Upon his return from his detached duties, he was too ill to resume his duties, being greatly "debilitated from long exposure and the effects of the climate". In addition he was possibly suffering from depression. His wife died in February 1860, and he had to turn the care of his six children over to his sister in Rockville, MD. When he was able to work, he was frequently intoxicated while on duty. Shortly after noon, October 31, 1862, he shot himself in the head with a revolver.

The following information is from Ralph W. Donnelly's *"Biographical Sketches of the Commissioned Officers of the CSMC"*

First Lieutenant Israel Greene -- Went on to command the Marine Guard aboard the *USS Niagara*. His ship sailed from New York on June 30, rounded the Cape of Good Hope, and arrived at Yedo (now Tokyo) on November 8, 1860. Fort Sumter had fallen just before he returned to the United States. Reportedly offered a Colonelcy of a Wisconsin regiment, he declined and cast his lot with Virginia and the South. He attempted to resign from the Marines, but was instead dismissed on May 18, 1861. He entered the Provisional Army of Virginia as a Captain on May 25, 1861, assigned to recruiting duty in Richmond. He was commissioned in the Confederate States Marine Corps as a Captain on June 19, 1861. This rank was confirmed on August 13, 1861, and on the next day he was nominated as Adjutant and Inspector General of the Corps with the rank of Major. This appointment was confirmed on August 14, 1861. He served at Marine Headquarters at Richmond, VA for the remainder of the war and left only upon the evacuation of the city. He seems to have joined the retreat of Lee's Army of Northern Virginia and took his parole at Farmville, VA between April 11 and 21, 1865. After the war, he resided in Berryville, VA for a brief period, and then moved to Minnesota. Because Minnesota was so "pro-Union", he moved farther West to South Dakota in 1873. There he farmed his government claim until his death on May 25, 1909, almost a full fifty years after striking down John Brown. He is buried in Mitchell, SD.

(More information about Greene's later years may be obtained from the Mitchell Area Historical Society, headquartered in the Carnegie Resource Center at 119 West Third Ave, Mitchell, SD 57301.)

Portrait of Israel Greene
While serving in the CSMC

(Photo from David M. Sullivan's Collection)

Family Tree

First Lieutenant Israel Greene, USM

and

Major General Nathanael Greene, Jr.

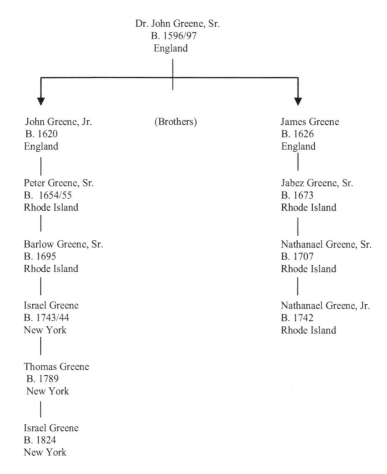

[Researched by Author]

The following information is from www.ghostgarrison.org

Uniform Cloth and Color

Dark blue cloth represented relatively expensive, smooth, finely woven broadcloth, dyed in the cloth. Sky-blue signified a much cheaper (and easily procured), rougher material, often dyed in the thread and woven afterward. Dark blue, considered a 'national' color, indicated formal dress wear; whereas sky-blue meant field or working wear. Until the twentieth century, the enlisted man's uniform was made of wool or wool mixed with cotton or flax. Kersey was a rough, coarse woven wool cloth, usually ribbed, used extensively for fatigue clothing.

Fatigue Coat

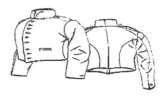

Fatigue Cap

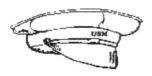

Greatcoat

Dennis Frye, Chief Historian at Harpers Ferry National Historical Park, standing inside the 'Fort' with a replica of the John Brown pike.

[Photo by Associated Press]

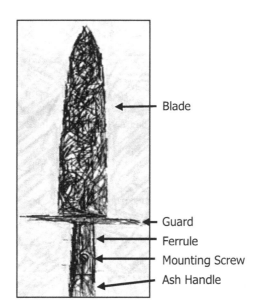

The 'working' end of a John Brown Pike

[Drawing by unknown]

Train Travel
Washington to Harper's Ferry
October 1859

Washington to Relay House is a Branch Line of the B&O RR
(single track)

Relay House to Harper's Ferry is part of the Main Stem of the B&O RR (multiple sidings)

Relay House is about 10 miles SW of Baltimore

The distance from Washington to Relay House is 27 miles
At an average speed of 22.5 mph, the trip
takes about 75 minutes

Marines depart at 3:30 and arrive at Relay House
at approximately 4:45
(Hooked up to 12 cars of Militia heading West from Baltimore)

Express heading South to Washington at 27 mph,
takes about 60 minutes

Lee has to wait 2 and 1/2 hours at the train station
before departing Washington

Lee departs Washington at approximately 6:10 and arrives at Relay House at approximately 7:15, only to find that the West bound "Military Train" had departed at 5:00 p.m.

The distance from Relay House to Harper's Ferry is 65 miles
At an average speed of 16.25 mph, the trip takes about 4 hours

Lee waits almost 90 minutes for train at Relay House
Sends telegram to Frederick Junction for Greene
Tells him to stop at Sandy Hook - about 1 and 1/4 miles from Harper's Ferry

Marines delayed at Frederick Junction for 10 minutes
Arrive at Sandy Hook at about 9:00 p.m.

Lee departs Relay House at 8:45 p.m.
Rides in the engineer's cabin of Engine #22
(At a top speed of 32 mph, trip takes a little over 2 hours)

Engine 22 arrives at Sandy Hook at approximately 11:00 p.m.

Lee's total transit time from the White House to
Harper's Ferry was roughly 8 hours

(Lee and Greene take the Marines to Harper's Ferry
at approximately 11:30 and arrive close to Mid-night)

[Researched by Author]

Col. Robert E. Lee's Report Concerning the Attack at Harper's Ferry
October 19, 1859

Colonel Lee to the Adjutant General

HEADQUARTERS HARPER'S FERRY

COLONEL: I have the honor to report, for the information of the Secretary of War, that on arriving here on the night of the 17th instant, in obedience to Special Orders No. 194 of that date from your office, I learn that a party of insurgents, about 11 p. m. on the 16th, had seized the watchmen stationed at the armory, arsenal, rifle factory, and bridge across the Potomac, and taken possession of those points. They then dispatched six men, under one of their party, called Captain Aaron C. Stevens, to arrest the principal citizens in the neighborhood and incite the negroes to join in the insurrection. The party took Colonel L. W. Washington from his bed about 1-~ a. m. on the 17th, and brought him, with four of l]is servants, to this place. Mr. J. H. Allstadt and six of his servants were in the same manner seized about 3 a. m., and arms placed in the hands of the Negroes. Upon their return here, John E. Cook, one of the party sent to Mr. Washington's, was dispatched to Maryland, with Mr. Washington's wagon, two of his servants, and three of Mr. Allstadt's, for arms and ammunition, &c. .As day advanced, and the citizens of Harper's Ferry commenced their usual avocations, they were separately captured, to the number of forty, as well as I could learn, and confined in one room of the fire engine house of the armory, which seems early to have been selected as a point of defense. About 11 a. m. the volunteer companies from Virginia began to arrive, and the Jefferson Guards and volunteers from Charlestown, under Captain J. W. Rowen, I understood, were first on the ground. The Hamtramck Guards, Captain V. M. Butler; the Shepherdstown troop, Captain Jacob Rienahart; and Captain Alburtis's company from Martinsburg arrived in the afternoon. These companies, under the direction of Colonels R. W. Baylor and John T. Gibson, forced the insurgents to abandon their positions at the bridge and in the village, and to withdraw within the armory enclosure, where they fortified themselves in the fire-engine house, and carried ten of their prisoners for the purpose of insuring their safety and facilitating their escape, whom they termed hostages, and whose names are Colonel L. W. Washington, of Jefferson county, Virginia; Mr. J. H. Allstadt, of Jefferson county, Virginia; Mr. Israel Russell, justice of the peace, Harper's Ferry; Mr. John Donahue, clerk of Baltimore and Ohio railroad; Mr. Terence Byrne, of Maryland; Mr. George D. Shope, of Frederick, Maryland; Mr. Benjamin Mills, master armorer, Harper's Ferry arsenal; Mr. A. M. Ball, master machinist, Harper's Ferry arsenal; Mr. J. E. P. Dangerfield, paymaster's clerk, Harper's Ferry arsenal; Mr. J. Burd, armorer, Harper's Ferry arsenal. After sunset more troops arrived. Captain B. B. Washington's company from Winchester and three companies from Fredericktown, Maryland, under Colonel Shriver. Later in the evening the companies from Baltimore, under General Charles C. Edgerton, second light brigade, and a detachment of marines, commanded by Lieutenant I. Green accompanied by Major Russell, of that corps, reached Sandy Hook, about one and a half mile east of Harper's Ferry. At this point I came up with these last-named troops, and leaving General Edgerton and his command on the Maryland side of the river for the night, caused the marines to proceed to Harper's Ferry, and placed them within the armory grounds to prevent the possibility of the escape of the insurgents. Having taken measures to halt, in Baltimore, the artillery companies ordered from Fort Monroe, I made preparations to attack the insurgents at daylight. But for the fear of sacrificing the lives of some of the gentlemen held by them as prisoners in a midnight assault, I should have ordered the attack at once.

Their safety was the subject of painful consideration, and to prevent, if possible, jeopardizing their lives; I determined to summon the insurgents to surrender. As soon after daylight as the arrangements were made Lieutenant J. E. B. Stewart, 1st cavalry, who had accompanied me from Washington as staff officer, was dispatched, under a flag, with a written summons, (a copy of which is hereto annexed, marked *A.)* Knowing the character of the leader of the insurgents, I did not expect it would be accepted. I had therefore directed that the volunteer troops, under their respective commanders, should be paraded on the lines assigned them outside the armory, and had prepared a storming party of twelve marines, under their commander, Lieutenant Green, and had placed them close to the engine-house, and secure from its fire. Three marines were furnished with sledge-hammers to break in the doors, and the men were instructed how to distinguish our citizens from the insurgents; to attack with the bayonet, and not to injure the blacks detained in custody unless they resisted. Lieutenant Stewart was also directed not to receive from the insurgents any counter propositions. If they accepted the terms offered, they must immediately deliver up their arms and release their prisoners. If they did not, he must, on leaving the engine-house, give me the signal. My object was, with a view of saving our citizens, to have as short an interval as possible between the summons and attack. The summons, as I had anticipated, was rejected. At the concerted signal the storming party moved quickly to the door and commenced the attack. The fire-engines within the house had been placed by the besieged close to the doors. The doors were fastened by ropes, the spring of which prevented their being broken by the blows of the hammers. The men were therefore ordered to drop the hammers, and, with a portion of the reserve, to use as a battering-ram a heavy ladder, with which they dashed in a part of the door and gave admittance to the storming party. The fire of the insurgents up to this time had been harmless. At the threshold one marine fell mortally wounded. The rest, led by Lieutenant Green and Major Russell, quickly ended the contest. The insurgents that resisted were bayoneted. Their leader, John Brown, was cut down by the sword of Lieutenant Green, and our citizens were protected by both officers and men. The whole was over in a few minutes.

After our citizens were liberated and the wounded cared for, Lieutenant Colonel S. S. Mills, of the 53d Maryland regiment, with the Baltimore Independent Greys, Lieutenant B. F. Simpson commanding, was sent on the Maryland side of the river to search for John E. Cook, and to bring in the arms, &c., belonging to the insurgent party, which were said to be deposited in a school-house two and a half miles distant. Subsequently, Lieutenant J. E. B. Stewart, with a party of marines, was dispatched to the Kennedy farm, situated in Maryland, about four and a half miles from Harper's Ferry, which had been rented by John Brown, and used as the depot for his men and munitions. Colonel Mills saw nothing of Cook, but found the boxes of arms, (Sharp's carbines and belt revolvers,) and recovered Mr. Washington's wagon and horses. Lieutenant Stewart found also at the Kennedy farm a number of sword pikes, blankets, shoes, tents, and all the necessaries for a campaign. These articles have been deposited in the government storehouse at the armory.

From the information derived from the papers found upon the persons and among the baggage of the insurgents, and the statement of those now in custody, it appears that the party consisted of nineteen men-fourteen white and five black. That they were headed by John Brown, of some notoriety in Kansas, who in June last located himself in Maryland, at the Kennedy farm, where he has been engaged in preparing to capture the United States works at Harper's Ferry. He avows that his object was the liberation of the slaves of Virginia, and of the whole South; and acknowledges that he has been disappointed in his expectations of aid from the black as well as white population, both in the Southern and Northern States. The blacks, whom he forced from their homes in this neighborhood, as far as I could learn, gave him no voluntary assistance. The servants of Messrs. Washington and Allstadt, retained at the armory, took no part in the conflict, and those carried to Maryland returned to their homes as soon as released. The result proves that the plan was the attempt of a fanatic or madman, who could only end in failure; and its temporary success, was owing to the panic and confusion he succeeded in creating by magnifying his numbers. I append a list of the insurgents, (marked B.) Cook is the only man known to have escaped. The other survivors of the expedition, viz: John Brown, A. C. Stevens, Edwin Coppic, and Green Shields, *(alias* S. Emperor,) I have delivered into the hands of the marshal of the western district of Virginia and the sheriff of Jefferson county. They were escorted to Charlestown by a detachment of marines, under Lieutenant Green. About nine o'clock this evening I received a report from Mr. Moore, from Pleasant Valley, Maryland, that a body of men had, about sunset, descended from the mountains, attacked the house of Mr. Gennett, and from the cries of murder and the screams of the women and children, he believed the residents of the valley were being massacred. The alarm and excitement in the village of Harper's Ferry was increased by the arrival of families from Sandy Hook, fleeing for safety. The report was, however, so improbable that I could give no credence to it, yet I thought it possible that some atrocity might have been committed, and I started with twenty-five marines, under Lieutenant Green, accompanied by Lieutenant Stewart, for the scene of the alleged outrage, about four and a half miles distant. I was happy to find it a false alarm. The inhabitants of Pleasant Valley were quiet and unharmed, and Mr. Gennett and his family safe and asleep.

I will now, in obedience to your dispatch of this date, direct the detachment of marines to return to the navy-yard at Washington in the train that passes here at 1 am to-night, and will myself take advantage of the same train to report to you in person at the War Department. I must also ask to express my thanks to Lieutenant Stewart, Major Russell, and Lieutenant Green, for the aid they afforded me, and my entire commendation of the conduct of the detachment of marines, who were at all times ready and prompt in the execution of any duty. The promptness with which the volunteer troops repaired to the scene of disturbance, and the alacrity they displayed to suppress the gross outrage against law and order, I know will elicit your hearty approbation. Equal zeal was shown by the president and officers of the Baltimore and Ohio Railroad Company in their transportation of the troops and in their readiness to furnish the facilities of their well ordered road.

A list of the killed and wounded, as far as came to my knowledge, is herewith annexed, (marked C;) and I enclose a copy of the" Provisional Constitution and ordinances for the people of the United States," of which there were a large number prepared for issue by the insurgents.
I am, very respectfully, your obedient servant,

R. E. LEE, *Colonel Commanding.*

Colonel S. COOPER, *Adjutant General U. S. Army, Washington City, D. C*

ABOUT THE AUTHOR

Dale Lee Sumner was born and reared in a very Navy family. His father was a retired Chief Petty Officer and his mother a Yeoman Third during World War II (both are buried in Arlington National Cemetery). His brother was a Navy SEAL and is buried with his parents at Arlington. His sister is married to a career Naval officer. After twenty-four years of his own Naval service (seven years enlisted and seventeen years commissioned), Dale retired in December 1991 as a Commander (O-5) in the Supply Corps.

While stationed at the Marine Corps Air Station at Yuma, Arizona, as a Navy Third Class Petty Officer (AZ3), he experienced the unusual privilege of being awarded the station's highest honor of 'Marine of the Month, June 1970'. An association with the Marines continued throughout the rest of his career. In 1996, Dale co-founded the first Civil War Federal Marine Re-enacting unit, "U.S. Marine Detachment, Washington Navy Yard, 1859-1865".

He acquired his Bachelor of Science Degree through the Navy Enlisted Scientific Education Program (NESEP) at Miami University, Ohio (1974). He later earned his Master of Science Degree from Golden Gate University, San Francisco (1984).

Dale has two sons and four grandchildren. He and his wife, Cindy, winter in Florida and travel the United States in their motorhome during the summer.

This is his first novel -- number one in an expected series of five about 'The Forgotten Marines' of the Civil War.

Synopsis of the planned series titled

The Forgotten Marines

Volume I – *"The Capture of John Brown"* -- The story of the Marines' preparation and participation in this historical event at Harper's Ferry (October 1859).

Volume II – *"The Outbreak of Civil War"* -- The Marines' participation during the little known surrender of the Pensacola Navy Yard (Jan 1861) and the historic burning of the Norfolk Navy Yard (Apr 1861).

Volume III – *"The Battle of Bull Run"* -- a necessary story intended to set the 'record straight' about the Marine Battalion's performance at this first major battle of the Civil War (July 1861).

Volume IV – *"The U.S.S. Cumberland"* -- The day before the C.S.S. Virginia (aka Merrimack) met the U.S.S. Monitor, the C.S.S. Virginia attacked and sank the U.S.S. Cumberland. The brave actions of the Marines aboard the U.S.S. Cumberland need to be told (March 1862).

Volume V – *"The Medal of Honor"* -- The first Marine recipient of the Congressional Medal of Honor served aboard the USS Galena at the Battle of Drewry's Bluff. This is his story (May 1862).

NOTES

Made in the USA
Columbia, SC
19 January 2018